Summer in the Highlands

Copyright © 2024 Mirror Press
Paperback edition
All rights reserved

No part of this book may be reproduced or distributed in any form whatsoever without prior written permission of the publisher, except in the case of brief passages embodied in critical reviews and articles. These novels are works of fiction. The characters, names, incidents, places, and dialog are products of the authors' imaginations and are not to be construed as real.

Interior Design by Cora Johnson
Edited by Meghan Hoesch and Lorie Humpherys
Cover design by Rachael Anderson
Cover Photo Credit: Arcangel with photographer Joanna Czogala

Published by Mirror Press, LLC

Summer in the Highlands is a Timeless Romance Anthology® book.

Timeless Romance Anthology® is a registered trademark of Mirror Press, LLC.

ISBN: 978-1-952611-42-1

TIMELESS
Victorian
COLLECTION

Summer in the Highlands

Nichole Van
Heidi Kimball
Michele Paige Holmes

Mirror Press

Timeless Victorian Collections
Summer Holiday
A Grand Tour
The Orient Express
The Queen's Ball
A Note of Change
A Gentlewoman Scholar
An Autumn Kiss
Summer in the Highlands

Timeless Regency Collections
Autumn Masquerade
A Midwinter Ball
Spring in Hyde Park
Summer House Party
A Country Christmas
A Season in London
A Holiday in Bath
A Night in Grosvenor Square
Road to Gretna Green
Wedding Wagers
An Evening at Almack's
A Week in Brighton
To Love a Governess
Widows of Somerset
A Christmas Promise
A Seaside Summer
The Inns of Devonshire
To Kiss a Wallflower

Table of Contents

Remnants of Love by Nichole Van _____ 1

Of Kilts and Courtship by Heidi Kimball _____ 123

Into the Light by Michele Paige Holmes _____ 255

REMNANTS OF LOVE

Nichole Van

One

May 20, 1858
Dinnet, Aberdeenshire
Scotland

MRS. CHRISTIANA NEWTON had not intended to end up face down in a Highland bog.

But then she also hadn't planned to be twenty-nine years old, a widow, and scrabbling for employment to feed herself.

Fate, she realized long ago, had reserved a great many indignities for her alone.

Chrissi attempted to push onto her knees, gloved hands groping for purchase in the dense mud.

"Och, Mrs. Newton! Dinnae move!" Fiona called down the embankment where Chrissi had slipped. "Ye might sink deeper into the bog, and it will catch ye like quicksand. Ye must stay precisely where ye are!"

Chrissi looked up at the younger woman—an innkeep's daughter hired with meager coin to act as a guide. Her wide eyes and the horrified "O" of her lips spoke volumes as to Chrissi's appearance.

"Are ye hurt?" Fiona continued.

Hurt? In body—no.

"'Tis only my pride that is wounded, Fiona." Chrissi wiped mud from her eyes. Or rather attempted to do so, but as the mud was everywhere—hands, face, bonnet, dress—she merely spread it around.

The girl swallowed, looking up the path. "Dinnae fret, Mrs. Newton. I'll fetch help and a good length of rope." She paused. "Just . . . dinnae move."

Fiona disappeared in a whirl of wool skirts.

Heaving a defeated sigh, Chrissi rested back on her heels, trying not to see the situation as a metaphor for the entirety of her life—mired in the Quagmire of Futility and Despair.

It sounded like the title of a penny dreadful.

Well . . . she felt like she was *living* a penny dreadful.

Generally, Chrissi preferred *not* to be covered in rank-smelling mud and sphagnum moss, particularly right before meeting an important client—Lord Farnell, in this case.

But, as usual, excited curiosity over the archaeological remains she would be excavating had overthrown her common sense.

Eager to begin the project, she had left The Boat Inn in Aboyne in the early hours of dawn, Fiona guiding her path. Chrissi wished to survey the glen around Kinord Castle, the ancestral seat of Lord Farnell, and conduct a preliminary study of the stone circle and large mound there before meeting with Lord Farnell himself.

Upon reaching Kinord Castle, she had noted the terrain. The castle stood atop an impressive rise, the mountainous Cairngorms towering behind. The standing stones and a large mound rested below the castle on a smaller hill. And to the side of *that* hill, a bog stretched across the glen—a mix of marsh and fen and swamp grass.

But as Chrissi approached the stone circle, she had spotted another solitary stone standing on an island of firmer ground in the middle of the bog. So odd, that stone, isolated from its brethren. Her feet had drifted toward it without conscious thought, heedless of the steep embankment alongside the path. A careless step on jutting rocks had sent her tumbling down the banked earth and into the bog.

The lone stone remained in her line of vision now, standing jauntily over the marsh. And if she craned her neck to the right, mud gripping her shoulders, she could see the tops of the standing stones on the hill above her—the ancient monument a silent witness to her folly.

Chrissi sighed.

A pair of magpies quarreled overhead. A fat bumblebee bobbled past, its rotund body defying physics by staying aloft. The swampy bog grass eventually gave way to heather and Scots pine in the distance. And all around her, the rolling hills and peaks of the Cairngorms loomed.

This excursion *was* to have been the beginning of Hope. A true chance to reverse the winds of fortune. To gain some semblance of financial stability for her future.

As it was, Chrissi would be lucky if Lord Farnell didn't show her the door immediately. Her stomach knotted at the thought despite being achingly empty. After all, she had chosen to spend her remaining coin on hiring Fiona rather than food. If Lord Farnell sent her packing, Chrissi would be paupered.

As an antiquarian specializing in ancient Scottish ruins, Chrissi already had to contend with male colleagues who considered her too unorthodox—translation: too female—to be a true archaeologist. However, that did not stem her attempts to continue the work she had begun with her late husband, Dr. Stephen Newton—a celebrated Oxford professor of British antiquities. Nearly thirty years her senior, Stephen had been more friend than lover, but together, they had devised new methods for documenting and understanding archaeological remains.

So when Chrissi had received a letter from Lord Farnell's secretary requesting her assistance in excavating a series of ancient ruins, she had leapt at the chance. His lordship wished to avail himself of her expertise and learn from her methodology, offering generous financial recompense.

Funds Chrissi desperately needed.

Unfortunately, Lord Farnell would certainly be informed of her foolish tumble and would justifiably question her ability to head an excavation safely.

Hopefully, she would be given the chance to bathe and right her appearance before facing his lordship herself—time to compose an argument that would convince the gentleman that despite her gender and uncharacteristic clumsiness, she was competent in her expertise. Anything to prevent her dismissal.

She flexed her fingers in her gloves, fighting the encroaching chill. Even in May, Highland mud was hardly warm, and the sun did little to battle the ever-blowing cold wind.

Ten minutes later, Chrissi heard the rumble of male voices.

Ah. Rescue and humiliation had arrived.

Three male heads, hats pulled low, bobbed down the path, Fiona's excited chatter leading them forward.

Reaching her, Fiona and two of the men—farmhands, Chrissi intuited, by the roughness of their clothing and the rope held between them—paused to look down the embankment. All three wore matching expressions of concern and, truth be told, suppressed hilarity.

Chrissi added "laughing stock" to the list of items she would need to address with Lord Farnell.

"Do we have enough rope to fetch her up, do ye ken?" the third unseen man asked.

"Aye, my lord," one of the men said over his shoulder as they began uncoiling the rope.

My lord?

Chrissi snagged onto the honorific immediately.

Please no!

Lord Farnell had come himself.

She could not imagine a more unbecoming scenario in which to meet her employer for the first time.

How much worse could her day become?

Truly . . . she should have known better than to ask the question, even rhetorically.

The third man peered over the edge—Lord Farnell, she gathered, due to the expensive superfine of his tailored coat and the sheen of his beaver top hat.

A jolt sizzled down her spine as she met his brown eyes.

It appeared that her day could indeed become much, *much* worse.

Blinking in shock, she stared up at the familiar face of Alistair Maclagan.

The only man she had ever loved.

There were likely worse ways to encounter your former betrothed after a separation of nine years.

However, at the moment, Chrissi struggled to think of one.

Belatedly, she remembered that Lord Farnell had been a distant relative of Alistair's. What tragedies had occurred to permit Alistair to inherit the Scottish title of Lord of Parliament?

Had she known Alistair was Lord Farnell, she would never have come. But then, if *he* had known she was Mrs. Stephen Newton, he would never have hired her, of that Chrissi was certain.

Once, Alistair Maclagan had been her . . . everything.

The sum of every poetic cliche.

The other half of her soul. The air that breathed life into her lungs. The man she could not wait to take as husband.

Seeing him now . . .

He has changed, she thought.

Broader, muscular, and deep of chest. Lines bracketed his eyes, wheel spokes stretching toward his temples. A beard framed lips that pulled into a taut line—lips she knew to be as soft as velvet beneath her own.

His gaze was fiercer—more Scottish raider than the youthful knight errant of her memory.

He had once laughed and smiled with ease, but intuition told Chrissi that his smiles were rarer now.

Hmmph.

Well, they *should* be.

Years. It had taken her years to recover from his betrayal.

The blackguard *should* have difficulty smiling after such villainy.

Betrayal and bitter regret. That was all that remained between them now.

She gazed at him, willing none of her surprise and roiling emotions to show on her face. Waiting for *him* to recoil in shock and astonishment.

But no.

Fate handed her one final, outrageous indignity of the day—

Alistair stared blankly at her and nodded politely, tipping his hat in greeting. Not a trace of recognition to be had.

"Lord Farnell, at your service, Mrs. Newton. I suspect this is not quite how either of us planned to meet," he called, Scotland winding through his rolled Rs and expansive vowels. "However, your bravery is to be commended. We shall have ye topside shortly."

Chrissi closed her eyes, swallowing back the thick lump of pain clogging her throat.

Of *all* the reactions she had envisioned if she ever encountered Alistair again—anger, sadness, recriminations.

Shouting, perhaps. Groveling, in her more maudlin moments. Tears, even . . . preferably his.

Never once had she imagined that Alistair would have simply forgotten her.

That her existence would be banished from his memory, as if she and her heart had been so much fairy floss, strands of spun sugar whisked away on a stiff Highland breeze.

But that had been the problem from the beginning, had it not? His lack of *seeing* her?

Deliberately, she forced her lungs to breathe in and out—to accommodate the lacerating agony of his dismissal sitting atop her sternum like a spike-studded chest.

What a nightmare.

She could hardly stay and continue with the excavation now . . . what with Alistair being Lord Farnell.

Working together would be impossible, no matter how desperately she needed this situation. She bit back the encroaching tears, refusing to add weeping to her list of humiliations.

Besides, surely at some point, Alistair would remember her.

Maybe once she was cleaned of mud and speaking of antiquities, some spark would ignite in his dark eyes—eyes her dreams still remembered all too clearly and frequently—and he would say in that puzzled way of his, head tilting to the side, "Ye seem a wee bit familiar, Mrs. Newton. Have we met before?"

And how would she reply?!

"Why, yes, my lord. I do believe we were betrothed once upon a time. Handfasted, even . . . in Florence, Italy. It was rather idyllic, what with Florence and the kissing and handfasting and all. Do you not recall?"

Awkward did not begin to describe the scene. To have to

explain to him what they had once been to one another. Or what she had *assumed* they had been.

Instead, she watched from her bog—mud-covered, cold, and miserable—as Alistair shrugged out of his tailored coat and gold-embroidered waistcoat, handing them along with his hat to Fiona for safekeeping from the muck.

With confident movements, he wrapped one end of the rope around his chest and ordered his men to tie the opposite end around a nearby pine. The men obliged and then held on to the rope, bracing their feet on the path as Alistair slowly walked backward down the slope, trusting the rope and his men with his weight.

Alistair had always been agile and sure-footed. Another detail Chrissi was annoyed to remember.

"Almost there, Mrs. Newton." He still faced the slope, but his voice was calm and assured. "Unfortunately, ye will need to cling to my neck in order for my men to haul us both up. Can ye manage that, do ye ken?"

"Yes, Ali—my lord," she replied, hating how his Christian name clung to her tongue.

He stopped mere inches away from where the bog began, feet braced against the solid embankment. Keeping one hand on the rope, he reached back with the other, beckoning her forward.

Inching on her knees, Chrissi wrapped her hand around his forearm, allowing him to pull her from the mud with a squishy *pop*.

Gracious, she had forgotten how strong he was. The coiled power in his arm, the muscles bunching and pushing against the sleeves of his white linen shirt.

"Now, wrap your arms around my neck," he ordered.

"The mud..."

"It will wash out. This is the only way to get ye up the slope. Ye will need to hold fast."

Swallowing, Chrissi did as he ordered, looping her arms around his neck and clinging tight.

She might as well have dipped her head into a witch's potion labeled Remembrance of Lost Love.

Wave after wave of memories washed through her.

The distinct smell of his cologne—warm ambergris with hints of sandalwood and citrus.

The tiny brown mole on his right earlobe, the very one she had loved to nibble.

The stubborn curl at his temple that poked outward, no matter how much pomade he applied.

The faint bump in his nose caused by a tumble from an oak tree when he was nine.

"I've got ye," he said, words gruff, face half-turned toward hers.

Only then, when he clutched her to him—when every finger of his right hand pressed into her midsection with scorching heat, when their noses practically touched and his breath was a puff of air against her own lips—did recognition *finally* flash.

He froze, head rearing back and eyes flaring wide. His jaw sagged and his hold on the rope slipped.

They both lurched backward before he secured his grip, steadying them and pulling Chrissi that much tighter against his chest.

"Chris?" he rasped, her name a surprised gasp of air.

"Alis," she replied with a nod.

They had always laughed at their nicknames—*Chris* for her, *Alice* for him. A humorous swapping of their genders.

She felt only slightly relieved that he had recognized her. Her vanity would have liked the moment to have occurred much, *much* sooner.

But his current reaction was gratifying.

He stared. And stared and stared.

The arm holding her trembled. From emotion? The heft of her body? The lingering weight of his treachery?

"Shall we heave yous up?" a voice called from above.

They both looked to the farmhand holding the rope.

"Aye," Alistair croaked.

Reflexively, his right arm tightened around her.

"Cling tight, lass," he breathed.

Chrissi nodded, not quite trusting herself to speak.

Gracious.

Surely the last time she had experienced so many emotions in such quick succession had been that final disastrous day of their disintegration.

She breathed in the scent of him . . . this former beloved, this long-ago traitor.

This Scot who had always completely overset her world.

ALISTAIR SCRAMBLED UP the embankment, every muscle in his body vibrating with tension.

Chris.

He was holding Chris.

His Christiana.

Though . . . hardly *his* anymore.

Mrs. Stephen Newton.

He had learned, years ago, that she had married some unnamed gentleman. The news had sent him careening, downing far too much whisky and shouting angrily at the silver moon, casting aspersions on womankind in general and her head specifically.

It had not been one of his finer moments.

Time had (mostly) healed the gaping wound of her loss.

Alistair had never known or even wanted to know the

identity of her husband—not wishing to torture himself by imagining her life with another.

Now... he knew. Chris had married Dr. Stephen Newton—an elderly colleague of her father's at Oxford and easily thirty years her senior. Why had she married *him*, of all people?

Scratch that.

Alistair knew why.

She had gotten her wish, in the end. To work and publish alongside her husband, feats she had definitively accomplished. And as she had always been listed as Mrs. Stephen Newton in publications with her husband, Alistair hadn't sussed her true identity—that Mrs. Stephen Newton was, in fact, the former Miss Christiana Rutherford.

And now she was here, in his arms.

His body more than remembered the womanly curve of her, the slope of her waist and arch of her neck. Her touch seared, a scalding brand of familiarity that hurt more than it healed.

He didn't want this. Not now. Not at this juncture.

She was his painful past, not his hoped-for future.

Reaching the top of the slope, he released her perhaps a bit too abruptly, causing her to stumble. But, as ever, Chris righted herself instantly. That had always been her way—chin up, shoulders strong.

"Thank you, my lord." She gave him a wan smile. "I most certainly did not intend to make such a dramatic entrance today."

The crisp vowels of her English accent washed over him, bringing with it memories of Tuscany that clung like sun-drenched honey—delicious and cloyingly sweet.

Chris racing ahead of him through a wisteria-draped loggia along Largo Leonardo da Vinci in Fiesole, skirts snapping as wind whipped her laughter.

Chris carefully brushing dirt off a wee Etruscan funerary figurine, narrating the find for him to scribe in their field notes.

Chris curled into the curve of his arm on a lamplit stairway, bosom hitching as she arched upward to touch her lips to his.

How he had loved her. Even now, the thought of that heady summer set his heart to racing and yearning ribboning through his chest—

No.

He had grieved her loss and moved on.

He refused to revisit the brokenhearted boy he had been.

And now...

He studied her. Categorically, she appeared a mess. Given the mud caking every inch of her person, it was a wonder he recognized her at all.

And yet, beneath the grime, he could discern the stubborn clench of her jaw, the hollow slash of her cheekbones. Gone was the round softness of girlhood, that gentle air of hope and childlike exuberance that had clung to her shoulders like magic.

No, like him, time had altered and changed her.

It was for the best.

She had her life. He had his.

Now... they simply had to untangle themselves from this debacle.

Two

April 20, 1849
Florence, Italy

Nine Years Earlier

HE STRODE OUT of the billowing haze like Apollo fallen to earth.

Standing at her father's side in the Maria Antonia railway station in the center of Florence, Italy—enormous locomotives belching steam and smoke—Chrissi could only gawk in wonder at the god-turned-mortal coming toward them.

Dark-haired and dark-eyed, her Apollo walked with broad-shouldered confidence—not arrogance, per se, but the gait of a man secure within himself. Clean-shaven and fresh-faced, he was tall but not loomingly so. As if even his height chose politeness over dominance.

And unlike other aspiring antiquarians who begged her father for a chance to assist on an archaeological expedition, this man appeared to be no stranger to physical labor—the depth of his chest and width of his biceps testified to this. *Strapping*, her Aunt Eunice would describe him.

He stopped in front of them, setting his leather bag on the ground and tipping his hat in greeting.

"Dr. John Rutherford, I presume?" the man asked.

Chrissi nearly shivered as the delicious rumble of his

Scottish brogue rolled over her. Moreover, he was younger than she had supposed, surely no older than her own twenty years.

"Yes," her father replied.

The man extended his hand. "Mr. Alistair Maclagan, at your service, sir."

Alistair.

It suited him, the name. Subtly refined and stuffy. The name of an elderly gentleman smoking a pipe in the library of White's in London. But the *dare* sound in *Alistair* hinted at danger. At a strand of devilry and mischief.

The twinkle in Mr. Maclagan's eye confirmed this as he turned to Chrissi, obviously expecting an introduction.

"My daughter," her father gestured, "Miss Christiana Rutherford."

Chrissi dipped a small curtsy and extended her gloved hand.

Mr. Maclagan paused before taking her fingers lightly in his own, bowing over her knuckles.

His touch might have been a vise for how thoroughly it affected her.

Her hand hummed with the contact. She felt branded. Scorched. As if in that simple gesture, he had marked her for himself and himself alone.

Chrissi would later describe the moment to him as they walked the sunlit path to the top of Mount Ceceri overlooking Fiesole, hands clasped once more and swinging between them, the drone of cicadas in the air.

How she had simply *known* that Alistair would be the gentleman to win her heart.

And even later, in the aftermath of his betrayal and their subsequent breaking, she would marvel at her initial sense of surety. At the confidence of her naive twenty-year-old self who believed the years between falling in love and leaving this earth would be merry ones, easily passed without heartache and trial, secure within the arc of true love.

But in the train station that first day, any thought of disaster was far from her mind. She was young and eager for her first love, her first kiss, her first . . . everything.

And so, as her father hailed a *carozza* to transport them home, she listened, rapt, as Mr. Maclagan described arriving in Pisa on a clipper ship from Edinburgh and the marvel of the railway line—opened only a year past—taking less than two hours to deposit him in the heart of Florence.

As he spoke, his eyes never left Chrissi's face. As if, like herself, his fingertips sparked with lightning and trembled to close the space between them.

Unlike other gentlemen of her acquaintance, he wasn't enamored with his own speaking voice. He asked questions, too, and listened intently.

"What is that church there?" he inquired as they stood waiting for the *carozza*, pointing to the enormous stained-glass Gothic windows overlooking the train station.

"Santa Maria Novella," Chrissi took great pride in informing him. After all, she had already been in Florence for several weeks. Long enough to feel native, she supposed. To show a newcomer around *her* city. "The frescoes inside are magnificent—Ghirlandaio, Filippino Lippi, Masaccio. There are even sculptures by Brunelleschi."

He grinned at her confident words.

"It sounds fascinating." Though he might as well have said, *Ye sound fascinating*, for how Chrissi heard the words. "Ye will have to show me yourself."

"I should be honored," Chrissi blushed.

On the hour-long carriage ride north to Fiesole—an ancient town perched on a hilltop overlooking Florence—

Chrissi and her father described the archaeological excavations underway.

Her father, Dr. John Rutherford, was a respected professor of antiquities at Oxford, ancient Rome and Etruscan cultures being his area of specialty. His excavations in Fiesole intended to uncover the Roman and Etruscan history of the city. For example, the remains of an amphitheater peeked out from the slope descending behind the main cathedral. Her father suspected there had been Roman baths and possibly a temple on the site as well. Why, just twenty years ago, a cache of a thousand silver Roman *denarii* had been found there—a fortune buried but never recovered.

Her father hoped to uncover more of such riches. As the carriage curved around hills and climbed upward, the three of them excitedly discussed the possibility of finding older Etruscan grave goods—gold necklaces, carved bronze mirrors, and alabaster vases as thin as glass—artifacts similar to those found in Cerveteri or Volterra.

Just an hour after stowing his things in his room in their *pensione*, Mr. Maclagan was tromping around the excavation site. Chrissi raced to join him, happily explaining how he would be assisting them.

"Papa believes in stratigraphy," she explained, motioning to a section where they had been digging.

"Stratigraphy? Like geology?" Mr. Maclagan asked, his brown eyes bringing to mind a pot of hot chocolate—indulgent and deliciously sweet.

"Yes, exactly!" she beamed at him. "Like sediments in the earth, archeology is laid down over the years. Our job as archaeologists is to carefully peel back the layers of each era, to study a time period thoroughly before moving down to the next. That is why we will start with the Roman ruins and then carefully dig farther back in time to the Etruscans who came before."

"So ye consider yourself an archaeologist in truth?"

"Women can be archaeologists." Chrissi hated the defensive note in her voice.

"I do not doubt it. How did ye begin?"

"My mamma died a week before my fourth birthday," she explained as they crawled over a toppled column, "and so it has always been just Papa and me."

"He adopted ye as his assistant, I ken," Mr. Maclagan replied.

"Yes, and I intend to follow in his footsteps." Fervency thrummed through her words.

He paused to stare at her, the Tuscan sun catching in the caramel flecks of his eyes. "I can see it in ye now—Miss Christiana Rutherford, archaeologist. Though I must state the truth: I rather suspect ye might be a bit of a bonnie distraction."

"To whom, sir?" she asked on a laugh, delight and outrage in her tone.

He said nothing . . . only smiled and looked away. But not before she registered the admiration in his eyes.

Before Alistair, had anyone asked, Chrissi would have described her physical person as abysmally undecided—average, unremarkable. Was her hair blonde or brown? Her eyes gray or blue? Her height short or average? Her face plain or pretty?

She supposed her personality *had* to become strong in order to marshal all that indecisiveness into order.

But under Alistair's gaze, her hair transformed into the golden brown of honey, fresh from the comb. Her eyes turned the color of the North Sea off the coast of Stonehaven, storm-blue and undulating with life. For him, her height was neither short nor average but the perfect size to tuck under his chin. And he declared her face to be an enchanting echo of the

Madonnas painted by Raphael or Botticelli in the Uffizi Museum.

Alistair made her feel she was anything but ordinary. He openly admired her love of learning and sympathized with her frustration that women could not attend Oxford.

Chrissi noticed his own distinct qualities, too.

How his brown eyes would stare intently into hers as she spoke of her aspirations. How the timbre of his brogue would deepen as he described Scotland and home.

The son of a solicitor from Aberdeen, with family ties to the aristocracy, Alistair had lived a life typical of the gentry—an excellent education in private school, followed by antiquarian studies at the University of St Andrews in Fife. He longed to become a professor, like Chrissi's father. To make learning his life-long profession. At twenty-one years of age, he had seized the chance to apprentice at her father's feet.

Falling in love with him was effortless. An exhilarating free fall. Chrissi and Alistair were puzzle pieces slotting together. As if they had always been destined to live and breathe as one entity.

Three

ALISTAIR PACED THE great hall of Kinord Castle as if wearing a path in the Axminster carpet would somehow help untangle the *fankle* of his thoughts.

Hands clasped behind his back, he walked from the impressive hearth to the enormous windows at the south end of the hall and back again.

Generally, Scottish castles were dark and dreary places with narrow windows built for defense, not illumination. But his predecessor had removed almost the entirety of the south wall of the great hall, replacing it with pane after pane of glass. Not only did the large window harness the warmth of the sun and flood the room with light, it also gave a commanding view over the surrounding landscape—the boggy marsh melting into rolling hills, thick with Scots pine and fields of fluffy sheep, stretching to the peaks of Ben Avon and Beinn a' Bhùird in the distance.

The scenery did nothing to quiet his mind.

Chris was here.

Alistair's stuttering brain could scarcely reconcile the absurdity of the situation.

After pulling her from the bog—truthfully, she was fortunate not to have broken her wee neck or been drowned in the fen, tumbling down the embankment as she had—they had retired to the castle. Alistair had summoned servants and a bath, both for himself and for her.

She was currently in his best guest room, surely attempting to wash moss and dirt from her hair and cursing the Fate that had deposited her on his doorstep.

As for himself, the mud had been easily dispatched from his person.

Would that thoughts of Christiana Rutherford Newton were banished as easily.

This was to have been his year.

The year that he reclaimed his life from the memories of her and their lost love.

Particularly, Alistair had resolved to recoup his love of archeology. He had abandoned the field after his tumultuous break with Chris. Even if he had wished to continue with his studies, Dr. Rutherford had made it clear Alistair would not be welcomed. Antiquarians were a tight lot, and Dr. Rutherford had stood beside his daughter.

But Alistair's ascension to the title of Lord Farnell two years ago had come with a respectable fortune attached. And as Dr. Rutherford had passed away, Alistair felt the time had come to again explore archeology.

Hence his hiring of Mrs. Newton. As the wife of Dr. Stephen Newton, she had gained a reputation for her own expertise in ancient Celtic excavations, working alongside her husband and even publishing the occasional paper jointly with him. Alistair had never heard a mention of her Christian name... pun intended, he mused to himself.

Dr. Newton had passed away over two years ago, but his widow had continued his work. Therefore, the professor's widow had been the most logical—nearly the *only*—choice when hiring an archaeologist to assist Alistair in understanding the history of his—

A rap on the door interrupted his thoughts.

"Come," he called.

Mrs. Craib, his housekeeper, entered, bobbing a polite curtsy. "Should I still plan on Mrs. Newton joining the party for tea, my lord? Or do ye ken she would prefer a wee rest? The poor thing was proper *clatty*, dripping mud on the flagstones as she was."

Yes, what would Mrs. Newton prefer? Well, likely to be quit of him. But until she said as much . . .

"Plan on Mrs. Newton joining us, Mrs. Craib. I shall inform ye if that plan changes."

The housekeeper bobbed another curtsy before leaving in a rustle of wool skirts and the clink of keys on a châtelaine.

Alistair resumed his pacing.

He paused at the window, gaze automatically straying to the hillside just south of the castle. From here, he could see the standing stone circle—five stones surrounding a larger central monolith. An impressive mound sat behind the circle, keeping watch as the hill descended to the boggy fen beyond. The landscape held a sort of hierarchy . . . castle to standing stones to burial mound to bog.

What was the purpose of the standing stones? And what was under the turf of the mound? A burial cairn? A barrow, like those found in England? The remains of a Pictish fort?

Without Mrs. Newton, he feared he would never know.

But *knowing* Mrs. Newton was Chris . . .

No. It simply wouldn't do. Alistair would prefer to spend the rest of his days staring at the mound and wondering than to endure months of Christiana Rutherford's presence.

All that remained now was to find a polite way to send her packing.

The door *snicked* open again at his back.

"Mrs. Stephen Newton, my lord," his butler, Jamieson, intoned.

Chris glided through, motioned forward by the butler.

"Will ye have Mrs. Craib send up some refreshment, Jamieson?" Alistair asked.

"Of course, my lord."

Jamieson bowed before retreating, leaving the door open as a nod to propriety.

And then . . . Alistair and Chris were alone.

Before today, he would have said that the pain of losing her had healed. That he had licked his wounds and grieved and come out the other end a revived man.

A better man, even.

But now . . . facing her again . . .

The gash of her loss pulsed anew. The haunting whisper of *what if.*

What if he hadn't done what he had done?

What if they had reconciled and married?

What if hers had been the face he had awakened to every morning for the past nine years?

What was done was done. The past had passed. He knew this. And yet the intervening nine years without her had not been gentle. He had spent them full of self-recriminations and mourning the loss of the only future he had ever wanted.

Given how upright and tense she stood just inside the great room door, Chris was likely working through similar thoughts.

He studied her, now cleansed of mud and the thunderstruck numbness of his surprise.

She was older. Obviously. Faint lines bracketed her mouth and a pair of wee wrinkles sat between her eyebrows, the remnants of years spent squinting into the sun.

Her hair remained a lustrous honey-woven brown, though damp now and slicked into a chignon. Her figure was, as ever, well-proportioned—trim waist and curved bosom.

Her storm-blue eyes met his.

Where to begin? Alistair wondered. Words and sentences, nearly entire libraries of thoughts, crowded his tongue. And yet somehow . . . language failed him.

Swallowing, she looked away. Her hands twisted and clasped before her, the only sign of her agitation.

"I didn't know," she began, gaze coming back to his. "I didn't realize that Lord Farnell . . ." She gestured helplessly, indicating his person and the castle as a whole. "I would never have come had I known."

"I believe ye." And he did. "I didn't know either, obviously. We have both sustained a shock today. Won't ye be seated?"

He motioned toward a red velvet settee placed perpendicular to the fireplace. If nothing else, good manners should see them through the awkwardness of this conversation.

Nodding, she crossed in a rustle of wool skirts. He waited for her to pass and tensed for the scent of her perfume—gardenias with under notes of something exotic—to assault him with memory.

But none came.

Instead, he smelled the faint tang of the lavender soap Mrs. Craib made in the stillroom behind the kitchen, bubbling lye in a vat for hours before stirring in lavender oil as the soap began to thicken.

Odd.

Chris had prized that flower-scented perfume, wearing it constantly. Did it hold too many memories, then? Had she abandoned it along with himself?

With a deep breath, Alistair shook the unhelpful questions away.

The less he embroiled himself with Chris, the better.

She sat.

He sat on a chair opposite.

She looked at the flames guttering in the hearth.

He stared at her profile and then rubbed at his eyes, helpless to know where to begin.

Finally, he simply asked the question he most wished to know.

"Was he kind to ye?"

Chris jerked her eyes back to his.

"Stephen?" She named her husband.

She needed no clarification as to his meaning. Even now, after the passage of so many years, their thoughts easily traveled the same path.

"Aye."

"He was." She nodded, eyes going back to the fire. "He . . . saved me, I suppose you could say."

"Did ye love him?" Alistair hated the words as soon as they left his lips. The petty jealousy of them.

Did ye love him as much as ye loved myself? he might as well have asked.

"Yes . . . after a fashion."

After a fashion?

Alistair frowned. What did that mean?

His gaze dropped once more to her hands, clenched into fists atop the bulk of her skirts.

"Chris—"

She flinched. "Please. Refer to me as Mrs. Newton, my lord. Let us not complicate this situation further with the intimacy of personal names."

Mrs. Newton. A woman who belonged to another man, even in his death.

The door creaked open, and Mrs. Craib entered carrying a tray laden with a teapot, shortbread, neatly cut rectangles of roast beef sandwiches, and Victoria sponge dripping strawberry jam.

The housekeeper set the tray on the table before the settee, curtsied, and retreated.

"Would ye be so kind?" Alistair gestured toward the teapot.

With a nod, Chris poured for them—her elegant fingers grasping the teapot and dispensing the tea with confident verve.

Once upon a time, that phrase had nearly been her personal motto—*confident verve.*

It had manifested in the way she troweled away dirt from a Roman mosaic, hand sweeping boldly as if she could already sense what lay beneath. Or in the way she skipped ahead as they strolled through the pine-forested hills behind Fiesole, walking backward to face him as she explained the difference between Etruscan and Roman pottery sherds, arms gesturing in her excitement.

Now, watching her drop a sugar cube and healthy splash of cream into his tea—remembering how he took it after all these years—

She seemed . . . thinner. Not just in her person but in spirit, too. As if the weight of living had dampened the vitality that had once shimmered like a ruby-chested hummingbird in the sun.

Perhaps . . . perhaps those months had simply been magical, in the way of conjuring or witch's spells. Perhaps Alistair had merely romanticized Chris and their time together. Had the Christiana Rutherford he knew ever truly existed? Or had she merely been a construct of his eager heart—the beautiful girl wrapped up inextricably with archeology and the glory of summer in the hills above Florence?

He took the saucer and teacup from her with a murmured thanks. "Tell me of yourself then, Mrs. Newton. Of your years since our last meeting in Fiesole."

Painfully formal, those words.

She stirred sugar and cream into her own tea.

"There is not much to say." She placed a roast beef

sandwich and triangle of shortbread on her plate. "As you know, I left Italy immediately after . . ."

She rolled her hand, as if that simple motion could somehow encapsulate the detonation of their relationship. Was it his imagination, or did her hand tremble slightly as she lifted her cup and saucer?

Perhaps she wasn't as unmoved at seeing him again as she appeared.

The thought cheered him. Misery always loved company, as his gran would say.

"And Dr. Stephen Newton? How did your marriage come about?"

"Yes, well . . ." Chris cleared her throat and sipped her tea, as if choosing her next words carefully. "I was rather . . . bereft, as you might imagine, upon leaving Italy. Once back in Oxford, I found myself often at loose ends. Stephen was caring and attentive to my needs, given that my father was still out of the country. As an old friend of the family, Stephen wished to ensure my well-being."

Of course he did. *Old* being the most significant word of her description.

Alistair, thankfully, managed not to say as much.

"Our friendship grew," she continued, "and we married. Stephen welcomed my insights and 'youthful energy,' as he called it, toward his archaeological work. And we were happy, after a fashion, for several years."

After a fashion. That phrase again.

"And then my father fell ill and passed away."

"I was sorry to hear of it."

"His loss was difficult." She looked to the window, eyes a wee bit too bright. Rallying, she took in a long breath. "Stephen followed the year after."

"And that was two years past, was it not?"

"Yes."

"And since then?"

She shrugged and shot him a wan smile. The sort that did not touch her eyes. "Since then, I have been doing what women do, my lord . . . getting on with life."

Getting on with life? What did she mean by that?

She reached for another sandwich.

Finally, Alistair slotted together the puzzle pieces—the things she was *not* saying.

It started with the fragile thinness of her arm stretched over the tea tray, her wrist bone protruding alarmingly as if begging to be fed. His eyes moved upward to the sleeve of her gown, the edge frayed and worn. The fabric had been turned, he realized—a painstaking process that required unstitching a dress entirely, turning the sun-faded fabric over, and restitching the whole. An economy when coin to purchase new fabric was scarce.

A faint frown creased his brow.

Abruptly, he feared he understood only too well what "getting on with life" meant. His chest ached as if the thought of Chris existing hungry and cold and ill-clothed violated the very laws of his heart.

Alistair cleared his throat. "I assume your husband . . ."—Blast it all. How to ask this politely?—"or your father left some sort of . . . of annuity . . ." He allowed the words to drift off.

The teacup rattled atop the saucer in her hand, but she said nothing for a long moment.

"As well you know, any possession of mine became my husband's upon our marriage."

She said nothing more.

It wasn't truly an answer, but Alistair read between the lines. Neither husband nor father had provided for her.

"And now?" he asked.

"Well . . . my mother's sister—"

"Your Aunt Eunice?"

"Yes," she replied too brightly, eyes finally lifting to his. "Aunt Eunice has been kind enough to offer me a place to stay." She pronounced Eunice's name in the Italian fashion—ay-oo-NEE-chay. "When I am not engaged in archaeological activities, of course."

From Alistair's memory, Aunt Eunice was a terrible skinflint. Showing such benevolence to her niece seemed... uncharacteristic.

And so he said as much. "Such generosity seems... unusual for your aunt."

Chris blinked in surprise, perhaps at his bluntness... or perhaps his unflagging recollection of her family dynamics.

"Yes, well, Aunt Eunice is nothing if not eccentric."

Memory washed over Alistair, unbidden and unwelcome—Chris laughing at her aunt's idiosyncrasies as they strolled the Roman excavation site, fingers clutching his arm. He could still recall the very words Chris had spoken, the playful cadence of her voice.

"Aunt Eunice insists on us all pronouncing her name as if she is an Italian lady—ay-oo-NEE-chay. Mind you, she was born and raised in Sussex and has never dipped a toe in the Mediterranean Sea. Aunt guards every penny of her fortune, as she wishes to pass it all intact to my cousin, Freddie the Feckless. Therefore, she will not hear of a single cent being spent unnecessarily. I haven't the heart to tell her that Freddie will likely lose the whole at the gambling table or the racetrack or both and will not give a fig (what with his feckless heart and all) that Aunt Eunice so scrupulously protected her fortune for him. I would put the coin to much wiser use. But as with most situations in life, Aunt Eunice feels that fortunes are better entrusted to the male line."

Now Alistair studied Chris, trying to discern the reality behind her emotionless words.

He gave up and asked directly. "Knowing Aunt Eunice's spendthrift ways, I must admit I am surprised."

Chris pursed her lips. "Well, I did not say she provided anything *other* than a place to lay my head, now did I?"

Her wit sparked with the woman he had known.

Unbidden, a smile touched his face. "And what, precisely, does that mean?"

"Merely that Aunt Eunice will permit me to grace one of the five empty bedrooms of her manor house, provided I pay for my own coal and meals."

"Ah. Freddie the Feckless will be safeguarded to the very end, I see."

"Aunt Eunice might have many foibles, but inconsistency is not one of them."

He smiled again, faint but there.

They sipped their tea in silence.

The bird-thin wisp of her wrist would not let him be. It flashed every time she lifted her teacup or reached for another roast beef sandwich. How many had she eaten now?

Did she not have the funds to feed herself properly? Was she often hungry?

Alistair had begun this conversation fully intending to dismiss her. To discuss the impossibility of them working together in any capacity, for both their sakes. To usher her out his front door and relegate Chris firmly to his past.

But now . . .

What would she do if Alistair sent her packing?

Return to Aunt Eunice's bleak bedchamber and even bleaker charity? Spend her days hungry and shivering?

To say nothing of what might befall her once Aunt Eunice drew her last breath.

Despite everything that had occurred between himself and Chris, how could Alistair leave her to such a fate?

 Four

CHRISSI TRIED NOT to squirm under Alis's direct gaze and the sharp probe of his questions.

Pragmatic and forthright—that was Alis. He had never been one to mince words.

Moreover, she had forgotten how unnerving he could be—how he listened with his entire body, leaning forward, eager to hear what she might say next.

Physically, he was just as overwhelming. His shoulders dwarfed the armchair where he sat, his long legs stretched before him. He had swapped his mud-splattered shirtsleeves for a tailored, superfine suit the gray color of wood ash, a blue-and-cream striped waistcoat underneath. The chain of a gold pocket watch winked in the light, as did the carved signet ring on his right pinky.

In short, Alis no longer resembled the impoverished student he had been, hungry to uncover artifacts. Instead, he looked like the wealthy lord he had become.

Chrissi felt every last inch of the worn fabric of her outdated dress. Depressingly, it was one of the nicer garments in her meager wardrobe. If Alis dismissed her this afternoon, the dress would not be replaced anytime soon.

Why? she wanted to scream, shaking an angry fist at the sky. Why did fate have to land her here, in this castle, seated across from the remnants of her broken heart? She wanted the past scrubbed from her brain. Heaven knew she had tried to erase Alis from memory.

And now, to find herself entwined with him once more, in desperate need of his charity . . .

"I have enjoyed your archaeological articles," he said after a moment. "Those ye did with Dr. Newton."

"Thank you. Stephen encouraged my writing." Chrissi didn't add "unlike others" to the end of her sentence, but she was rather sure Alis heard it anyway.

"Are ye no longer writing?" he asked.

"As you are well aware, my lord, a woman must generally have a man's name beside her own in order to publish." She set her teacup back on its saucer with an audible *clink*. "And even then, realizing one's work in print can be fraught."

He at least had the decency to wince at her jab.

"Ah." Alis sat back, saying nothing more.

Please don't turn me out, she silently pleaded.

She eyed the sandwiches remaining on the tea tray. How many could she eat without sparking more questions?

Though given the ponderance of Alis's stare and his probing queries about Aunt Eunice, she rather suspected he already understood the whole of her situation—impoverished with few prospects.

She and Stephen had wed without a marriage contract. So foolish of her, in hindsight, not to insist upon one. Not to demand over and over that the gentlemen in her life—father and husband—spare a thought for her future.

But then, she had made a tremendous number of foolish mistakes at that point.

Her father had assumed that her husband would care for her, as the significant sum she had inherited upon her father's death had become Stephen's to pass along. After all, as a woman, she had no personhood under British law; all her possessions were held by her husband. Chrissi was merely an extension of Stephen.

For his part, Stephen had promised he would amend his will to include her—a promise he had neglected, as she learned after his death. Stephen could be absent-minded, but she had trusted him to adhere to his word and heed her insistent nagging. By the time she realized Stephen's negligence, he was already gone.

And, therefore, all of Stephen's possessions—including the fortune she had inherited from her father—passed to her husband's adult son from his first marriage, Mr. Thomas Newton.

It had been a dreadful shock for Chrissi—listening to the solicitor read Stephen's will and not to hear a single mention of herself. To realize that her own inheritance had been lost.

Thomas had been recalcitrant, refusing to release a single penny of her own monies from his late father's estate. He considered his father's marriage to a much younger woman an affront to his deceased mother. According to him, Chrissi, in her poverty, only reaped what she had sowed. If his father had wanted her to have the money, he would have made provision.

A solicitor Chrissi had consulted about the matter had been equally unsympathetic. The man had stated, quite solemnly, that she must have been a difficult wife for her husband to so summarily dismiss her from his will.

And so, desperate to avoid the poorhouse, Chrissi had thrown herself upon Aunt Eunice's strained charity.

Chrissi's throat still tightened to think upon the bleak months after Stephen's death. The cold nights shuttered in Aunt Eunice's dingiest bedchamber, selling her mother's jewelry to pay a portion of Eunice's household expenses.

Archeology had been her only hope of income. She had penned letters to colleagues of her father and Stephen, inquiring after work or possible publishing opportunities. Some had responded. Slowly she had begun to eke a living from the work that came her way.

But this project with Lord Farnell was to have been her saving grace—a large commission that would finally see her coffers replenished and give her a modicum of stability. Perhaps a few coins for a new bonnet and dress. Or even enough clout to garner a publication under her own name.

As long as Aunt Eunice breathed, Chrissi would have a place to rest her head. And if she could continue to work and live by the strictest economy, she might eventually save enough to support herself once Aunt Eunice's "largesse" reached an end.

Sitting back in his chair, Alis nibbled on a wedge of shortbread, his gaze speculative and far too understanding.

Drat him for knowing Chrissi so well, even at this juncture.

He appeared poised to ask a dozen questions about her circumstances that she desperately wished to avoid.

"And yourself, my lord?" she inquired, a bit too brightly, helping herself to the last roast beef sandwich. "How did you come to inherit the title of Lord Farnell?"

His dark eyes pondered her for another long moment before replying. "As ye may remember, my great-uncle was Lord Farnell . . . a Lord of Parliament in the Scottish Peerage. His son inherited, and the title was to have passed to three cousins before myself. But illness and an accident claimed their lives one after the other. My predecessor, Captain Michael Maclagan, was a cavalry officer with the Royal Scots Greys and was badly wounded in the siege of Sevastopol. He returned home only to succumb to his injuries a year later. And thus I inherited the lot." He motioned to indicate the room, the castle, and all that lay beyond.

"Was it a dreadful shock?"

"The death of a family member is always a bit of a shock, I suppose." He sipped his tea. "And though I cannot say I dislike inheriting, I greatly dislike that it took Michael's death to bring it to pass."

"Wisely said."

Chrissi set a slice of Victoria sponge on her plate.

Alis drank his tea.

So civilized, she mused, the pair of them. An outsider would merely see two friends becoming reacquainted after the passage of many years.

None would suspect the roil of emotion churning like the wind-whipped North Sea within her ribcage.

How could she work with Alis on this project? To relive, day after day, the headiness of that long-ago summer? To ponder, again and again, her many mistakes and wonder if she should have forgiven his shattering choices in the end?

It felt impossible.

But then, returning to Aunt Eunice's drafty bedchamber felt equally impossible—perhaps literally so unless Alis lent her the funds for the train journey.

No.

She needed this opportunity, this paid commission, too badly to quit the field.

Swallowing, Chrissi decided to match his earlier directness and merely ask what she most wished to know.

"So, my lord, your proposed excavations?"

Those dark eyes continued to assess her, imparting nothing of his thoughts.

"Do ye think it possible to work together, lass, given everything?" His words wafted across the room to her, all the more devastating for their softness.

No. She absolutely did not.

But she had nothing else.

"I . . . I should like to try."

"Because ye value the archeology?" He studied her for another long moment. "Or because ye need funds?"

Blunt.

So very blunt.

But then, that had always been his way.

Alistair Maclagan would always say precisely what he meant.

"Well." Chrissi looked to the fire in the hearth, then to the ancient tapestries hanging from the walls before coming back to him. "Can it not be both?"

He shifted forward, elbows coming to his knees. "We both know ye would be on the first train out of Deeside if ye could manage it—happy, once more, to see the backend of my sorry carcass."

Chrissi bit the inside of her cheek.

True that.

"Nonsense," she replied. "I would watch the front end of you disappear just as happily."

The quip earned her a crack of laughter. Alis tilted his head back, white teeth flashing as he chuckled.

It hurt, that sudden burst of joy.

Chrissi had to forcibly resist pressing the heel of her hand to her breastbone to still the ache there.

"Ah, Chris—ehr, Mrs. Newton—how I've missed your humor," he smiled. "Ye were never one to let a proper jibe pass ye by."

Chrissi pressed her lips together, disliking how they ached to curve into a matching smile. Hating the warmth his words—her name upon his lips—ignited in her chest.

Only Alis had ever called her Chris.

A commotion sounded outside the door—people

climbing the stairwell leading from the entrance hall to the great hall.

The butler entered.

"Mrs. Rollins and Miss Rollins, my lord," he intoned.

A fashionably dressed matron and her daughter breezed past the butler into the room.

A palpable change swept over Alis—spine straightening, gaze eager. Smiling broadly, he stood and crossed the room to greet his guests.

"Welcome." He bowed first over Mrs. Rollins's hand and then Miss Rollins's. "It is a pleasure to have ye here."

Chrissi rose to her feet, studying the women.

With bright blue eyes and gleaming blonde hair, Miss Rollins appeared the picture of demure, maidenly innocence. She blushed prettily at Alis's words.

Mrs. Rollins was an older version of her daughter, supervising Alis and her charge with a benevolent expression.

"Please"—he motioned the pair forward—"come greet my houseguest."

Chrissi well understood her cue to cross the room and smile as Alis made introductions.

"Ye be much younger than I would have supposed, Mrs. Newton. Do ye not think, Mamma?" Miss Rollins smiled prettily at Chrissi and then her mother.

"Aye," Mrs. Rollins said, voice kind. "Lord Farnell has told us much of your accomplishments, Mrs. Newton. And to know that ye have done so much already in your young life, why it is even more a marvel."

Chrissi murmured her thanks, trying to understand why the pair were here. Had they stopped in for a visit? A mother looking to secure a husband for her daughter?

Alis motioned for them all to be seated. Mrs. Craib bustled in with another tea tray. Mrs. Rollins poured this time.

It appeared a well-versed routine between them all.

When offered, Chrissi shamelessly added another roast beef finger sandwich to her plate. The ladies chattered with Alis about the vicar's sermon Sunday last and the unwise changes Farmer McLean was making to his east field.

Clearly, theirs was an acquaintance of some standing.

The conversation finally turned back to Chrissi and her presence here.

"Do ye ken the excavation will uncover something dreadfully exciting, Mrs. Newton?" Miss Rollins asked, balancing a square of Victoria sponge on the edge of her plate.

Had Chrissi ever viewed the world with such wide-eyed innocence?

Perhaps once. Before Alis and heartbreak.

"I always hope to uncover something exciting and new on each excavation," Chrissi replied.

"Have I told ye the plan for the excavation, Miss Rollins?" Alis asked, gaze solicitous and, Chrissi disliked admitting, fond.

The reason for the ladies' visit was becoming more and more apparent with each passing moment.

"No," Miss Rollins beamed, "but I should dearly love to know."

"Come," Alis motioned, rising to his feet.

Setting down her plate, Miss Rollins eagerly followed him over to the large window, cooing and giggling as he gestured toward the hills outside, expounding his thoughts on the excavation.

Mrs. Rollins studied the pair from where she sat beside Chrissi. The woman loosed a contented sigh. "They make such a handsome couple, do ye not think, Mrs. Newton?"

"Yes. They do," Chrissi agreed. "Pretty as a picture."

And they were.

Alis's dark head bent near Miss Rollins's fair one, arm outstretched to point out features of the landscape. At one point, Miss Rollins turned her head to gaze up at Alis, a fetching blush on her cheeks and starshine in her eyes. Chrissi challenged the celebrated painter Sir Ewan Campbell himself to capture a more perfect expression of adoration.

Chrissi dropped her eyes to the Victorian sponge on Miss Rollins's abandoned plate—a bead of strawberry jam dripping down the side into a puddle. As if the cake were weeping.

Clearly, the emotions pricking Chrissi's eyes were clouding her thinking.

Enough. How many tears could one woman shed over Alistair Maclagan?

Any thought Chrissi had of fighting to complete the excavations died a thousand deaths at the sound of Alis's laugh over some witticism Miss Rollins murmured.

Better an empty stomach than having to stoically watch Alis court, and likely marry, another woman. Better the cold comfort of Aunt Eunice's "hospitality" than to drag the grief and pain of their splintered past into the light of day once more.

"I say, Mrs. Newton, your color seems off," Mrs. Rollins said. "Are ye feeling poorly?"

Bless the woman. She must be the Catholic Saint of Lost Lovers in the guise of a Scottish matron.

"I am rather unwell." Chrissi pressed a hand to her brow and rose to her feet.

Alis and Miss Rollins turned toward her.

"I do beg your pardon," Chrissi said, attempting to affect a look of pain. "I fear the events of today have given me something of a headache. Do you mind terribly if I retire to rest my head?"

And pack her trunk and abscond before she did

something ridiculous . . . like beg Alis for funds to purchase a railway ticket.

Alis frowned, likely seeing right through Chrissi's onion-paper of an excuse.

"Of course," he said.

"I do hope you feel well soon," Miss Rollins said, her blue eyes limpid with concern. "We are all so delighted to have ye here."

Not for long if Chrissi could help it.

"Thank you," she nodded, turning for the door.

But not before witnessing Alis and Miss Rollins bending their heads together once more, the sound of his deep bass chuckle all but chasing Chrissi from the room.

Five

May 2, 1849
Fiesole, Italy

"THERE YE BE, Miss Rutherford."

Chrissi looked up as Mr. Maclagan's shadow fell across the sketchbook she had spread atop her skirts, pencil gliding as she practiced her drawing skills.

Her heart frolicked in her chest, happy as a week-old lamb at the sight of him.

Over the past fortnight, she and Mr. Maclagan had shared stolen glances, speaking to one another whenever possible.

But this was the first time he had deliberately sought her out.

"Mr. Maclagan." She shielded her eyes to gaze up at him. "Well met."

Grinning, he sat down on the grass beside her.

"'Tis a bonnie spot ye have here, lass." He wrapped his arms around his knees, taking in the view.

It was indeed bonnie, as he had said. Set upon the hill rising to Fiesole, the grassy knoll—dotted with wildflowers and roses in bloom—provided a stunning vista of Florence. In the distance, a sea of terracotta roof tiles undulated beneath towers and domes—the medieval spire of Santa Croce, Brunelleschi's dome, the crenelated defenses of the Palazzo Vecchio.

Of course, Chrissi only wanted to look at *him*. To ponder the smooth skin of his neck and watch the wind ruffle his hair.

"I come here when I wish to think. And sketch, obviously." She tilted her sketchbook toward him.

He smiled politely, but Chrissi knew her drawing skills were average at best. Nothing like the drawings she had seen him produce—plants and stone and bits of history. The world came alive under his pencil.

Thankfully, he nodded approvingly at her sketch before lifting his warm brown eyes to her face. Chrissi willed herself not to blush.

"And what thoughts grace your lovely head, Miss Rutherford?"

Lovely.

Her cheeks burned.

Later, Chrissi would wonder if perhaps it was the compliment that loosened her tongue. Or maybe just the thrill of having Alistair Maclagan's attention focused on her, gaze earnest and listening.

Regardless, she confessed, "I wish to write. To see my ideas about archeology published in journals like my father."

His eyebrows rose in surprise. "Ye can do that as a woman?"

"No." The word emerged half sigh, half defeat. "That is the rub, obviously. My femaleness."

The fire in his brown eyes stated, rather clearly, that *he* considered her femaleness to be rather delightful.

"In order to publish," she continued, "I would need to have a man's name alongside my own."

His head tilted. "What about your father?"

Chrissi's mouth twisted to one side. "My father feels that tying my name to his in a publication would only cheapen both our work."

"As others would assume ye had only been published out of charity."

Chrissi nodded.

"It seems a shame," he said, "for your brilliance to remain tucked inside your head, no matter how pretty a package it is."

Her blush deepened.

"My *assumed* brilliance, you mean," she had to say. "Perhaps my ideas are drivel."

His gaze raked her from head to toe, sending gooseflesh skittering down the back of her arms.

"Ah, lass. After two weeks of working beside ye, watching how ye study and document things . . . Well, I ken *brilliant* is the only thing ye could ever be."

Chrissi rather forgot to breathe.

They stared and stared, her lungs struggling to take in enough air. Finally, she had to look away . . . anything to alleviate the giddy infatuation banding her rib cage.

They sat in silence for a long moment.

"What if . . ." he began, hesitantly. "What if another gentleman offered himself as tribute? A male scaffolding holding aloft those *brilliant*"—here he shot her a telling look—"ideas of yours. I am utterly unknown in the field, as of now, so no one could say I offered ye charity. If anything, 'twould be the other way round. Others would see me for the supporting buttress that I am."

Chrissi's jaw sagged as her mind scrambled to assimilate the reality of what he was offering.

"You would . . ." She blinked. "You would do that? Foster a joint publication between us?"

"Aye. I would. Ye write, and I will illustrate."

"Even making it clear to a publisher that I am a woman?"

"Ye should have more faith in your ideas. They are worthy of any man." He grinned. "I could be Alis to your Chris if a gendered name exchange helps."

Alis and Chris.

Oh! She very much liked the sound of that.

"Do you let all the ladies call you Alis?" she had to ask.

"Only the bonniest ones," he chuckled.

Chrissi feared her blush matched the red of the poppies ringing the field.

"Well . . . Alis . . . I should be honored to be your Chris." She extended her hand.

He stared at it before slowly, almost reverently, pressing his palm to hers.

The contact sent fireworks bursting beneath her skin. Chrissi briefly worried the heat licking up her arm would set the grass afire.

"Chris," he smiled. "I can't wait to see all the splendid things ye write for us."

Six

CHRIS HAD LEFT.

Alistair stared at the trunk sitting just inside the door of her bedchamber, neatly bundled and ready for the carter's wagon. The upstairs maid had alerted him to the fact—Mrs. Newton had ordered her effects packed and then, while Alistair was still *blethering* with Miss Rollins and her mother, had slipped out the front door.

Running away without a word of goodbye. Just as she had in Fiesole all those years ago.

It astonished him that it hurt . . . her leaving.

He scrubbed a tired hand down his face.

Wouldn't it be best to simply let her go? They had destroyed each other, he and Chris.

In truth, her death would have been easier to overcome than her abandonment. Ironic, perhaps, but accurate, nonetheless. Because in death, she would have remained his.

Instead, he had spent the intervening years imagining her married to another—loving him, sharing a life with him. Another man reveling in the crackling spark of her wit, enjoying the touch of her soft hands, the husky whisper of her voice in his ear. Another man giving her the renown and academic credit that Alistair had not provided.

And now, after so many years, he had come to peace with it all. There was Miss Rollins with her bright smiles and easy manner—never demanding, never pushing. Willing to be content with what he could share of himself and not insist upon more.

Not like Chris.

No. Chris had wanted to know everything—his hopes, dreams, the very dregs of his soul. And in his naive foolishness, he had let her in, eager to splay his heart at her feet. Heady with the euphoria of being so known.

It had made the crush of his failures and her subsequent rejection all the more devastating.

And yet now, he stared helplessly at her packed trunk sitting isolated between the foot of the bed and the hearth. The spare starkness of it—three battered leather straps reaching across the lid to brass clasps, one of which dangled broken—dents and scratches testifying to the drubbing that life had delivered.

Somehow, he knew the trunk contained her entire world—every treasured book and notebook, every presentable skirt and bodice.

The image of her too-thin wrist surfaced.

Nine years ago, brokenhearted and angry, he had let her go.

But now, he simply . . . couldn't. Not like this.

His feet pivoted for the stairs before any conscious thought surfaced.

ALISTAIR HAD THOUGHT to find Chris trudging on foot down the rutted road, attempting to reach Dinnet before everything was shut tight for the evening.

But as he crossed the road, he caught the flash of skirts whipping from behind the central monolith in the stone circle below the castle.

He found Chris there, her shoulder blades pressed to the ancient granite slab, shawl tucked tight to her chest, eyes staring out over the bog and the lone stone standing in the middle. As the solstice was only four weeks away, the sun still hung in the sky, bathing the marsh grass and rolling hills beyond in golden light.

Hearing him approach, she startled and swiped at her eyes with the corner of her shawl, fingers shaking.

Not saying a word, he dug into his pocket and extended a white handkerchief to her.

With a hiccup, Chris took it, dabbing the tears off her cheeks.

She had always been an elegant crier; he would give her that. Her eyes did not become red-rimmed, nor did her skin turn splotchy. She rarely made noise. Instead, the tears flowed soundlessly before she wiped them away.

Alistair rested his shoulders beside her own, content to dwell in silence with her and listen to a pair of cuckoos quarrel in the bushes.

The ever-restless wind soon wrapped Chris's skirts around his knees and whipped the ends of her bonnet ribbons across his chest.

He heard her swallow.

"Thank you," she whispered, twisting the handkerchief around her fingers.

"There is nothing to thank."

More silence.

"She seems lovely."

No need to clarify w*ho* Chris meant.

"Aye. I haven't officially declared my intentions, but Miss Rollins is truly a bonnie lass."

Chris nodded, the wind-reddened tip of her pert nose peeking out from the brim of her bonnet.

How odd.

Alistair had spent the entire afternoon with Miss Rollins, and yet he could not recall a single thing they had discussed or even the color of Miss Rollins's gown.

But he easily remembered every detail, every word spoken, with Chris.

"Are ye leaving?" he continued.

She ran her fingertips over his initials embroidered in a corner of the handkerchief.

"I do not see how I could stay, Alis."

"Alis, am I now? Not *my lord*?"

"That is the problem." She finally lifted her gaze to his, a storm gathered in her gray-blue eyes. "I realized that I cannot pretend you are anything but *Alis* to me. It is why staying is too difficult—reliving everything from Florence while watching you woo Miss Rollins."

"Aye." He heartily agreed with her.

Swallowing again, she wiped her cheeks with a frustrated growl.

"I *meant* to leave. But then I remembered that stone out in the bog there." She pointed to the rock standing tall on a wee island of firmer ground. "And it *hurt*... to leave without knowing if it was deliberately put there. And if so, its purpose."

"Ah. Curiosity always did get the better of ye."

"It did."

"'Tis what makes ye such an excellent archaeologist—ye aren't content to let something be until ye have sussed out an answer."

She gave a hiccupping sigh. "Do not c-compliment me, Alis. Not at this juncture."

My heart cannot take more bruising, she didn't add. But Alistair heard the words anyway.

His own heart panged in sympathy.

"Ye might need to let this mystery be, Chris. The bog makes reaching the stone treacherous. Best to wait until July when the sun has dried out the marsh somewhat. Besides, it's likely just a *gowk stane*." He pointed to where it stood above the bog.

"*Gowk stane?*"

"Aye. A cuckoo stone, to translate it from Scots. There are many here in Aberdeenshire."

Interest peeked out from her gaze. "They are marked somehow, then?"

"Nae. There is no logical reason why they are called *gowk stanes*. Some are marked or carved. Others are simply natural boulders. But if a community deems a rock to be a *gowk stane*, then it becomes one."

"That seems . . . arbitrary." Chris frowned.

He shrugged. "The *gowk stanes* are believed to be gateways between this world and the underworld—the place that cuckoo birds retreat in winter and emerge come spring."

"Ah. A visual reminder of rebirth."

"Aye."

Her eyes skimmed the landscape. "Spring comes so late this far north. It's nearly June, and yet the trees are only now budding. It was summer in Sussex when I boarded the train."

"True. But give it two weeks, Chris. The heather will turn green with new growth and gorse will paint the hills in lemon-yellow flowers."

"The very color of hope."

Alistair hated the wistfulness in her tone.

"Has hope been in such short supply, then?"

She shrugged, eyes dropping back to his handkerchief still wound around her fingers.

"I haven't—" she began, chest heaving again. "I h-haven't the funds to leave."

He had suspected as much, but it still sent a bolt of anger lancing through him.

"I am sorrier than I can say that your husband and father left ye nothing. That was a right damnable thing to do."

"It was."

"The funds from this excavation are important to ye."

"They are, but I was also excited for the work. To conduct an exploration of this magnitude is every archaeologist's dream."

He grunted. "Ye should have been born a man, Chris. Ye would have taken the world by storm."

The words were true enough, though Alistair would forever be grateful she was a lusciously curved woman.

"I would have," she sniffed, dabbing at her eyes once more. "I still might."

Helpless admiration swelled at her indomitable spirit. "There is the Chris I know."

Even as he spoke, the very air changed around him. An energy vibrated along his muscles as if a long-dead part of him was slowly awakening.

A sensation he had only ever felt in Chris's presence.

And in that moment, he knew.

He had to convince her to stay. He couldn't send her back to Aunt Eunice's rackety garret. To live with hunger and hopelessness.

"If I double the amount I proposed to pay ye, then would ye stay?" he asked. John McIntosh—his steward, or *factor*, in Scottish parlance—would surely berate him for the expense, but Alistair knew he could afford the funds.

Chris froze, the handkerchief half-raised to her face.

Her gaze skewered him.

"Why would you do such a thing?"

"Because it's the right thing to do. For yourself. For me."

They stared at one another as wind rippled the grass around them.

She still has that shard of gold in her right iris, he thought. A wee hint that her soul was lightning struck.

"It isn't pity if that is what ye be thinking," he continued.

She laughed, a sharp crack of sound. "I would hardly care, even if it were pity. Pride is the privilege of those with full stomachs and more than a handful of gowns to their name."

Alistair hated the reality her words implied.

"Double, you say?" She looked sideways at him.

"Aye."

"If I did decide to stay, how would you see this proceeding?" She motioned to the space between them. "I cannot think that the two of us working in close quarters would be advisable."

True, that.

How *did* he see this proceeding?

"We could work in shifts?" he offered tentatively, his mind scrambling to find solutions. "Ye could take the mornings and then leave me notes for the afternoon? I understand your methodology and know how to wield a trowel."

"Do you still refuse to sharpen your trowel?" she asked conversationally.

"I see no need to hone mine to a knife's edge, as well ye know, Chris."

"Amateur." She shook her head.

He couldn't stop a grin. "Not all of us wish to attack an excavation site with the precision of a surgical scalpel."

"Again. Amateur."

A beat of silence.

"So we wouldn't speak with one another?" she asked.

"Well . . . only when polite circumstances demand it." His gaze slid out over the landscape, puffy white sheep grazing in the distance. "Would ye prefer we interact more closely?"

"No." To the point. Pragmatic.

He spread his hands as if to say, *Precisely.*

"Heaven knows I could use your illustration skills," she said finally. "Are they still up to snuff?"

"They are. Better, even." He had never stopped drawing over the years.

"Well . . . I suppose we could give such an arrangement a go."

Alistair nodded in agreement.

This would be a disaster.

She dabbed at her cheeks one last time before handing back his handkerchief.

"This is going to be a disaster," she said, unerringly echoing his thoughts.

"Aye, most likely."

She glanced at him. "I give us a week."

"Confident of ye. I would have thought no more than three days."

Even hours on, Alistair could still hear the treacle-sweet echo of her choked laugh.

Seven

IN HINDSIGHT, THREE days might have been optimistic.

Chrissi pondered this the next morning as she walked the stone circle and earthen mound, Alis at her side.

After coming to terms with Alis the day before, she had used the remaining sunlight to comb the site with a groom as an assistant—getting her bearings, examining the layout of the various elements, and making notes of things she wished to explore.

But today, she and Alis needed to establish a methodology for their excavations. It felt surreal to be walking an archaeological site with Alis once more, sharing ideas and theories.

Chrissi tried to ignore how appealing he looked today, the wind snapping his frock coat and tousling his hair into wild shapes. He appeared unfettered. Free. He had given up on his top hat the second time the Scottish breeze had snatched it from atop his head. Standing at her side now, he tapped his hat against his thigh.

"I think we should start there." Chrissi pointed to a section where the mound dipped a few feet into the earth. Despite the early hour, the sun was already high in the sky. "That area faces east and is the most likely spot to find an entrance tunnel. Most mounds tend to be oriented toward the rising sun. If, of course, this is a burial mound."

"Do ye have doubts?"

"Not really. The standing stones there—" She pointed to the stones resting fifty yards from the mound. "—indicate that this was a site of some importance. But everything is conjecture until we put shovel to earth."

Nodding, Alis gave her a soft look, the sort she had once taken for granted.

As ever, she felt the siren call of him—the magnetism that had always spilled in his wake. It whispered at her senses, the teasing brush of a feathered wing luring her to throw off all caution and reach for adventure and far-off shores.

Well.

She had done that once and now knew that feathered wing belonged to an albatross—a harbinger of heartache and grief.

No more.

Granted, her personal vows were easier to remember without the scent of Alis's masculine cologne filling her nostrils and the coiled power of his large body at her elbow.

"What will we be looking for, then, as far as the entrance is concerned?" he asked, thankfully breaking the spiral of Chrissi's thoughts.

She lifted an eyebrow and tilted her head. "Typically, chambered cairns have three distinct features: a long tunnel-like entrance, a central chamber, and small niche side chambers. Given the height of the tunnel entrance, the earth leading to it needed to be shored up. Therefore, the ancient builders would have constructed a breastwork on either side of the entrance—large stone walls to hold back the dirt. The stones would have sloped from the height of the door to the ground, creating a channel of sorts. My goal is to begin hunting for a channel."

Alis stared at the landscape, obviously trying to envision

what she could already see in her mind's eye. Her father and her husband had always praised Chrissi's ability to think like people and cultures long since passed.

"You have a knack for seeing a landscape as the ancients would have," Stephen had said on more than one occasion.

He was not wrong. While on an excavation, Chrissi would often feel a hum, a sense of how past peoples would have viewed and interacted with their surroundings. It had led to more than one find.

"Your instincts were always uncannily accurate," Alis said now, unwittingly agreeing with her late husband. "I'll send my men up so ye can begin."

He had designated a crew of five men to do the digging—field hands who welcomed the extra coin, he said.

"Thank you."

"I look forward to your notes. Just leave a list of what ye would like me to do each day, and I will see it done."

Chrissi looked up at him, wind tugging at her bonnet.

Alis gazed back, his dark eyes reflecting the green grass at their feet and the clouds racing overhead. A whole world contained there, Chrissi supposed.

A world she had once adored with every atom that comprised her body.

A world she would have to fight daily not to tumble headlong into once more.

That was the problem.

She could (and would) work with Alis on this excavation.

She would earn funds that were pivotal to her future.

But could she do both of those things without pining for him? Without stewing in a mire of jealousy as he courted and wed another woman?

Without ending up alone and clutching the tattered shards of her heart?

She forced her eyes away from his, afraid he might see the truth there.

That her love for him had never ebbed. Never died.

Swallowing, she took in a deep breath.

You can do this, she encouraged herself. *Just focus on the excavations. Just breathe through each day.*

NATURALLY, TELLING HERSELF to focus on the excavations and ignore Alis as much as possible was rather different than actually accomplishing said goals.

Theoretically, Chrissi and Alis were to see one another sparingly.

In reality, they both lived in the same castle and worked at the same excavation site.

Often, Chrissi would be snugged into her bedchamber of an evening, listening to the crack of Alis's laughter as he drank whisky with a visiting friend.

Or she would be passing his study and hear the rumble of his voice speaking with his factor, Mr. McIntosh.

And each evening, as was proper, they would dine together. It would have set servants' tongues to wagging had she avoided the dining room altogether and taken a tray in her bedchamber.

Mr. McIntosh would always join them for dinner, for propriety's sake, if nothing else.

But Miss Rollins and her mother were frequently in attendance. Or the vicar and his wife. Or any assortment of local gentry who Alis counted as an acquaintance.

It was torture, pure and simple.

To witness Alis happy and content in his life. To endure the crackle of his wit and the intelligence of his mind.

And worst of all, for Chrissi to imagine herself within it. To see clearly what her life might have become had she been willing to forgive and accept the terms of marriage Alis had once offered her.

But that future had been lost nine years ago when she had chosen to turn her back on him and marry Stephen instead.

A choice she now recalled almost daily.

Would the horror and pain of those days ever cease to haunt her? How long would she pay penance for her rash decisions?

True to his word, she and Alis communicated mostly through notes about their work.

We uncovered a row of eleven cut stones today, she wrote to him on the third day of their excavations. *At the moment, they do not appear to be sloping toward an entrance, but we are in early days yet.*

His replies were always thorough, his notes detailed.

As with his personality, Alis dove in head-first:

Excavations today have uncovered another seven stones, continuing along the line you began. Troweling around the base of the stones revealed seventeen pottery sherds and various animal bones. Given the depth of the finds, I presume them to be of medieval origin, not from an earlier primitive time. But I await your expert eye.

His faith in her expertise soothed her battered ego. He had even included drawings of the pieces of broken pottery, the sherds illustrated with exacting precision.

However, when Chrissi had agreed to stay, she had not thought to prepare herself for the gut-punched ache of his handwriting—confident but neat, as her father had once described it.

With each missive, she found herself staring at his notes for minutes at a time—the sight of his bold letters evoking the lazy hum of cicadas under a drowsy Tuscan sun, herself curled into Alis's side as he wrote.

This was why working with him was doomed to failure—the enterprise held a thousand memories just waiting for the right moment to pounce. For the wrongs between them to spill out, sharp as knives. Or the beauty of what might have been to snatch the air from her throat.

For example, on the fifth day of their excavations, Chrissi caught sight of Alis helping field hands restack a section of stone fencing a rambunctious bull had knocked down. As he often had in Italy, Alis shed his coat and waistcoat, preferring to work in just trousers and shirtsleeves.

Mesmerized, Chrissi stared at the shadow of biceps flexing beneath the lawn of his shirt, the muscles bunching between his shoulder blades as he hefted a large rock. And suddenly, she was remembering what those arms had felt like around her, how the dips and ridges of his back had moved under her palms.

Who knew how long she would have stared if a worker hadn't cleared his throat at her side.

How was she to manage it, this constant onslaught of memory?

The never-ending pang of what might have been.

And the hollow terror of having to face the chasm of his loss yet again.

CONVINCING CHRIS TO stay was a mistake.

Alis knew this shortly after he walked away that first day, leaving her to assess the site.

His initial thought had been to view the excavations in

Scotland as a bookend to their summer in Italy—the Highlands and their relationship as chilly and barren as Florence had been warm and indulgent and welcoming. A final curtain before Chris exited his life for good.

But even hours after that first meeting, a humming buzz still vibrated along his skin. A sense of . . . what? Anticipation? Excitement?

He could hardly say. But it was a sensation he remembered well from their time together.

Chris, as ever, ignited a fire within his breast. An energy. A desire to reach for more—to learn and know and *become*.

And try as he might, he simply could not ignore her . . . this will-o-wisp come to haunt the halls of his memory.

Days on, he would find himself standing before the window in the great hall, watching her skirts billow in the never-ending Scottish wind as she drove stakes into the ground, sighted lines, and scribbled in her field notebook. Sometimes her bonnet would hang from its strings down her back, forgotten in her eagerness to examine some artifact one of his men had uncovered.

In that moment, he would feel it keenly—the tug of her light and intellect. The spell of her classical beauty. And he would hunger to explore the earth with her.

Her field notes—dispatches that should have been dry and matter-of-fact—held the essence of her inquisitive voice.

Success! Today we uncovered a series of ascending stones, stretching toward the top of the mound. Every instinct screams that this must be the long-sought channel leading to the cairn entrance. My mind cannot help but ponder the last people to see these stones. Who were they? Some weary medieval traveler, perhaps, who broke his cup, leaving sherds for us to find? Or a Viking raider, intent on pillage? My mind spins with imagined scenes.

Alistair felt tossed into the past, reliving Chris's excitement, her enthusiasm for archeology.

Her teasing notes were even worse:

I reached a limit today, if you must know—I sharpened your pathetically dull trowel. It practically begged me for help, the poor thing. I could no longer endure to remain a silent bystander to its abuse.

Her pithy tone left him laughing.

Alistair knew he needed to keep his distance, both physically and emotionally. Certainly, he needed to avoid being alone with her. Even the briefest exchange felt indulgent. Like the lemon bonbons his grandmother used to give him— a sweet he could not help but devour in one gluttonous afternoon and still pine for more.

Chris had made it clear she did not forgive his past actions.

Yet, when she asked to show him something in person, he abandoned plans to call upon Miss Rollins and rushed to the excavation site instead.

"My lord!" she cried, waving her hand in greeting from a hole that swallowed her to her shoulders.

They were mindful, the two of them, not to use Christian names around others. No need to set tongues wagging.

But she was pure Chris as he approached, eyes gleaming and expression animated.

"Come!" she beckoned. "You must see. I think we have found the beginnings of an entrance tunnel!"

Approaching, he crouched to examine what she had uncovered.

Were she anyone other than Chris, he would have jumped down in the hole with her.

But he thankfully still retained a shred of self-preservation.

"What have ye found, Mrs. Newton?"

"Look at this line of stones here." She drew her trowel down the wall, indicating a straight-cut edge. "These stones have been finished similar to the ones at Clava outside Inverness. This must be where the entrance begins."

Turning, she beamed up at him, the wind burnishing her cheeks rosy pink.

Alistair had to remind himself to breathe. That he wasn't at liberty to lean in, slide his hand around the nape of her neck, tug her onto tiptoe, and capture her mouth with his.

"Oh! And let me show you this. Here. Assist me." She reached her hand upward, indicating for him to pull her out of the hole. Several workmen stepped forward to help, but Alistair waved them off.

Chris, as ever, was no shrinking flower. Grasping his hand, she braced a boot against the wall of the hole, dirt sloughing off as the soil had yet to be stabilized.

He pulled her up. But upon reaching the top, she did not let go of his hand.

No, instead she tightened her grip.

"You must see!" She tugged him toward the standing stones. Alistair followed her willingly, a helpless grin on his face.

How could he have forgotten the infectious nature of Chris's joy?

Arriving at the stones, she took his shoulders and pushed him against the center stone, positioning herself beside him—the two of them standing just as they had on the day he persuaded her to stay on at Kinord Castle.

"Look!" She pointed excitedly toward the hole where she had uncovered evidence of the tunnel. "The entrance appears to line up precisely with this central stone. I am an idiot not to have thought of this sooner—that the standing stones might have been aligned to, and used in conjunction with, the chambered cairn or earthen house or whatever is under that mound. That the sites are linked."

"Like . . . ceremonially?"

The large stone at their back amplified his voice, making the timbre richer, deeper.

It felt like a microcosm of moments spent with Chris—life simply became more *alive* in her presence. Birdsong swelled, the sky grew bluer, flowers held their petals longer. Perhaps even past civilizations gathered in the wind, singing.

"Yes!" Her arms waved in excitement, sending the scent of lavender soap and sunlight swirling around his head.

Alistair nearly closed his eyes at the onslaught.

Chris, of course, prattled on, oblivious to his olfactory crisis. "Perhaps they held funeral rites here amongst the stones before escorting the dead to their final rest within the chambered tomb. Or perhaps it was a bacchanalian celebration, with bonfires lit to pagan gods amid the stones and goods left as offerings within the cairn. Who can say?"

Or perhaps, Alistair mused to himself, the cairn held the bones of formerly sound-minded men pining for women whose hearts they had broken.

It seemed a fitting punishment.

"That is astonishing," he said. Though given how she blushed, he might simply have said what he meant: *You are astonishing.*

And she was. Bubbling with ideas, leaping from bright thought to thought.

No wonder he had fallen so madly in love with her all those years ago.

Turning toward her, he leaned a shoulder into the stone. "So, what now?"

"That is an excellent question." She ticked off on her fingers. "We need to shore up the sides of the hole. Write down measurements of everything and ensure every find is carefully cataloged. I would also adore a preliminary sketch of the stones we have uncovered."

"Permit me to do that."

"Excellent."

They talked more, ideas and theories flitting between them—firefly sparks of spirit flashing back and forth.

He left her to the work an hour later.

But thoughts of Chris would not leave him be.

They continued to dance a merry jig in his mind, taunting and teasing him.

The crisp sense of her observations, the draw of her spirit, always moving, infusing the very marrow of life.

With her rich brown hair and lovely periwinkle eyes, she called to mind wisteria in full bloom. The sheer exuberance of the vine, blossoms hanging in purple-blue clumps over rock walls and woody tendrils climbing up gables as though desperate to expend every last drop of energy in brilliance and beauty.

That, in essence, was Chris.

He happened to be watching out the great hall window the next morning when she opened his sketchbook to the illustrations he had created the previous afternoon.

Holding the illustrations in one hand, she touched her fingertips to the drawing.

Alistair felt the touch as surely as if she had skimmed her hand across the back of his neck.

As if sensing his gaze, she whirled her head, eyes lifting to his.

Grinning wildly, she waved at him and then hugged the sketchbook to her chest, simultaneously communicating her gratitude and approval of his drawings.

He raised a hand in reply, his heartbeat tingling in his palms.

Alistair had thought his love for her dead.

Instead, he feared that he had merely buried it deep.

And like her excavation, day by day, she unearthed a wee bit more of the adoration that had once flowered in his own chest.

Was it even possible to return to what they had once had . . . to regain trust and harmony? Or would his sins forever stand between them?

And, most importantly, did he wish to try to make amends for his folly?

He continued to see Miss Rollins, and though he appreciated her sweet nature and gentle ways, he recognized the simplicity of his feelings for her. There were no depths to be explored there. No mounds to excavate or promises of hidden treasures.

Being with Miss Rollins felt akin to a stroll through Princes Street Gardens in Edinburgh on a fine day—pleasant, easy, enjoyable.

Nothing like the heady joy of chasing Chris through an olive orchard in Fiesole, her helpless giggles drawing him onward. Or the euphoria of catching her about the waist and turning her to him, her arms reaching to pull his head down for a scorching kiss.

Granted, it was hardly fair to make such a comparison.

He was not the carefree youth he had been at age twenty-one, starry-eyed and believing in the power of love. Trusting that he and Chris would transcend every problem, every issue that might arrive.

And yet . . .

The memory of that love would not let him be.

A spark remained between Chris and himself. An ember slowly glowing back to life.

Three days later, he sat in his study pondering that ember, contemplating the wisdom of fanning the spark of their attraction into something more.

The room hung with afternoon light, the tall case clock in the corner ticking away the seconds.

A pounding of boots on the stairs preceded McIntosh bursting into the room in a whirl of overcoat and fresh Highland air.

"I am so sorry to disturb ye, my lord," the man said breathlessly, "but ye best come quickly."

Alarmed, Alistair rounded his desk. "Whatever is the matter?"

"'Tis Mrs. Newton."

"Mrs. Newton!" A clanging bell sounded in Alistair's mind.

"Aye. There has been an accident at the excavation site."

Eight

July 29, 1849
Fiesole, Italy

"You love me? Truly?" Chris whispered against his lips.

Alistair snugged her tighter against his chest, fighting the urge to kiss her again and again.

"Always, lass," he pledged.

They stood on Via delle Cannelle—an ancient series of steps linking the lower and upper sections of Fiesole. Around them, night jasmine clung to the ancient walls, cascading sheets of green dotted with tiny white flowers that perfumed the evening air.

"When all is right, love is like breathing—natural and easy," his gran had told him once.

Now he understood her words. Loving Chris was effortless. A dizzy free fall into happiness, like a burst of laughter on Christmas morning or tumbling backward into heaped autumn leaves.

He felt as if she had always belonged at his side, and yet the joy of her presence refused to abate.

"Marry me, lass." He touched a palm to her cheek.

He sensed more than heard her gasp.

"Marriage?" Her blue-gray eyes searched his.

"Aye. I cannot bear it, wondering and hoping ye will be mine."

A smile lit her cheeks, elation in her gaze.

"Oh, Alis!" She wrapped her arms tightly around him. "I cannot bear it either. Please. Let us marry! Let me take you as husband."

Let me take you as husband. How like Chris to accept his proposal in such a manner. No simple yes for her, no acquiescence. She would always insist on meeting him as an equal.

"We shall take the world by storm," she continued. "You and I . . . married archaeologists. We can research and travel and publish and always be together."

"Aye."

This, he decided.

This was one of the many things he loved about Chris—she would always "drink life to the lees," as Tennyson described.

"In Scotland," he continued, "when a couple decides to marry, we plight our troth with a handfasting."

"A handfasting? Don't Scots consider that a form of legal marriage?"

"Aye, several generations ago, it was. Family lore says my gran and grandad married via handfasting. Now, marriages must be solemnized by a vicar or the local sheriff. But the tradition remains. Many couples handfast when they first plight their troth."

Chris smiled. "Let us handfast, then. We shall do everything properly."

She stretched to her tiptoes and quite thoroughly kissed the grin from his lips.

Nine

ALISTAIR HAD NO memory of how he came to be standing at the edge of the excavation site. The words *Mrs. Newton* and *accident* had sent him racing from the castle without a hat or coat.

What had occurred?

He needed to see Chris. He needed to understand what had happened.

Pushing through the gathered workers, he finally comprehended the situation.

Chris lay at the bottom of the excavation trench, a pile of stones and mud atop her legs. A trickle of blood ran from her temple onto her cheek, a stark slash of crimson against the dirt and pallor of her skin.

Odd, he would ponder later, how a single moment could clarify one's heart.

Chris was hurt. *His* Chris.

And it was unbearable.

Rushing down the steps his workers had cut to access the trench, he yelled at McIntosh to summon the doctor before joining the other workers in shifting the rubble off Chris.

"We broke through tae the entrance tunnel proper," one of the men said to him as they worked. He pointed to the rectangular opening behind where they stood.

It was indeed an entrance tunnel, perhaps four feet high

and scarcely more than two feet wide, all capped by enormous cut stones bearing the weight of the mounded earth above it.

"Mrs. Newton stepped forward tae inspect the tunnel, but we hadnae stabilized the surrounding walls yet. They broke loose," the worker continued, indicating stones and earth near the entrance. "We couldnae do anything tae stop it afore Mrs. Newton were buried."

Chris whimpered softly as they lifted the largest stone off her legs.

Instantly, Alistair moved to crouch beside her, taking her filthy hand in his.

"I'm here, lass," he murmured. "I have ye."

"Alis," she whispered, eyelids fluttering, her fingers tightening around his.

He wanted the fast hold of her hand to be a promise, he realized. He wanted it to be a beginning.

"The tunnel—" She winced as the men moved the last of the dirt and rubble off her body.

"Can ye tell where ye might be hurt most?" Alistair rasped.

"What about the tunnel?" she asked instead. "We need to investi—"

"Devil take it, Chris! Ye nearly crushed your wee head, and ye still be on about the tunnel?!"

Her eyes blazed with life. "We broke through!"

"Aye, and it's been here for thousands of years. I ken it can wait another day or three afore feeling the scrape of your razor trowel. Where are ye hurt?"

Chris shifted a wee bit. Relief poured through him as her legs moved easily beneath her mud-caked skirts. Her spine appeared uninjured.

She moaned and winced again. "My left ankle is afire."

"We need to get ye back to the castle as quickly as

possible." Gently, Alistair slid his arms under her back and knees, lifting her into his arms.

"I can try to walk," she protested as he staggered upright. "Or let the men fetch a litter to—"

"Nae, lass," he said gruffly, shifting her in his arms. "Let me carry ye."

She stopped arguing, not mentioning the tunnel or protesting his touch. Instead, her head sank into his shoulder as she gave her weight over to him. All of which only ratcheted Alistair's alarm.

If she were not truly injured and hurting, his fierce, independent Chris would insist upon walking, upon investigating the tunnel further instead of being carried away.

Carefully, he tucked her against him and climbed the steps out of the trench, striding toward the castle. She was far too light in his arms, only reinforcing his worry over her underfed frame. Her shoulders trembled, her body likely descending into shock.

He quickened his pace.

How many years had it been since someone had watched over this woman?

And if he wished that person to be himself, what would it take to convince her?

CHRISSI SAGGED INTO the heat of Alis's chest.

Her ankle pulsed with a blinding pain that set stars to sparking behind her closed eyelids.

She didn't want to find comfort in his arms. It felt too much like home, and she feared for her heart if she permitted herself to bask in it.

Love held too much risk. *His* love, in particular.

Forgiveness, as well, felt out of reach.

But... she hurt. In her soul, in her body. In her ankle, throbbing in time to her heartbeat.

And she hadn't the strength to fight.

How she had missed the smell of him—his cologne, yes, but also the scent of his skin, sun-warmed and delicious. It called to mind lemon trees in bloom and lazy summer afternoons cuddled in his arms after a hearty *pranzo* of linguine and *bistecca alla fiorentina*.

She must have drifted off at that point, her mind awash in memories that buzzed as pleasantly as honeybees along the surface of her mind...

The shock of cool sheets at her back awoke her with a start—Alis laying her atop the bed in her room.

Time passed in a blur.

Mrs. Craib appeared and, with the help of a housemaid, stripped Chrissi of her muddy clothing and gently washed the worst of the grime from her skin.

Then a doctor arrived, sure hands feeling bones and testing bruises to see where she hurt most.

"A severely sprained ankle, I should think. Nothing feels broken. Some lightly bruised ribs and several cuts. And perhaps the slightest concussion," he pronounced. "All in all, you are most fortunate not to have suffered worse, Mrs. Newton. When the wall came down, the mud at your back and the volume of your skirts appear to have cushioned your bones from more serious harm."

The doctor prescribed a drop of laudanum for her pain and copious amounts of rest.

Chrissi sensed rather than saw Alis hovering nearby.

Now what? she thought, drifting in a haze of aches and twinges, laudanum slowly overtaking her senses.

The thrumming pain in her body made it clear she would not be crouched with a trowel in hand anytime soon. And the archaeological excavations could scarcely continue without her presence. Moreover, it was hardly fair to expect Alis to house and feed her throughout the duration of her recovery.

How bitter to have reached this point in her excavations only to be forced to abandon them. To never know what lay at the end of the tunnel.

And Alis... to leave him so soon. Already her heart trembled at the prospect.

I'm not prepared to depart. Let me have a little while yet.

Sleep tugged at her senses.

Tomorrow.

She would deal with it all tomorrow.

Voices murmured just outside the edge of her understanding... Alis, speaking with someone. The doctor, perhaps?

The rumbling timbre of his bass lulled and soothed.

My favorite sound, whispered through her mind.

A strong hand wrapped around hers, lacing their fingers together.

And as she slipped into sleep, soft lips pressed a lingering kiss to her knuckles.

CHRISSI AWOKE TO sunlight shimmering against her eyelids and dull pain pulsing through her ankle.

Squinting, she blinked into the bright daylight for a full ten seconds before memories of the previous day rocketed through her brain—

The euphoria of breaking through to the entrance tunnel of the cairn.

A shout of warning.

The pummeling force of dirt and rocks tumbling over her.

Truthfully, she was lucky to have escaped with only a

concussed head, a sprained ankle, and what felt to be an impressive collection of bruises.

A sound had her turning her head in time to see a maid slip from the room.

In a mere blink, Alis took the girl's place, the bedchamber door ajar for propriety's sake. Had he set a watch upon her?

"Good morning," he said, a smile on his lips and warmth in his eyes.

Chrissi remembered that warmth well. Like everything else about him, it evoked their months together and a thousand exchanged glances.

It didn't help that he looked more like her Alis this morning—hair still damp around the edges from a bath, cravat slightly loose, coat unbuttoned.

She stared.

He sank into the chair at her side.

"How are ye feeling, lass? As poorly as last night?"

Wincing, she struggled into a sitting position.

"My ankle pains me yet. And . . ." She paused, surveying her body. ". . . my head aches and perhaps my ribs?"

Why it came out a question, she couldn't say.

"Would ye like more laudanum?"

"No." That answer was simple enough. "The pain is bearable for now."

"Excellent." His grin was far too open and charming for Chrissi's peace of mind.

It lit a fluttery flame in her chest that she valiantly attempted to smother.

"How fares the excavation site?" she asked, changing the topic. "Was anyone else hurt?"

"Nae. My men are building scaffolding at the moment to shore up the entrance channel to the tunnel. We don't want any more accidents."

They both turned as a maid entered bearing a tray of breakfast fare. The scent of baked bread, sausage, and coffee filled the room.

Leaping up, Alis took the tray from the girl with a nod of dismissal.

And then he busied himself with ensuring Chrissi was comfortable. He set the breakfast tray on the counterpane beside her hip and elevated her sore ankle atop a cushion. He adjusted and fluffed the pillows at her back.

And with each kindness, each accidental brush of his hand, each lungful of his cologne ... Chrissi felt herself tensing and resisting the depths of his care. Terrified to sink into the comfort of being cherished and treasured.

It was simply too much—a bellows fanning the flame of her love into a roaring conflagration.

She simply couldn't do this ... to risk placing her heart into his hands once more.

Fear tightened her chest.

And so, when Alis returned to his chair, gesturing at her to eat, Chrissi merely stared helplessly at him instead.

"Eat, lass," he said on a laugh, pointing to the tray. "I won't be accused of starving ye."

It was such an *Alis* thing to say and so she loosed the thought.

"That is such an *Alis* thing to say."

"Is it?"

"Yes. Is it not odd to you ... that we know one another so well, and yet not at all? Not anymore."

He certainly didn't know her ... not the things she had done to survive. Things he would rightly condemn.

He stared at her for so long, Chrissi nearly squirmed, worried that perhaps he would pluck her sins from her brain.

She reached for a *bap* instead, the bread still warm from the oven.

Crossing his arms over his chest, he sat back in the chair. "What if I said I wished to know ye as ye be now?"

Chrissi froze, butter knife in hand poised to spread jam on the *bap*.

He appeared... serious.

Her heart kicked off, drumming in time to the ache of her ankle. Moisture evaporated from her throat.

"What of your Miss Rollins?" she countered.

"She is not *my* anything."

Chrissi's eyes narrowed as she pointed the butter knife at him. "Have you clarified that point with Miss Rollins herself? Because I am quite positive that—"

"Ye be avoiding my question, Chris."

She set her *bap* and knife down and matched his pose with arms crossed over her chest. As if that could protect her from the onslaught of memory. Of him. Of everything that had broken between them. Of her own actions that he did not yet know... actions she would have to tell him if he continued to press this issue. She couldn't live with herself otherwise.

"Why?" The plaintive word tumbled from her lips, a world contained within.

Why me? Why now?

Why do you wish to revisit what we once were?

And, as usual, Alis immediately understood. Their minds, as ever, attuned.

It was why Chrissi knew from the beginning what the heartbreaking outcome of this conversation would be.

"Can we not try, Chris?" He leaned forward, elbows on his knees. "Having ye here... seeing ye hurt yesterday and feeling so helpless. Angry, too."

"Angry?"

"Aye. Angry with myself. That I didn't pursue ye nine years ago. That I let ye leave without truly attempting to reconcile our differences. That I didn't write ye, that—"

"You *betrayed* me, Alis."

He at least had the decency to flinch. "Does it help to know that I have regretted my actions ever since?"

Ten

August 23, 1849
Fiesole, Italy

JUST AS HE had months past, Alis strode out of the steam and smoke of the Maria Antonia railway station with godlike swagger.

Only this time, instead of remaining stock-still and awestruck, Chrissi squealed in delight and ran to him, giggling wildly as he caught her in his arms and spun her in a circle.

"You're home!" she cried. "I missed you so."

Laughing, he set her down. "It's only been three days, lass."

"Three days of eternity, you mean. I feared some demonic deity had tampered with Time itself, the minutes passed so slowly." She pressed her palms to the lapels of his coat.

"*Och*, I paid the demon myself, lass," he grinned. "I wanted to ensure ye were as miserable without me as I was without your bonnie self."

Heedless of onlookers, Chrissi kissed him right there, the tang of coal smoke eddying around them. It felt imperative. Necessary, even, to express the *loveadorationhappiness* overflowing in her chest.

"Tell me!" She pulled back, bouncing on her tiptoes. "I want to hear every detail. Your telegram was ridiculously brief."

"I told ye the important bit—"

"*Success!* That is all you said. I want all the details of your—no, *our!*—triumph!"

She tugged him toward the stand where a *carozza* could be hailed for the return trip to Fiesole. Her father, ever indulgent, had permitted her to make the short jaunt into Florence alone.

The entire journey had felt so adult. Grown-up.

Another confirmation that hers would not be a life confined to hearth and home as other women.

No, she and Alis would dominate the antiquarian world—researching and publishing side by side. Case in point, he had just returned from meeting with an English publisher of archaeological articles who resided in Rome.

Chrissi had hated that she could not travel with him. Not alone. Well, not without fueling scandal.

"Next time," Alis had promised, his lips against hers. "Soon, we shan't ever be apart again."

Now, Alis handed her into a *carozza*, giving the driver their direction in Fiesole before stepping into the carriage himself.

Chrissi grabbed his hand in both of hers. "Tell me!"

"Why so impatient, my love?" he laughed. "Do the details truly matter? Your words will be published."

"Of course details matter." She kissed his cheek. "This publisher only prints a journal every two years; it's an honor to be included. I want to hear every last word that was spoken of my brilliance."

He laughed again, but Chrissi finally noticed that he appeared . . . tense. Nervous, perhaps? His knee bounced in time to the clatter of the carriage wheels, and he kept glancing away, his grip on her hand growing tighter.

She frowned, a trickle of unease chasing her spine.

"Tell me," she repeated, less exuberantly. "*Did* the meeting go well?"

"Aye!" His tone too bright. "The publisher very much admired the detail in my illustrations, as well as your clever insights into archeology as a practice."

As well he should, Chrissi thought.

Alis's illustrations had been works of art, so precise and lifelike, they seemed to bound off the page.

As for herself, she had spent weeks crafting just the right tone to the paper—insightful and intelligent with droll pops of humor. In the end, Alis had only offered a few suggestions for correction. The words of the article were, for all intents and purposes, entirely her own work. But she didn't mind sharing the limelight with Alis. Surely as they continued with their publications and excavations, he would begin contributing to the writing as well.

"But . . ." Chrissi prompted.

Alis took in a long, deep breath. The sort of breath that preceded unpleasant news.

Something that tasted like dread settled into her throat.

"It is just . . ." he began, eyes studying their joined hands on the seat. "The publisher was not willing to permit a woman's name to be listed alongside mine on the publication."

Chrissi blinked, her eyelids drifting up and down, and she listed toward him.

Or perhaps it was merely the sense of her entire world tilting on its axis.

"What do you mean?" She tugged her hand free of his.

"Precisely what I said. The publisher will pay handsomely to print the article, but he insisted on my name being listed as its author."

"But . . ." Chrissi wrapped her arms around her middle. "Surely you explained . . . the writing is all mine—"

"Not all," Alis protested. "I *did* help."

"A sentence here and there!" Her voice rose.

"Let us not forget my illustrations."

"Yes, and they are lovely. But the ideas, the research, the insights, the very tenor of the argument—those were all my own. What did the publisher say when you told him as much?"

"Chris—" Alis began, voice so very weary.

She sat back against the carriage squabs, her heart a frantic, rabbity thing.

"You didn't tell him." She could hear the heartbreak in her voice.

"Who wrote what or how much . . . it simply didn't come up."

"Didn't come up?! Women writing academic articles is not a place conversation naturally leads, Alis. You must direct the conversation there—"

"And what would ye have had me say, Chris?! *Oh, see here, sir. My betrothed actually wrote this, and I insist her name be on it as well?*"

"Yes! Yes, yes, yes! That is *precisely* what I would have you say!"

"And what then? Be made to feel like a laughing stock? That I am so henpecked, my betrothed directs all my endeavors?"

Chrissi was appalled to feel tears pricking her eyes.

"No," she choked. "You would say such things because you are proud of my accomplishments. Because you are honest. Because you wish my work to be acknowledged. Because you see me as more than chattel or a mere possession that—"

"What does it hurt to work together under one name? When we marry, we will become one under the law. What is yours will become mine regardless."

"Yes! Under *your* name. I will cease being a legal person entirely!"

"Ye ken well that isn't how it is, Chris. Not between yourself and me."

"But the world is not just you and me, Alis. You delude yourself if you think it is anything *but* that. You know my feelings on this matter—how important it is for me to retain my sense of self, even within marriage. To have you trample on my wishes like—"

"There is nothing to be done at this juncture. The publication is done and dusted." Alis threw up his hands. "I already signed a contract under my name and—"

"You what?!"

"I already signed the contract," he repeated, exasperated.

"Why? We could have tried another publisher—"

"Who? There are few publishers of this sort of antiquarian research and certainly no others in Italy. I would have to return to London, and even then it could take years, given the snail's pace of publication schedules. *This* publisher will have the article to print in just two months. We can begin to establish ourselves as a force to be reckoned with now."

"But . . ." Chrissi trailed off.

"What's done is done, Chris." He pinned her with his dark eyes. "And truly, once we are married, it will be as if our efforts were joined. Because *we* will be joined!" He motioned between them.

Aghast, Chrissi could only stare at him.

This was what he thought of her?

No matter all the pretty words they had exchanged—goals and aspirations she had thought they both shared—he felt justified in claiming her hard work as his own.

And how could she marry him, knowing this was his true nature? That he would never view her as an equal?

"When we write our next article," he continued, "we can negotiate better how to proceed with—"

"Another article?! Why would I trust you enough to attempt this a second time?"

"Chris . . ."

"No! Do not *Chris* me, as if I am a child you need to reprimand. You knew how I would feel about this, and yet you acted anyway. You have shattered the trust between us, Alis!"

He blanched and then, just as quickly, scowled. "I think that might be a wee bit dramatic, lass. Ye must be more pragmatic about this. In order to establish a household, we need the money and recognition *now*, not in five years. Ye be a woman, Chris. A brilliant one, aye, but a woman nonetheless. A female attempting to publish in an academic world. It simply isn't done. It should be enough to know that a publisher thought your ideas fine enough to pass as my own—the man you will *take* as your own!"

"So that is your true opinion, then? That I should simply be grateful that my work was esteemed so fine, a *man* might have done it? Those are the lofty heights to which I should aspire?"

"Aye! That is the reality of the world in which we live. Ye are usually so level-headed. I thought ye would understand the practical nature of this."

"Practical nature?! I have a dowry, Alis. You cannot convince me this is *only* about money."

Scowling, Alis turned to look out the window. "Let us discuss this once we have both had some time to think more rationally."

Chrissi stared at his profile, her stomach a tangle of rope—twisted and pulling.

What was she to do? How could she marry him—despite the love still burning in her chest—when he assumed she would be happy to work in his shadow? When he cared more about finances than honesty?

The very thought was a beast's claws sinking into her breast.

Because there was only one conclusion to be reached here—

Alistair didn't know her. Not truly. He certainly didn't understand her—not the yearnings that drove her heart, the desires that gave her life meaning and breath.

Nor, if his current attitude were to be believed, did he *wish* to understand her.

Oh dear.

She bit her trembling lip.

No!

Her heart angrily rejected the conclusion her brain had already determined.

And yet...

She couldn't.

She simply could *not* marry Alis. Not like this.

Time.

Perhaps they both simply needed... time.

Eleven

ALISTAIR STARED AT Chris propped against the bed pillows—pale, disheveled, hair frayed in its braid and slowly unraveling...

She had never appeared more lovely.

"Regretting your actions does not remove the consequences of them," she said, voice quiet.

"Aye, I agree. But can we not try? Can ye find forgiveness in your heart for me?"

He would never forget the gut-punched horror of realizing that Chris had simply... left. That after their argument in the carriage, she had decided to leave Fiesole without another word. With her father's assistance, she had packed her trunk and taken the next train out of Florence.

She had left a note, at least. A terse missive that he could still recall word for word nine years on:

I am too angry and wounded in my soul to be with you at present. I am returning to Oxford for a while. I shall write when I feel able to speak without screaming. You, of course, may write me at will. May I recommend you begin with groveling apologies?

Her eyes dropped to the *bap* on the tray, her finger touching its crusty exterior.

"You never wrote," she whispered. "I waited and hoped—"

"I should have. I was twenty-one years old, clod-headed, and an arrogant arse. That is the only justification I can offer."

She nodded. "I should have written, too. I planned on it, but then . . ."

"Your father was angry."

"Yes. He was. So very angry over your actions."

"A few weeks after ye left, he tossed me out on my ear. He prevented the publication of your article in Rome and told me that I would never work in archeology again."

Dr. Rutherford had been true to his word. All doors into antiquarian work had been shut to Alistair. Surely Dr. Newton, Chris's husband, had played a part in that as well, Alistair now realized.

"Papa told me as much."

"I ran into your father two years later in London. He roundly informed me that ye had married well and were the happier for it."

Chris nodded again, her eyes still downcast. "Stephen helped me heal. Not from the article, per se, but from loss." A pause. "From the loss of *you*."

Silence hung for a long moment, neither of them moving or speaking.

Alistair stared at her profile—the sloping curve of her pert nose, the plump roundness of her lips, the stubborn jut of her chin.

So close.

He had come so close to losing her forever yesterday. The sight of her pale and half-buried under rubble would haunt him to the grave.

It rushed through him then—emotions and memories of their shared past . . .

The sound of her helpless giggles as he mimed antics from his days at St Andrews.

Chris reaching for him, tugging his mouth down to her hungry lips.

Her whispered words in the dusk of a Tuscan evening, fireflies winking in his peripheral vision—*I shall love you forever, Alistair Maclagan.*

Her love might have faded, but his . . .

No.

He loved her.

It was truly that simple.

She awakened him and made him see how dreary and Chris-less his life had been.

Once, he had permitted wounded pride to stem his apologies.

Never again.

This time he would fight for her. For them.

Without thinking, he reached for her slim hand resting on the counterpane.

Unlike other ladies, Chris's hands were not paragons of milky-white ease—soft and unblemished.

No. Hers were the hands of a woman at work—chafed knuckles, dirt beneath nails, the raised white scar on her thumb from a cut, courtesy of her absurdly sharp trowel.

Slipping her fingers through his, he could feel the calluses on her palm, the strength in her grip.

And like him, she gasped at the unexpected touch, her eyes flying to their joined hands.

Electricity hummed at the connection, licking heat up Alistair's arm.

He ached to kiss her. To lift her chin with a finger and draw her lips to his. To crawl into the bed beside her and urge her head to nap on his chest.

He merely studied her instead.

"Please, Chris," he whispered. "Can we try again? It's been

nine years. Could ye possibly forgive the hurt of my betrayal and learn to trust me once more?"

She stared at their hands, threaded together.

And then she shifted, her palm moving to rest atop his hand, her thumb tracing the blue vein from his middle knuckle to his wrist bone.

Alistair rather forgot to breathe.

Finally, she lifted her gaze. Something haunted and pained lingered there. Perhaps merely a reflection of his own beating heart.

"I am not sure forgiveness will be possible, Alis. I cannot say . . . given all that—"

"Please, lass. I ken that I am nine years too late with my groveling, but can we not give it another go?"

"Alis—" she began, tone so weary.

"Please."

Her bottom lip trembled and she bit it, her top teeth sinking deep to stem her tears. Reaching for the napkin atop the breakfast tray, she dabbed at her eyes.

"It w-won't end well," she gasped.

"Perhaps not. But I think we owe it to the memory of our past selves, to those happy months in Fiesole, to at least try."

Chris didn't agree with him in words.

But she did nod before picking up her *bap* again and reaching for the jam pot.

It wasn't a resounding declaration, but Alistair's heart took flight.

He would give her space. A chance to breathe freely again.

And in the meanwhile, he would do everything in his power to rebuild the trust he had once shattered.

"I COME BEARING gifts," Alis announced the next day, shouldering his way into Chrissi's bedchamber, a large wooden box in his arms.

Chrissi looked up from her position on the bed, ankle propped once more on an obliging cushion.

"Gifts?" she asked, alarm chasing her spine.

Normally, she adored presents.

But given the current state of matters between herself and Alis, gifts made her leery. She could not bear growing more indebted to him, losing more of herself in his happy smile.

"I ken ye might be a wee bit *crabbit*, being forced to rest as ye are," he grinned. "So I brought ye some cheer."

Alis placed the box on the counterpane with a grunt. Battered and somewhat dirty, it appeared anything but a gift.

She eyed it warily.

Alis busied himself with opening the wooden lid.

"You chose this box . . . why?" she asked. "Because you find wildflowers too pedestrian?"

He froze, pinning her with a look. "Would ye have liked flowers?"

"They are pretty. And spring has finally arrived."

As Alis had predicted, the landscape around the castle had come to life over the past week—trees leafing out and gorse blooming. Even the *gowk stane* had yellow Scots broom brushing against its side.

"Noted," Alis nodded before turning back to the box.

Chrissi's curiosity rose.

Thankfully, he didn't keep her long in suspense. With a flourish, he lifted out several jute bags.

She instantly recognized the telltale clink of pottery.

Her expression brightened. "You brought me sherds to sort! What type of sherds? Italian? Scottish?"

"And ye claim to prefer flowers," he snorted. "Ye regard

pottery sherds with the same excitement that a débutante views bonnet ribbons."

"Nonsense. Sherds are much more interesting."

Laughing, Alis set about prepping the sherds, placing a large square of canvas atop the counterpane for her to spread out the bits of broken pottery.

Oh! She had forgotten this—the thrumming delight of being the focus of Alis's care.

Emotion pricked her eyes.

"How goes the excavation today?" She cleared her throat.

"Excellent." He dumped a bag of mixed sherds on the canvas... Scottish pottery, by the look of it. Chrissi immediately recognized bits of Grooved Ware and perhaps a few pieces of Rothesay. Her fingers reached for them.

"You know I need more information than merely 'excellent,' correct?" She rubbed a piece of pottery between her fingers, testing its texture.

He laughed. "Today, the workers hope to finish the scaffolding to retain the embankment surrounding the entrance tunnel. Once that is in place, I thought perhaps I could begin a careful exploration of the tunnel. It appears to have some debris and dirt blocking it about three feet in."

"Ah." She glanced at her foot, hating that her injury would prevent her from being on-site to witness it all. "Thank you for moving slowly and methodically. Many archaeologists would simply shovel out the dirt in their eagerness to reach the center chamber."

"Aye, but I learned from the best." His fond look gave no doubt as to his meaning. "I shall do ye proud, Chris."

Such glowing affirmation...

Chrissi had to swallow again, her throat aching.

Sunlight streamed through the window at his back, rimming his head and catching coppery highlights in his dark hair. The beard suited his features, she decided. It lent him a dangerous air, as if he had just set down his sword after an afternoon of marauding.

At twenty-one, he had been virile and unnervingly attractive.

Now at thirty, he seemed a fortress unto himself. An immovable block of muscle and determination.

She ached for that strength. To crawl into the comfort of his arms and let him battle her demons and the memories that still haunted her. To grow old together, secure in the other's affections.

But that wasn't how their story would end.

The more he pushed, the more inevitable it became that her own sins would tumble loose, burying them both in a rubble pile of hurt and betrayal.

Chrissi had survived his loss once, if just barely.

But a second time?

No.

Alis would destroy her in truth this time around.

Particularly when he left her bedchamber and returned an hour later, a bouquet of freshly cut wildflowers—Highland thistle, wild rose, and dog violet—clutched in his fist.

CHRIS WAS MELANCHOLY.

The development puzzled Alistair.

When he had determined to woo her, he had expected resistance—anger and recriminations.

Instead, with every kind act, she seemed to sink a wee bit more inside herself, becoming more wan with each passing hour.

After two days, Alistair decided a change of scenery was in order.

Surely, Chris was simply upset to relinquish the excavations to his care.

He ordered a roaring fire built in the library and installed her there, ankle propped on a footstool and the pottery sherds on a table within easy reach.

She seemed content enough, sorting and cataloging as he read across from her.

From time to time, he would feel her eyes upon him. But when he glanced up, she would immediately look away. And the one time their eyes met, Chris blushed.

He considered that to be progress.

But his attempts to draw her into easy conversation were stymied.

The next day, he moved her to the great hall, placing her in an overstuffed chair before the enormous windows.

"If ye lean to the right here, lass"—he pointed—"ye will be able to see the excavations."

Her expression brightened at that.

"And how fares the digging?" Chris pressed him for updates.

"Well! The workers are slowly removing the dirt I marked from the tunnel. They are to summon me should they find anything. In the meantime, I shall enjoy keeping ye company."

"Thank you," she replied, almost absently, adjusting her ankle on the footstool.

Alistair frowned. Her words felt . . . *blasé*.

For not the first time, he wondered if something was wrong. It was as if the more he wooed her—the kinder his actions—the sadder she became.

Was she melancholy, in truth? The Chris of his memory had never suffered from a depression of spirit. But perhaps she had over the intervening years, particularly given the twin losses of husband and father and the financial instability their deaths had brought.

Regardless of its source, Chris's sadness weighed on him. Was there some piece of this puzzle that he was missing?

He thought of it as he watched her stare listlessly out the window. Her stark expression remained with him as he troweled away the remaining dirt blocking the tunnel, revealing a path to the chambered cairn beyond.

Chris was clearly eager to return to the excavation site. Refusing crutches, she began limping across the great hall, testing her ankle for how much weight it could sustain.

A week after her injury, Alistair arrived at her bedchamber to find her bed tousled and empty.

No Chris to be seen.

Mmmm.

He knew where he would find her.

THE MEN HAD been busy in the week since her injury.

Chrissi stood in the center of the chambered cairn, a flickering candle in her hand. Her ankle had loudly protested the crawl through the long entrance tunnel, but she simply could not remain in the castle a moment longer.

Not with Alis hovering so solicitously.

Not with her own heart slowly cracking in her chest.

Not with the pain of their past racing toward her like a runaway locomotive.

Losing herself in work seemed the wisest course.

Lifting her lantern, she studied what Alis had uncovered.

Corbel-vaulted, the chamber rose to well over fifteen feet in the center, but the sides were sloped and low. Square holes were cut into the perimeter at regular intervals, suggesting niches or side chambers. The weight of the turf overhead and the tight fit of the stones ensured that, unlike the entrance tunnel, this part of the cairn remained free of mud and debris.

Setting the lantern atop a jutting stone, she bent to brush dirt from one of the possible niches, regretting that she had not thought to place her trowel in her pocket.

A noise and dimming of the daylight from the tunnel had her turning her head.

Alis emerged from the entrance, stooped and crouching.

Of course he would run her to ground. Alistair Maclagan watched over those in his care.

The cracks in her heart trembled.

"I thought I might find ye here, lass," his voice reverberated around the small chamber.

He stood, crossing to join her, rimmed in sunlight from behind and flickering lamplight in front.

How odd, Chrissi mused. The chamber had felt large enough just moments before. But now . . . it suffocated her, the walls too close and confining. Alis saturated the space, the potency of his large body setting hers to vibrating.

Enough.

How could she continue to play this doomed dance?

"You have been hard at work here," she said. "The space appears—"

"Ye shouldn't be venturing so far afield." He frowned. "Your wee ankle won't heal if ye abuse it so."

"I had to see the progress myself. Surely, you know that no twinge in my foot would stop me." She pivoted away as she spoke, needing to avoid his gaze. To prevent him from seeing the anguish in her eyes.

But she turned too quickly, and her ankle faltered. She teetered to the left, but his strong hand around her waist quickly righted her, pulling her spine against his hard chest.

"A minor twinge," he groused in her ear from behind. "Ye be barely mobile, Chris."

Chrissi closed her eyes, trying to swallow past the delectable feeling of him wrapped around her. The press of his pectorals to her shoulder blades. The heat of his palm branding her stomach.

I will not survive this, a dry part of her mused.

Helpless to resist, she sagged into his strength. His grip tightened around her, feeling her capitulation.

"I . . . uhm . . ." she began, voice far too breathless for her liking. "I was contemplating the purpose of this chambered cairn."

"Were ye now, lass?" This time, his breath brushed over the sensitive shell of her ear, sending a shower of reciprocal goosebumps flaring down the backs of her arms.

"Y-yes," she replied on a warble. "Other similar monuments have burials in them."

"Mmmm." Soft lips pressed to the hollow just below her ear, before trailing down her neck. His beard provided a delicious counterpoint to the slide of his mouth.

She gasped.

Her eyes fluttered shut and her knees loosened, sinking further into him.

Only his firm grip around her waist kept her upright.

"Tell me more," he rasped.

More?

What had she been saying?

"Uhm . . . I . . . I imagine the cairn aligns with s-sunrise during the winter solstice and—"

She broke off as he spun her effortlessly in his arms, crushing her body to his.

Helpless, her arms looped around his neck, fingers threading into his hair as if they instinctively understood where they belonged.

It was simply . . . too much. Too overwhelming.

Her mouth found his. Or perhaps he reached first?

Regardless, Chrissi nearly moaned at the contact. At the feel of his fevered lips on hers once more.

She rose upward, heedless of the ache in her ankle, eager for more, more, more—

Over the past weeks, Chrissi had wondered from time to time what kissing him again would be like.

Would it feel like kissing a stranger? Or perhaps like donning a cast-off gown, one that didn't quite fit any longer—familiar and yet not?

But no.

Kissing Alis sent fireworks bursting behind her eyelids.

He felt like silk and electricity and happiness.

Like homecoming.

As ever with them, a simple kiss turned into three . . . and then twenty, lips and teeth nipping along jaws and throats.

Her body undulated, seeking somehow to draw closer to him, to subsume herself *into* him. To allow the shocks of sensation skittering along her skin to somehow merge them into one.

Her name was a litany of synonyms on his tongue: "Chris. Love. Darling."

She swallowed them down with her lips.

This closeness could not—*would not*—last. It might be the last time she felt his arms around her, the approving rumble from his chest, the delicious weight of his palm skimming her spine—

Something of her desperation must have communicated itself to him.

"Hush, love," he murmured softly, attempting to quell her urgency. "There is time. All the time."

But there wasn't.

He didn't know. He didn't understand.

And once he did . . .

Tears swelled upward from her chest, an ocean of sorrow for what might have been.

As ever, Alis heard the words that she did not say.

Pulling back, he pressed his forehead to hers. "I haven't felt this happy since we were last together, but that doesn't seem to be the case for yourself. What am I missing, lass?"

"Alis—" Chrissi attempted to back out of his arms, but he stopped her.

"Don't retreat, Chris. I love you. I've never stopped loving ye. I see that now. Please. Love me, lass. Be with me." He searched her face, eyes tracking the tears falling in earnest now.

"I don't think there is enough f-forgiveness for that."

"Ye truly can't forgive me? I was young and thoughtless and—"

"No, y-you misunderstand." Her fingertips skimmed his beard.

He turned and pressed a kiss to her palm.

How Chrissi had wanted to avoid this. Anything but this.

To witness his love turn to hatred before her very eyes.

But now . . .

The reckoning had come.

"I forgave you years ago, Alis." She told him the spare truth. "It is you who will not be able to forgive me."

He stilled at that, brows drawing down. "Pardon? What do I have to forgive?"

Chrissi stepped back, and this time he let her go.

His brow drew down, his expression turning wary.

Her heart fractured into pieces.

A sob tore from her lungs. And then another.

Anguish and loss and grief . . . long buried and yet, somehow, never far.

Alis took a step toward her, but she stayed him with an uplifted hand.

Her ribs heaved. A terrible shivering wracked her muscles.

"What is it, Chris? Tell me."

It took two more spasms of her lungs to get the words out.

"I was increasing, Alis. When I left Italy, I was with child."

ALISTAIR FROZE, HIS body cemented into place as immobile as the stones around him.

"Pardon?" he whispered.

Chris had covered her face with both hands, hiccupping gasps lifting her chest.

Surely, he had misheard.

She would never have kept something so vital from him.

"Chris?" he asked, voice rising along with his agitation.

She lifted her head at that, expression so anguished. "I-I was pregnant . . . with your babe."

Alistair staggered back, the impact of her words like a horse hoof to the chest.

They both knew what had occurred between them . . . the anticipation of their marriage vows. He had loved her so much, so dearly. And they were betrothed. Handfasted.

Why are we waiting for a signature in a parish record? she had whispered to him on a sultry Tuscan evening. *Can we not become husband and wife now? We have plighted our troth and handfasted one another, after all. Your ancestors married in such a way. Why can't you and I?*

He had needed no further encouragement.

She *felt* like his wife. And he wanted her—the life that they would have together.

Their coming together—clothed only in moonlight and the hum of cicadas—had been a first for each of them. A glorious promise of the awaiting future.

Somehow, he had never once considered that their indiscretion had incurred consequences.

Perhaps because he had supposed that Chris—his beautiful, forthright Chris—would never have kept a secret of such magnitude from him.

"I didn't realize, not until I was on a ship bound for London. My seasickness simply would not abate. And then my courses didn't come. I d-didn't know . . . I didn't know what to do."

"Me!" He pointed at his chest. "Ye return to me, lass! That is what ye should have done!"

She leaned back against the rocks of the cairn, sobs shaking her shoulders.

Pivoting, Alistair faced the entrance tunnel, hands coming up to clasp the back of his head.

His heartbeat pounded in his ears.

And yet Chris's words still reached him, clogged with tears and heartache.

"Return to you? I was angry and hurt. It felt like a betrayal of my very self to return. And so I continued to Oxford, assuming you would write. That you would perhaps be on the boat behind mine, apologetic and remorseful. That I would receive something from you other than *silence*." The word emerged on a knife's edge—a heartbreak of syllables.

"Ye should have written regardless." Alistair turned back to face her.

"I know that now . . . I have been granted many, *many* years to ponder the folly of my actions."

But where is the child? he thought. *What happened to our babe?*

The thought of it nearly broke him. That he had a son or daughter wandering the globe, unaware of Alistair's paternity. That he had missed so many years of a child's life.

"Not hearing from you, I assumed the worst," she continued. "I supposed that you had stopped loving me, that our love had not meant as much to you as it had to me—"

"Lies. I never stopped loving ye."

"But how was I to have known?!" She pinned him with her gaze, red-rimmed and anguished. "You didn't write!"

"Again, ye should have written me!"

"Well . . . I didn't. I hadn't the courage to *beg*. My maid—a gossipy thing from Bristol—began to spread the rumor that I appeared to be increasing. And I simply . . . I panicked. What was I to do? I understood only too well the fate of women who bear children out of wedlock. It was unbearable to think that all my dreams of archeology would be dashed. That my father would be shamed. Not to mention the child itself, born a bastard. Dr. Stephen Newton—a family friend who I had always viewed as a sort of kindly uncle—stopped in on a particularly bleak day. I ended up confessing the whole sordid tale to him, and he offered to marry me. His wife had passed a few years before, and he longed for companionship. And so I accepted—anything to give myself and my unborn babe a normal life."

Alistair stared at her, part of him surprised that she hadn't morphed into a different woman—one he had never known—the words and sentiments coming out of her mouth were so foreign.

"Ye married another man, knowing he would claim paternity of my bairn? Ye denied me a relationship with my child?!"

"I d-didn't—" Chris pressed shaking fingers to her forehead. "I don't know if I would have truly gone through with the marriage had I—"

He stalked toward her. "Chris, where is my child?"

Her palm, flexed outward, stopped him.

"I m-miscarried." She licked tears off her lip. "A week before the wedding, I began bleeding. The midwife said it was likely due to nervous attacks from . . . everything. Our babe was born months too early to survive." She stifled another sob. "A boy."

A son.

He had nearly had a son.

Pacing away, he walked from one side of the cairn to the other.

"And then ye married Newton anyway," he said, tone scathing.

"Yes," she gasped. "I didn't know what else to do. I was ruined and—"

"Were ye ever going to tell me?" The question emerged nearly at a shout. "If ye hadn't accidentally ended up here, would ye have ever told me?"

Her crumpling expression was his answer.

No.

She would never have told him.

In fact, she had already had *weeks* to disclose the truth.

And she had remained silent.

He didn't . . .

He couldn't . . .

He and Chris had made a bairn together.

And instead of writing him, instead of permitting him to step into his rightful place as her husband and father of her child, she had cut him out.

Excised him as precisely as she wielded the sharp edge of her trowel.

Yes, he had betrayed her, but this . . .

It was simply too much.

Alistair's feet strode out of the cairn, across the stone circle, past the castle, and into the forest of Scots pine beyond.

His thoughts tied into such a *fankle*, he doubted he would ever untangle them.

Thirteen

CHRISSI LIMPED BACK to the castle and spent the remainder of the day weeping into her pillow.

Never had she hated herself more.

She had been too much of a coward to tell Alis nine years ago. Too hurting over his betrayal—his lack of *seeing* her and supporting her most cherished aspirations. And then the misery of his subsequent silence.

But he had deserved to know. And regardless of how he felt about her, he would never have abandoned his child. No. He would have rushed to her side and married her immediately.

But she hadn't wanted their married life to begin that way, with Alistair essentially forced to marry her. To always wonder if he would have, of his own free will, returned to her.

Of course, she got her answer in time—

He did not return.

And so, in a way, it felt like absolution. That Chrissi had made the correct decision in keeping news of the child from him. After all, the only thing worse than marrying a man who viewed her as property would have been feeling that she had entrapped him.

In contrast, Stephen had chosen her, even knowing she carried another man's child. He had nurtured her dreams and fulfilled her wish to see her research published.

And yet...

The horror in Alis's gaze when he had realized what she had done. She had imagined it so many times. But the reality had been even more terrible, more awful—to witness his heart shatter, to see betrayal freeze his handsome features into stone.

Perhaps the bleak desolation of her current life was deserved. A just punishment for her actions.

Finally, puffy-eyed and weary, she hobbled over to the window.

It was done.

Alis finally knew the truth she should have confessed years past.

Would he evict her now? Cast her person and belongings out of his castle and return to his placid Miss Rollins?

Chrissi hated the sharp derision of her thoughts.

Pressing fingertips to her brow, she took in several steadying breaths.

A knock sounded on her bedchamber door.

"Come," she called.

A maid entered, carrying dinner on a silver tray.

It felt decadent to be catered to when surely Alis simply wished her gone.

"Your dinner, Mrs. Newton." The maid set the tray atop a small table beside the fire and bobbed a curtsy before quietly exiting.

The smell of steak and ale pie filled the air.

Only then did Chrissi see the note placed atop the cutlery, her name scrawled in Alis's bold hand.

Scarcely breathing, she opened the foolscap, tipping it into the light.

I do not know what to say. Our conversation this afternoon has overset me in ways I cannot explain. Had I any sense at all, I would terminate our contract for the excavation. However, I cannot, in good conscience, deprive ye of much-needed income, or myself of long-awaited answers to the ruins on my land. Please continue your work. I shall remain out of your sight, just as I am sure ye wish to remain out of mine.

That certainly spelled out his feelings, did it not?

He had only loved her when *his* were the deeds to be forgiven.

But forgiveness for herself . . .

Well, she had known, long ago, that it was likely impossible.

She wiped away another fugitive tear as she penned a reply, telling him she agreed with his terms.

Chrissi would remain to finish this excavation and give him the answers he sought. It was the least she could do. Her ankle was healed enough for her to resume work, regardless of what anyone else said. Perhaps if she hurried, she could have it done and dusted close to the summer solstice.

And then, once she had uncovered what she could, she would pack up her trowel and disappear into the ether, bothering him no more.

TRUE TO HER word, Chrissi worked tirelessly.

And true to his word, she scarcely saw Alis.

Every day, she limped back and forth from the excavation site, her ankle still twinging but on the mend. She took meals in her bedchamber, consolidating her notes from the day's labors—writings she sent to Alis.

He said nothing in reply.

Ten days after their conversation in the cairn, Chrissi was

scraping the floor of a side niche when her trowel hit upon something rather extraordinary.

A few hours of excited exploration later, she sat back on her heels, surveying what she had found.

How... unexpected.

She tore a sheet from her notebook, scribbling a message to Alis.

No matter his anger toward her, he would find this discovery thrilling.

ALISTAIR WAS IN his study, reviewing estate expenditures, when his butler delivered Chris's note.

Come down to the cairn. I have found something remarkable, unlike anything I have ever excavated. Never fear, I shall make myself scarce so you needn't see me.

He contemplated her words for a long moment—the most she had written to him directly in over a week and a half. What had she found?

His anger over her deception had faded into a glum sorrow that hung over his mood like a *dreich* rain cloud.

Yes, Chris should have told him about the babe.

But having overcome the initial shock, he couldn't help but put himself in her shoes—a girl scarcely twenty years of age, alone without her father's protection, unmarried, and with child. Her babe's father had betrayed her and hadn't bothered to write, giving every impression that he had washed his hands of her.

Chris would have known only too well the fate of women bearing a child out of wedlock. It was more than merely shameful. Once her condition became widely known, she would have found herself rejected by Polite Society, unable to find employment or provide for herself and her child. Her father certainly couldn't have permitted her to remain in his home. In order to salvage his own reputation and career, he would have had to cast her off.

What was she to have done?

Of course she had panicked and taken the first viable solution that offered both her and her unborn bairn respectability and a future—marriage to Stephen Newton.

Alistair could hardly fault her.

But now what was he to do?

Simply forgiving her and accepting her deception felt . . . difficult. Absurd, even.

But letting her exit his life once more also seemed nothing short of impossible.

He sighed and rubbed his eyes.

Snatching up his hat and coat, he made his way down to the excavation site, Chris nowhere to be seen.

A worker beckoned him forward eagerly, handing him a lantern.

Lamp in hand, Alistair crouched along the tunnel, emerging into the cairn proper. A second lantern flickered on a pole, adding illumination to the space.

The central chamber appeared untouched. But Chris had been hard at work excavating the side niches. One, in particular, had been scraped down to the same level as the main chamber.

Lifting his lamp to examine it more closely, he froze, breath catching in his ribcage.

Chris's unexpected find lay on the floor before him.

Shaking his head in wonder, he bent forward, eyes drinking in the story before him.

Two skeletons lay side by side, knees bent, hands mingled

together, heads turned to face one another. Their foreheads had likely touched when first placed into the earth.

A romantic embrace.

As sure a depiction of love as any poem ever written or vows declared.

Alistair stared at the entwined skeletons for far too long, pondering how they had come to be here together. Had they both died at the same time, the loss of one causing the other to falter? Or had one been unwilling to be parted even by death itself, and so had willingly joined their lover in the afterlife?

He would likely never know.

But standing there, his lamp casting long shadows on the surrounding stones, he knew one thing clearly:

Whoever they had been—husband and wife, illicit lovers—and whenever and however they had lived and died . . .

They had loved.

It was writ, despite time and decay, in their very bones. Stated as clearly as an epitaph. Or as an immortal poem. Two lines from Shakespeare's sonnet, "Shall I compare thee to a summer's day?" drifted through his mind. Would-be suitors often recited the first line or two, but neglected the final couplet:

> *So long as men can breathe or eyes can see,*
> *So long lives this, and this gives life to thee.*

And like Shakespeare in that sonnet, the skeletons before Alistair loudly declared their love. So that he, thousands of years onward, knew and understood what had passed between them.

It stole his breath and caused his own bones to tremble.

Because . . .

If he let Chris go, if he were content to watch her walk away, no one would ever know. There would be no trace of their love. No remnant. It would dissolve like sea foam, melting into the sands of Time and utterly forgotten.

And that . . .

That would be simply unbearable.

That she would be so forgotten.

That *they* themselves—Chris and Alis—would be forgotten.

How odd.

That the largest decisions were, in many ways, the simplest.

He loved Chris.

He couldn't bear to let her go. To let their love pass away, uncelebrated. Unmarked.

No.

He forgave her.

Just as she had forgiven him.

The surety of it washed through him, as cleansing and life-giving as summer rain.

Together, they could find a way back to what they had once had.

He just had to take the first step.

Fourteen

ANOTHER DAY.

And Chrissi was, once again, mired in a bog.

This time . . . quite literally.

One would suppose she had learned over the past weeks to avoid the fen like a sensible, rational person.

But no.

Just as on the day of her arrival, she could not stop studying the *gowk stane* standing alone on its little solid island amid the marsh. Given that Alis could send her packing any day now, she felt some urgency to solve the mystery of the stone.

And after much contemplation, she had a hunch.

But confirming her hunch required standing beside the stone at sunrise. Which at this time of year, with the solstice looming, was more akin to staying up late than rising early. Being so far north meant that sunrise and sunset were scarcely two hours apart.

And so Chrissi had simply not gone to sleep.

Once the house was quiet, she had donned wellies, hiked up her skirts, and trudged into the muck. The sky was so twilight-bright, she didn't need a lantern to light her way.

Of course, she had learned her lesson in the past. This time, she entered the bog with a plan. The workers assisting her on the excavations had charted a way to the stone—a path to follow that avoided the more treacherous holes.

The ground was, indeed, less swampy than it had been when she first arrived—the marsh grasses green and lush.

And she would have reached the stone without incident had her good foot not slipped and sent her toppling onto her hands and knees, covering her to the neck in cold, muddy sludge.

Fortunately, the ground under the mud was solid, enabling her to push herself upright. She stood, shaking mud from her hands. It was apropos, she supposed, to be covered in mud once more—ending her time at Kinord Castle as she had begun it.

This time lost and alone in the dim twilight.

Biting her lip, she blinked back tears.

Had she not shed enough over the past week?

But given the flood trickling down her cheeks, the answer was clearly no.

Why? she longed to scream at the sky.

Why did life have to be so difficult? Why did Alis have to betray her heart with both his words *and* his silence? Why did their babe have to die?

Why, why, why?!

She was crying in earnest now, muddy fists to her eyes, terrible loud sobs wrenched from her chest. Those in the castle probably feared a wild animal prowled the night.

A sound to her right had her lifting her head.

Alis trudged through the muck toward her, a scowl on his handsome face.

Similar to herself, he was dressed in wellies, shirtsleeves, and a long overcoat that dragged behind him. Unlike her, he hadn't taken a cold mud bath, though his red nose testified to the chill of the pre-dawn air.

She shivered to see him.

Surely he would cast her out now. His good grace could only extend so far.

"Chris," he growled.

"A-Alis," she hiccupped, chest spasming as she fought to stop her tears.

He stopped two feet in front of her, eyes flicking up and down the muddy, disastrous expanse of her.

"I dislike finding ye covered in mud, lass."

"I d-dislike *being* covered in m-mud."

"Ye be mad to be out in the bog. And in the cold dark, no less. Have ye no concern for your wee neck?"

Chrissi wanted to reply. Truly, she did.

Something pithy and witty like, "Oh yes, well, I understand a chilly mud bath is excellent to invigorate circulation. 'Tis all the rage in Paris."

Nothing came out but a wail.

She expected him to ask the meaning of her tears. To berate her or . . . something.

Instead, Alis's expression turned soft and . . . and loving.

He pulled her into his broad chest, a large hand coming to cover the back of her head.

"Hush now, lass," he whispered.

Chrissi melted into him, drenching his shirt with her grief and hopelessness. And, truth be told, a goodly bit of mud.

Unconcerned, his arms held her tightly and she felt him press a kiss to her sodden hair.

"Ah, Chris," he murmured. "Could ye not have had a good *greit* in your bedchamber? The bog seems a wee bitty dramatic."

His teasing words simply made her cry harder.

How she had missed him . . . missed this sense of closeness.

She had longed to be in his arms once more. To feel the

thump of his heartbeat under her cheek, to burrow into the warmth of his body.

They stood for a long while, emotion pouring from Chrissi as the sky lightened around them.

"Oh!" She pushed off his chest with a start. "The sunrise. We can't miss it!"

Hurriedly, she wiped at her tears and looked toward the eastern horizon and the light swelling there.

"Sunrise?" Alis asked.

"Yes!" Somehow, a warbling half laugh made it past her tears. "It's why . . ." She reached for his hand. "It's why I'm here. I promise; I am not entirely mad yet."

He wrapped his strong fingers around hers.

"The stone." She pulled him forward. "Hurry."

Hand in hand, Alis steadying her, they reached the small island of sturdy ground where the solitary stone stood.

He scrambled onto the mound first, extending a hand to help her up.

Chrissi reached the stone just as the first rays of dawn streaked across the landscape. Standing beside the granite slab, she sighted along it back toward the chambered cairn and stone circle below the castle.

"Oh!" She clasped her hands to her chest.

Alis followed her gaze.

"Bloody hell," he whispered in awe.

From their vantage point beside the *gowk stane*, the gleam of the rising sun threaded precisely between two of the standing stones and illuminated the center monolith, turning it into a pillar of fire rising above the rest.

"The summer solstice sun," Chrissi said quietly, reaching for his hand once more. "A symbol of life and renewal. Of course the *gowk stane* would help light the way."

Alis looked around them. "The celebrations must have been enormous, eons past. An entire population gathered to witness this single, miraculous moment." He shifted, wrapping an arm around her waist and pulling her tight against him once more. "How did ye know?"

"A hunch. Other similar sites align to the winter or summer solstices, so it seemed probable that this one did, too. The lone stone out here felt key."

"Ah. Ye merely had to brave the bog to reach it. I imagine a poet would make a lovely metaphor for life and living out of that. We can only truly see the light after toiling through perilous muck to reach it."

Helpless to stop herself, Chrissi leaned her head on his shoulder.

They stood like that for a long while, watching the sunlight creep up the pillar until it crested the top and bathed the entire glen in golden light.

Words crowded her tongue, but she didn't know what to say.

Alis had come to her. That had to signify something.

But what?

"Ye be a bit of a witch, lass, bringing long-hidden worlds to light."

"A bog witch?" She lifted her head to look up at him.

He grinned, brushing a bit of sphagnum moss from her shoulder. "The moniker does appear to fit."

"Alis!" She tried to step back, but he held her fast.

"If ye be a bog witch, then consider myself enchanted."

Chrissi stilled.

"Ye know I am not skilled with declarations, Chris. But seeing those skeletons yesterday . . . knowing that they loved despite loss or doubt or betrayal . . . a love that is emblazoned on history for all to see. I simply couldn't bear it. That yourself and I would never have a similar record of our love."

Somehow, Chrissi still had tears to shed as Alis and the surrounding bog suddenly turned blurry.

"I love ye, lass," he continued. "That simple fact has never changed. I should have come to ye after our fight in Florence. And for that, I am eternally sorry."

"There is nothing to forgive there, Alis. I should have written you about our babe. I should have—"

"Hush, my love." He pressed the softest of kisses to her lips. "I cannot begin to imagine your terror at finding yourself increasing. We have both suffered loss and betrayal. But we are not the same people we were nine years ago—young and broken and hurting. Can we repair that pain with new life, do ye ken? I want to spend the rest of my days proving that love to ye. I want bairns and laughter and joy so bright it burns our souls. And when death finally comes for us, I want to be buried in a tomb at your side. A testament to future kin"—his hand swept an arc in the sky—"here, in this place, Alistair Maclagan loved Christiana Rutherford Newton."

It was too much. Too much longing for her heart. Too much happiness to contain.

Nodding her joy, she collapsed onto his chest again. Only this time, she lifted her face to his, their lips tenderly meeting.

A kiss of promise. Of hope. That out of painful remnants, love can be reborn—strong, forgiving, and bright.

"Marry me, Chris," he whispered. "For keeps, this time."

"Y-yes," she hiccupped.

He kissed her in reply, the sort of kiss that crumpled her knees and made her heart gallop.

"Be warned," he said against her mouth. "I will likely track down the sheriff this morning and ask him to marry us. I cannot bear another day without calling ye my own."

"Please," she gasped. "I want that life with you."

As he had on the fateful day of their first handfasting, he clasped her hand in his. "Forever, Chris—yourself and me."

"Forever," she repeated and sealed the vow with a kiss.

September 10, 1859
Kinord Castle, Aberdeenshire
Scotland

ALISTAIR AWOKE WITH a start.

Moonshine streamed through the window, the curtains pulled open and the shutters unlatched.

Blinking, he sat up in bed, looking to his right where Chris should be but noted only rumpled sheets and the coverlet thrown back.

"Ah, my love. We didn't mean to wake you," Chris murmured stepping in from the dressing room, bouncing a fussy white bundle in her arms. "Our Alice is having another rough night. Who knew growing teeth would be so painful? I could hear her crying in the nursery and simply couldn't bear it. Besides, Nurse could use some sleep."

Swinging his legs out of bed, Alistair was already halfway across the room before Chris finished speaking.

"Ye should have awakened me, Wife. Let me tend to our lass." He held out his arms and Chris nestled their daughter into the crook of his elbow.

Alice scrunched her wee face, preparing for another bout of *girning* and lament.

Accustomed to his daughter's fussy ways, Alistair transferred her to his shoulder, rubbing firm circles on her back as he paced the floor. As usual, the babe instantly settled down.

Chris watched, an amused grin on her lips.

"Well, we always knew you had a way with the lasses, Alis. Our tiny Alice never stood a chance." She pronounced their daughter's name in the Italian way—Ah-LEE-chay—to ensure that father and daughter were never confused.

"Go back to bed, Wife," Alistair scolded. "I shall wake ye if she needs to feed."

Chris grinned. "And miss watching you cuddle our child? I think not." She sat in the armchair before the fire, leaning forward to stir the glowing coals to life before adding a brick of peat.

The sweet scent of burning moss and grass filled the room.

Alistair continued to pace, adoring how wee Alice melted her weight into his.

Scarcely four months old, Alice had arrived, red-faced and screaming, on a *dreich* day in May. Her birth had been a profound moment of healing for both Alistair and Chris—to welcome another child into the emptiness left by the bairn they had lost. Alistair had looked into his daughter's newborn eyes and offered a humble prayer of gratitude.

But then, everything about life with Chris kindled thankfulness in his breast. Like a robust apple tree that simply kept shedding fruit, the sheer magnitude of his blessings overwhelmed him at times.

Together, they had continued excavating the burial cairn, finally finishing right before the first snowfall last autumn. Now, a manuscript lay atop Chris's desk—a detailed article chronicling the excavation and everything they had found, all illustrated in Alistair's hand. Together, they had already reached out to several publishers and had hopes that the article would be jointly published next spring. Never again would Alistair be content to relegate his wife to the shadows.

At the moment, Chris was anything but shadow. She watched him from her chair, gaze hooded and laden with intent.

"If ye keep looking at me like that, Wife, ye shall find yourself with child again far too soon."

Chris smoothed her dressing gown. "You make it sound like a threat, Husband, but all I hear is a promise."

Alistair chuckled, causing wee Alice to squirm.

"Come here," he beckoned toward Chris.

Grinning, she came, a glide of colorful silk, her hair a long braid down her back. "What do you have planned? You are still holding our daughter, in case you have forgotten."

With one hand supporting Alice on his shoulder, he slipped the other around Chris's waist, pulling her flush against him.

Bending his head, he kissed her.

A kiss of knowing, of tenderness.

A kiss that originated in the well of joy she inspired.

Chris looped one arm around his neck, the other coming to rest on Alice's back.

Popping onto tiptoe, she kissed their daughter's head.

And then Alistair's cheek.

"I love you, Alis," she whispered in his ear.

"And I you, Chris."

Chris leaned her head into his free shoulder, relaxing into him.

Swaying, Alistair danced his two lasses in a slow circle. The crackle of the fire and the soft *shush* of Alice's breathing blended with the beating of Chris's heart against his chest.

The most beautiful music, he thought.

A symphony of love.

AUTHOR'S NOTE

As this novella contains historical information, I thought I would provide some context and explanation.

Archeology as a field of study was very much in its infancy in the 1850s. Many supposed archaeologists were little more than glorified grave robbers/treasure hunters. But some archaeologists were beginning to advocate for more methodical approaches to excavations, such as stratigraphy and graphic mapping of a site.

Of course, very few archaeologists were women. However, Miss Christian Maclagan (1811–1901) stands out as a notable exception. A Scot and an heiress, Maclagan never married, preferring to dedicate her time and money to archaeological excavations in Scotland. Though a woman, she published articles and was named a "Lady Associate" of the Society of Antiquaries of Scotland. As an homage, I used her name as inspiration for my two main characters in this novella.

Neolithic stone circles and burial cairns abound in Scotland. However, most cairns are located in northwest Scotland and Orkney. Maeshowe, on mainland Orkney, is a particularly striking example of the type of burial cairn I describe in the novella. That said, there are some stone circles and cairns in Aberdeenshire and Moray, the setting for my story. Most notable are the stone circle and cairns at Clava, which are aligned to the summer solstice. *Gowk stanes* are still prevalent in Aberdeenshire and easily located with a Google search, if you find yourself in the area and would like to see one.

Fiesole, in the hills outside Florence, is as charming and beautiful as I describe. In ancient times, it was considered a getaway for the elite of Etruscan and Roman society. During the Renaissance, Leonardo da Vinci conducted some of his most famous experiments with flight and gliders there. And to be honest, even today it is still a welcome reprieve from the bustle of Florence.

For those reading one of my Scottish stories for the first time, allow me to also comment on the Scottish language. I've used modern spellings of Scottish pronunciations and, even then, restricted myself to a few key words to give a Scottish flavor to the text. I recognize that the accent as written is not perfectly consistent; this was done to aid readability. That said, I have continued to use more common Scots words wherever possible—e.g. *ken/kent* (think, know), *eejit* (idiot), *fankle* (metaphorically tied in a knot), *muckle* (enormous), *yous* (you all), *greit* (to weep), etc.

Thank you to my daughter, Austenne, for her help with the archaeological aspects of this book. Who knew archaeologists sharpen their trowels on the regular? As usual, I owe a huge debt to Erin Rodabough and Shannon Castleton for their brilliant editing suggestions. And an extra thank you to Nuria Martinez for doing a last-minute gut-check read for me.

And if you have made it this far, thank you for reading!

An international bestselling author, Nichole Van is an artist who feels life is too short to only have one obsession. In former lives, she has been a contemporary dancer, pianist, art historian, choreographer, culinary artist and English professor.

Most notably, however, Nichole is an acclaimed photographer, winning over thirty international accolades for her work, including Portrait of the Year from WPPI in 2007. (Think Oscars for wedding and portrait photographers.) Her unique photography style has been featured in many magazines, including Rangefinder and Professional Photographer. She is also the creative mind behind the popular website Flourish Emporium which provides resources for photographers.

All that said, Nichole has always been a writer at heart. With an MA in English, she taught technical writing at Brigham Young University for ten years and has written more technical manuals than she can quickly count. She decided in late 2013 to start writing fiction and has since become an Amazon #1 bestselling author. Additionally, she has won a RONE award, as well as been a Whitney Award Finalist several years running. Her late 2018 release, Seeing Miss Heartstone, won the Whitney Award for Best Historical Romance.

In February 2017, Nichole, her husband and three crazy children moved from the Rocky Mountains in the USA to Scotland. They currently live near the coast of eastern Scotland in an eighteenth century country house. Nichole loves her pastoral country views while writing and enjoys long walks through fields and along beaches. She does not, however, have a fondness for haggis.

She is known as NicholeVan all over the web: Facebook, Instagram, Pinterest, etc. Visit http://www.NicholeVan.com to sign up for her author newsletter and be notified of new book releases. Additionally, you can see her photographic work at http://photography.nicholeV.com and http://www.nicholeV.com

OF KILTS AND COURTSHIP

Heidi Kimball

One

ARABELLA HUGHES HAD been sentenced to one of Dante's nine circles of hell for the summer.

Scotland, to be precise.

After five days in a carriage jolting over Scotland's muddy roads, dealing with grumpy innkeepers, and the Scottish accent thickening with every mile they traveled north, Arabella was at her wits' end.

She was out of the country, out of reach of civilization, and out of patience.

And now this.

She stared down at herself, damp and mud-spattered, then lifted her eyes toward the damaged carriage, feeling a growing sense of helplessness. She wanted to throw something. Instead, she settled for kicking the broken axle. A streak of pain shot up her toe and she winced.

That was her reward, she supposed, for being unladylike.

Ironic, since being unladylike was what had gotten her into this mess in the first place. She wouldn't be here—cold, wet through, and foul-tempered—if she'd been the ladylike paragon her parents expected her to be. She'd still be in London, enjoying the end of the Season.

"Miss Hughes?" The driver cut through her melancholy thoughts. "The village is about a mile up. I can unhitch one of the horses for you, though you'd have to ride—"

"I've no intention of riding bareback." She pulled her cloak tighter around her. "We'll walk."

"But Miss Hughes!" came Molly's whine. "Walk in this?" Arabella's lady's maid gestured up at the sky, still letting down a steady rain. "Why, it'll be the death of us both, it will. We should wait here, in the carriage, for someone to—"

"Rescue us?" Arabella interrupted. "We'd be here the whole summer. No, we'll walk." And ignoring Molly's protests, Arabella turned and started up the hill, cursing the day she'd ever thought kissing Mr. Gresham was a romantic idea.

The thick mud sucked at her boots, and she kept her head down, trying to keep the rain out of her eyes. Molly's piteous cries followed her all the way up the hill, and by the time she entered the village's one small inn, The Fox and Crown, Arabella felt ready to snap.

Instead, she found the ruddy-faced proprietor who took one look at her and grunted. "Ye're drippin' water a' ower mah flair 'n' mah guidwife wull nae be happy."

While she didn't understand *exactly* what he was saying, she certainly understood the gist. It took a great deal of effort not to inform the man that his country had dripped water all over *her*.

She drew in a slow breath. *Be a lady.* "Yes, sir, and I am sorry. We've had some trouble with our carriage and need assistance. And perhaps a room where my lady's maid and I could dry out while we wait."

The man grunted again, returning to his ledger. "Thir's na yin wha kin hulp ye th'day."

His dismissiveness cut through her. "No one who can help us *today*? What about tomorrow? How about by next Tuesday?"

He didn't even bother to look up. "Ah will hae th' missus see aboot a room fur ye. Mrs. Ferguson!" he shouted.

Arabella was seething. She'd never been so ill-treated in her life. Her parents hadn't been exaggerating about the ills of Scotland.

The innkeeper's wife appeared, a short plump woman, hair laced with gray.

The man gestured toward Arabella. "A room fur th' lassie 'n' her maid tae freuch oot."

"*Seòmar don bhoireannach. Ach gu dearbh!*" She turned to go. "*Lean mise.*"

Thus far, the thick Scottish accent had been difficult to make sense of. But this woman's words sounded like another language entirely. Arabella could feel a headache coming on.

Yet she dutifully followed, and the woman settled them in a cozy parlor, leaving their cloaks drying by the fire. A quaint table sat in the middle of the room and Arabella took one of the wooden chairs.

"A whole summer here," wailed Molly, retreating to one of the corner chairs. "In this uncivilized country. Oh, what did I do to deserve it?"

Arabella was already tempted to leave Molly here at the end of the summer. After a week of the girl's whining, she was beginning to think Mother had hired Molly as part of her punishment.

Luckily, Molly's complaints were soon quieted as she drifted off to sleep. Arabella leaned back against the chair and closed her eyes, shutting out the world. Welcome though the reprieve was, Arabella couldn't help but let her thoughts drift back to London, to the missteps that had led her here.

It had started out innocently enough.

A harmless flirtation with Mr. Gresham.

Meaningful glances. Whispered words. Brief meetings in Hyde Park on the rare occasion she managed to escape her mother's watchful eye. The thrill of those secret moments had filled her with a heady sense of freedom.

Arabella hadn't been in love with him. She was certain of that. But she had loved having something, for once, that was all her own.

Arabella had grown tired of being a puppet on a string, her parents controlling her every move. The speed at which she walked. How often she smiled. Who she danced with. Her circle of friends.

So, when she'd met Mr. Gresham, who cared nothing for her parents and their rigid rules, he'd carried her away on a current of desperation. At first, she'd been so careful. So cautious.

Until she hadn't.

The door to the parlor swung open, and Arabella sat up, smoothing her skirts.

"*Cup tí dhut.*" Her hostess bustled in with a tea tray. "*Feumaidh tu a bhith gorta.*"

Pretending she understood, Arabella gave her a weak smile. "Thank you."

The woman set the tray on the table. "*Leig fios dhomh ma tha dad a dhith ort.*"

Arabella could only nod again.

Thankfully, the woman seemed to take that as some sort of agreement and retreated from the room.

Arabella leaned back again, closing her eyes, loathing Scotland more and more by the minute. "Does no one in this infernal country speak a *word* of English?" she asked aloud.

"I do." The deep voice came from somewhere behind her.

Arabella's eyes flew open and she whipped her head around, only to see a pair of boots descending a set of steps near the back of the room. A man in a caped greatcoat came to stand at the foot of the stairs, a half-smile lifting one corner of his mouth.

She tried, in the space of a few short seconds, to take his

measure. He was undeniably striking, with dark hair that curled over his brow, laughing eyes, and an angular jaw. His finely tailored clothes and polished boots were fit for London's finest drawing rooms. And the way he stood—the casual yet attentive stance of a man of consequence.

Where had he come from? And how, exactly, did one respond to a stranger who was so *direct*? Normally she would ignore such impertinent behavior. They hadn't been introduced, after all, and he had to have known she wasn't speaking to *him*. But even in those two words he'd spoken, she'd heard that perfectly familiar, perfectly clipped English accent. The sound of home.

Which is why, Arabella convinced herself, she answered back. "I suppose that makes two of us."

His mouth twitched. "If we find a third, perhaps we should start a society."

Try as she might, she couldn't find much humor in it. "It isn't as though I have anything else to do to pass my time here," she said, voice laced with bitterness.

The man looked at her more closely, raising a questioning eyebrow. "You are visiting, then?"

She nodded. "Unfortunately." And then, remembering she really shouldn't be conversing with a stranger, she began making herself a cup of tea.

Even as she added some cream and sugar to her cup, she could feel the man's eyes on her. "It sounds as if there's a story there," he said, his words a bit softer. Inviting Arabella to share, if she would.

And perhaps, if she hadn't felt so very forlorn, she wouldn't have answered. But she was friendless, hundreds of miles from home, and worn down from days of travel. The thought of having someone to confide in was . . . unexpectedly comforting.

She glanced toward Molly's sleeping form. They weren't alone, not really.

"There is," she admitted, taking a long sip of tea.

Without waiting for an invitation, the man took the seat across from Arabella, settling back in the chair. Ready to listen.

Arabella set her cup down. "I'm to spend a summer here in Ballintraid with my grandmother as a . . ." She looked up and met his gaze, his eyes a rich green. "A punishment," she confessed.

"A punishment," he repeated. "Does your grandmother beat you?" His eyes danced with amusement.

She laughed despite herself. "Certainly not. At least I *hope* not. I've never met her. This is my first time visiting Scotland," she admitted. "But in the five days since I crossed the border, I've discovered everything my parents warned me about is true."

"The whole country offends you?" He didn't bother to hide his curiosity.

"Well, yes, if you must know. The accent is impossible."

He nodded, expression grave. "It can be."

She thought of the rain and mud she'd trudged through to get here. And in June! "The weather is atrocious." A bit of her frustration melted away as he listened. Attentive. Empathetic.

"It is that," he agreed, face stoic.

"But it's more than that." Arabella lowered her voice, as if the whole country might be listening. "Scots are . . . well, swarthy and bad-tempered. And you must have noticed how very backward Scottish etiquette is. There's an off-putting bluntness of manner that is so very . . . un-English." She leaned forward, whispering, "I fear they're all brutes."

The man quirked his lips. "Quite savage," he said. "Most Scots can't be trusted a bit."

"Yes," she said. "Exactly!"

A crease formed between his brows. "I'm surprised your parents allowed a young woman such as yourself to travel alone in a country where there are so many dangerous men about."

Arabella gestured toward where Molly slept in her chair, head lolled to one side. "I've my lady's maid. And I daresay she could easily scare most men off with the force of her complaints."

He leaned forward, looking at her with an intensity that made her insides flutter just a bit. "Still, I must insist you be on your guard. Never accept a ride from a Scotsman. No matter how well-intentioned he may seem."

"I won't," Arabella agreed, touched by his concern. "I promise."

The man pushed back from the table and stood. "You must excuse me, Miss . . . ?"

"Hughes," Arabella supplied, startled. "Miss Hughes. But where are you off to? The rain hasn't let up."

"Ach, but a wee smirr never keeps a Scotsman from his destination, ye ken. And I really must be getting home." He had a thick Scottish accent now, a noticeable rolling cadence in his voice.

Arabella blinked and shook her head, worried exhaustion was finally catching up with her. After five days in Scotland, perhaps she was only imagining his brogue. "A Scotsman? But . . . you're English."

He grinned, a full mouth of straight white teeth on display. "Nay. Though I was educated in the finest schools England has tae offer."

She shook her head in disbelief, stomach sinking. He was Scottish. And he'd been trifling with her this entire time.

He retrieved his hat from a peg on the wall and placed it

on his head. "Your grandmother's estate is adjacent tae mine, Miss Hughes, so perhaps I'll be seeing ye aboot this summer."

"My grandmother? You know my grandmother?"

"Oh aye. We've been neighbors all my life. She's a fine woman." Eyes twinkling, he tipped his head forward, whispering conspiratorially. "She won't beat ye."

Discarding her shock, Arabella's mind caught hold of an important fact. "You said your estate is adjacent to hers? And you have a carriage?"

"Indeed. And I do wish I could offer ye a ride, but—"

A helpless sort of desperation welled up within her. She pushed back her chair. "You needn't worry about the impropriety if I bring Molly. We won't be a bit of trouble. I promise."

"I wish I could, Miss Hughes. But I . . ." He seemed to consider it, but at last he shook his head. "Nay. I would not wish ye tae put yerself in danger with a savage such as myself. Ye *did* promise not tae accept a ride from a Scotsman, after all. And I, Mr. Gavin McKenzie, am most certainly a Scot."

And with one last smile, he and his greatcoat swept from the room.

Two

GAVIN MCKENZIE LEANED against the mantel, still grinning like a schoolboy.

"What has ye in such a jovial mood?"

He turned to see Nan striding across the sitting room to greet him. He stepped forward and pulled her into a hug, her familiar mint-and-honey scent washing over him.

"Can I not just be happy tae see ye?" he asked.

Nan pulled back and gave him a knowing look. "Ach, I ken ye better than that."

He still remembered the day he'd met her. Her hair had been mostly gray, and she'd stood over him as he'd sat crying, his scraped knee throbbing. It wasn't until after she'd patched up his knee and his britches that it had occurred to him to ask for her name. "Ye can call me Nan," she'd replied kindly.

Now her hair was white, her back stooped, her round face lined with wrinkles. But the passage of time hadn't dimmed the perception in her gaze.

He gave her a roguish smile. "I met yer granddaughter."

She set a hand on her chest. "Arabella? Ye didn't."

"I did. She was just as lovely as ye said she'd be." With her lustrous dark hair and sea-blue eyes, Gavin had found himself quite taken with her. Until she'd opened her mouth.

"How? Where?" she demanded.

All these years she'd been waiting, hoping to meet her

only grandchild. What Gavin hadn't known that first day they'd met? That she was lonely, grieving the daughter who'd cut her off. But fate had been kind, bringing him and Nan together. He'd filled an empty part of her heart just as she'd come to fill an empty part of his.

"At The Fox and Crown. There was a mishap with her carriage."

"Well, where is she?"

Gavin had the good sense to look a bit remorseful. He rubbed the back of his neck. "I left her there."

"Left her there... in the hands of cantankerous auld Mr. Ferguson? Gavin Alexander McKenzie! Whatever for?" Nan gave him a hard stare.

He crossed his arms over his chest, remembering the snobbish look on the young woman's face. "Tae rid her of some of her prejudices against Scots."

Deep grooves formed in the old woman's forehead. "It's as I feared, then."

"Worse than ye feared, I think." Gavin guided her over to the settee by the window.

She sat down heavily, sighing. "Do tell."

Gavin sat beside her and leaned forward, forearms resting on his thighs. "If ye'd heard how she talked aboot Scots, as if we are a species barely above coos or sheep. She used the words 'swarthy' and 'brutes.'"

If it had been anyone else, Gavin would have found the whole situation quite comical. What did he care for the young chit's opinion? But this was Nan's granddaughter. The young woman she'd ached to know for as long as he could remember. If her prejudices hurt Nan in any way... *that* would be another matter entirely.

His mouth tightened into a hard line. "Ye'd have been tempted tae disavow her."

Nan clasped her gnarled hands together. "Her mind is made up, then. Her parents have poisoned her against me. Against her own roots."

He couldn't bear the note of defeat in her voice. "Well, we'll just have tae change it then, won't we?"

"We?" One corner of her mouth lifted. "Based on what ye've told me, I doubt *ye* are in her good graces."

Gavin shook his head. "I don't think ye . . . or we . . . should try tae get in her good graces."

She cocked one white eyebrow. "Go on, then. This plan sounds more and more promising by the moment," she said, words laced with sarcasm.

He leaned back and stared at the wainscotting on the ceiling, a strategy forming in his mind. "It seems tae me that since she's expecting the worst . . ." A smile crept over his face. "We should give her exactly that."

"Ye really think leaving her tae rot in that inn will endear her tae me? And Scots in general?"

"Not exactly. But the alternative is what? Beg for a morsel of her affection? Hope that with enough shortbread and Dundee cakes, we can cajole her intae thinking better of us?" Everything within Gavin bristled. He shook his head. "Nae."

"All right, then. What exactly did ye have in mind?" Nan looked dubious, but she was warming to the idea.

"We cannae be too extreme or we'll arouse her suspicions." He imagined Miss Hughes in the chair across from him, sitting so prim and proper, yet so eager for connection that she'd confided in a stranger.

What was going on behind those crystal-blue eyes of hers? As a lad, Gavin had taken apart clocks and pocket watches, captivated by their inner mechanisms. How each piece worked together to make the instrument tick. As a man, he was even more intrigued by the inner workings of the human mind.

And Arabella Hughes promised to be a fascinating case, indeed.

"We'll start with a few basic misconceptions, the types of things she thinks she already kens aboot Scots. Strong brogues. Tartan plaids."

Nan rose and began to pace. "I dinnae ken, Gavin. This is my granddaughter. And she's ainlie here for the summer. I'll likely not get another chance. After losing Ada . . ." A fleeting look of hurt passed over Nan's face, remembering the daughter who'd wed an Englishman and never looked back. Never visited. Kept her daughter out of reach of her Scottish grandmother. "I cannae lose Arabella, too."

Gavin nodded. "I ken ye miss your daughter. That ye still grieve her." He let out a slow breath, hating that these words would hurt her. "But have years of pleading and begging with her changed anything?"

Eyes on the floor, Nan shook her head.

"Perhaps 'tis time tae try something different," he said softly. "Pleading and begging has not worked with her mother, and I do not think it will work on Arabella either."

The last thing he would ever want to do is jeopardize Nan's relationship with her granddaughter. But he also knew what he'd seen in Miss Hughes. "Ye cannae coddle her. Ye cannae hope tae change her mind or heart by making things easy for her. She's a stubborn lass. And she needs tae be shown a bit of stubbornness in return."

"For how long?" She pursed her lips together.

"No more than twenty-four hours."

She stopped pacing. "One day?"

"At most," he promised.

She hesitated. "I'll think on it. But first, I think ye should take your carriage back down tae the village and bring her home tae me."

"You!" An accusatory voice rang out from the doorway.

Gavin and Nan turned in unison.

There stood Arabella Hughes, so wet that it looked like she'd taken a dip in the loch. Her boots and dress were thickly coated with mud, her hair plastered to her head. Flecks of dirt and mud spattered her cheeks like an artist's smock.

The lass had *walked*.

Three miles.

Uphill.

In the rain and mud.

She had spirit, Gavin would give her that. Or perhaps it was sheer Scottish stubbornness. Either way, he was impressed.

But given the look of contempt on her face, the feeling wasn't mutual.

She spoke through gritted teeth. "I wouldn't get into a carriage with that man if he were the last person on earth."

Cargill, the butler, holding a sodden cape and looking more flustered than usual, peeked his head around her. "May I present Miss Arabella Hughes, ma'am. She insisted on seeing ye at once."

Three

ARABELLA COULDN'T BELIEVE it.

That . . . that *man*.

Here, in her grandmother's sitting room.

Relaxing on the settee, one leg crossed over the other, looking casually at home. As if he belonged. As if *he* were a family member and *she* the interloper.

She glared at him, blood boiling so hot that she feared her wet clothes might begin to steam.

But under the force of her scathing stare, his mouth only tipped up in half a smile. A smile that she, not two hours past, had thought handsome. Now she was certain he bore a striking resemblance to the devil.

He got to his feet and ambled toward her. "Ach, women are such changeable creatures, are they not, Miss Hughes? An hour ago, ye were quite desperate for a ride in my carriage." He cocked his head. "But dinnae fash yerself. I'll do my best tae keep up with yer changing preferences."

The . . . the *nerve*.

Arabella didn't have the words for what she'd like to do to Mr. Gavin McKenzie. But it involved things like boiling vats of oil, the rack, and a dank, dark dungeon.

"Arabella!"

Preoccupied as she'd been with the unexpected sight of

Mr. McKenzie, she'd barely noticed the white-haired woman at his side.

Her grandmother.

The old lady was short and stout, with kindly features and the same bright blue eyes as both Arabella and her mother. One hand rested over her mouth as if to keep emotion from spilling out.

Relief spread through Arabella at the sight of her. At last, someone who would save her from the nightmare of this past week.

The woman stepped forward. "Ach, it feels as if I've waited my whole life for this moment. And just look at ye, a grown and beautiful woman! Here in Scotland at last!"

Arabella's smile faded. Was her grandmother daft? Senile? Could she not see that Arabella had risked life and limb scaling treacherous highland terrain? That she was muddy and soaked through, and it was all the fault of that dreadful Mr. McKenzie?

"Oh yes," Arabella replied, tone biting. "And what a welcome your country has given me."

Her grandmother paused mid-step, features frozen. She exchanged a look with Mr. McKenzie, then gave him a small but determined nod that Arabella couldn't decipher.

All at once her face broke into an unnaturally bright smile as she reached out to pat Arabella's cheek. "It appears ye took a pleasant walk. There's certainly naething better for one's constitution than some nice brisk air and a wee bit of rain."

A pleasant walk? Brisk air and a bit of rain? It was hardly—

Just then the spritely woman threw her arms around Arabella. For a moment, the gesture threw her off balance. Her grandmother came up only to her chin, but there was nothing feeble about her embrace. It was far different from the awkward way Mother patted her shoulder after they'd had one of their "talks" and Arabella had agreed to one of her requests. Grandmother's embrace was fierce and heartfelt and seemed to warm Arabella in a way even the warmest quilt couldn't do.

"Have some towels brought up tae her room at once, Cargill. And water for a hot bath." Grandmother released her, then linked her arm through Arabella's. "We'll get ye warm and dry in no time."

"But my trunks are still a mile outside the village. And my lady's maid is back at The Fox and Crown . . ."

"We cannae send for them until the weather clears, ye ken. But 'twill be nae trouble at all tae pull out one of yer mother's auld dresses."

She led Arabella to the door, pausing to turn and speak over her shoulder. "Gavin, ye will be joining us for dinner, won't ye?"

Arabella turned back to find Mr. McKenzie watching her, amusement dancing in his eyes. She could have cursed him for sitting there with such nonchalance, looking more dashing than any Scotsman had a right to be.

Or any Englishman, for that matter.

While she, sodden from head to toe, looked no better than a drowned rat. A drowned and muddy rat. Inwardly seething, she swore to herself before the summer was over she'd see *him* covered in mud.

Almost as if he knew exactly what she was thinking, he gave her a piratical grin. "I would like that very much. Very much, indeed."

GAVIN STOOD IN the dining room near the head of the table, still grinning.

He couldn't remember a better day in recent memory.

Part of that was due to being back in Ballintraid, where he belonged. Far from city life, away from the crushes of London and the manifold obligations that met him whenever he visited Edinburgh.

But the other part was thanks to Miss Arabella Hughes.

Did he feel a modicum of guilt as he thought of all that lay in store for her? Perhaps. But with her English airs and outlandish prejudice against Scots, the young lady had brought it upon herself.

Nan slipped into the dining room, shaking her head. "I look ridiculous, do I not?"

Gavin measured his answer, for she did look a wee bit ridiculous. Like some sort of matriarchal clan leader come back from centuries past. A tartan shawl was crisscrossed over her chest, and on her head, another plaid had been fashioned into a turban.

"'Tis for a good cause," he said diplomatically.

Truth be told, Gavin was a bit self-conscious as well. He and Nan had rummaged through several chests in the attic before they'd found her late husband's kilt. And while he didn't mind the swath of fabric across his chest, he found the kilt itself to be a bit . . . breezy.

"'Tis for a good cause," he repeated, reassuring himself.

She glanced toward the table. "Is everything arranged, then?"

Gavin kept his voice low. "Aye. All is ready."

Nan blew out a breath. "What about Rory?"

He smiled. "He was more than willing."

The sound of a throat clearing put an end to their conversation.

Miss Hughes stood just inside the doorway on the other side of the room. "Good evening," she said, her voice perfectly cool.

His breath snagged in his chest as he locked gazes with her. When he'd met her back at The Fox and Crown, even disheveled as she'd been, he'd known she was uncommonly pretty. But now, dark hair gleaming in the candlelight, cheeks high with color, and attired in an old-fashioned dress that accentuated her every curve, she was much more than that. Gavin struggled to find his voice.

Fortunately, Nan had no such difficulty. "Ach, lass. Ye look just like yer mother. I can hardly believe it."

Miss Hughes smoothed the fabric of the dress. "It's a little short. I'm a bit taller than her."

"Ye need not worry aboot that. Come, let us eat. I'm sure ye are famished."

"I am," she agreed, coming to join them at the head of the table. And that was when she saw the two of them fully. Her eyes moved from Nan's tartan turban to Gavin's kilt.

Her jaw went slack. "What are you... your... your *knees*," she gasped.

Gavin lifted his kilt a little to give her a better view. "Fine specimens, wouldn't ye agree?"

Now it was Miss Hughes who was at a loss for words. Her mouth opened and closed several times before she looked sharply at her grandmother.

"Dinnae worry, we have a tartan for ye as well," Nan assured her.

Miss Hughes shook her head. "Oh no. That won't be necessary."

"Ach, but ye must," Gavin said. "We cannae begin dinner until ye are wearing a plaid of yer own." He shrugged his shoulders. "'Tis tradition."

And before she could protest again, Nan took the extra plaid she'd brought down and looped it over her granddaughter's neck.

"Tradition?" Miss Hughes asked while Nan crossed it over her chest and moved behind her to tie it. "Are we celebrating something special for the seventh of June?"

"Well, yes," Gavin replied, as if it were the most obvious thing in the world. "Same as we do every night. We're celebrating the repeal of the Diskilting Act."

"The *Dis-kilt-ing Act*?" She broke diskilting into three distinct parts as if it were a foreign word.

"Ye must ken what happened in 1746," said Nan. "After the Jacobite uprising. When all forms of Highland dress, including kilts, were outlawed?"

Miss Hughes shook her head.

"It wasn't until 1782 that the act was finally repealed," Gavin went on. "And ever since, we Highlanders have worn our kilts and tartans every night for dinner in celebration of our victory."

"*Every* night?"

Nan cinched the knot and patted Arabella's shoulder. "But of course, dearie. Now, come. Let us eat."

Gavin helped both women into their chairs, watching Miss Hughes as he took his own seat.

And she did not disappoint. Her eyes drifted over the table, widening when she saw the four mugs at her place setting.

Gavin took a long drink out of one of his mugs and let out a pleasurable sigh.

"Grandmother," Miss Hughes said. "Why do we each have four . . . *glasses*?"

Gavin hid a smile at her choice of words. Did she find the word *mug* distasteful?

"For our drinks, of course," Nan said patiently.

"*Drinks*?" she asked, pitch growing higher. "Is one not sufficient?"

"One for each, yes. Ale, port, brandy, and whisky." Nan gestured toward her mugs. "We cannae very well mix them all together, ye ken."

Gavin had no doubt that Miss Hughes had been given the finest English education money could buy. She'd probably learned deportment, elocution, and etiquette, and spent considerable time at an expensive finishing school.

But, he noted with some satisfaction, nothing could have prepared her for this.

"Your granddaughter is likely accustomed tae the English way," Gavin told Nan. "Where ainlie weak wine is served at dinner." He took another drink. "The English never could hold their liquor verra well."

Miss Hughes struggled, opening her mouth, then snapping it shut as if remembering it wouldn't be proper for a gently bred lady to speak about whether the English were prone to becoming drunk.

Finally, she chose a different avenue of conversation. "And how do the two of you know one another, did you say? You are neighbors?"

"Ach, yes." Nan smiled, eyes crinkling. "I met Gavin on the steps down tae the beach. He'd fallen and scraped his knee and was greetin' like the world was at an end. I took him home, bandaged his knee, sewed up his trousers, and fed him a scone." She looked over at him, expression soft. "And he's been following me around ever since. The grandson I never had."

Awkward silence filled the room.

"I see." Miss Hughes stared down at her lap.

Nan realized she'd misspoken immediately. "I dinnae mean it tae sound..."

Gavin thought he detected a hint of wistfulness in Miss Hughes, the feeling of being an outsider. He felt a small prick of sympathy, for he knew the feeling well.

Cargill set a bowl of soup in front of each of them. Fish stew, from the smell of it.

"You mentioned a beach?" Miss Hughes asked, attempting to steer the conversation back to safer topics, as a lady would.

Her fortitude was something to be admired.

Nan smiled in relief. "Aye, the beach is breathtaking. Just beneath the cliff 'tis rocky, but it stretches out intae a mile or so of sandy white beaches. If yer willing tae brave the steep steps down, that is."

"I've still a scar on my knee that attests tae the hazards they pose," Gavin said. "Perhaps ye noticed it earlier when ye were admiring my knees?"

Miss Hughes nearly spit out her sip of wine. "Admiring your . . . I was *not* admiring your knees, Mr. McKenzie. On the contrary, I—"

"There's no shame in it, lass. Ye're not the first Englishwoman tae have fallen prey tae such temptations." He winked at her. "Methinks it may be one of the reasons the English outlawed kilts in the first place."

Even as a flush spread over her neck and into her cheeks, Gavin didn't look away. She squirmed under his brazen stare, probably wishing him at the devil.

"*Methinks*," she nearly spat, "you Scots have very high opinions of yourselves."

"Aye," he agreed. "We can only hope yer own opinion of us is a bit improved by summer's end."

Her smile was half-feral. "We shall see."

He'd have been an *eejit* not to understand her true meaning: *Not a chance.*

Gavin lifted his mug toward her. "A toast, then. May ye enjoy a long and glorious summer in the Highlands, Miss Hughes. Welcome tae Scotland."

Four

WRETCHED MAN.

As if she'd be tempted by his *knees* of all things.

Willing her blush away, Arabella looked down at her soup. Not only was she starving, but it was a relief to have something to focus her attention on besides her grandmother's ill-mannered guest. Her gaze skirted from one side of her soup bowl to the other, searching for a spoon.

"Grandmother," she said at last, attempting to keep the irritation from her voice. "I don't seem to have a spoon."

"A spoon?" Mr. McKenzie picked up his knife. "Nae, ye wouldn't. We dinnae bother with spoons. Or forks. A good, sharp knife is the only utensil ye need."

She lifted her hands in exasperation. "You cannot be serious. One cannot eat soup with a *knife*."

In answer, he speared one of the pieces of fish from his stew, then raised his brows in question as if to say, *Is anything the matter?*

In the space of a few short hours, they'd managed to develop a wordless communication they both understood perfectly. Which was ideal since there were plenty of things Arabella wanted to say to him that she didn't want her grandmother hearing.

She was beginning, however, to wish she knew a few more curse words.

Holding her gaze, Mr. McKenzie raised the fish to his mouth, lips closing around his knife as he slowly pulled the utensil away.

Arabella could only stare at him, hating the way her toes curled in her slippers at the sensual way he'd taken a bite of fish stew. With a *knife* of all things.

A knife! She refused to believe it.

Scots were known for kilts and plaids, their propensity for drinking . . .

But *this*? No.

This had to be some ghastly joke.

Surely Scots used spoons and forks.

Surely.

Beside her, Grandmother stabbed a piece of fish and took a bite.

Arabella drew in a slow breath. "But one cannot eat broth with a knife."

"Of course not," Mr. McKenzie said, winking at her for the second time this evening.

If ever any man was asking to be slapped, it was him.

"Ye drink it, like so." He picked up his bowl and lifted it to his mouth, slurping down the broth.

Her jaw dropped. In less than a day, every one of her worst fears about Scotland had been confirmed. If anything, her parents had downplayed the ills of the country to which they'd relegated her.

She watched her grandmother and Mr. McKenzie eat for several minutes, stabbing at pieces of fish with their knives, then drinking the broth.

Arabella's stomach growled, loudly.

"Yer famished, Arabella." Grandmother frowned. "Well, go on. The fish won't bite ye."

Arabella glanced down at her knife. She couldn't.

Wouldn't. But the alternative was what, exactly? Refuse to eat on principle? Starve herself for the entire summer?

Tentatively she picked up her knife, eyed the largest piece of fish in her bowl, then speared. As she did, she could almost imagine the gates of hell through which Dante had passed, inscribed, "*Lasciate ogne speranza, voi ch'intrate.*"

Or, in English, "Abandon hope, all ye who enter here!"

She put the fish on the tip of the knife to her lips and took a bite, swallowing hard.

One bite, then another, then another.

Much how the summer would have to be endured.

One day at a time.

Five

WHAT *WAS* THAT dratted noise?

Arabella buried her head under the pillow, trying desperately to drown it out.

But the sound persisted, loud and melancholy...

A rooster perhaps? A *deranged* rooster? The poor thing sounded as if it were singing a death dirge. But in the middle of the night?

She pressed the pillow around her ears, but her exhaustion was no match for the tenacity of that... noise. As Arabella had closed her eyes last night, the thought of sleep had been a relief, her bed a fortress that would provide an escape from the misery she'd endured since her arrival in this wretched place.

She'd been wrong.

It seemed Scotland was even capable of ruining her precious sleep.

Arabella threw back the covers in frustration, her eyelids so heavy that it took several long blinks before she could keep them open. To her surprise, small rays of light shone around the edges of the curtains.

Already?

It seemed only a few minutes ago she'd lay her head on the pillow. Her mind had still been reeling from tartans and kilts, the drinking, the knives. Had it all been a dream?

But the touch of her bare feet on the ice-cold floor assured her she was very much awake.

Arabella dressed quickly, pulling on last night's dress, slipping into her boots, and throwing the tartan shawl Grandmother had given her around her shoulders.

She took no pains to keep quiet as she stomped down the stairs. Whatever that noise was, she was determined to put an end to it. And if it was a rooster, she'd ... well, she could always use a knife.

They seemed to have plenty of those here in Scotland.

The house was quiet and dark. Arabella pulled open the heavy front door and stepped outside.

It was there she paused, spellbound.

For the entirety of her journey northward, Scotland had been rainy and dismal, with low-hanging clouds and persistent fog that had obscured any real view of the countryside. On her long trudge from the village yesterday, she'd questioned why anyone would want to live in such a bleak and gloomy place.

But now, as Arabella got her first real glimpse of the Highlands, she knew.

With soft rays of sun sweeping over the crags and ridges in the distance, Scotland looked otherworldly. The Highland peaks were painted in every shade of green, stretching down into valleys with so vivid a color that it hurt to look at them. A thin mist covered the sweeping hills, softening their intense beauty, giving the scene an almost ethereal feel. Nestled in a nearby dell was a winding river, a quaint bridge arcing over it.

Somewhere inside her, Arabella felt a little tug. As if the exquisite beauty before her had hooked around her rib cage, pulling her forward. Urging her to explore. And Arabella might have given in if it hadn't been for that dratted noise. But for now, she had to discover its source. The screech of it almost sounded like ... music?

It was coming from the north side of the house. She hurried around the corner, then pulled up short, coming face-to-face with a man she'd never seen.

His cheeks were round and red from puffing air into some sort of instrument she didn't recognize.

Not a rooster, then.

He wore a feathered black hat, a woolen coat, knee-high socks, and a kilt, the pleated fabric blowing in the cool morning breeze.

But why on earth was he so determined to make music—if it could be called such—at this early hour? There were twenty-four hours in each day, after all. She saw no need for him to choose the ones in which she preferred to sleep.

"Do ye enjoy the bagpipes, Miss Hughes?" The familiar brogue came from behind her.

Mr. McKenzie.

She turned to find him leaning against the house in a casual pose, sporting the same grin as yesterday.

She frowned, crossing her arms over her chest. Wasn't he supposed to be at home, sleeping off all the ale and whisky and whatever other drinks he'd consumed last night?

Instead, he looked rested and refreshed, his hair combed and his face cleanshaven, and unlike her, it appeared he'd taken his time dressing for the day. Arabella pulled her shawl more tightly around her shoulders, resisting the urge to touch her sleep-tossed braid.

She cleared her throat. "The bagpipes, Mr. McKenzie?"

"Aye, don't ye love the plaintive sound of them?" He raised his voice to be heard over the garish notes.

"Is that how they're *supposed* to sound?"

One corner of Mr. McKenzie's mouth quirked. "Rory may not be the most accomplished piper in Scotland."

She looked askance at him.

He shrugged. "In fact, it may be more accurate tae say he is still very much in the *learning* phase. But he certainly gives it his all. Wouldn't ye agree?"

Arabella glanced over at the man who continued to struggle through the song, rounded cheeks puffing. "But that doesn't explain why he is playing them *now*. It's five in the morning!"

"It's how we wake every morning, Miss Hughes. Ach, ye see. Here comes your grandmother."

Just as he said the words, Grandmother came around the corner, face wreathed in a smile. "I worried I'd have tae wake ye for the playing of the bagpipes, but ye were up and gone before I could get these auld bones oot the door."

"I wish I'd been informed of this *ritual* last night," Arabella said, quite ready to be done with Scotland's many surprises.

"Ach, 'tis my own fault. I'm so accustomed tae it, I dinnae even think tae warn ye."

"And how long will he play?" All she wanted was to go back to bed.

"An hour at most," Mr. McKenzie assured her.

"An *hour*? Each morning?"

"Refreshing, isn't it?" Grandmother smiled contentedly. "A wonderful way tae start each day."

Arabella wanted a pen and paper. If she couldn't sleep, she planned to write a *long* letter to her mother, outlining the many woes she'd been subjected to.

But Grandmother and Mr. McKenzie were already walking around the back of the house, murmuring about some of the wood that needed to be replaced due to salt rot.

At last the man finished, breathing hard, forehead beaded with sweat.

"Thank you," Arabella said, hoping he would interpret it

to mean she was thankful for his playing and not surmise the truth—that she was grateful he had stopped.

"O' course. 'Tis always a pleasure tae play my pipes."

She offered a polite smile. "You must be quite dedicated to play every morning."

"Well, yes. Though not usually fer an audience. And not at five in the morn."

Arabella frowned. "You don't *usually* play at five in the morning, to wake everyone?"

The man looked confused. "Nay. Why would I?"

"Of all the . . ." Arabella strode forward but then stopped. "Do you, by chance, use forks and spoons? When you eat?"

His forehead creased. "I do," he replied, the words long and drawn out as if she might be slow of intellect. "Doesnae everybody?"

"And do you wear this garb"—she gestured up and down, indicating his Highland clothing—"every evening to celebrate the Diskilting Act?"

"The Diskilting what?"

She nodded. "Thank you, sir. You've been very helpful."

He tipped his hat at her, a puzzled look on his face, but she was already turning, running to catch up with Mr. McKenzie. Of all the uncouth, abhorrent gentlemen she had ever met, he was the worst.

In fact, he wasn't a gentleman at all. He was a Scot.

She caught up to them at the back of the house, where they stood looking out at the ocean.

"You cad!" she shouted, unwilling to communicate in their silent language this time. Her grandmother was as guilty as he.

Mr. McKenzie turned. "'Tis a bit early tae be throwing insults, isn't it?"

"How long?" she demanded. "How long would you have

let me go on, believing you wear Highland attire every evening and drink like madmen and only use knives?" Now that she stopped to think about it, she felt foolish, for she'd been served with forks and spoons at every one of the inns she'd stayed at in Scotland.

Mr. McKenzie crossed his arms over his broad chest. "That depends," he replied. "How long were ye willing tae believe it?"

Shame and humiliation singed her as she thought of last night. Of how she'd believed and gone along with every one of their machinations. The amusement she'd provided them. "And you," she said, facing her grandmother. "I'd never have expected my own . . . why would you . . ."

"'Twas my own foolish pride," Grandmother cried, immediately contrite. "And I am sorry. I should never—"

"If the fault is anyone's, ye ken it is mine," Mr. McKenzie broke in.

Arabella's eyes snapped to his, hot tears burning down her cheeks. She batted them away. She did *not* want this man to see her cry. "Of that, I have no doubt." Her voice shook with anger.

And then, looking for escape, her eyes caught on the path that led down to the beach, and she fled.

Six

ARABELLA FLEW DOWN the steep steps.

What was it about Mr. McKenzie? Arabella rarely gave way to emotion. And she never cried. Mother always said it was a weakness a woman could ill afford. But somehow, *he* managed to . . .

Another tear splashed down her cheek.

She was nearly halfway down the cliffside when Mr. McKenzie called her name. "Miss Hughes!"

She ignored him.

"Miss Hughes, please. Hear me out." His voice was closer now, only a few steps behind her.

Anger mounting, Arabella whirled to face him. "And why should I? You lied to me from the first moment we met. Why should I listen to a single word you say?" Her chest was heaving, hair coming loose from her untidy braid.

He peered at her, gaze inexplicably soft. "I didn't lie tae ye. I spoke with an English accent, yes. But I never said I *was* English. The assumptions ye made were yer own."

She gritted her teeth. "You knew exactly what I thought and were all too willing to take advantage. A true gentleman would never have done such a thing," she said icily.

"And a true lady would never have spoken the way ye did." He leaned forward, the softness in his expression vanishing.

"Ye sat at that table, slinging insults at me and my countrymen, so full of prejudice, ye couldn't see what was right in front of ye. So yes, I took advantage. And just as ye made assumptions about Scots, I made some assumptions about ye."

Somehow the words were both an apology and a rebuke, which only heightened her fury. "You do not know me, Mr. McKenzie. You know nothing about me or what brought me here—"

"I knew enough tae fear ye'd hurt Nan," he interrupted. "That with yer ridiculous preconceptions ye'd wound the woman who has only ever wanted one thing—tae be a part of your life. I'll not stand for it, Miss Hughes. So blame me. Hold me responsible. Hate me, if ye must. But do not fault your grandmother."

She stared at him, caught off guard by his defense of her grandmother. The protectiveness in his voice. The love.

But she was too angry to give him credit for such feelings. "You needn't worry, Mr. McKenzie. I hold *you* fully responsible."

He cleared his throat. "I am sorry if I hurt ye, Miss Hughes. 'Twas only meant as a bit of fun."

Arabella raised a brow. "At my expense." It was not a question.

"Can ye not find even an ounce of humor in it?"

Her jaw tightened. "No, Mr. McKenzie, I cannot."

"Then I feel sorry for ye, Miss Hughes." He shook his head.

"I do not want your pity. I do not need it." She sounded childish, she knew. She felt childish. As if she were throwing a favorite toy on the ground just to prove a point.

He stepped onto the stair above where she stood. "Very well, then. Ye do not want my pity. Might I at least offer ye a word of advice?"

"I've no interest in your advice."

"Your grandmother is a fine woman," he said, ignoring her. "The very best. Do not let whatever your parents told ye keep ye from spending time with her and getting tae know her. Ye only have one summer here. Ye might as well make the best of—"

Arabella refused to listen to another word. She turned to go.

He set a soft hand on her arm. "Miss Hughes—"

She spun around and wrenched back her elbow to pull herself free from his grip. But, already realizing his mistake, he'd released her, and the motion only caused her to lose her balance. Her arms flailed, stomach dipping as she wobbled. She balanced precariously on the edge of the step, a hair's breadth away from dropping toward the rocky shores below.

And then Arabella felt herself falling, tumbling backward—

Quick as a flash, Mr. McKenzie caught her about the waist and pulled her against him. Cheek pressed against his chest, she inhaled deeply, the air seeping into her lungs, cool and sweet. She held to him tightly, the wall of his chest like a shield.

It was a long moment before Arabella was aware of anything besides being blessedly, unexpectedly alive.

Alive.

When she could so easily have . . .

She turned her head, staring at the sheer drop of the cliffside.

Mouth agape, she shuddered, the shock of it splintering through her.

It was then that she saw her shawl. It must have come loose in the struggle, snatched away by the strong coastal breeze. She and Mr. McKenzie both stood, transfixed, their breaths coming hard.

Neither moved as they watched the shawl's slow but

steady descent. It fluttered in the air for several seconds before being whisked away, pulled and pushed by the invisible hands of the wind until it finally landed on the rocks below.

"Are ye all right?" Mr. McKenzie murmured, his lips close to her ear.

Arabella's entire body was trembling, her pulse thudding in her ears. "I . . . I think so."

"I blame myself. I should have insisted we finish this conversation somewhere else. These steps are dangerous, even when one is taking the greatest heed."

She swallowed, willing her heart to slow. Willing herself to step out of the comfort of Mr. McKenzie's arms. Instead, she allowed herself to stay a moment longer, breathing in the masculine, windswept smell of him.

"Promise me ye'll be careful on these steps," he demanded. "Ye must go slow. Ye must take care."

It was the authoritative note in his voice that made her remember herself and pull back.

He released her slowly, inspecting her as if to convince himself she was truly all right.

Once free of his embrace, Arabella's frustration came flooding back. "Thank you, Mr. McKenzie, for your unsolicited advice. And now, I hope you'll excuse me."

He sighed. "Good day, Miss Hughes."

Arabella felt his eyes on her as she continued down the stairs. Her steps were slower now. Cautious. But it wasn't until she'd descended the last stair that Mr. McKenzie turned and left.

Alone at last, she heaved out a breath.

She stared out at the churning gray ocean, where wave after wave hammered the rocks. Her tartan shawl was nowhere in sight, likely already swept out to sea. The mood of the scene perfectly captured her feelings. Anger. Frustration. Helplessness.

She picked up a rock, turning it over and over in her hand, its rough surface scraping the soft skin of her palm. Then she hurled it into the ocean, watching as it hit the water with a satisfying splash.

She picked up another one and threw it, this time aiming for a rock that jutted up out of the incoming tide. Imagining it was the back of Mr. McKenzie's head.

She threw another.

And another.

And another.

She'd thrown a great many stones before she realized that although she was far from ready to forgive Mr. McKenzie, the bulk of her resentment wasn't truly for him.

It was for her parents.

For sending her away, far from everything and everyone she knew.

For not even trying to understand her and why she'd done what she had.

Arabella still couldn't think back on that awful day without her stomach becoming a tight-fisted knot. In the quaint gardens of their London townhome, it had been a sunny day. Several friends had called, Mr. Gresham among them, and they'd congregated out by the marble fountain, where they'd spent the morning talking and laughing. Then one by one, they'd left, until only Arabella and Mr. Gresham remained. When she'd turned to go inside, he'd caught her hand, pulled her to him . . .

And kissed her.

Within seconds the back door had slammed open, her father striding toward them. Ire in his eyes. Fury in his words. He'd demanded Mr. Gresham's silence and sent him away, then accused Arabella of risking her future for a nobody.

She'd known the risks.

She just hadn't expected the consequences to be so dire.

An entire summer sequestered in the Highlands of Scotland, far from anything that resembled civilized society.

Arabella looked up the shoreline, where the rocks and stones gave way to white powdery sand. The sun glinted off the water, the waves ebbing and flowing with a calming regularity.

Her parents had wanted her to regret what she'd done.

And she did.

Just not for the reasons they believed.

The kiss had been an utter disappointment. As brief as it was unexpected. Mr. Gresham's arms around her back, while she stood frozen in his arms, the stiff press of cold lips against her own. Arabella had been too shocked to do anything but stare at him, wide-eyed, wondering if kissing was always so . . . *rigid.*

She picked up one last rock, surprised at its polished exterior. Instead of throwing it, she rubbed her thumb back and forth over the smooth surface.

The sandy white dunes farther down the beach beckoned to her, and she wandered up the shoreline, still holding the stone. Between two dunes that sheltered her from the wind, she lay back on the sun-warmed sand, listening to the wash of waves and the gulls overhead, trying to push out the thoughts crowding her head. But it was no use.

Mr. McKenzie's words echoed in her mind.

Your grandmother is a fine woman. The very best. Do not let whatever your parents told ye keep ye from spending time with her and getting tae know her.

Arabella was sick to death of everyone telling her what to do. Her father. Her mother. And now Mr. McKenzie.

The glint of sunlight off the water began to hurt Arabella's eyes. She laid an arm across her face to block the brightness, wishing she could as easily block out thoughts of him. But her mind seemed determined to relive that moment on the steps when Mr. McKenzie had pulled her to safety, encircling her in his arms.

There was only one other time in her life she'd been so close to a man: Mr. Gresham. Both times the contact had been initiated by the man. Both times the proximity had taken her by surprise.

And yet they hadn't been the same at all.

Mr. Gresham was thin and blond, and his grip had been demanding. And the way he'd kissed her—as if her lips were something to be taken. Stolen.

Mr. McKenzie's hair was dark, his large frame muscular. Yet his hold on her had been both secure and gentle. Safe. She'd stayed in his arms longer than necessary, her cheek pressed against his chest.

The way her body had responded to his had left her dazed and confused.

And curious.

Unable to stop herself from speculating what kissing *him* might be like.

Perish the thought.

She sat up at once, staring out at the ocean, reminding herself of Mr. McKenzie's deceit. His audacity. Of the amusement he'd had at her expense. Of his . . . Scottishness.

Heaving back her arm, she threw the polished stone into the waves where it disappeared with a splash.

And thought of how very grateful she'd be if she never saw him again for the entirety of the summer.

Seven

AS GAVIN TRUDGED up the steps, he was certain of one thing: he'd never met a more stubborn woman than Arabella Hughes.

He wanted to dismiss her. Wanted to dislike her and her infuriating arrogance. Wanted to relegate her to a forgotten corner in his mind and never think of her again.

But she was Nan's granddaughter. Which meant all of that was impossible.

Because Nan loved her.

And because *he* loved Nan, he had to make an effort with Miss Hughes.

But deep down, if Gavin was honest with himself, there were other reasons he couldn't dismiss the lady out of hand.

Her enchanting blue eyes, for one.

Maddening as she was, he found himself mesmerized by their depths. Blazing blue crystals that flashed like the hottest flames in a fire.

And grudgingly, he had to admire her spirit. He'd never much enjoyed the company of English women, for most were too soft, too missish. Miss Hughes was anything but. Much as she tried to affect the airs of a gently born lady, she was a stubborn lass and one whose temper flared quite regularly.

At least when he was present.

Nan was waiting for him at the top of the path. "Well?" she demanded.

Gavin rubbed his chin, stalling. "It did not go *exactly* as well as I wished it to," he admitted, unable to be anything but honest. "She merely needs a bit of time for her temper tae cool."

Nan pursed her lips. "I should not have listened tae ye."

"Strange. That is exactly what Lord Andicott said after I advised him on some of his wagers at Newmarket."

"Cheeky lad." Nan scowled, but he knew she wasn't truly angry. Just worried.

Gavin offered her his arm.

As he led Nan along the path that divided their two estates, his mind wandered back to that moment on the steps, when he'd tried to offer Miss Hughes some advice. She was a difficult woman to read, but he'd been almost certain something he'd said had pierced her. "She'll come around. I promise ye. But it may take some time and patience."

Nan looked up at him, a wry expression on her face. "Gavin Alexander McKenzie, I think ye ken I've patience aplenty after dealing with ye all these years. 'Tis the matter of time that worries me."

Gavin grinned. "A person's opinion can change a great deal in three months, ye ken. She won't be able tae help but love ye."

"It's her opinion of *ye* that worries me."

"Ye need not . . ." But suddenly, Gavin knew exactly what she was thinking. He couldn't believe he hadn't seen it coming. "Nan—"

"Ye'll forgive an auld woman, but I had high hopes for the two of ye."

"Even if I had any interest in . . ." Gavin shook his head. "Your granddaughter hates everything about Scotland. She's been poisoned against Scots her entire life."

She gave him a devious smile. "And?"

Devil take it, when Nan got an idea in her head... "Ye ken I have no intention of marrying an English lass. Related tae ye or nae." He'd marry a Scottish lady, one who loved this land like he did.

"Don't think I haven't seen the way ye look at her." Nan raised her brows. "And she's ainlie half English, Gavin."

"And *ye* are ainlie half blind," he replied. "Now, I think perhaps I'd better lie low for a few weeks. Give the two of ye some time together."

"Nonsense. Ye must dine with me every Tuesday, as ye always do."

"Not tomorrow," he said firmly. "Or the week after. She needs some time, remember?"

Nan grudgingly agreed and the conversation meandered on, but Gavin's mind kept returning to that moment when he'd placed his hand on Miss Hughes's arm. The obstinate set of her chin, the way she'd jerked back.

And he couldn't help but continue to think about what Nan had said. What her hopes were. He hated that he'd have to disappoint her.

Not because Miss Hughes wasn't lovely. Not because of her ridiculous pride. Not because she was English.

But because, for the first time, Gavin had decided there might be such a thing as *too* stubborn.

Eight

ARABELLA SAT AT the dressing table, the ink on the letter she'd written her mother still drying. Instead of joining her grandmother for dinner, she'd requested a tray in her bedroom, claiming a headache.

She was still hurt and humiliated. Whenever she allowed herself to think of last night's dinner, it was all she could do not to groan. Remembering her willingness to believe every one of the ridiculous claims made by her grandmother and Mr. McKenzie.

Arabella touched her finger to the paper, testing to see that the ink was dry. Satisfied, she looked over the letter that held an account of all she'd been subjected to since setting foot here. Scathing words. She was certain, once they received it, her parents would come for her. All that remained was to send it off and wait.

One week? Two?

Three weeks at most, she decided.

Surely she could last here for three weeks.

She glanced around the room she'd been given, cozy and quaint, though quite outdated. Several decades out of fashion, at least.

Arabella's gaze was drawn to where her empty trunks sat near the foot of the bed. She hadn't expected to find them waiting for her when she'd returned from the beach, but there they'd been, Molly humming as she unpacked them.

She'd frowned, watching as Molly aired out her dresses. "However did you manage to get my trunk up that steep hill? Grandmother said the roads were still impassable."

"A Mr. McKenzie came for me. Said he'd retrieved your trunks and offered me a ride."

Molly had chattered on, complaining about her stay at the inn last night, the roads, the weather. But Arabella had stopped listening. After the way she'd dismissed Mr. McKenzie, after the argument they'd had . . .

He'd fetched her trunks.

But why?

A knock sounded at the door, rousing Arabella from her thoughts. Probably a maid come to collect her dinner tray.

"Enter," Arabella called, folding the letter. "The tray is just here." She slipped the letter into the drawer of the dressing table and looked up, only to meet her grandmother's gaze in the mirror.

"Oh," she said softly. "I didn't . . ."

"I hope ye dinnae mind."

Arabella cleared her throat. "Of course not."

She stepped forward, coming to stand behind Arabella. "I am sorry. For dinner last night. And for this morning. I . . ."

The uncertainty of her words made Arabella soften, just a little. She waited.

"Ye cannae even imagine the shock I received when yer mother wrote, asking if ye could come for the summer. It was so unexpected. After she's kept ye from me all these years.

"And I've been so worried aboot what ye'll think of me, or what yer parents have told ye that . . . And Gavin, well. Ye cannot blame him. Ultimately, it was my own pride that made me do it. But I certainly dinnae do it right, did I? And it's been agony today, ye see, worrying that I've made ye think ill of me..."

Her grandmother reached out a wrinkled hand to set on Arabella's shoulder. But at the last moment she drew back as if worried her touch wouldn't be welcome.

Arabella's heart pricked, remembering the way her grandmother had hugged her yesterday, even sopping wet and muddy as she'd been. Now the woman didn't even dare touch her. And she recalled, with some shame, the first words she'd spoken to her. Some bitter comment about Scotland. No wonder the woman was hesitant.

And so, biting back her pride, Arabella said, "I need to apologize as well. I've been arrogant and judgmental... and, well, I think you know my parents sent me here as a punishment. But that is no excuse for my behavior since my arrival. No excuse for *me* punishing *you*."

Grandmother shook her head. "Ye could never be a punishment, lass. 'Tis a blessing tae have ye here." She looked at Arabella with undeniable hope. "Do ye think we might begin again?"

Mr. McKenzie's advice from this morning echoed in her head again.

Do not let whatever your parents told ye keep ye from spending time with her and getting tae know her.

Arabella bit her cheek. She'd had every intention of interacting with her grandmother as little as possible this summer. She wouldn't be rude, just reserved. Distantly polite.

But she'd never intended to get to know her.

Admitting that made Arabella feel unexpectedly callous. What other person, offering to play hostess to her for several months, would she treat with such indifference? And how had she come to the decision that she wouldn't make an effort with her own grandmother?

Because her parents, whether they'd said it aloud or not, had made it perfectly clear she wasn't worth knowing.

Arabella wasn't sure exactly what it was that made up her mind. Perhaps it was regret for the way she'd acted. Perhaps it was a desire to contradict her parents. She didn't wish to examine her motives too carefully.

But she nodded. "Yes," she said softly. "Let's begin again."

Her grandmother smiled, wrinkles gathering in the corners of her eyes.

It was such a small thing Arabella had offered, but seeing how much it meant made her determined to make good on her word.

Grandmother picked up the brush from the dressing table. "May I?"

Surprised, Arabella nodded.

One by one, she removed Arabella's hairpins, then began brushing her hair in long strokes. Her withered hands were capable and strong, but she was gentle, brushing all the way from Arabella's scalp to the ends of her hair.

Arabella closed her eyes, enjoying the soothing ministrations.

"This was yer mother's room, ye know," Grandmother said quietly.

Arabella opened her eyes, curious. She looked around, trying to imagine her mother here. Mother, who never said a word about the past. Who never spoke of Scotland without derision in her tone.

Grandmother continued brushing. "I used tae do this for her every night while she sat in that verra seat."

"Did she not have a lady's maid?"

Her grandmother's eyes grew distant. "Ach, yes. But I loved tae do it. I think yer hair is even thicker though. So long and lustrous."

"It's impossible to manage," Arabella retorted.

"It's beautiful." She gave a sad sort of smile. "*Ye* are beautiful. Almost hurts me tae look at ye."

The ghost of her mother's memory lingered between them, and Arabella couldn't meet her grandmother's eyes in the mirror. Nor could she think of what to say.

But Grandmother seemed content to talk, her soft Scottish brogue rolling over her words. "I've a portrait of her down in the gallery. Painted when she was just a wee bit younger than ye. I can show ye tomorrow, if ye'd like tae see it."

Arabella had so many questions about her mother, so much she wanted to understand but didn't. "Yes, please. I'd like that very much."

GRANDMOTHER MADE GOOD on her word. Right after breakfast the next morning, she took Arabella down to the gallery. They started on the far end, where the oldest pictures hung.

Grandmother pointed up at a dashing man wearing a kilt, a sword sheathed in a scabbard at his side. "Did your mother ever tell ye about yer great-grandfather? Neil Callender?" she asked hopefully.

"She . . ." Arabella shook her head. "No. She never did."

Grandmother sighed. "I see."

"Would you tell me about him?" she asked. Her grandmother was trying, and she would, too.

Grandmother looked up at the portrait. "Ach, he was a daring man. A smuggler."

"A smuggler?"

"Yes. And a successful one at that. Smuggled all sorts of things. Right under the noses of the British patrols."

Arabella studied the picture. The kilt. And tried very hard not to think of Mr. McKenzie. "And this Neil Callender—my great-grandfather. He was never caught?"

Grandmother smirked, the expression making her look years younger. "It depends on what ye mean by 'caught.' As the story goes, there was one occasion where Neil Callender was caught and arrested. But just as they were ready tae cart him away, a man dressed in the uniform of a British captain told them Neil Callender was on a special errand for the Crown and ordered the soldiers tae release him at once."

Arabella grew impatient. "Who was it?"

Her grandmother chuckled. "Tae this day, no one kens. But it was a good thing. Neil had eleven children. If he'd been hanged, they'd all have been left fatherless."

"Eleven?" As an only child, Arabella couldn't imagine such a thing. "His wife must have been a saint."

"Nay. Freya Callender was more of a spitfire. She's in that picture, right there." She pointed to a portrait of a woman with fiery-red hair. "After Neil was nearly captured, she gave him an ultimatum. Give up smuggling, or she'd turn him in herself. Said her children deserved tae have a father that wasn't always living on the brink of danger."

Arabella laughed. "Good for her."

There were more stories after that. A great-great-grandfather who'd been a trusted advisor in Bonnie Prince Charlie's court in France. A cousin who had served during the war of American independence and brought home an American bride.

"And who is this?" Arabella gestured toward a large painting of a man with auburn hair, looking off into the distance.

"That is yer grandfather. My Hamish," Grandmother said fondly, then grinned. "Wasn't he handsome?"

Arabella nodded, sad that she'd never met him. He'd died before she was born. "How did the two of you meet?"

"Our marriage was arranged by our parents. 'Twas awkward at first, two strangers living under one roof."

"But the two of you fell in love," Arabella guessed.

"Aye, that we did. Long walks on the beach are very romantic, in case ye are wondering."

Arabella blushed at her grandmother's implication.

They moved down the hall and Arabella's eyes caught on a portrait of her mother. It was like staring at a painting of herself. Same glossy dark hair. Same high cheekbones and full lips. Same blue eyes, shining with just a touch of arrogance.

Strange to see her mother's picture here, almost like a piece of evidence. Proof that this was where she had come from.

Grandmother came up behind Arabella. "Beautiful, isn't she?"

Arabella could only nod. "Will you tell me about her?"

"Oh, where tae begin?" Grandmother asked. "Yer mother was a determined child. Ambitious. We always said it was dangerous tae get in the way of anything she wanted. As a young woman, she was forever pushing the boundaries we set for her."

Her staid mother, who was forever disciplining her for the smallest infractions? "What changed her?"

"'Twas a slow process. Gradual. But I fear it began when we sent her tae finishing school in England. One of my cousins suggested we send our daughters there together, and your mother was quite keen on the idea. So we agreed tae let her go." Grandmother stared at the portrait—with what? Regret? Resignation?

She turned to Arabella. "She came home acting differently, speaking differently. And she was determined tae have a

Season in London." Grandmother made a clicking sound with her tongue.

Her eyes returned to the picture, tracing over the face of her daughter. "Hamish and I were quite set against it at first. We told her no. But then . . ." She paused for a long moment, making Arabella wonder if there was something she was leaving out. "After a while we relented. In London, she met your father. Several months later, they were married." Grandmother's voice had turned flat as if the story was over.

But Arabella's curiosity wasn't satisfied. "But that still doesn't explain what changed her so drastically. It had to have been more than finishing school."

Grandmother's lips pinched together. "Has she told ye nothing of her past? Of her life growing up here in Scotland?"

The truth would give her pain, but Arabella couldn't lie. "She doesn't speak of it."

"And ye have never asked?"

She shook her head. Somehow, she'd always understood she couldn't. Shouldn't.

Grandmother's shoulders sagged, her eyes distant. "There are some things I can share, Arabella. And there are some things that are yer mother's tae tell. If ye'd like tae know more, I'm afraid ye'll have tae ask her yerself."

Nine

GAVIN STOOD OUTSIDE the stables, waiting for his horse. It was early—before eight—and the air was still crisp, the sun's rays peeking over craggy green mountains. After several long days of gray skies and drizzly rain, it was a welcome reprieve.

Not that he hadn't gotten out these past weeks. He'd been down to the pub a time or two, had dinner with friends on several occasions. But in giving Nan time and space with her granddaughter, he'd spent one night too many alone, with only the fire for company.

Finlay his groom, stepped forward, leading Baird by the reins.

"Thank ye, Finlay." Gavin put one foot in the stirrup and swung himself into the saddle.

"My pleasure, Mr. McKenzie. I always say yer horses are like my children. I ken I am not supposed tae have a favorite, but if I did . . ." He gave a furtive glance over his shoulder. "Baird would be mine."

Gavin chuckled. "I'll not tell the others."

And then he was off, urging Baird into a trot. Gavin turned north, toward the low sweep of hills where new lambs bleated at their mothers. A soft breeze blew in off the coast, pulling at his coat.

"Sir!" Mr. Murray stood near the fence line, arm raised.

"What can I do for ye, Mr. Murray?"

"I took that rowboat down the river tae test it out like ye asked, but I dinnae think the patch job held, sir. It took in water, slow but steady."

Gavin sighed. He'd spent an entire morning patching that hole. With a decision about an upcoming investment weighing on him, he'd needed a change of scenery, needed to work with his hands while he mulled things over in his mind. He'd busied himself repairing the boat and thought he'd done an adequate job of it. Apparently not.

"Where is it now?"

"I stacked it atop the other one." His eyes flitted toward Gavin's. "Thought we might send it down tae the village for repairs."

"I'll ride down and take a look. I might want tae have another go at it."

Mr. Murray sighed, as if he knew he'd not talk Gavin into allowing someone with actual carpentry experience to repair it. "If ye'd like, sir. Good day."

The sun climbed higher as Gavin set off up to the steeper climbs where many of the herds grazed. He gave Baird his head as they rode toward the northern edge of his property. His eyes swept over the hillsides, green and verdant, spring edging into summer.

He surveyed the land, unable to keep his thoughts from his father as he rode. It was he who had taught Gavin the importance of inspecting his properties with his own eyes. *Ye'll have a steward. And a land agent. And they'll be invaluable tae ye. But no one will care for the land the way ye do, Gavin. Not one.*

Next he turned west, where the mountains gave way to rolling hills. The impossible beauty never failed to move him. Mother had loved this time of year. Said it made living in dreary and dreich northern Scotland the other three-quarters of the year worth it.

He turned south, toward the river, where his property bordered Nan's. Since the death of his parents, she'd become his family. Which is why it felt strange having Miss Hughes here, taking the time and attention that were usually his own. Not that he begrudged Nan time with her granddaughter. It was only that these past weeks had been impossibly dull.

Save for the times he'd crossed paths with Miss Hughes.

Gavin was not a man prone to exaggeration. But he very nearly considered himself a *saint* for the restraint he'd shown in his interactions with her these past few weeks. Not that he'd been perfect.

The first week at kirk, sitting in the pew behind her, he'd made a point to sing the hymns out of tune and with a stronger-than-usual Scottish brogue. Miss Hughes had shifted in her seat, trying to figure out who was responsible for singing off-key, only to look back and realize it was him.

He'd grinned at her unrepentantly.

She'd hurriedly turned back toward the front, nose in the air.

Unable to resist, Gavin had whispered, "Come, now. My voice isn't as bad as Rory's bagpipes."

Obviously struggling to maintain godly thoughts, she'd replied under her breath, "I wouldn't be so certain about that."

A few days after that, when he'd run into Miss Hughes on the steps down to the beach, he'd purposefully misinterpreted which way she was going, continually bumping into her until she was so flustered that she could barely string two words together.

And the following week, when he'd seen her through the window of the town's small haberdashery, the temptation had proved too great. He'd eased the door open quietly. She'd been talking to Mrs. Weatherspoon near the window display. "I need a good, strong bonnet. One that can withstand the winds here. My other bonnets have already been torn to pieces."

"I am certain we can find something that will please ye, Miss Hughes. Now let me see—"

Gavin closed the door with a loud bang.

Both women looked up. Miss Hughes frowned. Mrs. Weatherspoon rushed over and greeted him with a smile. "Mr. McKenzie, whatever are ye doing here? Though make no mistake, 'tis a pleasure to see ye!"

Gavin gave her his most charming grin. "And ye as well, Mrs. Weatherspoon. I find myself in need of your help."

"Certainly, Mr. McKenzie. How can I be of service?" she'd asked eagerly.

"I need your help in choosing a bonnet."

"A bonnet?" Miss Hughes narrowed her eyes.

Mrs. Weatherspoon blinked, still smiling. "A bonnet?"

"Aye. For my . . . cousin."

Just as he'd anticipated, Mrs. Weatherspoon had forgotten all about Miss Hughes and her needs and sprung into action, offering poke bonnets and wide-brimmed bonnets and showing him all sorts of possible trimmings. Flowers. Lace. Birds. Feathers.

Miss Hughes had stood across the room, glowering at him.

At which point he'd admitted it was quite difficult to imagine how the bonnet would look on his cousin. "She and Miss Hughes have similar coloring, I think. Do ye mind holding it near her face?"

"Better yet," said Miss Weatherspoon, "I am sure Miss Hughes would not mind trying it on for ye, if that would help. Would ye, dear?"

"Of course not," Miss Hughes had said, voice laced with irony. She'd joined them up at the counter and glowered at him at much closer range while Mrs. Weatherspoon tied the bow beneath her chin.

"My cousin smiles a bit more, Miss Hughes," Gavin had

said, unable to help himself. "Do ye mind smiling for a moment so I can get a better idea of how it will look on her?"

If not for Mrs. Weatherspoon's presence, Miss Hughes likely would have pulled the bonnet off and strangled him with the ribbons.

Even still, Gavin couldn't help but notice how fetching she'd looked in the wide-brimmed bonnet with a blue velvet ribbon tied beneath her chin.

"Aye," he'd said. "That will do verra well. Mrs. Weatherspoon, ye are a bonnet genius."

Mrs. Weatherspoon had blushed and tittered, promising to have the bonnet delivered two days hence. Only after she'd bid him farewell three times did she finally turn back to Miss Hughes.

So maybe he hadn't *quite* been a saint.

But there had been several times when he might have teased her and hadn't. And he'd kept his promise to Nan and stayed away for several weeks. That had to count for something.

By the time Gavin had finished his route and made his way to the river, it was mid-morning. He tethered Baird by one of the trees near the bank, then walked down toward the boats. But instead of finding the two he'd expected, there was only one. The damaged boat was gone.

Gavin looked around, but besides the long grass and the reeds, he saw nothing. He frowned. Perhaps Mr. Murray had forgotten to move the leaking boat away from the bank? With all the rain, the river was high, and it might have been carried away by the current. With any luck, the damaged boat had gotten caught in a tangle of reeds along the riverbank and he could retrieve it.

Remembering the skepticism in Mr. Murray's voice, he set his jaw. He'd find that boat and fix it if it was the last thing he did.

Ten

ARABELLA MADE HER way down the hillside, boots struggling for purchase on some of the steeper inclines. The same "dreich" weather that had kept her indoors the past few days had left the path slick and muddy.

The last several weeks had been . . . surprising, to say the least.

As promised, she and Grandmother had begun again. And once Arabella had let go of some of the preconceived notions she'd had, she found she liked Grandmother. Quite a bit.

She certainly wasn't as prim and proper as Mother.

Nor as strict.

Arabella would almost venture to say she was . . .

Well, for lack of a better word . . . *fun*.

She hated formal meals, loved gothic novels, and was an avid and competitive game player.

This had all come as a bit of a shock to Arabella, who had grown up in a home where *everything* was formal, novels of any sort were forbidden, and Mother had taught her it wasn't ladylike to show any interest in the outcome of a game.

But several nights before, after being soundly beaten at piquet three times in a row, Arabella had had enough. "Again," she'd demanded.

Grandmother had only laughed as she'd begun to deal a new hand. Instead of making small talk during that fourth game, Arabella shifted her attention to each card and trick played.

Grandmother, after taking an early lead, needled Arabella relentlessly.

Arabella had retorted with a snide comment or two of her own, redoubling her efforts.

And she'd won.

Another thing Arabella had quickly discovered about her grandmother was that she didn't follow any sort of schedule. One night she'd retire at eight o'clock, another they'd stay up reading *The Mysteries of Udolpho* together until well after midnight. One morning she'd come down in a formal gown to join Arabella for breakfast, the next she'd invite Arabella to her room for tea and still be in her wrapper.

But what Arabella liked best about her grandmother was how very easy it was to relax in her company. She didn't protest if Arabella slouched or ate a second biscuit or wished to take a nap.

So different from Mother, who never seemed to be satisfied with anything Arabella did. Forever reminding her to eat tiny portions and small bites. If she was playing the pianoforte, it was too loud. If she laughed, she was acting childish.

Even after three weeks away from home, she could still hear Mother's voice in her head, imagine her disapproving looks, the silent scolds Arabella had learned to anticipate and avoid.

Perhaps that was why she still hadn't sent that letter, demanding her parents come for her. It sat in the drawer of her dressing table, untouched.

The river was even more enchanting up close—the water

a jewel-toned aquamarine, the soft murmur of the water soothing. Grandmother had been adamant she get out and explore. "There are plenty of cloudy days here, Arabella. Ye must take advantage of the sunny ones."

Grandmother's rheumatism had been bothering her this morning, so she'd sent Arabella off on her own, encouraging her to walk down the hill path to the river. "Mr. McKenzie keeps several small boats down by the river. The river divides our property, ye see. But the bank on his side is steep, so I allow him tae keep the boats on my property, and he allows me tae use the boats whenever I wish." Her eyes twinkled as she said, "Though since I dinnae use the boats, I suppose he's getting the better end of the deal."

Though Arabella had avoided Mr. McKenzie whenever possible, their paths still crossed plenty. And always he found some way to provoke her, ruffling her composure. Even when he wasn't around, the man had the audacity to occupy her thoughts, and she often had to force her mind in other directions, which was difficult to do, since Grandmother talked about him constantly. In the past few weeks, she'd heard enough stories about Gavin Alexander McKenzie to last a lifetime.

Exactly in the spot Grandmother had described, there were two boats, one stacked atop the other. Initially, she'd been hesitant about taking one of the boats out by herself, but seeing the river up close, her worries faded. The river was slow-moving and not more than about forty feet across.

Arabella tugged the top boat away and began pushing it down the bank. She grunted with effort, but with one final shove, the boat hit the water with a satisfying splash.

What she hadn't considered was how quickly it would begin to drift away. Having no desire to get her boots wet, Arabella had only one choice. She leapt.

She hit the far side of the boat, her weight tipping it, water splashing up over the side. Heart thumping, Arabella stayed low as the boat settled. With slow movements she positioned herself onto one of the seats, then used an oar to push against the shallow river bottom, maneuvering out toward the deeper part of the river.

The boat was sucked into the slow-moving current, making the use of her oars unnecessary. Arabella sat up straight as the boat glided through the water.

Her gaze was drawn upward. Birds winged over the river, darting low and then riding sharp gusts of wind high overhead. Sheep dotted the rolling green hills in the distance, grazing lazily, low bleats drifting across the valley.

But there wasn't a single person in sight.

Arabella was utterly and completely alone.

It was a strange feeling. She was far more accustomed to the busy streets of London or the press of a crowded ballroom. At seeing and being seen.

Here there was none of that.

After several long minutes she began to relax. She scooted toward the edge of the boat and leaned over, staring out at the water, letting her fingers skim its surface.

Her breaths came slow and deep. The tension in her shoulders eased. And somewhere in the back of her mind, she admitted to herself that she was beginning to enjoy her summer here in Scotland.

Her thoughts drifted, back again to that day in the garden with Mr. Gresham. Trying to decide if she wished she could undo it. Undo that moment, that kiss, and the punishment that came with it. She wouldn't have had the opportunity to get to know her grandmother. Or explore her mother's past.

A cold slosh of water filled one of Arabella's boots. She looked down, horror filling her as she realized the entire bottom of the boat was filling with water.

Grabbing the oars, she rowed desperately, but the boat hardly responded, heavy as it was. Arabella looked around, but just as before, not a soul was in sight. Even if she yelled and screamed there was no one to hear her.

She glanced down at herself, cursing her heavy dress. She was barely proficient as a swimmer, and the bank now seemed very far away. Ice-cold water swilled around her skirts.

Why did this country seem so intent on getting her wet?

She turned, heart sinking to see the bridge so far away. But up ahead and off to her left, her eyes locked on a tree that rose out of the water, holding firm against the pull of the river.

It was her one chance. Heart thudding with both relief and desperation, she rowed hard. Water lapped the bottom of her thighs now and her arms burned from the effort of her struggle.

But she didn't dare stop. The rush of the current pushed her steadily forward, and she rowed furiously to the left. By the time she was a few feet away, she had no choice but to try and lunge for the tree.

Arabella gasped at the shock of cold river water as she slipped beneath the surface before her head bobbed up and her hands closed around the trunk. Legs locked around the tree, she held on tightly, watching as the boat disappeared beneath the water.

She leaned her forehead against the trunk, breathing hard. Should she try to swim for shore? Or wait for someone to cross the bridge and call for help?

"Well, well, well," came a voice behind her. "Miss Hughes, we meet again."

Arabella stiffened.

She knew who it was before she turned.

Mr. McKenzie. The man himself, perfectly dry. His boat, perfectly unsunk.

Oh, she could curse.

He managed to maneuver his boat near the tree and grabbed at one of the branches, holding his boat in place beside her. The lines of his body were relaxed, his mouth curved up in a shameless smile. "It seems I always find ye in a spot of trouble, Miss Hughes." He spoke to her as casually as if they were in the sitting room sharing afternoon tea.

She was half tempted to grab for the side of his boat to tip him out. "I'd appreciate very much if instead of being the cad I've come to expect, you kept your mouth closed and assisted me into your boat," she said through gritted teeth.

"And I'd very much like tae do just that." His mouth twisted as if in consideration. "But if I recall correctly, ye said ye wouldn't get intae my carriage if I were the last man on earth. Do ye feel differently aboot boats, then?"

 Eleven

MISS HUGHES HAD occupied more than her fair share of Gavin's thoughts this past week, remembering the suspicion she'd eyed him with during dinner that first night. The fierce look of displeasure she'd given him on the cliffside stairs. And the hostility she'd shown him during the bonnet incident.

But that was nothing to the look she was giving him now.

She scoffed and turned her head away, unwilling to answer.

He had to give her credit. She was nothing if not consistent. To hold on to her pride even with the icy river water swirling around her...

Stubborn lass.

But as the owner of an extensive property in the Highlands, Gavin had dealt with his fair share of stubborn sheep. And he'd learned that sometimes the best way to deal with such obstinacy was with brute force.

Gavin leaned over and hooked his hands beneath Miss Hughes's arms, tugging her upward. Fighting against the drag of the current and the weight of her saturated clothing, he pulled her back against his chest and heaved her over the side of the boat.

For one breathless moment, they remained in a heap at the bottom of the boat as it rocked back and forth.

She tried to lift her head from Gavin's shoulder but fell back, too sapped of strength to move.

"There now." Gavin slowly eased both of them up.

Her teeth began to chatter.

"I think we'd best get ye warm." One arm behind her back, supporting her, he used his other to remove his coat. Then he drew it around her shoulders, tucking it close.

"I would have been just fine," she whispered, teeth still chattering, "without you."

He gave her a wry look. "Now, now. Careful not tae flatter me. I might begin tae believe ye like me."

"We cannot have that," she huffed, though one corner of her mouth edged up.

Smiling, he reached for the oars and then began rowing upriver, straining against the current. He'd been part of the rowing team back at Cambridge, and it felt good to work his muscles, urging them to remember the familiar rhythm.

He glanced at Miss Hughes, sitting across from him. Though her teeth had stopped chattering, she still shivered, and her face was pale. Even now, sopping wet and chilled through, she sat with her back straight, posture perfect.

"Ye've been here close to a month now," he said, hoping to distract her from her miserable state. "Do ye still see your time in Scotland as a punishment?"

She burrowed deeper within the thick folds of his coat. "Now might not be the best time to ask me."

"Ye never did tell me what ye did tae deserve such a punishment."

She lifted her chin a notch. "That is because it is none of your business, Mr. McKenzie."

A smile escaped before he could stop it. "I'm verra good at guessing," he warned. "Did ye step on a gentleman's foot while ye danced?" he asked.

She straightened, unable to resist answering. "No."

He nodded thoughtfully. "Did ye perhaps use the wrong title while addressing a person of import?"

She sighed. "Hardly."

He was enjoying this little game, slowly luring her in. "Did ye cheat at cards?"

Miss Hughes looked heavenward. "Of course not. Now you are just being ridiculous."

"Did ye kiss a man?"

Her eyes flew wide.

Gavin grinned as he pushed the oars through the water. "Aha. I guessed it. Ye kissed a man."

"I did not," she said firmly, lips pressed in a thin line. "He kissed me."

"Ah." There was something charming in the way she protested. "Were ye an unwilling participant, then?"

"I . . . no. *No*," Miss Hughes said more forcefully. "I meant only to say he was the one who initiated it."

"Ah. I see." He nodded gravely. "'Tis important tae be clear aboot who initiates it."

Her cheeks turned red, and she looked pointedly away. "If you say so." She fiddled with the buttons on his coat.

It was the strangest thing, seeing Miss Hughes in something of his. It almost felt like a statement of possession, of claiming. Which was absurd. He'd sooner claim a cantankerous donkey than such a headstrong young woman.

He returned his attention to the river, to his rowing. The boat's sounds made a steady rhythm—the creak of wood as he pushed and pulled the loom, the splash of the oar blades as they cut through the water. He eased off as they approached the bank, the bottom of the boat scraping against the shallows.

Gavin released the oars and stepped over the side, boots splashing through the water. He pulled the front of the boat up to the bank, then held out a hand to help Miss Hughes. "My horse, Baird, is waiting just there. I can take ye home—if ye don't mind sharing a horse. Ye need tae get out of your wet things."

Miss Hughes only nodded, still shivering. After taking several tentative steps forward, she grasped his hand.

His warm palm closed around her slender, icy fingers. And though he knew there was nothing in it, that she had only taken his hand to keep her balance, he couldn't deny the surge of attraction he felt for her.

Nor could he resist trying to make her blush again. "And was it worth it, Miss Hughes?"

She looked up, confusion clouding her gaze. "Was what worth it?"

Gavin steadied her as she stepped up onto the bank. "That kiss. 'Twill be a long summer."

She pulled her hand away, scowling.

He shook his head. "That's a right shame. The next time ye are kissed . . ." He raised his brows suggestively. "I can only hope the man makes it worth your while."

Her cheeks bloomed with color. "There won't *be* any more kissing, Mr. McKenzie," she retorted, stomping toward the tree where Baird was tethered. "My parents will make certain of that."

"No more kissing?" he called after her. "Even *after* ye marry? I'd like tae ken how they intend—"

Miss Hughes stopped beside Baird, her back to Gavin, and spoke through clenched teeth. "Be flippant if you will, but you'd likely not find the matter so amusing if you were a woman—with no rights of your own, and parents determined to choose every step of your life's path."

Gavin stayed silent for several seconds, surprised at the pain in her admission. He stepped up behind her, releasing a long breath. "And what path would ye take, Miss Hughes? If ye could choose for yourself?"

Twelve

AND WHAT PATH would ye take, Miss Hughes? If ye could choose for yourself?

The question was so surprising, so unexpected, that it stunned Arabella into silence.

Because the truth was that she'd never truly taken the time to consider what she wanted.

What was the point, when she'd never be free to pursue it?

When it could only mean disappointment?

The horse nickered, sniffing at her.

Arabella turned, coming to face Mr. McKenzie. Her voice was smaller than she would have liked when she answered him. "How could I know when I have never been given the luxury of such a choice?"

He looked at her then, and there was something rough and jagged in his gaze, something discerning that seemed to slash through her defenses, as if by a mere look he could unlock the secrets inside her.

"I'm afraid," she whispered, "that I'll go through an entire lifetime having all my choices made for me. First by my parents and then by the husband they choose for me. And I'll die an old woman, one who never knew who she truly was or what she wanted."

It was, perhaps, the most honest thing she'd ever said.

The space between them seemed to contract.

She froze as Mr. McKenzie settled his hands on her waist. Her breaths grew shallow. He looked down at her, brow creased. She softened a little under his gaze. She couldn't help it when he looked at her that way, almost as if he were going to . . .

And then he was lifting her, up, up, as if she weighed nothing more than the breeze. He settled her in the saddle before releasing her. Arabella bit her lip, hating herself for the thud of disappointment that echoed through her. She grabbed for the reins, needing something, anything to hold on to.

Mr. McKenzie looked up at her and shook his head. "So I ask ye again. What is it ye *want*?"

He was a man who wouldn't tolerate platitudes. Who wouldn't accept a lie. Who, for some inexplicable reason, seemed hungry for the truth. Her truth.

An ache grew in Arabella's center, pulsing like the throb of a finger after a cut.

What did she want?

What did she *want*?

"I want time, Mr. McKenzie," she said finally. "Time on my own, where I can learn my own mind. Where I can figure out who I am without the influence of my parents."

They locked eyes and he gave the barest nod. "It seems tae me," he said, stepping a fraction closer, "that's exactly what ye've been given. An entire summer in Scotland without them."

"But they expect—"

"The devil take their expectations." He leaned forward, hand on the horse's neck, a V forming between his brows. "Ye'll forgive me for speaking my mind, Miss Hughes, but I spent most of my youth in English schools where my teachers tried relentlessly tae mold me into an English lad. Tae change my accent, my opinions, and my attitudes tae conform tae their ideal." He shook his head.

"Do ye know the only time I was truly able tae escape? To throw off the weight of their expectations? When I didn't have tae fight tae keep what they were trying so hard tae take from me?" He swallowed hard. "My summers at home in Scotland. This place became my refuge."

It was the strangest moment. Not two minutes ago, Arabella would have said the two of them were enemies. Adversaries. Opposites. Now she wasn't so sure. Would an enemy share something so private, so deeply held? Would he bare such insight into his past, the very threads of the tapestry that made up his whole? Could she and he really be so different when he seemed to instinctively understand the battle she'd been fighting all her life?

Earnestness filled Mr. McKenzie's expression—in the set of his jaw and the slant of his brow. "There is something here. I cannot put it intae words, exactly. But there is a wild sort of freedom here, one that will make ye examine who ye are and who ye wish tae be. And that . . . *that* is the Scotland I'd have ye know."

His voice softened to a plea. "So take your summer, Miss Hughes. Take the time ye've been given. 'Tis not a punishment but a *gift*. A chance. And from the sounds of it, one ye'll likely not have again."

He was right. Her parents had already begun to make arrangements, the plans that would decide her future. She'd be married by the end of next Season.

But somehow that made what Mr. McKenzie was asking all the more futile.

Her teeth began to chatter again, not from cold this time but from fear. "I—I'll have to think on it. It's only . . . I don't know if I can." She looked up, away. Anywhere but in his eyes. "You probably think me a coward, Mr. McKenzie."

His chest was near her thigh, and she could feel the warmth coming off his body. Feel the magnetism that forced her to meet his gaze. "Since our first meeting, Miss Hughes, I've thought of many words that might be used tae describe ye." His jaw tightened. "But not coward. Never a coward."

Arabella could scarcely breathe. She was caught off guard by the realization of how much she cared to have Mr. McKenzie's good opinion.

He leaned closer, his eyes locked on hers, their rich green depths churning with brown and gold and gray like a summer storm. "I dare ye not tae take it. Tae look back in years tae come, when ye're the auld woman ye're afeart of becoming. And still be holding on to the regret of the opportunity ye let pass by."

A taunt.

A challenge.

It was too much, all at once.

Contemplating freedom when all she'd ever known was a cage.

Considering recklessness when all she'd ever shown was restraint.

On impulse, she grabbed at the reins, forcing the horse to step backward, away from Mr. McKenzie.

"What are ye—"

She tugged harder, urging the horse to put a little distance between them. "I'm sorry. I need time to think."

"Think all ye want," he said, stepping forward slowly, hands outstretched as if approaching a skittish colt. "But that is no reason tae steal my horse." He lunged forward. "Ye cannae just—"

She guided Baird to the left, easily sidestepping Mr. McKenzie. "Cannot just what?" The horse pranced impatiently, but she held the reins firmly. "Abandon you and leave you to find your own way home?" She cocked her head. "I daresay I would be leaving you under better conditions than you left me. It isn't raining, after all."

Mr. McKenzie nodded, long and slow. "'Tis a fair point ye make, Miss Hughes. But I did just rescue ye." He took a step toward her. Then another. When he was within three feet of her, he stopped, setting his hands on his hips. "Could we not simply put the past behind us?"

"Allow me to set the record straight, Mr. McKenzie." It was a heady feeling to have the upper hand for once. "I find I do not mind occupying a boat with you. And I may, at some point, be forced to reconsider my stance on joining you in a carriage."

He nodded, mouth lifting in the beginnings of a smile.

Arabella leaned forward, face perfectly grave. "But I can say without hesitation that I will never, *ever* share a horse with you."

Mr. McKenzie tried to grab the reins, but she was too fast. She kicked forward, even as he gave chase, bending low over the saddle as the horse began to gallop, wind whipping at her wet things as she headed up the hill toward home.

Thirteen

GAVIN SPRINTED HARD, but it was no use. He slowed, growling in frustration. "Minx!" he called after her, hands cupped around his mouth. "When I come for dinner tomorrow, I'll expect your answer! *And* my horse!"

The only reply was the flapping of the coat—*his* coat—in the wind, billowing out behind her.

He bent over a little, hands resting on his thighs, panting from the exertion of his run. And then he laughed aloud. Every time Gavin thought he had the woman pegged, Miss Hughes managed to surprise him.

She'd surprised him with her resilience after her dip in the river. Yes, she'd been obstinate. Grumpy. Yet even though she'd been wet and cold, she hadn't complained.

More surprising still? The way one simple question had unlocked such vulnerability in her. Listening to her plight, as she'd confided the truth of her fears and her future, had stirred something in him. And while Miss Hughes was no doubt beautiful, in those moments where she'd been real and raw, she'd been something more. Free of pretension and affectation she'd been . . .

Exquisite.

It had almost hurt to look at her, lips twisted in uncertainty, her eyes blue pools of yearning.

Gavin blew out a breath and ran a hand through his hair. He needed to get ahold of himself. This . . . *thing*—whatever it was growing between them—could never be.

But there had been a moment, hadn't there? When he'd set his hands on her waist. The look on her face—surprise and then something else. Almost as if she'd been torn between propriety and longing.

What would she have done if he'd kissed her then? For he'd wanted to.

If he was honest with himself, Gavin had wanted to kiss her since that first day, when she'd stormed into Nan's sitting room, soaked through. She'd been a goddess of fury—head high, eyes flashing. He'd liked the fact that she hadn't let him best her. And despite her constant grumblings about Scotland, he liked *her*.

But that didn't mean he was eejit enough to kiss her just now. The moment hadn't been right. She was too vulnerable. And he'd already asked too much of her.

Gavin sighed. Though he was in no hurry to report to Mr. Murray that the leaking boat couldn't even be used for kindling now, he resigned himself to it and began the long walk home.

A soft breeze rustled the long grass. The green hills were speckled with purple thistle blossoms. He stopped to examine one of them. The blossoms themselves were beautiful, a full vibrant purple. But the stems and leaves were covered in prickles, making them almost impossible to pick.

A great deal like Arabella Hughes.

She was a woman of layers. Prickly at first. Almost as if daring anyone to get close. But if one ventured near enough and risked getting pierced . . .

Gavin had confronted her, challenged her. And he'd watched as her defenses had fallen away. He had felt more than seen the maelstrom of uncertainty, the turbulence created by turning over such questions in her mind. He'd sensed the courage it would take to be something other than what her parents wanted her to be.

And in that moment, he'd been granted a brief glimpse of the woman she could be if she tore off the shackles of their expectations.

She would be, in a word, magnificent.

As brilliant and majestic as the thistle blossoms that covered these hills.

And so as he started forward, seeing Nan's house up on the rocky cliffside, he half feared the answer she'd give him tomorrow.

For Gavin suspected that if the true force of Arabella Hughes was set free, his heart would be in very great danger.

ARABELLA DRUMMED HER fingers on the arm of the settee.

"Arabella? Is everything all right?" Grandmother sat across the room in a chair before the fire. "Ye're driving me tae distraction, dearie."

Arabella stood, clasping her hands together. She was driving *herself* to distraction. "I'm fine. Just restless. And hungry."

It wasn't a lie. But it wasn't exactly the truth either.

Arabella had been wrestling with herself since yesterday, ever since that unexpectedly intimate conversation with Mr. McKenzie. Turning possibilities over and over in her mind.

She kept coming back to that moment on the cliffside stairs, when she'd almost fallen. Remembering the stark and wondrous feeling that had surged through her when Mr. McKenzie's arms had closed around her, the intense relief at being alive.

But was she alive—really *alive?* When she was constantly being prodded and poked, molded into the ideal her parents expected? When she allowed them to make every decision, big or small?

The answer, now, was plain.

No.

Up until now, she had lived—at best—half a life.

A life of invisible chains. They'd been there so long, Arabella had learned to live with them. She'd grown so used to them, she sometimes forgot they were there. The thought of breaking free was daunting. Like an animal kept in captivity all its life, she wasn't sure how to live in the wild. Or if she even could.

But for the first time, she wanted to. And she'd finally decided that succeed or fail, this summer she was going to try.

So why did she feel so nervous to give Mr. McKenzie her answer?

Grandmother looked up from her embroidery. "Ye've been restless all day, dearie. Is it the rain?"

"Mmmhmm," Arabella replied, her mind still far away.

"Good evening, ladies." Mr. McKenzie appeared in the doorway, not bothering to wait for Cargill to announce him.

Arabella froze. Knees locked. Back straight.

He went to Grandmother first, sweeping her into a bear hug. "Miss me?" he asked.

She chuckled, batting him away. "I haven't missed ye that much."

"Ye wound me," he teased, placing a hand over his heart. Then he turned and met Arabella's gaze.

A charged energy crackled through the air as they stood facing one another.

He, impossibly handsome, dark hair damp, as if he'd walked through the rain.

Her heart, beating ridiculously fast.

His eyes met hers, gaze unrelenting. "Ye'll have tae forgive me for being late. Someone stole my horse and hadn't the decency tae return it."

So he *had* walked. To make a point.

He wanted his horse.

And her answer.

And suddenly, Arabella knew exactly why she'd been nervous. Why she'd feared this moment.

On her own, Arabella was conventional. A rule follower. Save for her one indiscretion with Mr. Gresham, she was quite boring. About as exciting as a blank sheet of paper.

But Mr. McKenzie was like the spark coming off flint.

And when she was with him, her blank sheet of paper ignited, tinder catching fire. She felt it even now. A snarl of emotion swirling in her chest, a fidgety feeling in her fingertips.

Grandmother came and stood between them, waving them toward the dining room. "Ach, the time is nae matter. But let's not keep Cargill waiting."

Dinner was a very different affair than it had been the last time Mr. McKenzie had come. There was still tension between them, but a different kind. One of anticipation, of expectancy.

As if something new was beginning to unfurl between the two of them, and they each waited, on bated breath, to see what it might be.

Only a single wine glass was placed at her table setting. Arabella couldn't help but smile a little as she looked at it. Had it only been three weeks since that fated evening—when she'd believed Scots drank four different types of liquor at dinner? The whole affair seemed a distant memory, as if instead of weeks, months had gone by, altering her perceptions of Scotland, her grandmother . . .

And Mr. McKenzie.

"How have ye been?" he asked, gaze intent. "Since your dip in the river?"

There were questions beneath his questions, but she wasn't ready for them. "Warm and dry, as you can see." Arabella cut a bite of potato. "But enough about me, Mr. McKenzie. I am curious to know how your . . . *cousin* likes the bonnet you purchased for her?"

"Cousin?" Grandmother looked at Mr. McKenzie. "I did not ken ye had a cousin, Gavin."

He cleared his throat, trying not to smile. "'Tis my second cousin . . . three times removed."

Arabella raised a brow. "*Three* times removed?"

"Ach, yes. Quite removed." He nodded vigorously. "She lives in India. It may be a good while before I am able tae give it tae her."

"You took such pains to choose it," she said, all innocence. "You can see why I am anxious to see what she thinks of it."

"Ye'll be the first tae ken," he assured her, "when I do."

Grandmother laughed as Gavin regaled her with the story of how he'd rescued Arabella from the river. Arabella protested through the entirety of the tale, correcting his exaggerations and embellishments, while secretly amused.

"Are the two of ye attending dinner at the Wallaces'?" Gavin asked, setting down his knife.

"I told Arabella it is up tae her," Grandmother replied. "I always enjoy time with my neighbors. But I am equally as content at home, just the two of us."

"The Wallaces—the vicar's family?" Arabella took a sip of wine.

"Aye, dear. Ye met Maisie Wallace, their oldest daughter, at kirk."

"Ye should come," Mr. McKenzie said. "It should be a good crowd."

It was tempting. Especially after coming from London's social whirlwind.

"I shall think on it," was all she promised.

When the last of the meal had been cleared away, the three of them gathered around the small table in the sitting room. Mr. McKenzie scooted his chair close to Arabella, so close that their knees brushed beneath the table. She couldn't look him in the eye. She wasn't ready to face him. Not yet.

"What do ye think, Arabella?" Grandmother asked. "Would Mr. McKenzie enjoy *The Mysteries of Udolpho*? We could take turns reading aloud."

"No," she said, a little too quickly. "No, I think not." The last thing in the world Arabella needed was to hear Mr. McKenzie read the romantic passages of that book aloud. She removed a deck of cards from the drawer. "I believe he'd much prefer a game of piquet."

Grandmother frowned. "Piquet is a game for two." Then a slow smile stole over her face. "But nae matter. The two of ye can play while I make myself cozy by the fire."

Arabella panicked. "We can certainly find something—"

"Nae, I insist." Grandmother stood and gave an exaggerated yawn. "I'm feeling quite tired. I'll look forward tae hearing who wins." And with that, she pointedly left the two of them seated together at the small table.

In a bit of a panic, Arabella began dealing the first hand. As soon as she'd finished, she picked up her cards and began examining them. Mr. McKenzie didn't touch his. He stared at her across the table.

"Yes, Mr. McKenzie?" she said, the muscles in her jaw tense. "Is there something I can get for you?"

"I think ye ken what I want, Miss Hughes."

There was no mistaking his meaning. She shifted in her seat. Ordered her cards. "You want my answer."

"I do." A lock of hair fell across his forehead.

"Very well, then." She took a breath, needing just a heartbeat longer before she spoke the words out loud. "I've decided to accept your challenge."

He smiled, but this was not the smile she had come to expect. This one was slow, unhurried. Smooth as silk and warm as sunshine. A small dimple appeared in his chin. "I knew ye wouldn't disappoint me, Miss Hughes."

Why did those words spread through her middle like melting butter? "Did you? I wasn't sure myself until a few hours ago."

One corner of his mouth lifted. "Ah, but from our first meeting, I recognized in ye a woman who always rises tae a challenge."

She swallowed hard, scooting toward the back of her seat.

He leaned forward. "Which is why I thought it would be appropriate tae come up with a series of challenges for ye tae complete."

"Challenges? As in plural?" This seemed . . . dangerous. Even having made up her mind about this summer, she still couldn't drown out the whispered warnings of her parents.

He nodded. "*Challenges*."

"I will *not* be wearing a kilt."

His eyes piqued with interest. "I can see your ideas are more interesting than mine, Miss Hughes."

"And what, exactly, did you have in mind?"

"I dare ye tae dispatch your use of the formal Mr. McKenzie."

Arabella's mouth went dry.

"And call me Gavin."

She felt the intensity of his gaze all the way down to the pit of her belly. "That is what you want? For me to call you by your first name?"

"Aye. That is what I want."

She bit the inside of her cheek, trying for composure. "So long as it is understood that I am by no means giving you leave to call me anything but Miss Hughes."

He sat forward, eyes twinkling. "Ach, I never intended tae wait for your permission, Arabella. I'm far too impatient a man for that."

Fourteen

Two days later, Arabella found Molly rifling through her dresses. "I'd like to choose my own dress for this evening," she informed her.

Molly stared at her. "But your mother instructed me to—"

"I know," Arabella said simply. "And I'm changing those instructions. From now on, I'll be choosing which dresses I wear and when. And tonight, I'd like to wear the rose-colored silk velvet."

"But I—"

"Please, Molly."

Molly sighed. "Very well. Though I do hope your mother doesn't find out. You know she has opinions."

"Yes," agreed Arabella, "I know."

After Molly helped her dress, Arabella insisted they try something different with her hair—gathering it more loosely around her face, leaving curls cascading over one shoulder.

Arabella cut off Molly's protest. "And yes, I know it isn't what Mother instructed. But Mother isn't here."

Arabella could practically hear the litany of complaints in Molly's head and was grateful that, for once, the girl had the sense not to speak them out loud.

Once Molly had finished, she examined Arabella from every angle, face pinched. "If you hoped to look different, you've certainly succeeded."

Arabella looked at herself in the mirror.

She *did* look different.

And she felt different.

She couldn't help but remember the small thrill that had coursed through her the other night when Mr. McKenzie—*Gavin*, she reminded herself—had used her given name.

I never intended tae wait for your permission, Arabella.

And though she'd laughed in the moment, her heart had constricted a little.

She'd heard her parents say her name hundreds of times. When they said it, it was always infused with a reprimand, as if her name itself was a scold. But when Gavin had said her name, his Scottish brogue skirting over it, *Arabella* almost sounded like a different word.

Wild.

Untamed.

Full of possibility.

And that possibility was what Arabella saw now when she looked at herself in the mirror. Even though the changes she'd made were small—choosing what dress to wear and how to style her hair—they were a start. A few steps forward in discovering who she was and what she wanted. And she felt braver for having taken them.

Grandmother was waiting for her downstairs. "Are ye ready? The carriage is waiting."

Arabella's stomach fluttered with nerves. Even though she'd agreed to this dinner at the Wallaces', she instinctively knew it would be nothing like an event in London. And she knew her parents would not approve. No doubt they imagined her sequestered at Grandmother's house, passing the summer in isolation. And for the most part, she *had* stayed secluded.

Until now. The summer stretched before her, full of possibility.

And so, in a moment that felt very much like crossing the Rubicon, she nodded. "Yes, Grandmother. I'm ready."

ESTATE BUSINESS HAD kept Gavin occupied well past six that evening, so by the time he arrived at the Wallaces', he was half an hour late. But as he was ushered inside, he was gratified to see Nan and Arabella being enthusiastically greeted. He hadn't been certain they'd come.

Gavin suddenly found himself looking forward to the evening. At gatherings like this, he was often pestered by all the old women about why he wasn't married. In truth, Gavin adored all the grannies, many of them Nan's friends. He'd flirt with them until they laughed and shooed him off, urging him to use his wiles on one of the young women who'd caught his eye.

And tonight, there happened to be one who had.

Arabella stood behind Nan, lovely as always. But from where he stood, angled toward her profile, he could see there was something different about her. Something softer.

Mrs. Wallace pulled Nan into an embrace, then curtseyed to Arabella. "We are so honored tae have ye." Smiling, she lowered her voice. "I feel I must warn ye, however, that there will be plenty of young men vying for your attention."

"I am happy tae shoo them away if need be," the vicar said.

Arabella laughed. "I'll keep that in mind."

Mrs. Wallace turned and caught sight of Gavin. "Mr. McKenzie, come in, come in. I'm sure ye've met Miss Hughes."

He found Arabella's eyes. "I have, in fact."

"No doubt Mr. McKenzie has been charming ye," Mrs. Wallace chirped.

"Oh, most certainly." Arabella gave him a meaningful look. "Mr. McKenzie knows how to make one feel right at home."

Before any more could be said, Mrs. Wallace's older daughters approached and began peppering Arabella with questions about finishing schools, London, and what it was like being presented to the Queen. Gavin chuckled, watching a wide-eyed Arabella be whisked away and swallowed by the crowd.

Dinner began briefly thereafter, an informal affair with a large buffet, and Gavin saw Nan settled before being pulled into a conversation with several of his father's old friends.

Gavin scolded himself for continually searching for Arabella, who was always at the center of attention, surrounded by a circle of admirers. But it brought him a great deal of satisfaction to note how often Arabella looked in *his* direction. At one point, when he caught her gaze, he speared a piece of meat with his knife and put it to his mouth.

She coughed, stifling her laugh.

It was nearly ten o'clock when one of the younger Wallace girls asked if they could move the furniture and have some dancing.

Mr. Wallace smiled and nodded. "I dinnae see why not."

Soon everyone was helping, scooting chairs across the floor and rolling back the rugs to make space. Someone pulled out a fiddle and Arabella's hand was immediately claimed.

Gavin waited on the periphery, watching as the dancing began. As he'd expected, Arabella was unparalleled. Her posture perfect, her movements graceful, every step flawlessly executed. Next came a quadrille. Then a waltz.

The room grew noisy and warm as people talked and danced and laughed, while those watching called out teasingly when someone made a misstep. Several windows were propped open to help cool the room.

As soon as the fiddler began a Scotch reel, Gavin made his move toward Arabella. He edged through the crowd and came up behind her, bending to speak in her ear. "May I have the next dance, Arabella?"

She turned and suddenly they were face-to-face, her blue eyes sparkling, her rosebud mouth just inches away from his. "You should not use my name in so public a setting," she breathed, her shoulder brushing against his chest as they were jostled by the crowd.

"Shall I take ye somewhere more private?" he teased.

Her mouth fell open. "Certainly not."

"Then dance with me," he said low.

"I shouldn't." She wiped her brow. "I'm already exhausted."

He could see her warring within herself. Against propriety. Against her strict upbringing. He leaned closer, forcing her gaze back up to him. "Your next challenge, then. A dare. Dance the reel here, in the country where it originated."

Arabella raised her chin. "Me? Dance with a brute like you?" She set her mouth, trying not to smile.

And then he was taking her hand, and couples were finding their places, and the fiddler's tune led them into the first steps of the reel. The light in the room was soft, and the corners of Arabella's lips curved up as they turned around the room in their circle of eight. She performed the intricate steps of the reel perfectly as they whirled through an exchange of partners, forming circles and arches, doing the cross springs and the traveling step.

The pace of the fiddle quickened as the next song began. Gavin grinned at her. "Ready for another?"

Her eyes widened as she realized there would be no break before they started into the next reel, one that wasn't as well known in London circles. He raised his brows at her in question, in challenge, but she only lifted the hem of her dress and followed his lead, catching on to the rhythm and formation with ease.

"I can see what ye're thinking, lass," he said to her when the dance brought them close.

Her brow wrinkled in confusion, though she didn't miss a step.

"Ye wish I'd worn a kilt."

"Gavin," she scolded low, laughing as they whirled away from each other. Skirts were swirling, chests heaving, and several couples retired from the circle, unable to keep pace. The room was stifling now, even with the windows open. The open step, a whirl and exchange of partners, a double kemkossy. Arabella was smiling wide, cheeks flushed, her heels clicking on the hardwood floor.

Gavin spun her in a clockwise turn. "For an English-woman, ye're doing quite well."

The staccato rhythm of their steps kept time with the beat. "Just see if I can't best you at your own Scotch reel, Mr. McKenzie."

The fiddle grew louder and faster, bridging into the next song, and more people dropped out. There were only three couples left now, including Gavin and Arabella, and they pushed forward, every move made on instinct because there was no thinking, only dizzying movement, the clapping of the crowd around them, the shouts of encouragement to the remaining couples.

Sweat beaded on Gavin's brow and Arabella's breaths came hard and fast as they circled right, then back again. The open step, a side hop and back, the fosgladh. Now there were only two couples remaining. Their feet were a blur.

The speed of the fiddle continued to mount, urging them on. Arabella was laughing now, her curls flying out behind her as Gavin spun her around. Unable to keep up, the other couple stepped back, both doubled over in laughter and in search of breath.

But neither Gavin nor Arabella was ready to stop, and they continued in a dizzying fashion, in and out, forward and back, circling, stepping, until finally, finally, Gavin couldn't keep up. He stepped back while Arabella continued on, feet whirring, keeping time with the music until at last the fiddler slowed and played the closing chord with fanfare.

Gavin reached for Arabella's hand and held it up in triumph. "Your victor," he shouted, breath still heaving. The room broke out in a cheer and Arabella was laughing, beaming, and panting all at once.

"Open the back doors!" someone called, then the French doors at the back of the house were being pushed open, light spilling out into the darkness.

Gavin grabbed a drink from a nearby tray, guiding Arabella through the crowd that was slowly dispersing on the back lawn and into the gardens. A delicious breeze swept down the hills.

Several small saplings on the side of the house provided a quiet place for the two of them to catch their breaths. Arabella turned to face him, the moon lighting her features. "I've never been so tired in my life. You should have warned me!" she accused, laughing.

He grinned. "And risk ye refusing? Never." He placed the drink in her hands, his fingers brushing over hers. The mood between them shifted in an instant as she stared up at him, eyes sparkling.

Gavin had guessed there would be dancing tonight. And from the moment he'd laid eyes on Arabella earlier this evening, he'd planned to dance the reel with her, wanting to see what he saw now. A woman free of constraints. Hair coming undone. Cheeks flushed. Smile wide.

He'd known, or at least suspected, that Arabella Hughes, if freed from stricture and propriety, would be a woman who would prove a formidable foe for his heart.

What he hadn't expected was how quickly he might fall. Already there was this tugging inside him, a kind of pull he'd never experienced before. The strength of it, of *her*, took him aback. The realization that if he gave in to these feelings, they could be deeper, stronger than any he'd ever known. That already, this woman had a hold on his heart.

Nan's *granddaughter.*

It was a realization he wasn't prepared for.

Wasn't sure what to do with. At least not yet.

For now, he needed something, anything between them. "Ye were impressive in there, Arabella Hughes." His mouth tipped up in a half smile. "Must be your Scottish blood."

"More likely my English dancing master," she shot back, finally taking a large gulp of the drink he'd given her. And then she coughed, spewing liquid all down her front, sputtering as she gasped in air.

Arabella pounded a fist against her chest, still coughing. "What *was* that?" she demanded.

Gavin winked at her. "Why, what did ye expect after putting us all tae shame doing the reel? It's whisky, of course."

Fifteen

ARABELLA SLEPT LATE the next morning. It had taken hours for her to fall asleep, mind whirring through last night's events, replaying certain scenes again and again. The whole evening held a rosy hue. The chatter and informality. The camaraderie among neighbors.

And the dancing. So different from the ballrooms in London, cold and formal, everyone glittering with jewels. But there'd been something invigorating about it—the spontaneity, the young and old dancing together, the fiddle music.

And the reel with Gavin . . .

Arabella's cheeks flamed every time she thought of it. Remembering the way he'd teased and goaded her. Remembering the warmth of his hands, the warmth of his gaze. The dizzying and exhilarating speed, the energy of the crowd, her moment of triumph when she realized she'd outlasted everyone, including Gavin.

It was a night she'd not forget.

And it was a night she knew her parents would not approve of.

Lying here in bed, a nervous guilt churned in her stomach. And she wondered why she should feel so culpable when all she'd felt last night was joy.

A knock sounded at the door, and Molly entered. "I've a

letter for you, Miss Hughes. From your parents. I thought you'd want it at once."

She handed the missive into Arabella's hands.

And just like that, Arabella's sunny mood burst into something far more somber. It was only a letter, only paper, but it felt heavy in her hands. Like a paperweight.

Her name was written on the front in Mother's impeccable handwriting. Just looking at it made her feel guilty, as if her parents could sense from miles away that she'd been doing something wrong.

"What did you say you'd spilled on your dress again, Miss Hughes?" Molly asked. "I'm having a difficult time removing it."

"Whisky," Arabella said absentmindedly.

"*Whisky?*" she choked out.

"Yes, whisky," Arabella said firmly, pulling the covers back.

After helping Arabella dress and arrange her hair, Molly stopped her as she was leaving.

"What about your letter, Miss Hughes?" she asked. "Don't you wish to read it?"

"Maybe later," Arabella said. "For now, you may put it in the drawer of my dressing table."

Putting the letter from her mind, Arabella went downstairs. When she'd first arrived at Grandmother's, Arabella remembered feeling anxious about how the days had stretched before her, with nothing to fill them. No events. No schedule.

Now she relished the freedom, letting each day fill itself with a walk down to the beach or taking a nap in the library or drying some of the flowers she'd picked in the hills.

After breakfast, she found Grandmother in the sitting room, looking out the window. She turned, smiling when she saw Arabella. "Did ye enjoy yourself last night?"

Arabella fought a blush. How could she even answer such a question? "I did. It was a very . . . nice . . . evening."

"Nice?" she challenged.

Arabella smiled despite herself. Grandmother had a way of getting straight to the heart of the matter. "It was much more than nice," she admitted. "I loved every minute of it."

"That's more like it." Grandmother glanced back out the window. "'Tis sunny today," she said abruptly. "I think a walk outside would do ye good. Go fetch a shawl."

"It's early yet. I thought perhaps we could—"

Grandmother shook her head. "My rheumatism is giving me trouble this morning. I'll need tae rest."

Had last night been too much for her? Arabella should have paid better attention. "Are you—"

But Grandmother made a shooing motion. "Off with ye now. One never kens how long the sunshine will last."

She seemed so insistent that Arabella obeyed at once. After debating between her pale-yellow gauze shawl and her white cashmere one, she chose the latter, knowing it was probably chillier than it looked outside.

Grandmother met her at the bottom of the stairs. "Nae need tae hurry back. I'll just be resting."

Arabella's forehead wrinkled. "You are sure you don't wish to come? Or I could stay, perhaps play some music for you while you rest?"

"Dinnae worry aboot me. I'll rest this morning and perhaps I'll feel better this afternoon."

But Arabella had only made it down the first three steps before she realized why Grandmother had been so insistent about getting her out the door. Mr. McKenzie was riding up the drive, leading another horse along behind him.

He dismounted from Baird and continued forward, leading a beautiful bay roan toward Arabella.

"What is this?" she asked.

"I couldn't help but notice ye are an excellent horsewoman." He met her eyes, his gaze even. "And I am here on a mission tae reform ye."

"Reform me?" She quirked a brow.

"Aye," he said, face grave. "I ken your grandmother's stables are not well stocked. And I hoped loaning ye a horse for the summer might cure ye of your thievery."

Arabella bit her lip to keep from smiling. "Seeing as how I left you stranded the other day, one might call it self-interest."

Gavin tipped his head forward, grinning. "One might." He held out the bridle for her. "Do ye want tae give Willow a try?"

GAVIN WAITED OUTSIDE while Arabella hurried up to change. He'd stayed up late last night, sitting by the fireplace in his study, staring into the flames. Thinking. About what he wanted. About what to do with the realizations he'd had about Arabella Hughes.

After the deaths of his parents, Gavin had traveled a great deal. To different cities on the Continent. To London. Searching, hunting for something to fill the empty spaces inside him. And when he'd realized they were just as hollow as he, he'd returned home.

To the Highlands. Where slowly he'd healed. Where happy memories of his parents assuaged his bruised heart. Where his emptiness was slowly filled by friends and neighbors, especially Nan, who'd become family.

And for a while, that had been enough.

But the past several years, a different kind of hollowness had opened up inside of him. A hunger not for more friends. Not for a grandmother figure. But for a woman.

A wife.

The decision he'd made last night to pursue Arabella was not a logical one. If he were wise, he'd find a young woman who lived here. Or perhaps in Edinburgh. But it was too late for that. Arabella already had a foothold in his heart. And fool that he was, Gavin had no desire to pry her loose.

Instead, he'd decided to court her. Slowly. Cautiously.

Such patience was not in his nature. Gavin was accustomed to going after what he wanted with reckless abandon, throwing himself wholeheartedly into the things he cared about.

But Arabella deserved his caution. She'd only begun to test the boundaries of a life out from under the shadow of her parents. He couldn't ask her to consider more. Not yet.

Willow snorted and stomped. He brushed a hand down her nose, trying to calm her. "The best things in life require a bit of patience," he whispered. Pulling an apple from his pocket, he let her nibble at it from the palm of his glove.

A few minutes later, Arabella returned wearing a sharply cut riding habit of dark blue, one that made him consider whether he should throw caution to the wind and kiss her here and now. Patience be hanged.

He took a steadying breath. "Ready tae give Willow a go?"

Eyes bright and cheeks glowing, she nodded. "Yes, please."

Today, Gavin didn't trust himself to put his hands around her waist. Instead, he interlocked his fingers and offered Arabella a step up. Resting her hand on his shoulder for balance, she mounted Willow easily.

They set off, Gavin leading them south along the slowly descending cliff line. "I meant what I said about your riding," he told her.

"Rest assured, if it's an area in which my parents believe a young woman should be proficient, I am more than accomplished. Dancing, painting, music, riding, needlework." She said it without conceit, stating a fact rather than bragging. The wind was at their backs, blowing some of Arabella's curls into her face, and she used one hand to brush her hair back behind her ear.

"Languages?" he asked.

She looked heavenward as if making a mental list. "French. Italian. And a fair bit of Latin."

"But not Scottish," he teased.

She held back a laugh, but barely. "I'm learning, ye walloper. Bampot. Eejit."

"A little too well, I think." He chuckled. "Though as I recall, insults have always come quite naturally tae ye."

Her mouth twisted into a smirk. "Only where *you* are concerned."

He shook his head. "I've never quite been able tae understand what ye have against me. That day we met at the inn I was only protecting ye from brutes and savages."

She laughed. "Your nobleness astounds, Gavin Alexander McKenzie."

"I see your grandmother has been telling stories about me."

"She has," Arabella acknowledged. "Knowing all that I do, it's quite shocking that I've agreed to be seen in the company of a man like you." The cliffside descended, giving way to more even terrain.

He sighed heavily. "Nan told ye about the time I stole the collection plate, I take it?"

Arabella nodded. "And about the time you tried to hold up a carriage like a highwayman."

He shrugged. "Turns out that was a profession that didn't suit me."

"*And* about the time you set her stables on fire."

"A stroke of misfortune."

"A *large* stroke, it seems. It sounds as if your parents allowed you to run completely wild." She shook her head. Such a thing was probably unfathomable to her.

"I'm not so sure 'twas a matter of *allowing*. More that, as a young lad, I was unstoppable. But yes, I was given a great deal of freedom during my summers home."

"That's right. You spent the other parts of the year at school in England."

He nodded. "Eton. And then Cambridge."

"I remember," she said quietly. "Did you hate every moment of it?"

"Of school?" He considered the question. "I did. At first. I was teased about my accent quite mercilessly. Boys that age ... they can be quite cruel." He led Baird down a path where long grass gave way to soft white sand.

She followed him, guiding Willow down onto the beach. Arabella brought her horse up alongside Gavin and they rode together in silence for several minutes, save for the rhythmic sounds of the waves as they pounded the shore.

When he glanced over at her, a groove had formed between her brows. "Why were your parents so intent on sending you to school in England if you hated it so much?"

He looked down the shoreline. "That was the doing of my mother. A wise woman. She was a lowlander and a widow. She'd been married to an Englishman before my father and knew plenty about the prejudices that existed against Scots.

"And because she never wanted me tae feel less than, she decided I would be educated as well as any Englishman's son. And I was. And aye, while it was hard at first, I made friends—loyal friends who didn't care about my background or heritage. And my education, my experience, has served me well. I'm grateful for it now."

Gavin squinted against the rays of sun sparkling off the ocean.

"You love your mother very much," she said softly. It was a statement. An observation.

"I do." He cleared his throat. "I did. I loved both of my parents. My father was the kindest, most tender soul ye'd ever meet. A gentle giant." His mouth curved in a sad smile. "And perhaps a little too forgiving of his ramshackle son."

"They're . . ." She blinked. "Gone? Both of them?" Arabella pulled her horse up abruptly.

"Aye." He reined in Baird, emotion thickening the back of his throat. "They died in a shipwreck when I was twenty-one."

"Oh, Gavin," she breathed. The eyes she turned on him were as soft as the fading blue of a summer sunset. The tenderness in her voice made a bit of the hollowness inside him recede.

"When I think how you let me go on about my own parents." She bit her lip. "About silly things, little things . . ."

He eased Baird closer to her and reached out his gloved forefinger to set it softly on her lips, quieting her. "They aren't little things, Arabella. Not tae ye. Not tae me."

Tears sparkled on her lashes, balancing on the tips as if she was determined not to let them fall. "I'm sorry, Gavin. Truly." She tried for a smile. "Your mother sounds wonderful. And wise. Wise enough to send you to school in England to prepare you for those ridiculous people who are prejudiced against Scots." Her lips twisted in a sad sort of smirk. "Like me."

"That was her intention, Arabella. No doubt," he said, laughing softly. "Though I doubt anything could have prepared me for the likes of ye."

Sixteen

WHEN ARABELLA RETURNED home a few hours later, she headed straight up to change. There was a lightness in her steps as she walked down the hall to her room. Her cheeks hurt from smiling.

After riding down to the beach, she and Gavin had dismounted and given the horses into the groom's care, then spent almost an hour walking the shoreline, finding shells, throwing rocks, and . . . talking.

About nothing and everything. Their favorite foods and books and places. Gavin's were scones, *Gulliver's Travels*, and the ruins of an old abbey several miles north, which he'd promised to take her to. When Arabella had confided that *The Mysteries of Udolpho* was the first novel she'd ever read, he'd shown mock outrage and immediately recommended several books he thought she'd enjoy.

While they'd walked, he'd extended a third challenge: to take off her shoes and stockings and wade out into the ocean in her bare feet. The cold had been shocking, and she'd yelped when an unexpected wave had snuck up on her, soaking the bottom of her riding habit. But it had also been exhilarating. Within several minutes, her feet had grown numb, and she'd begun to enjoy the sensation of the lapping waves, laughing as Gavin reenacted her shrieks with great fanfare.

Later, after she'd put her shoes and stockings back on,

they'd discussed weightier matters. Gavin had told her more about his parents and about the dark period after their deaths. About how Nan had come over every day to make sure he'd eaten something and gotten dressed. Arabella had confided in him about the secret widow's walk on the roof of their townhome where she went at night when she couldn't sleep. About how few friends, real friends, she had in London.

One thing was certain. Gavin Alexander McKenzie was nothing like any of the men Arabella had known in London. He wasn't stuffy or conceited, nor did he believe he had all the answers to life's many questions. He laughed and joked about everything, including himself.

And what's more, he made *her* laugh. Often.

While undoing the top buttons on her riding habit, Arabella caught a glimpse of herself in the mirror. At first glance, she was a mess. Her hair disheveled, bonnet askew, riding habit flecked with mud. But she also looked . . . happy. Nothing like the staid and proper young woman who had arrived here just over a month ago.

The next two weeks passed in a joyful blur. Rounds of piquet and playing the pianoforte for Grandmother. Looking through some of her mother's old chests, trying to piece together the puzzle of the girl she'd once been. Rising early to try and capture the beauty of the Highlands in watercolor. Dinner with neighbors. Accepting new challenges from Gavin as they rode the hills or walked down to the beach.

She'd just returned from one of these long rides and was going upstairs to freshen up when Molly appeared at her side. "You wanted the blue organza for this evening, was that right?"

Arabella nodded. "Thank you, Molly."

Molly followed her upstairs, chattering about the habits of the other servants, about how slowly time was passing, about how they still had another six weeks to endure here in Scotland.

Only six more weeks?

The thought made Arabella freeze. She remembered having similar feelings when she'd first arrived. Her first week here, even as she'd gotten to know Grandmother, had inched by, each day stretching interminably.

But now it had begun to feel as if time was going too fast, as if the sand in an hourglass was slipping through her fingers.

Molly opened the door to Arabella's chamber. "Your grandmother told me to tell you dinner will be served at seven. Will you be needing anything else?"

Arabella's thoughts jumped to the letter her mother had written, the one she still hadn't opened. "No, I think I'll rest for a while."

But when Molly shut the door, Arabella didn't go to the bed. She took a seat at her dressing table and opened the drawer, pulling out the letter. There was no need to open it to know what was inside. Chastisement for not writing. A list of expectations. Threats of what the consequences might be if she failed to live up to them.

Opening it would be akin to holding out her wrist to be fitted with a manacle, and she wasn't ready to do that just yet. Not when she was finally beginning to learn who she was; not when she was at last discovering what it meant to be free.

To read an afternoon away because she wished to find out how the book ended.

To go hunting for shells along the shoreline for hours at a time, delighted by the variety of their size and shape and color.

To listen to Grandmother telling stories of her childhood over breakfast.

To begin to feel, as she wandered the hills and valleys, as if this country, this place, even with all its rugged wildness, was in her blood.

Images of Gavin flashed in her mind, of all the moments,

big and small, they'd shared these past weeks, and a lump formed in her throat.

To spend time with someone, not because of how they might improve one's status, not because the rules of etiquette required it but for the sheer pleasure of his company.

Arabella's thumb brushed over one corner of the letter.

In a small vase on her dressing table was a single white rose, one Gavin had picked for her when he'd given her and Nan a tour of his glasshouse. The petals were just beginning to unfurl, the rose on the cusp of blooming. Arabella lifted the bloom to her nose, careful not to touch the fragile petals, breathing in its sweet scent before gently placing it back in the water.

She couldn't open the letter. Wouldn't open it. Like the rose, her newfound freedom and her feelings for Gavin were fragile. Her mother's words would bruise and break them as surely as a clumsy hand would crush the petals of a blooming rose.

Which is why, instead of opening it, she placed it back in the drawer of her dressing table.

It was only then that she noticed that the letter she'd written to her parents that second day at Grandmother's was missing.

Seventeen

"'Twas a fine meal, Gavin. Ye'll have tae give my compliments tae the cook." Grandmother leaned back in the chair. "Ainlie problem is, I'm not sure I'll be able tae get up."

Gavin laughed. "Let me help ye." He rose and went to her side.

Arabella watched the scene, surprised by the emotion billowing within her chest, a soft sort of joy. The smallest details that no one else would notice but that said a great deal about the two people who had come to mean so much to her.

The gentle way Gavin took ahold of Grandmother's elbow and helped her rise.

The affection shining from her eyes as she looked up at him.

The way he murmured in her ear, making her laugh.

Arabella couldn't remember ever feeling as content as she had this past month. In many ways, the time felt like a soap bubble, sitting on the rim of a tub. One that might burst at any moment. But for now, as she followed Gavin and Grandmother into the parlor, she allowed herself to revel in it.

Gavin saw Grandmother settled in a chair by the fire. She lifted a hand to cover a wide yawn. "We cannae stay too late if the two of ye hope tae get an early start tomorrow, but will ye play a little something for us, Arabella? Gavin has a fine instrument."

Gavin led her over to a handsome pianoforte, painted and carved with intricate figures of a lake scene with swans. She ran her hand over the top of its smooth surface. "It's beautiful."

He nodded. "'Twas my mother's."

She started to pull her hand back. "Are you sure you don't mind—"

"I dinnae mind," he said, setting his hand over hers, thumb brushing over her knuckles. Butterflies fluttered low in her belly. "I'd like tae hear ye play it." He squeezed her hand gently before releasing it.

"She'll need someone tae turn the pages," Grandmother called.

They both chuckled. Gavin pulled back the bench while Arabella leafed through the sheet music until she found a song she knew.

Her fingers glided over the keys, the tone of the instrument warm and mellow. Arabella had seen a painting of Gavin's mother, her laughing eyes and easy smile so much like his, and she couldn't help but think of her while she played. Did hearing Arabella play make Gavin miss his mother, or did it bring back happy memories?

Perhaps both.

Her mind drifted back to a few days before when Gavin had gifted Arabella the bonnet he'd purchased for his supposed cousin in India. With perfect grimness, he'd explained that she'd met her unfortunate end in a tiger attack. And though Arabella had been in stitches, Gavin unwilling to admit his second cousin three times removed had been a ruse, she'd wondered, even then, if it was from his father that he'd had inherited the ability to give thoughtful gifts.

How she wished she knew them, the parents who had formed and molded and shaped the man she was coming to love.

When she'd finished, fingers lifting gently from the keys, she put her hands in her lap. "Thank you," she said. "For letting me play."

Gavin stood behind her, and the space between them had its own sound, a buzzing, an insistent hum. Arabella moved to the edge of the bench and got to her feet, but she was unprepared for the proximity in which it would place them. Gavin, inches away, green eyes muted in the dim room, jaw shadowed with soft stubble.

Her breath caught in her chest because the look of aching desire on his face made her realize she'd been wrong. This wasn't a bubble at all. The feelings that had been growing between them these past weeks were real. And they were becoming more and more difficult to ignore. Instead of satiating her, every minute, every hour spent with him only made her hungrier for his company, his stories, his teasing.

His touch.

They stared at each other a long moment before Gavin lifted a hand, brushing the back of his fingers down her temple. He leaned closer, his breath whispering against her cheek. Arabella closed her eyes, her heart pounding.

Gavin pressed a kiss to her hairline, his lips soft. Tender.

Arabella's breath was trapped in her chest.

A loud snore broke the silence, and she jerked back in surprise. Silence followed before both of them burst out laughing. Arabella clapped a hand over her mouth to keep from waking Grandmother.

"Is she faking, do ye think?" Gavin whispered.

Arabella nearly giggled. "It always starts out that way," she said, thinking of how many times in the past weeks Grandmother had fallen asleep for twenty minutes at a time, conveniently giving Gavin and Arabella a bit of privacy. She wasn't particularly subtle. "But usually within a few minutes, there is nothing fake about it."

"I can hear ye," Grandmother called. "And Gavin, if ye missed your chance tae kiss her, 'tis through no fault of my own."

Gavin tipped back his head and laughed. "True enough, Nan. True enough."

THAT NIGHT, BACK at home, Arabella remembered to ask Molly about the missing letter. "Do you know what happened to the letter I wrote my parents? I left it in this drawer, but it isn't there anymore."

Molly was plaiting Arabella's hair, smoothing her thick tresses into a long braid down her back. She looked up. "Yes, Miss Hughes. I found it when I was putting away the letter your mother sent you and gave it to one of the footmen to add to the post."

Arabella's fingers froze around the hairpin she'd been toying with. "You sent it?" Her voice was a strangled whisper.

Molly frowned, tying off the braid with a rag. "Did you not wish me to?"

"I—" Arabella wasn't even sure what to say. A cold, sick feeling slithered through her stomach. "How long ago did you send it?"

She pursed her lips. "Three weeks ago, I think? Maybe a little less."

Arabella began calculating in her head. Three weeks. Three weeks meant they'd received the letter and could already be on their way. Depending on how quickly they'd left, three weeks meant they could be here any day.

Molly began picking up the hairpins littering the top of the dressing table. "Did I do something wrong?"

Arabella shook her head. "It doesn't matter now." But it

did matter. All at once it became hard to breathe. She stood abruptly, nearly knocking over the chair.

"Miss Hughes—"

Arabella didn't hear any more. She was racing down the corridor, down the stairs. Needing air. Needing the wide-open spaces of the mountains and the ever-present gusts of wind and the vast feeling of peace that the Highlands opened up in her.

She burst out the front door, heaving in deep breaths as if she were gasping for air. In the month and a half since she'd arrived in Scotland, she'd already forgotten what it felt like to be in the presence of her mother and father. It was a vise-clamped-around-her-lungs feeling.

She stood, bent over, still breathing hard, guilt bearing down on her, hovering like the mist that clung to the Highlands each morning.

After almost two months of freedom, going back to her cage in England felt impossible. Not just because of how she'd changed, not just because of all she'd experienced.

But because of her feelings for Gavin McKenzie.

It was becoming difficult to remember what her life had been like before him. She had laughed less, certainly. And she'd been so wary, so restrained. Frozen in place for fear of making a single misstep.

But with Gavin, she felt free. Completely unfettered by expectation or demand. Even tonight, in that stolen moment by the piano, that almost kiss, her heart had been soaring, winging skyward on a wind of longing.

But with threat of her parents' arrival looming, she could see herself more clearly.

She was a trained hawk, her parents falconers. And though these past months she'd been flying free, soaring through the sky at exhilarating heights, that freedom was merely an illusion. With a simple raise of the arm, she was being called back.

And as much as she wanted to remain untethered, and despite the strength of her feelings for Gavin, obedience was intuitive. She'd been tamed, after all. Carefully disciplined for the past twenty years.

Deep down, Arabella feared that when her parents came for her, she, like the well-trained hawk she was, wouldn't have the strength to resist their commands.

Eighteen

GAVIN STOOD IN the front entry, waiting for Arabella. Today, he was taking her to one of his favorite places: the old abbey ruins about five miles north of there. They'd arranged to go several other times, but bad weather had always managed to sabotage their plans. And today, though there was a strong wind blowing in off the ocean, the skies were clear.

Nan came in to greet him as he waited.

He bent to kiss her on the cheek. "Ye are sure ye don't wish tae join us?"

"I would ainlie be an imposition." She cocked her head, smiling. "In a way the groom ye are bringing along, will not."

"Ye, Ailsa Callender, are quite the schemer."

"I dinnae deny it." She gave him a sly wink. "But ye dinnae seem tae mind . . . am I wrong?"

Nan wasn't wrong. He'd taken advantage of every opportunity she'd provided to spend time with Arabella these past weeks. Spent hours in her company at kirk, at meals, showing her his property, talking quietly before the fire after dinner. And in that time, he'd fallen deeply, irrevocably in love with her.

That part had been easy.

The part that would be more difficult?

The battle that loomed at the end of the summer. Gavin was no fool. He knew Arabella cared for him, that perhaps she was even coming to love him. Just as he knew her parents would never approve of a match between them.

She'd never said as much, but she hadn't needed to. He knew it from the way they manipulated her, controlling her every move. Knew it from what she'd said of the lofty ambitions they had for her marriage.

And he saw it. The shadows that occasionally passed over her face. The worry she held in the groove between her brows. When she laughed too loud or said something unladylike. Or, heaven forbid, when she felt the pull of desire between them.

What he feared more than anything was that he was running out of time. He was trying, every moment he spent with her, to tear down the lies her parents had made her believe. That her value was somehow tied to doing and acting and being exactly what they wished for her to be. That she had to fit a certain mold in order to be loved.

"Wrong about what?" Arabella asked from the top of the staircase.

Gavin and Nan both looked up.

"Wrong aboot the weather," Nan said easily. "I suspected it might rain today, but the sky is clear."

Gavin wasn't certain he could have answered. He'd thought, these past weeks, that he'd become accustomed to Arabella's beauty. But as she descended the stairs today, wearing her dark blue riding habit, her loveliness hit him anew. It was different from that first night when she'd rendered him speechless. No longer was her beauty an impersonal thing to be admired from afar. It was an intimate, cherished thing.

He'd seen her curls flying out behind her as they raced Baird and Willow along the beach. Watched her nose wrinkle while losing at a card game. Noticed how her cheeks flushed with color when he teased her. Observed her blue eyes light with pleasure when he pointed out a view that delighted her.

Seeing her now, each of those features so precious to him, made his throat constrict, making him more certain that even though the future was uncertain, Arabella Hughes was a risk worth taking.

She reached the bottom of the staircase. "Good morning, Mr. McKenzie."

Arabella still insisted on a degree of formality whenever they were in the company of others, even her grandmother. But today, there was no hint of playfulness in her voice.

He stepped forward. "Arabella?"

She smiled, but there was something forced about it. "Shall we go?"

Gavin shot Nan a look, but she looked as perplexed as he. He offered her his arm. "I've the horses waiting out front."

In no time they were mounted and heading north. Gavin kept an eye on Arabella, but she kept her gaze straight ahead, lips pursed, expression tight. The wind whipped around them, blowing so fiercely that it made conversation impossible.

Despite the wind, they made good time, cresting the hill that led down toward Lochinvar Abbey by a little past ten. At the top of the ridge, Gavin reined in Baird, waiting for Arabella. She pulled up beside him, cheeks rosy from the unrelenting wind.

Arabella's eyes went round as she caught sight of the abbey ruins. She stayed silent for several long seconds, taking in the view.

Lochinvar Abbey was set in a small dell, surrounded by hills on every side. The two largest walls that remained jutted up into the sky, like fingers pointing toward heaven. Ravens flew in and out of the pane-less windows, over low walls, and out over the small stream that wound its way through the valley. Tall clumps of grass grew at the base of the crumbling stone walls, and several climbing vines seemed to be nature's way of trying to reclaim the structure.

"It's haunting," Arabella said quietly. "And beautiful."

"We could walk for a while," he offered. "And perhaps ye could tell me what is bothering ye?"

She looked at him sharply.

"Ye dinnae hide your emotions as well as ye believe. 'Tis clear ye're upset."

Arabella bowed her head, lines of agony in her features. He wanted to smooth away the hurt, to offer comfort. Gavin dismounted and helped her down, giving their horses into the care of the groom.

Arm-in-arm they walked, silence pressed between them.

"The morning after I arrived here," she finally began, "I wrote a letter to my parents. Outlining every single one of the ills I'd endured. I said scathing, hurtful things. About you." Her lips twisted. "About Grandmother."

He nodded, keeping his face expressionless.

"I begged for them to come for me. To take me back home." She paused, taking a breath, her features smoothing. "But I put it away and never sent it."

"Why?" he asked softly.

"I'm not even sure myself. Only that by the time I remembered it, I'd already softened toward Grandmother."

"Not quite as soon tae me," he teased.

"No, not quite as soon." Her smile was brief. "Last night I discovered that Molly sent it," she whispered, voice tortured. "I thought I had another month here in Scotland, but if they've received my letter . . ."

A sense of dread grew low in Gavin's stomach.

She looked up at him, brows knitted together. "They could be here any day," she finished.

Gavin's mind was racing. "So they'll come. And what? Ye'll tell them . . ."

"I doubt I'll have much of a chance to tell them anything."

"Arabella, I ken what your parents are like. Ye've told me enough—"

She laughed, but there was no warmth in it. "Do you think they won't see the truth? That this summer hasn't been the exile they imagined? That I've broken every rule they ever . . ." She paused, face crumpling. "They'll take me back to London, Gavin. As quickly as they sent me north to Scotland."

He stared down at her, willing her to see him, to see all that he felt for her. "Ye dinnae have tae go back with them."

Her eyes squeezed shut. "But I do."

"Arabella, ye're a grown woman."

She turned away. "I'm only twenty, Gavin. Not yet of age. And you don't understand what they're like. What *I'm* like when I'm with them. When they come, I'll go with them. I might hate myself for it. I might regret it. But I'll go."

"But—but *why*? Ye've told me yourself they dinnae care about what ye want. Why would ye put your future in their hands?"

"They are my *parents*, Gavin."

"And ye are a different daughter than the one they sent tae Scotland. Ye're a different woman than the one I met back at The Fox and Crown. Ye've changed."

"I have," she said quietly. "But perhaps not enough."

Gavin grasped her upper arms, desperate to reason with her. "I dinnae believe it. Why do ye give them such power, Arabella? Ye've a fierce heart. Ye can make your own choices."

She set her mouth. "I've watched Grandmother this summer. My mother's choice broke her heart. It's a wound that won't heal, not even with time. And perhaps I'm weak and perhaps I'll regret it, but I cannot do to my parents what Mother did to her. I cannot." Her voice broke on the last word.

Pain cut through him, sharp and deep, and he released his hold on her. "But ye can walk away and leave me without a second thought. What did ye think all this was, Arabella?" He sucked in a breath. "A game?"

"No," she whispered, arms folded across her middle. "But perhaps a fairy tale."

"A fairy tale," he repeated, voice laced with disgust.

"I wish I were stronger. But you don't know—"

"I ken the woman I've come tae love would not be satisfied with the life she left back in London!" he shouted. And then softer, breath ragged, "She wouldn't be satisfied tae live in a world where she had no say, no choices, no freedom."

Arabella stepped backward, shock filtering across her features.

And no wonder. He'd gone and lost his head, declaring himself while shouting at her. But this unanticipated turn had him reeling, frantically grasping for something that seemed to be slipping out of his reach.

He took a step toward Arabella, but she held up a hand to stop him. "I cannot . . . do this. I cannot think straight. Please, Gavin. I need some time alone." And with that she whirled away, stalking toward the ruins.

Gavin dropped to his haunches and blew out a long breath. This was not what he'd imagined for today. He'd brought Arabella here hoping to show her pieces of himself and his history he'd never shown anyone.

Instead, he'd lost his temper. He'd let his fear of losing her get the best of him.

He was not that man. Not the kind that would force or coerce. Not the kind that would use what she felt for him against her.

Growing up in the home she had, Arabella had had enough of that to last a lifetime.

But one thing was certain. He'd not give up on her, or a future with her, so easily. And he had to believe that deep down, in the stubborn part of her soul that he loved so much, she wouldn't either.

ARABELLA WALKED, UNCONSCIOUS of her path. Over crumbling stone walls, through muddy bogs, up steep inclines. Her boots were filled with water, her stomach churned, and her heart ached.

She kicked at a stone, remembering that morning at the beach when she'd thrown rock after rock in the water. She'd thrown a great many before discovering it wasn't Gavin she was angry at but her parents.

And just now, she'd done the exact same thing. Taken her anger and frustration out on Gavin when the person she was truly angry with was herself.

She stood at the center of the ruins, full of self-loathing.

She wanted to be strong. Wanted to be the woman Gavin seemed to think she was. But deep down she feared if he truly knew her, he'd turn away and not look back.

Why couldn't she be stronger? Why couldn't she take her future into her own hands? And what would her future look like if she did? Would Gavin be in it?

Those words . . . what he had said . . .

I ken the woman I've come tae love would not be satisfied with the life she left back in London.

Gavin loved her.

He *loved* her.

Knowing that . . .

Could she be satisfied returning to her cage back in England? Falling into old habits and patterns? Allowing her parents to make her choices and decide her future? Marrying a man of their choosing?

"Arabella?" Gavin's voice echoed off the stone walls. It sounded as if he wasn't far away. "I'll give ye the space ye wish for, but I need tae make sure ye are well."

Hearing his voice set Arabella's insides aswirl with confusion. Her indecision felt like a noose, tight around her neck. She wanted to throw something.

She stared down at the mud beneath her boots, catching hold of a memory—a promise she'd made herself. One that might serve as a vent for all the emotion swirling inside her.

"Arabella?" Gavin's voice was closer now.

She scooped up a handful of mud, edging back behind a taller section of wall.

Gavin jumped down through a low-arched window, about twenty feet away. She stood ready, taking aim. When he turned, she hit him square in the chest.

He stared at her, jaw slack.

The shock on his face was more satisfying than Arabella had even imagined.

"I ken ye are angry, but mud?" He tried to wipe it off but only managed to spread it down the front of his coat.

"I'm not angry." Arabella was ready with another handful. "I only thought to give you a taste of the mud bath I had the pleasure of taking the first day we met. When you left me back at the inn." She threw another handful, this time hitting his leg and spattering his boots.

Gavin began stalking toward her. "Don't think ye will come away unscathed, Arabella Hughes."

Arabella bent down for another handful, but Gavin was already running at her. She shrieked, launching one final throw. Mud splattered across his cheek.

He stopped briefly to scoop up a handful of his own. The low slant of his brows promised revenge.

Heart thumping, she turned to run. She'd gone three steps

when she hit a patch of mud. Her left boot slid sideways, and her arms shot out. Gavin caught her flailing wrist and pulled her toward him with mud-covered hands. She squirmed and squealed, wrenching her arm away, trying desperately to elude his grasp. "Gavin, don't!" He pulled her closer. "I'm sorry," she yelped, still trying to pull free.

But even coated in slippery mud, Gavin's grip was unrelenting. "As am I," he told her with a wicked smile, one hand closing around her waist. "Because any remorse I might have had for that day is long gone." He lifted his hand.

"No!" she shrieked.

But he was laughing, slathering thick mud across her cheek. She turned her head, but he only trailed his muddy hand down her neck. "Fiend!" she yelled, yanking one of her hands free and spreading mud across his brow.

"Savage, I think ye mean," he said low, painting her other cheek, her nose, her ear. "Or perhaps brute." He grinned, white teeth flashing.

She struggled against his hold, half panting, half laughing. "Let me go!"

"Never," Gavin promised.

He was using both arms to hold her in place. They were both breathing hard, chests rising and falling, and suddenly she wasn't squirming anymore. Suddenly, she was staring into Gavin McKenzie's eyes, a green so deep that she felt as though she could lie down in their mossy banks.

Something changed as he saw the way she was looking at him, all hints of playfulness melting away. His gaze grew hard, the lines of his face carved from granite.

What had he said earlier?

What did ye think all this was, Arabella? A game?

She remained frozen, her lips parted. Whatever this was, it wasn't a game. The drumbeat of her heart said there was much more at stake. There would not be a winner or loser.

But there was a very real possibility she might break Gavin's heart.

Or her own.

Pain and longing flashed across his face. That face that was infinitely dear to her.

He grasped her arms tightly. "What do ye want, Arabella?" he said roughly. "What do ye *want?*"

He'd asked her that before, but this time she knew the answer.

What she wanted was standing right in front of her.

There was fire, desire, a warning in his eyes. Something that said what happened next would not easily be undone. But Arabella didn't care. Didn't consider. Didn't think.

"You," she said. "I want you."

His lips came down on hers.

They'd clashed against one another for so long that when they came crashing together, mouths meeting, time seemed to stop. Gavin cupped her face with both hands and his lips were not gentle. But Arabella didn't want gentle. She wanted the rapture of his mouth claiming hers, matching her passion, her hunger, her need. But with the way his hands moved through her hair, over her shoulders, around her neck it seemed he was more than willing. The way he held her said he was ravenous. Not just for her lips. But for all of her. Her mind, her body. Her soul.

His hand slid down her neck, thumb touching her collarbone. She melted against him, flames dancing behind her eyelids as his mouth traveled over her cheek, finding the hollow beneath her ear. Longing and yearning and desire all twisted together at her center, urging him closer.

And despite the water in her shoes and the mud on her hands, every detail became the brilliant facet of a jewel. The pad of his thumb brushing her jawline. The earthy, silty taste of his lips. The stubble on his jaw beneath her fingertips. The saltwater scent of his skin. The ravens squawking overhead.

They'd long ago perfected a silent means of communication, able to understand what the other was saying without speaking a single word. And they did so now.

She tugged at the hair on the nape of his neck. *I cannot do this without you, Gavin.* One of his hands moved to her lower back, pulling her up, closer. *Ye could. But ye will not have to.* She sighed against his mouth. *I love you.* He nuzzled her nose, teasing her with his mouth. *Of course ye do, lass. Of course ye do.*

Arabella let out a half sob, half laugh. Against all odds, Gavin McKenzie, with his irreverent grin, his constant teasing, and his stubborn Scottishness, had worked his way into her heart. He'd challenged, entreated, and emboldened her. He'd shown her the possibility of a future she'd never imagined, a future that had become a consuming ache at her very center.

He pulled back, looking down at her. His heart in his eyes, his face solemn. "I did not expect ye, Arabella Hughes. I did not plan for ye." He shook his head and heaved out a breath.

Green eyes shining with emotion, he reached for her muddy hand, taking it in his and holding it against his chest. "But what does that matter when I've come tae love ye like I do? When if ye leave, ye'll break me? Cleave my very heart in two?" He swallowed hard, his voice rough. "I love ye." He pressed her hand to his heart. "And I ken what I'm asking ye tae give up, Arabella. I ken. But I'm asking anyway. Stay. Stay here in the Highlands and marry me."

It had been almost two months since she'd arrived in Scotland. Two months since this place had begun to work on her mind and heart, its winds tugging at her, its vistas soothing her, smoothing away her sharp angles, softening all the rigidity that had been bred in her from the day she was born.

Scotland. She remembered the journey north, thinking it was one of Dante's nine circles of hell. But now she saw it as a haven. A heaven. A place where she'd come to know herself, to know what she wanted.

And even covered head to toe in mud, she wanted Gavin Alexander McKenzie.

"Yes," she said simply.

"Yes?" he pressed.

"Yes, I'll stay."

"And?"

She smiled up at him. "Marry you."

Heart bursting, all of Arabella's hesitations, every qualm and fear and worry were razed under the force of Gavin's gaze. His mouth was on hers again, yearning and sweet. Impossibly soft.

"Gavin," she whispered.

"I think I loved ye from that very first day," he said between kisses. "The haughty set of your chin. Your insults. The way ye tried tae be so prim when inside of ye was a fiery Scottish lass."

She laughed against his lips. "It took me a little longer."

"I dinnae believe it." His fingers brushed behind her ear. "Ye loved me from the moment I stabbed that piece of fish and put it in my mouth."

She giggled, not denying it.

He kissed her again, slowly, tenderly, as if sealing the agreement between them.

When they finally pulled away from one another, Arabella's skin was humming, her heart singing. She took his hand, threading her fingers through his. "Do I still get that tour of the abbey you promised me? I'd like to know why you love this place so much, Gavin."

"Of course." He nodded, face grave. "But before I do, I have just one question."

"Yes?" Her voice was a breathless whisper.

He grinned down at her. "Now who, exactly, would ye say initiated that kiss?"

Nineteen

It was late afternoon as Gavin guided Baird up the hill toward Nan's house. He glanced over at Arabella, riding with her usual faultless posture even though she looked as if she'd fallen into a muddy bog. Gavin was halfway certain the groom trailing behind them thought them both mad, but he didn't care. Not when Arabella had agreed to marry him.

Not when, after he made her his wife, he would finally have a family again.

"We cannot let Grandmother see you," Arabella told him, laughing. "Heaven knows what she'd think if *both* of us come home covered in mud."

"I have a fair idea of what she'd think." He flashed her a roguish grin. "And she'd be right."

Arabella shook her head at him but then turned, catching sight of something. Her body stiffened.

Gavin followed her gaze to a carriage parked at the top of Nan's drive.

Arabella's face had drained of color. Eyes distant, she jerked on the reins. Her grip was tight, but he could see that her hands were trembling.

It was her parents. It had to be.

Gavin was trembling himself, not with fear but with anger, watching the way their mere presence affected her. He had the instinctive urge to step in front of Arabella, to shield her from what was coming.

"It's my parents," she said on a short burst of breath. Willow whinnied. "You should go."

He drew Baird closer. "Arabella, I'll not leave ye tae face them alone—"

"Gavin," she interrupted. "They cannot see you like this."

He looked down at himself, his coat and trousers covered in mud. Frustration flared in his chest.

A feminine figure came and stood on the front steps of Nan's house, but it wasn't Nan. Which meant it must be Arabella's mother.

"Please," Arabella whispered. "I must do this on my own. Go!" She urged Willow forward, not glancing back.

Everything within him wanted to go to her, to reassure her of his love, to be there as a support as she faced her parents. Gavin knew the hold they had on her. He'd seen the stricken look on her face. It took all his willpower to turn Baird away.

He could hardly recall the rest of the ride home. He was handing the groom his reins and walking inside, heading up the stairs and calling for a bath, but it was as if it was all happening outside of his body.

His mind and heart were with Arabella, desperate to know how she was faring.

When the tub had been filled, Gavin stripped off his filthy clothes and climbed in. The heat of the water turned the dried dirt on his hands and face back to mud, the sludge and silt slowly settling on the bottom of the tub. He stared at his hands. The only trace of that earth-shattering, heart-consuming moment he'd shared with Arabella was the hint of mud beneath the crescents of his fingernails.

He hated this. Hated that he felt so powerless. Who knew how long it might be before he received word from her?

Tonight? Tomorrow? And what damage might her parents do, what hurt might they inflict in the meantime?

He wanted to hold Arabella in his arms and provide a barrier against it all. Wanted to tease her, provoke her into laughing to lighten her heavy heart. And he wanted to tell her that she didn't need to be anything other than the magnificent creature she already was.

Because by the heavens, he *loved* her.

Mind numb with worry, he stayed in the water until it had grown cold. Forcing himself out of the tub, he dried and dressed himself, heading down to the dinner he hardly tasted. And then he paced back and forth in his study, uncertain what to do.

Gavin was accustomed to action, to doing. Fixing things that were broken. Inspecting the state of his property with his own eyes. Offering Nan his arm when he could see her rheumatism was causing her pain. But here, with Arabella, he could do nothing. This was something she would need to do on her own. And he understood why.

In the years to come, she needed to know it had been *her* decision. Not one he'd pushed her into. The choice had to be hers.

But that didn't make it any easier.

Gavin knew he'd go mad if he stayed here and paced the whole night. Instead, he called for Baird to be saddled again and headed toward the village, to The Fox and Crown where he'd met Arabella that first day.

He needed a whisky. Badly.

It was almost ten when he walked through the door. The inn had its usual patrons, but Gavin wasn't interested in talking. He was hardly in the mood to be good company. He took a seat at a dark corner table, grateful when he was served almost immediately, a tumbler of whisky set in front of him.

He took a sip of the amber liquid, enjoying the burn as it slid down his throat.

"In and out the same day, she was," said Tom Abercrombie, sitting at a table with friends.

Gavin turned away. When the man drank, he always blethered on.

"Aye?" said his companion.

"Aye." Tom set down his mug. "She was always a proud one, even when she was young. Thought she was too good fer the likes of us."

Gavin was on his feet and across the room in three strides. "Ada Hughes?" he asked. "Is that who ye're talking aboot?"

"Is it Hughes now?" asked Tom, blinking up at Gavin.

"Ada Callender?" he tried, impatient.

"Thasss the one." His words were slurred.

"And she came back through? Headed south?"

"Isn't that what I said? In and out the same day."

Fear struck Gavin's core. "Ye're sure? Was she traveling alone?" He grabbed the man's collar, resisting the urge to shake him. If her parents were gone, why hadn't Arabella come to him?

"Nae. She had a young chit with her, a pretty thing. Ainlie stopped tae change their horses."

His words gutted Gavin. Arabella was gone.

He staggered backward, trying to make sense of it, to understand what might have happened to so drastically alter Arabella's plans after the promises they'd made one another today.

Tossing a few coins on the table, Gavin headed out the door. He needed air.

He stalked outside, where cool wind rushed into his lungs. Sweet Highland air.

He shook his head, still trying to fathom that Arabella was gone.

Everything within him bucked against such a thought. He knew what he felt for her, knew that this thing between them was not some passing, fleeting flare of attraction. For him, at least, it went deeper than that. Bone deep. As if somehow the woman had worked her way into his veins, through his bloodstream, and straight to his marrow.

He couldn't see a future without her. Her presence was everywhere. At The Fox and Crown, where they'd first met. At the haberdashery, where he'd purchased a bonnet for his made-up cousin. On the beach. In the hills. And now at the abbey.

There would be nowhere he could go to escape her. No place she'd left untouched.

This place that had always been a refuge for him would become haunted with memories of her. Her smile, her insults, her scent, her laugh. Arabella had become a part of this place for him.

And he wasn't sure he could bear to stay here if she was gone.

Twenty

MOTHER STOOD AT the top of the steps, ice in her gaze.

Arabella's limbs were so wobbly that she nearly tripped as she dismounted. "Mother, what are you doing here? I thought—"

"I would think it obvious, Arabella," Mother said. Her bearing was rigid, her voice unforgiving. "I came to fetch you. You sounded so desperate in your letter. So anxious to escape the 'Scottish swine,' as you called them." She walked down the steps and looked Arabella over, nose wrinkling just enough to show her distaste. "But now it seems you prefer to roll in the mud right alongside them."

Arabella glanced down at herself. The front of her riding habit was covered in mud and her face . . . She lifted a hand and felt the crusted mud Gavin had smeared there. "I—"

"Go inside, Arabella. I'll call for a bath."

Arabella's heart stuttered in her chest. But the commanding voice was so familiar that her body obeyed on instinct. She handed over Willow's reins to the waiting groom and headed up the steps. Through the door. Past the entry. Up to her room.

She closed the door and leaned against it, her heart still pounding. In five minutes, it had all come flooding back. The strength of her parents' grip on her. The way she so easily bent to their will.

Her hands were still trembling. She looked down at her

shaking, dirt-caked fingers. She'd felt so certain of everything just minutes before, but now . . .

Arabella walked over to her dressing table as the door swung open. Mother stared at her in the mirror. "How could you?" she asked, voice soft. Dangerous. "Again?"

"It isn't what you think," Arabella said, trying for composure. "Mr. McKenzie and I—"

Her mother crossed the room in three quick strides. "No?" She scoffed. "What's this?"

With two fingers she reached out and touched Arabella's cheekbone. The softest brush. And there Arabella could see, in the crusted mud . . .

A thumbprint.

Gavin's thumbprint.

"Save your lies, Arabella. You have a future waiting for you back in London. One you seem to have lost sight of. After that incident with Mr. Gresham, I feared we were being too hard on you. Now I can only be grateful your father and I had the foresight to send you so far north, where the chances of anyone learning about your indiscretions are slim."

"Where is he?" Arabella asked. "Father."

"Back in London, keeping up appearances. Doing his best to make the connections that will secure your future. We've secured an invitation to a house party—"

"I don't want the future you and Father have chosen for me." Arabella's voice was quiet but firm.

Mother's lips curved in a condescending smirk. "And what is it you want, Arabella?" So different from the way Gavin had asked that very same question.

Arabella let out a breath. "I want to stay here."

Mother laughed. "There is nothing for you here."

Arabella met her gaze. "Grandmother is here." She stepped forward. "And I don't know what made you turn your back on her and all of Scotland, but I love her. I love this place. And I love Gavin McKenzie."

Mother's look was one of scorn. "And you've come to realize all this in two short months? My, my. You have been busy."

Arabella held on to the back of the chair tucked beneath the dressing table, searching for strength. "Why did you leave? What happened—"

"That is none of your concern."

"You're my mother, of course it's my concern," she said, voice sharp.

Mother's eyes widened. Arabella had never raised her voice before.

"Help me understand, Mother, why you left. And why you never looked back."

Something flashed across Mother's face. It was the first time Arabella could recall ever seeing any real emotion there. She was silent for several long moments before she seemed to come to some sort of decision.

Mother leaned against the bed that had once been her own. "I'm sure my mother told you what I was like when I was young. Impetuous. Ambitious. Daring. The worst sort of combination.

"After I returned from finishing school in England, nothing back here seemed the same. There was so little to do, to see. The social opportunities were few and far between. I longed for London, for a Season."

Arabella nodded, remembering what Grandmother had told her.

"There were few young men here," she went on, "fewer still who were the kind of man I wanted to marry. Until a certain gentleman returned from his grand tour, a Mr. Oliver Cameron."

Arabella angled toward Mother, tensing. This was something she'd never heard before.

"When I made a passing comment to my mother about my interest, she grasped at it. She wanted so desperately to keep me here. To that end, she did everything she could to encourage the match and give us time together. And I, Ada Callender, at the age of twenty, fell head over heels with Oliver Cameron." She spoke with derision, as if she despised the spirited young woman she'd once been.

Mother shook her head. "I was such a fool."

Arabella drew in a breath. "He didn't return your affection?"

"He was secretly engaged to another, a woman in Edinburgh. I was nothing more than a way to pass the time until he married." Her features tightened. "When I learned the truth . . . it broke me. I hated him. I hated my mother for encouraging something that had brought me such heartache. And I hated this place for all the memories it held.

"Mother felt guilty and heartsick over the whole thing. *That* was why she finally agreed to let me have a Season. And there, in London, I made a very different choice. Not one of the heart, but one of the head. I found safety and security with your father. A certain future."

Arabella swallowed. It was the first time she'd ever truly understood her mother. How hurt she must have been. Why she'd made the choices she had. And why she'd tried to mold Arabella into a young lady who never took risks. Never took chances. Who took the safe path.

Mother looked up and met Arabella's eyes. "Don't you see, Arabella? The heart's choices are not always in one's best interest. I'd like you to come back to London with me. I know you think you love this Mr. McKenzie, but give it time. Come home for a while. Give your head time to reason with your heart."

One moment of heartbreak had shaped every decision Mother had made in the years since. But Arabella was not her mother. And she didn't want the safe path. Not anymore.

She kept her tone gentle. "I'm sorry for your pain, Mother. But both my heart and my mind are made up. I'm going to marry Mr. McKenzie."

Mother's brows arched. "I see."

"And I know it must be hard to forgive Grandmother," Arabella rushed on. "But to have cut her off so completely? With no mercy, no forgiveness? She's heartbroken. Don't you see how you've hurt her?"

A little crack appeared in her mother's façade. "And if you choose this Gavin McKenzie, you'll be doing the same to me."

The words pierced Arabella. Because her mother was right. If she chose Gavin, she'd be rejecting the future her parents had chosen for her. When they married, she and he would make a life together here. It was the very reason the decision had been so difficult, knowing how much it would hurt her parents.

But now, realization flooded her.

"No, Mother," she said, certainty gathering within her. "Marrying Gavin doesn't mean I'm rejecting you. I am *choosing him*. Choosing the path that will bring me happiness. And if you reject me because of it, that would be your choice, not mine."

A heavy weight, one she'd carried far too long, slid from Arabella's shoulders. But it didn't prevent the weepy feeling that was climbing up her throat. "You made your choice, Mother, as you had every right to do. But that doesn't mean I have to make the same one."

Twenty-one

AS SOON AS Arabella's mother left, Grandmother came straight up to her room.

Before Arabella could say a single word, Grandmother's arms went around her, and she was encompassed in the warmest, fiercest hug the woman's petite frame would allow. Arabella sobbed, her body shaking with a rush of emotion. And once she started, she couldn't seem to stop, as if the reality that it was over, her decision made, was finally catching up with her.

Grandmother led her to the bed, arms still around her, as she continued to cry. They were not tears of regret, but rather an exclamation point that marked the end of her parents' control and the beginning of Arabella's self-determination. It took a long while before she'd cried herself out. When she'd finished, streaked tears drying on her face, Grandmother urged her to lie down, placing a pillow beneath her head and rubbing circles on her back while Arabella fell into a deep sleep.

When she woke, it was nearly nine o'clock. Her skin, still caked with dirt, felt dry and cracked. Her throat was parched. Grandmother called for a bath and a dinner tray, tending to Arabella herself. She was slow and thorough as she washed Arabella's hair, her ministrations gentle.

Molly was long gone, insisting she be allowed to

accompany Mrs. Hughes back to England, and Arabella hadn't voiced a single protest. Indeed, she felt a quiet sort of satisfaction at the thought of her mother being subjected to Molly's incessant whining on the long journey back to London.

After she'd bathed and eaten, Arabella had desperately wanted to ride over to Gavin's, knowing he was probably frantic with worry. But it was long past dark and far too late.

And Grandmother had a better idea.

They sent off a brief note, making the necessary arrangements for the next morning.

Arabella rose at five. She took special care with her appearance, wearing a sky-blue gown that would bring out the color of her eyes and arranging her hair in a loose chignon.

And then, shawl draped about her shoulders, she walked outside, drinking in the vista as the first rays of sun broke over the mountains. How different it felt now than when she'd first arrived, still heart-wrenchingly beautiful, still wreathed in an ethereal mist, but now the sight was familiar. Now it felt like home.

She kept a brisk pace up and over the hill toward Gavin's home. It was there she met Rory, dressed in full Highland attire, all ready to play. She nodded for him to begin.

Seven minutes later, no doubt following the awful sounds of Rory's bagpipes, Gavin emerged from his house. At the sight of him, Arabella's heart skipped a beat as if racing forward to meet him. This time, *he* was the one rumpled and half-dressed, purple shadows beneath his eyes. Had he not slept at all?

She waited, leaning back against the wall of the house, arms crossed over her chest.

He turned and their gazes met. His steps were measured as he approached her, as if he somehow thought this might be a dream.

When he stopped three feet in front of her, her face broke into a grin. "Do ye enjoy the bagpipes, Mr. McKenzie?"

There was a single heartbeat before he was sweeping her into his arms, pressing her so close that not a whisper of a Highland breeze could fit between them. "Ye stayed," he whispered against her hair.

"I stayed," she laughed, face pressed into the hollow of his neck. But then she pulled back a little, wanting to meet his gaze, wanting him to feel the truth behind her words. "Because I love you, Gavin Alexander McKenzie. And I cannot imagine my life without you."

He pressed a kiss to her brow, his arms tightening around her. "Nor I without ye."

They held each other for a long moment before a note of teasing crept into her voice as she asked, "But are you sure you want to marry me, Gavin? I'm stubborn. And hardheaded."

He touched his forehead to hers. "Am I not just as stubborn? Just as hardheaded?"

"I'm a horse thief," she reminded him.

His breath became hers. "All my horses are yours, Arabella Hughes."

"And I'm prone to throwing things," she warned. "Rocks. Mud."

"Insults," he continued for her, eyes laughing. "Yes, my darling, I ken. And I love ye all the same."

And then, so there could be no question about who initiated it, Arabella went up on tiptoe, framed his face in her hands, and kissed him.

At a young age Heidi perfected the art of hiding out so she could read instead of doing chores. One husband and four children later, not much has changed. She is a champion napper, has an abiding love for peanut butter M&Ms, and loves long walks on foggy days.

After a long stint of moves all around the country, Heidi recently settled down in the shadow of the Wasatch Mountains.

Website: https://www.authorheidikimball.com/
Instagram: https://www.instagram.com/authorheidikimball/
Facebook: https://www.facebook.com/AuthorHeidiKimball/

INTO THE LIGHT

Michele Paige Holmes

One

Inverness, Scotland, June 1857

THE TRAIN SLOWED as it approached the station, the wheels grinding against the steel rails as the whistle signaled its arrival.

"Inverness! End o' the line." The conductor's heavy brogue carried along the narrow corridor as he strode the length of the car.

Beatrice Worthington's hand squeezed around the letter that had been frozen tight in her grasp since Edinburgh when she had learned of her cousin's latest mischief. *How am I ever to explain?*

A belch of steam accompanied the final lurch as the train ground to a stop. If only she might remain in this uncomfortable seat indefinitely. She'd gladly stay just as she was, unmoving, for the entire return journey, as penance for having allowed this to happen. Facing her aunt and uncle would be difficult, but at least she could predict their reactions. She knew what consequences she could expect there—her aunt's screeching and the subsequent burden of additional back-breaking chores that would follow as soon as her uncle was out of town again. Her uncle's look of disappointment would be hardest to bear. He might not blame Beatrice, but she *had* let him down, had failed at the task assigned to her.

But she could not face her aunt and uncle until she had

faced *him*—Theodore Hughes, Earl of Langston, recovering war hero and her cousin's fiancé. Or he had been, at least. Before Violet had eloped with another man.

Beatrice swallowed hard, pushing back both panic and tears. All around her people were standing, claiming their belongings, chatting happily about having reached their destination. She ought to feel happy as well, to be free of these close quarters and the people packed so tightly together. The views of the countryside were lovely for almost the entirety of their journey. But the last day especially had been stunning—shimmering lakes, meadows of flowers, hills, and crags, and towering trees. She had hoped to escape into that scenery once she and Violet were settled at the earl's residence. Long walks in the garden at home were her solace, and though she'd been loath to come on this trip, she could not deny the allure of summer in Scotland's Highlands, with idle hours to walk about as she pleased, free from her aunt's tyranny, and the constant reminder that she was a burden to everyone. She ought to have known such a vision was too good to be true. Now she faced walking back to England if the earl did not take pity on her.

And why should he? She was to have escorted his fiancée to him, safe and sound. *Instead, I have lost her.* Beatrice felt lost as well. She soon would be if he turned her out once she had explained Violet's absence. With no return ticket nor money to purchase one—Violet had seen to that, no doubt as a safeguard against Beatrice coming after her—she had no means to return to England. No means for anything at all.

THEODORE WHEELED HIS chair toward the window, tipping his face toward the light he could feel coming through the panes, though he could not see it. Not yet. That day would come. Doctor Hulke had all but promised him. His eyes would be healed. His legs, too, though at present neither showed much improvement. *I am not working hard enough.*

Not for the first time he wondered if he ought to have insisted upon waiting to reunite with his betrothed, instead of allowing her to come to Broughleigh to spend the summer with him—chaperoned, of course. Her mother had insisted that Violet was shy and needed the time to become reacquainted with him. He did not recall her being shy at all, but perhaps their brief interaction a few years prior had not impressed upon her mind as greatly as it had his—or perhaps it had and she was simply eager to be with him again.

He had been smitten with her those few days they'd spent together at the Milfords' summer soiree nearly three years past. Before the end of the week, he had both requested that she write to him while he was away and had asked her father's permission to marry her upon his return from Crimea. With both parents and the lady amiable to the idea, he had gone away content that he had a future to look forward to after he had done his duty to the queen and country. *Who knew that it would all end up such a bloody mess?*

Theodore's fists clenched at his sides, and his head fell forward as he fought off the demons of his past. The quiet room suddenly burst with gunfire. Explosions rocked his chair. Men screamed and then went silent in death. The twin smells of gunpowder and blood tinged the air. The bitter taste of blood filled his mouth; he'd bitten his tongue. He cursed and gulped in a lungful of air. *Breathe. Breathe. Breathe.* He brought a trembling hand to his chest. He was still alive.

Blood from the cut on his tongue dribbled out the side of his mouth. He wiped at it with his sleeve, then realized how that would look to Violet when she arrived.

Violet. He pictured her face in memory, focusing on it with all his might. She was his lifeline. The reason he was still here.

Her letters had been sparse, but Theodore blamed that on the war. Undoubtedly, many she'd sent had been lost. Those he had received were kind and filled with the wonder and beauty of England's changing seasons—poetic almost in their descriptions of autumn leaves, winter's snowfall, and springtime blooms. Though not the declarations of love and devotion he had hoped for, the letters had nevertheless warmed his heart and helped him feel closer to home. Her tender caring seeped through the ink as she promised to pray for his safety and wished him a speedy return.

And now, at last, they were to be reacquainted in preparation for their marriage. He wanted her to feel comfortable. *More than comfortable.* But how would she feel getting to know a blind cripple? At the Milfords' they had danced the nights away. Now he could do little more than stand long enough to get himself into and out of bed each day. And though he hoped neither blindness nor lameness plagued him by the time their September wedding arrived, both still did on this first day of June. His body was healing, and there wasn't much he could do to speed that process.

His head bent toward his legs as he momentarily forgot that he could not see them. He'd told Ian to leave off the blanket this morning. Trousers would do fine to hide the scars, and Theodore didn't need to appear any more invalid than he presently was. He was not some decrepit man, left in his chair in the corner, huddled beneath a blanket. At thirty-two he was not yet ancient. The war had just made him feel so—in mind as much as body. His decade-younger bride was sure to notice when she saw him again.

Theodore straightened in his chair and tilted his face toward the sun. A bit of color would do him good. He would suggest to Violet that they walk in the gardens each day. With a little guidance, he could wheel himself alongside her, and the fresh Highland air would aid his healing. It was one of the reasons he'd chosen to spend his recovery here instead of in England. Despite their recent popularity with the queen and members of the *ton*, the Highlands were still far removed from the usual requirements of life in London or even at his estate in Derbyshire. He was not ready to face those again, to return to life as he had known it before the war. It had changed him, and he was not certain how to go back to the man he had been—or if he ever could.

But would Miss Worthington—young, vivacious Violet—be able to love him as he was now? Even if his infirmities were eventually healed, he feared this darkness of soul would continue to plague him.

The sound of carriage wheels crunching on the drive outside drew Theodore closer to the window as if he might view the scene below. He wished he could and felt deprived of that first glimpse of Violet emerging from the carriage. She had traveled far to be with him and was no doubt weary. Yet was it not a good portent that she had come so far, had wanted this time with him?

"Milord." Logan's voice carried across the library only a few minutes later.

Theodore swiveled from the window to face the unseen butler. "Has Miss Worthington been shown to her rooms?"

"Nae, milord." The butler drew in a slow breath as if pained.

"Whyever not? She has arrived, hasn't she?" Theodore wheeled himself closer to Logan's voice.

"Aye, but—nae. Not exactly."

Theodore held his tongue, waiting for Logan to explain. In the ensuing pause, he imagined the butler shaking his head and the grimace that lined his face whenever something did not go as planned.

"A Miss Worthington *has* arrived, but she isnae the Miss Worthington ye expected."

"Explain yourself," Theodore demanded more sternly than he'd intended, silently reminding himself that the Scottish staff here at Broughleigh were not used to being ordered about or having to answer to anyone at all; he was so seldom in residence here. "Violet has not come?" He must have misunderstood. All that cannon fire hadn't done his hearing any good either.

"She hasnae. There was some trouble on the train. Her escort will be telling ye."

No Violet? Disappointment pierced his heart as surely as the bullet had his leg, shattering his hopes into splinters as sharp and painful as the fragments of bone had been. He had not seen Violet in so long. He'd clung to the memory of her beautiful face these three years past. It was for her that he had fought so hard to come home. For her he had endured the agony of the surgeries that would make him a whole man again.

"Send the escort in," Theodore heard himself saying, but his voice sounded far away. If only he could see, could verify what was happening. But tearing the bandages away now would only hurt his eyes and decrease the likelihood of their full recovery. Instead, he listened intently as the door closed and then opened again a minute later. Soft footsteps came toward him across the room. They stopped and then a quiet voice spoke.

"Milord, I am Beatrice Worthington, Miss Violet Worthington's cousin and escort on her journey from London."

Theodore gave a curt nod. He recalled the letter, stating that a spinster relation would be accompanying Violet. "And where have you escorted my fiancée to, Miss Worthington?"

"Nowhere, Milord. What I mean to say is that it was not my doing. I was with her the entire way until Edinburgh. We had tea there and changed trains, and then I fell into a deep sleep. I cannot know for certain, but I believe she must have put something into my tea to cause me to sleep. I am not usually given to napping, and as the views of the countryside were so riveting, it is not likely I would have—"

"Miss Worthington, *what* has happened to my fiancée? Where is she?" Little wonder the woman was a spinster when she prattled on so. No man could be expected to endure that kind of nonsensical company for long. And just how *old* was she to have fallen asleep so easily in the middle of the day?

"I don't know where she is!" the woman exclaimed, sounding as if she were near to hysterics. "She only left me a note telling me she had gotten off the train and would not be going to Inverness."

"Off the train? Of her own accord? And you were tricked into sleep, you say?" Fear unfurled in Theodore's gut, a waving banner that all but proclaimed something terrible had happened. Something nefarious. Even now, this very minute, Violet could be in grave danger. The gunfire started in his head again, and it took everything he had to force it away.

"What did the note say?" he demanded. "Did you recognize the handwriting?"

"I did. It is written in Violet's hand. I have no reason to believe that it was anyone other than her."

"What did it say?" he repeated.

A long pregnant pause filled the room. He heard the spinster's shallow breaths and imagined a grey head bowed in sorrow.

"Miss Worthington," he tried again, marshaling patience he didn't feel. "Will you please read the note to me, as you can see that I am presently unable to read it myself?"

More silence met this request. Theodore counted to ten and resisted the urge to reach out to grab the woman's arm and shake her. *Violet may be in danger. Every second counts!*

"She said that she was not going to marry you after all."

Theodore reared back as if she had slapped him. Of course they were to marry. It had been agreed upon. He had her father's permission. Violet had danced in his arms, laughed with him, even allowed him to kiss her out on the balcony that summer. Her letters were proof as well, even though they had not expressed much affection. That she had taken the time to write to him meant she cared for him at least a little. Didn't it? "What are her exact words, if you please?"

"Pardon, milord, but I do not please. Trust me when I say her message is best delivered as it has been."

"I do not trust you. For all I know, you have been involved in some plot to hurt Violet or to keep us apart. Perhaps you are against the institution of marriage and intend her to become a spinster like yourself."

A sharp intake of breath met this statement, and Theodore felt a niggling of his conscience for lashing out so. But the fact remained that his fiancée was not here, and the woman before him had been entrusted with her care. She was to have seen Violet safely to his home, and Violet was not here, nor were her whereabouts even known. *What if she is lost somewhere? Alone? Abandoned?*

"I would like you to read the letter exactly as it is written," he insisted. "*Word for word.*"

"Please, milord. I cannot. I—"

"You cannot read? You are uneducated?" He should have arranged for a chaperone himself.

"You misunderstand." The woman had regained a portion of her timid voice. "It is only that my cousin's words will do you no good, and I do not wish to add to your pain. Suffice it to say, she is not coming. She is not going to marry you."

"The letter!" Theodore ground out, hating her pity, hating himself and his present inabilities. "Read it," he ordered in a low, severe voice.

"I will not, but I shall leave it with your butler. You may ask him—"

"I wish *you* to read it, Miss Worthington. You were the one traveling with Violet. I wish to hear the complete tale from you."

"Please—"

"Or is there no letter at all? Have you made this entire story up to somehow benefit yourself?"

"No!"

Theodore could not deny the sincerity in her tone, yet neither could he feel any sympathy for her. "I will ask you once more to read the letter you claim to have. If you refuse, I will have you escorted from my house, and you may walk back to Inverness on your own."

He waited several heartbeats, praying her will would bend to his. Turning her out was not a threat he wished to make good on. More than an hour by carriage separated his home from any other civilization. To turn a woman—even an exasperating, untrustworthy one—out on her own was unthinkable. His mother would have boxed his ears for even suggesting such a thing.

A weary sigh reached him, followed by the sound of paper unfolding.

"Very well." The spinster's voice quavered. "I apologize in advance for my cousin's words. She has never thought of much beyond herself, as you will soon realize."

"This does not sound like the Violet that I know."

"She is also an accomplished actress," the woman said. "But believe what you will. Here is the letter—word for word.

"Beatrice,

I hope you enjoyed your nap. At the least, you looked better when resting. All that pressing your nose to the window was rather ridiculous. Trees and hills are the same anywhere. Why those in Scotland should so interest you is beyond reasoning. At any rate, you shall be well rested for delivering this message to the earl. I will not be continuing to Inverness with you for a summer in the Highlands. I have no intention of marrying the old cripple Father has chosen for me. William and I have eloped, and we will be starting our life together. By the time you wake and read this, we will already be married, so there is no point in coming after me—not that you will be able to. Good luck with the old chap.

—Vi"

Old. Cripple. Eloped. No intention of marrying... Stunned, Theodore sat unmoving as his mind tried to make sense of the words and his body absorbed the instantaneous pain they caused. In the past quarter-hour, he had felt disappointed, fearful, frustrated, and now deeply hurt. *Humiliated.*

"I am terribly sorry."

"Did you go after her? Did you even try?" This was *her* fault. The chaperone's, who had not chaperoned well at all. "You might have gotten off at the next station, might have gone back. Who knows but that this man forced her to write that note before he abducted her!"

"I could not go after her," the woman—this other Miss Worthington—said. "Violet took my reticule and all the money I had with me. If I exited the train, I would not have been able to board again. And I knew that I must let you know what had happened."

"You fell asleep. That's what happened!" Theodore's shout

surprised even himself. His initial shock was being quickly replaced by anger, and the only one to whom he could direct it was this mystery woman before him. The one who was supposed to have delivered his fiancée safely to his home and had instead slept while who knows what had happened. "Who is this William fellow? Are you familiar with him?"

"I—I have heard of him. He is a local man Violet's parents did not wish her to continue association with. I did not realize it was he when we made his acquaintance on the train on the first day of our journey. They acted as if they had just met as well, and he identified himself as Mr. Fitzwilliam."

"It is he who has done this," Theodore exclaimed. "He has stolen her out from under your not-so-watchful eye. It was he who arranged this, who also took your money—who put a sleeping draught in your tea, if that part of your story is indeed true. And now Violet is in grave danger."

"If she is, it is of her own doing," the woman said calmly. "I have known her since I was twelve years old, and during that time she has been involved in one scheme after another—always for her benefit, with no thought given to the feelings of others nor the consequences of her actions."

"But she agreed to marry me," Theodore argued. "She wished it when last we parted, and I have her letters of the last two and a half years as proof of her devotion."

"Did she write to you often—or recently?"

Theodore had no answer—other than the one that pointed at the possibility that this Miss Worthington spoke the truth. Had Violet's affections changed? If so, why had she not simply told him, told her parents? Why the charade of coming to spend the summer with him?

Because it provided a means for her to elope. Theodore still could not believe it. He would not until he had proof. He would send a message to Violet's father and have it delivered posthaste, but not by this fool of a chaperone her family had arranged for. He'd send a messenger to the train station with a telegraph that could be posted at Glasgow.

"I see that I am not going to convince you, so I will bid you farewell. I apologize once more for my cousin's unkind words and her absence. I hope someday you will come to realize that the latter was a blessing."

"That hardly seems likely," Theodore mumbled, already mentally composing the message to Lord Worthington. Theodore wheeled his chair to the bellpull and rang for Logan. A minute later the door opened.

"I need a message taken to the train station straight away." With brevity, Theodore dictated the words but felt no measure of satisfaction when they had been dispatched. *Would they make the train today? Or was it already gone?* It might be that Miss Worthington would know, having just come from the station herself. Theodore opened his mouth to ask her, then realized the stillness of the room meant that he was alone. Where had she gone? How long ago? Had she taken him at his word that he would turn her out?

He rang for the butler once more. Logan returned almost instantly as if he had been awaiting the summons.

"Please send Miss Worthington in," Theodore said. "We ought also to post a notice in the papers and notify authorities in Edinburgh. Miss Worthington can assist with that by describing this William fellow, as well as what he and Violet were wearing."

Logan cleared his throat as if he had an uncomfortable particle lodged there. "Miss Worthington isnae here, milord. I dinnae ken where she's gone either. She was bletherin' on about some such. I asked if she required a ride somewhere, but she didna wish it. Said she'd walk."

"To where?" Theodore brought a hand to his temple,

rubbing absently at the near-persistent ache that had only increased this afternoon. "Nothing is a walkable distance from here."

"Aye. But she didnae wish tae trouble ye more."

"Well, she has." Theodore wheeled himself toward Logan. "Have the carriage readied. I am going after her."

Two

The afternoon sun was no doubt pinking her nose, but there was no help for it. Her hat, along with all of her other belongings, had disappeared from the train along with Violet. Beatrice supposed it was fortunate that she'd had her shawl draped around her as she slept, or Vi would have taken that too.

A hollow beneath the dirt twisted her ankle and nearly sent her sprawling. Beatrice righted herself just in time and fought back the latest wave of tears that threatened.

Do not cry. She wouldn't. Years of practice holding in tears, lest she suffer more at her aunt's hand, had helped her master that skill. If she'd cried before her uncle or spoken at all of her misery and abuse, Aunt Margaret would make life that much more miserable when he left again. And he was always leaving, hardly ever home, given his assignments in the House of Lords—and his dislike of his wife, Beatrice guessed. So she pretended as best she could when he was home, even admitting to mischief and misdeeds that ought to have been credited to Violet.

This time it will be my misdeed that disappoints him. Beatrice could imagine all too well the frown that would turn down his lips when he heard how she had allowed his only daughter to run off.

To distract herself from such thoughts, Beatrice lifted her

eyes to the stunning scenery—to her left, green hills crisscrossed with flowing contours made by the sheep grazing there. They were like the sea, with sculpted waves cresting one after the other, but with blades of grass in different shades of green instead.

Below these, growing right up to the narrow road, a palette of purple and blue wildflowers seemed to be cheering her on as they waved delicately in the gentle breeze. Farther up, the hills darkened with the thick clusters of sturdy pines covering the slopes. On her right, a stream gurgled over and around rocks and was steadily growing wider. Above it all, the sky stretched pale blue and wide, curving down to meet the surrounding beauty. She'd never seen a place so picturesque, and her eyes feasted upon every detail, committing them to memory. She would never be able to paint this scene—even if she'd had artistic talent, her aunt would never have abided the expense of the materials—but she could hold them in her mind and heart, recalling this solitary walk as the best hours of her exceedingly shortened summer in the Highlands.

Carriage wheels sounded behind her, and Beatrice hugged the side of the road, hoping the vehicle would pass quickly without taking note of her. Instead, it slowed as it approached.

"Miss Worthington."

Lord Hughes. Her body reacted as it had upon hearing his voice the first time, an almost liquid warmth flowing through her. Somehow his voice had been everything she'd ever imagined—deep, rich, melodious. *Until it turned angry.*

"Lord Hughes." She glanced at the carriage and saw him leaning out the open window as if he might see her, though his eyes were still bandaged. Thank goodness they were bandaged. It was terrible of her to think such a thing, especially considering the pain he must have suffered, but his inability to see had likely saved her. She'd not had the practice of events in polite society to learn to hide her emotions. She tended to feel—either joy or sorrow—with her whole heart. And it seemed her expressions reflected that.

What might Lord Hughes have seen in their first moments together? Initially, she had imagined that he would pay her little heed, as he'd be so swept up in his reunion with Violet. And while that would have been painful to witness, Beatrice had hoped it would have protected her, and her secret as well. But without Violet to buffer their interactions . . .

He is handsome. The thought came unbidden once more as she glanced at his strong chin and cheekbones and the chestnut curls topping his head. Muscled arms and broad shoulders gave him the appearance of health and strength, though he was confined to a wheelchair.

"I did not mean for you to walk back to Inverness. My earlier words were spoken in haste, and I apologize."

She had not expected this. No one ever apologized to her. "Thank you, milord. It is a fine day for a walk, so no harm done." Beatrice continued, picking up her pace as the carriage rolled alongside.

"May I give you a ride?" he called.

She shook her head, though her feet were already sore. "I do not wish to trouble you." *I do not wish to land myself in trouble.* More than she already had.

Violet was a fool. Beatrice had realized that within the first moments of meeting Lord Hughes. He had truly cared for her cousin. That much had been evident in his crestfallen expression and utter denial of Violet's betrayal. *To have someone who cared for me like that, who maybe even loved—*

Foolish thoughts. An impossible dream. Any man who had ever shown interest in her had been put off by Aunt Margaret's lies. No man within fifty miles hardly dared even say hello anymore, such was her reputation. Little wonder Lord Hughes had thought the worst of her immediately. Tired and distraught as she was, she did not feel she could face his censure again so soon. Better to have sore feet and sleep out on the moor if necessary.

"Please, Miss Worthington. I would appreciate the pleasure of your company."

Beatrice stopped and slowly turned toward the carriage as it also came to a standstill. No one had ever said please to her either. Her instructions were given as orders, never requests. Neither had she ever been told that her company would be a pleasure.

"Please come back to Broughleigh with me." Lord Hughes leaned forward and pushed the door open. "In your haste to leave, you've forgotten your trunk. We can retrieve it and take you to the station after that."

"My belongings disappeared with Violet. I have nothing to retrieve."

A frown turned down the earl's mouth, and Beatrice imagined a matching furrowed brow beneath his bandages.

"This situation points more and more to a robbery and abduction. Why should your cousin wish to take your clothing when she has plenty of her own?"

"Because she hates me," Beatrice blurted, then instantly realized it was the wrong thing to say. He would think she *was* involved in Violet's disappearance, that they had quarreled or some such thing.

Instead, he asked quietly, "Why should she hate you?"

"Because her mother does," Beatrice said, defeated. She had told the first truth; there seemed little sense in denying him the second. He would certainly think the worst of her now—a thought that hastened the return of tears that had threatened earlier. Why should his opinion of her matter? She was used to the disdain of others after so many years.

"Regardless of your feelings for each other," Lord Hughes said, "I would like you to come with me to describe what Violet was wearing and what the man—William—looked like as well. We'll send a notice to the authorities in Edinburgh. Perhaps, if they find them, you will have your belongings restored."

Beatrice swallowed back disappointment. He had not spoken to her kindly because he wished her company or truly regretted his earlier words, but because he still wanted to discover Violet's whereabouts. Beatrice held in a weary sigh. Denying his request now would make her appear even more guilty. She walked toward the carriage. At least riding would keep her out of the sun. "I shall be glad to assist you, milord."

The earl held a hand out to her as she stepped up. His grasp was strong and sure, and after she was safely inside, he held her hand a few seconds longer than necessary and gave a gentle squeeze of sincerity. " *Thank you.*"

Beatrice nodded as the hovering tears spilled over. *He thanked me.* Her third first in as many minutes. He released her hand, and she brought it near to her heart. His simple touch upended her even more than his generous words. When had someone last touched her with kindness? With any sort of affection at all—even if it was only gratitude for her assistance? She could not recall this either, and so she held her hand close and blinked away tears, thankful that he could not see her gratitude or the way she savored their contact.

Violet was a fool.

Three

"What's his lordship thinkin'?" Mrs. McNeil, the head housekeeper, tsked as she led Beatrice along a hall in the servants' quarters. "A fine lady like yerself doesnae belong down here."

"It was my doing," Beatrice insisted. "There are no more trains today, so I must stay—the night, at least. Possibly longer? And if I must stay, then I told Lord Hughes I wished to work in exchange for my return fare to England. He is already out a fiancée. He need not be out additional money as well."

"He can afford it." The housekeeper waved her hand in the air, then turned to look at Beatrice, her eyes appraising. "What is it a lass like yerself thinks to help with?" She looked down at Beatrice's hands, smooth and free of calluses and blemishes, excepting her old scar. "Sewing on a button, mayhap? But beyond that—" Mrs. McNeil shrugged and held her own work-worn hands up as if already exasperated with Beatrice's efforts.

"You'd be surprised." Beatrice smiled, grateful for the first time in her life for all of the labor her aunt had heaped upon her. Her hands were soft because of the abhorrent goose grease paste her aunt had insisted that Beatrice use every night—until she had discovered that beeswax had a similar effect. Rough hands would have given away the reality of her life during her uncle's long absences. Aunt Margaret had been fastidious in hiding the truth, from making certain Beatrice's hands remained soft to ensuring that she had no easily visible bruises.

Mrs. McNeil planted a hand on her ample hip and arched a brow. "Nae as fragile as ye look, eh?"

"Not fragile at all." Beatrice's smile widened. Already she liked the woman much better than the waspish Hortence, who ran housekeeping at her aunt's house.

"Come along, then." Mrs. McNeil resumed her steps down the hall. "It's nae as if we cannae use the help, what with his lordship deciding tae stay the summer and him injured."

"I am grateful the earl is allowing me to earn my ticket," Beatrice said truthfully. *Grateful to spend at least one night in this magnificent house in such a beautiful place.*

As if echoing her happy thoughts, the sound of bagpipes filled the hall. Beatrice turned to see a kilted, white-haired, white-whiskered man, pipes in arms, blowing for all his might.

"Arthur!" Mrs. McNeil marched past Beatrice toward the piper. "How many times have I told ye? Dinna play yer pipes in the house. Nae when the earl is here." She poked a finger into the man's chest.

The sound died as Arthur stopped blowing. "*Haud yer wheesht*, woman. I thought him could use a bit o' cheerin'."

"He needs healin', that's what. I'll be scunnered if ye bring the man more harm. Take yer pipes outside tae the hill. Off with ye." Mrs. McNeil grabbed Arthur by his shoulders and spun him around, marching him toward the kitchen.

Beatrice found herself smiling as she watched them go. She wasn't certain what the meaning of scunnered was, and neither did she wish to find out. She'd already brought more harm to the earl today and wished she could take away the pain he must feel at Violet's betrayal. But what could she do?

He didn't trust her, that much was clear. She wished he

could see that she wasn't a terrible person, that she hadn't come to take advantage of him, hadn't had anything to do with Violet's disappearance. She was used to the looks of disdain, used to people either ignoring her or speaking about her behind her back. But here . . . *Let it be different. Let him see the real me.*

Just this once. If the earl would only believe her instead of blaming her, then she might return to England content.

Or as content as one in her position might be, anyway.

THEODORE RAN HIS fingers over the paper resting in his lap as if that might somehow allow him to read it. Logan had already read it to him three times. Simple words. Short, as telegrams were of necessity. Theodore had them memorized, yet the cryptic message had told him nothing.

> DO NOT TRUST B W   STOP
> STARTING SEARCH FOR V W   STOP
> WILL BE IN TOUCH   STOP

The initials were easy enough to decipher. B. W. had to mean Beatrice Worthington, the woman currently employed as a maid downstairs—at her own insistence. *Strange, that.* He had offered that first day to send her home, but she had asked instead if she might work to earn her fare before departing. He had acquiesced, believing that having her here might help discover Violet's whereabouts, though he regretted that decision now. Beyond her initial descriptions of what Violet had been wearing the day of her disappearance, Beatrice Worthington had said nothing more to him about her cousin. And now she'd had six days here, during which she might have done any number of deceitful things, taking advantage of both his blindness and her proximity to his household. He would have Logan check the safe today as well as the paperwork in his office. And he'd ask Mrs. McNeil to check the silver and the storeroom and make sure nothing had been disturbed there. He would also have her dismiss Miss Worthington immediately—without pay—if he discovered she had indeed been into things she ought not have.

But why, if she was not to be trusted, had his fiancée been given into her care? What had Violet's father been thinking? The man had seemed sane enough the last time they'd met. He'd seemed particularly hopeful about the match. So why would he allow Violet to be escorted by an unworthy chaperone? It made no sense.

As for the telegram—why had a reply taken so long? And as for starting the search for Violet ... where did her father intend to search, and how? *Six days later.* She could be anywhere by now. *Already married, as her scathing note had promised?* Theodore slapped a hand on the arm of his chair, frustrated that he was unable to search for her as well. Instead, he sat at home, lame and blind and fearing the worst. It would not do. She was at least partly his responsibility. He would send more men—in addition to those he'd already sent—in his stead. He would get to the bottom of this and get his fiancée back. But first, he needed to remove the cause for her absence.

Theodore wheeled his chair across the library, maneuvering slowly to avoid the furniture scattered about the room. Reaching the bellpull, he rang for Mrs. McNeil. No doubt she, too, would be pleased to dismiss the untrustworthy newcomer.

Four

"Nae milord. She's done nothing wrong at all," Mrs. McNeil declared adamantly. "Truth be, Miss Worthington's better help than most. I gave her the worst tasks, as we do all the new ones, and she did them well and cheerful-like too—sweepin' out the ashes and startin' the fires afore dawn, emptyin' the chamber pots, scrubbin' the floors, bringin' in the firewood. Cook asked for Miss Worthington yesterday, so I sent her tae the kitchens. I peeked in a few hours later and found the two of 'em up tae their elbows in dough and workin' together amiable-like—no small miracle, that. Ye ken how particular Cook is about her kitchen. She doesnae care for most of the girls who are sent tae her. She asked for Miss Worthington again today—said she's a far sight more helpful than Molly, who comes from town twice a week."

"Is that so?" Theodore tapped his toe on the floor as he considered. "You've checked the silver and the stores?"

"Aye, milord. Nothin' amiss there. I dinnae think she's the type tae take somethin'. I offered her another dress tae work in, and she declined, sayin' she'd wear an apron over her own and wash her things at night as needed. She doesnae wish tae be beholden tae ye for anythin'."

"Hmmm." Theodore hadn't been expecting this report. It did not at all match up with the note about B. W. being untrustworthy. What was it she'd said that first day as he had tried to convince her to return to the house with him? Something about her aunt hating her. And Violet feeling the same as well. Lord Worthington obviously did not feel much differently, given the telegram. There had to be a reason for their contempt.

The simplest thing would be to pay Miss Worthington the wage owed and send her on her way. She wasn't his problem, and he had troubles enough at present.

"Thank you for your report, Mrs. McNeil. It was most enlightening. I shall consider it."

"It isnae my place tae say it, but if ye dinnae mind a suggestion, milord—"

Theodore restrained the downward pull of his lips. Unlike his housekeeper in England who ran his household efficiently and rarely made an appearance anywhere outside of her domain, Mrs. McNeil was both outspoken and seemed to be present everywhere. She and Logan had managed the running of Broughleigh for years, and both had little use or regard for the behavior typically found in their English counterparts. Here, in the Highlands, things were simpler, free from the rules and conduct of the English aristocracy. Here a housekeeper might offer advice to the earl she served.

"What is it? Go on." She would anyway, so he might as well act as if it was at his request.

"Ye might consider asking Miss Worthington tae stay on—nae doin' the work she is now, of course. She *is* a proper lady. Anyone can see such in her speech and manners. But she might be a good companion for ye. She's real pleasant and helpful at every turn. She has a way about her, almost anticipatin' everyone's needs. Half the time this week she'd a task completed before I'd asked it of her, like she knew my mind aforehand and went ahead and acted on it."

Just what he needed—a spinster mind reader as his

companion. Was the staff feeling sorry for him, then? The poor, blind cripple whose fiancée had left him for another more whole man. "So, you're telling me she is some sort of witch or psychic?"

"Nae, milord!" Mrs. McNeil sounded properly horrified. Even in this day and age, it was not good to be thought of as a witch in the Highlands.

"It's only that she's—observant and thoughtful. Kind."

Someone to wheel him around and make sure he didn't spill his tea. A nursemaid, she might have said.

"Hmm. I shall consider that as well." He would do no such thing but redouble his efforts to get out of this chair sooner than the doctor's prediction. "Thank you, Mrs. McNeil. That is all I require at this time."

"Good day tae ye, milord."

Theodore felt a shift in the air and imagined the swish of her skirts as she left the room. He waited only a minute or two before ringing for Logan. A visit with Miss Worthington herself might be the only way to sort out the contradictory information he'd received. He would ask why her relations thought so little of her. Surely, she would not be able to lie her way out of such a direct question. He might be unable to see her expressions at present, but he'd wager he would be able to hear truth or deception in her voice. And then, his curiosity satisfied, he would send her on her way, regardless of her answers. He'd no need of her help or companionship this summer.

MISS WORTHINGTON HUMMED as she worked. The snip of the kitchen shears kept time to the unusual tune, and Theodore imagined her kneeling between the rows, cutting herbs. He listened a moment, safely hidden behind the hedge where Logan had deposited him earlier. Though it was galling to have to be carried downstairs and guided outside, it was the only solution for a trek outdoors—something Theodore felt very much in need of each day. Today that timed well with his errand to speak with Miss Worthington and send her packing.

But just now he hesitated, indulging in a rare moment of peace. His place behind the hedge was shaded, the fresh air soothing—made more so by the lilting notes carried to him on the afternoon breeze.

What did she have to hum about? Would silence not have been preferable while performing a monotonous chore? Or was the melody helping her cope with her present circumstances by carrying her far away, to some other place and time? Maybe he ought to try humming to endure his current monotony, waiting for his body and mind to heal and his life to begin again.

He might have stayed there indefinitely, listening and wondering, if not for the nagging of his conscience. It wasn't good to spy like this—even if it was only with his ears. Besides, he'd come out here to get a distasteful task over with. Lingering behind a bush was cowardly.

Theodore cleared his throat and wheeled his chair down the path and around the hedge, careful to turn widely so it didn't catch his chair.

As expected, the humming stopped abruptly. A spade or some other tool clattered on the stone walk.

"Milord. Good to see you out of doors today."

"Would that I could say the same." Theodore's mouth twisted in irony as he touched the bandage covering his eyes.

"Oh! How thoughtless of me. I didn't mean—"

"I was in jest," Theodore said, surprised to find that he had been. *A difficulty is always better endured when humor is applied.* Where had he heard that, and when? And why had he only recalled it now, after months of grumping through his trials? "I came to request your company on my afternoon walk—er, roll—through the gardens. Logan usually joins me, but today he is otherwise occupied." He was setting up the walking bars that had been delivered this morning. *God willing, I won't need this chair much longer.*

"I would be happy to join you on your walk, but first, may I run my basket into the kitchen? Cook is expecting these herbs."

"Go on." Theodore waved a hand in what he hoped was the direction of the kitchen.

Miss Worthington's footsteps were quick and light as she hurried away, leading him to picture her as a slim, straight-backed spinster rather than one on the portly side. Only a few minutes passed before she returned.

"Cook said to tell you—" She hesitated.

"What?" Theodore asked, though he supposed he knew already. "She is displeased with me for taking you from her?"

"Ye-es. Though she used somewhat stronger words than that. Or at least I assume they were. I find it difficult to be entirely certain of what she says most of the time. Though the way she waved the knife she was holding and then pointed at me rather implied her meaning."

Theodore's mouth quirked at the image invoked by her words. "No doubt she did. She'll have more to say to me when I tell her that you are done working in her kitchen." He wheeled his chair around and started the way he had come.

Miss Worthington stepped up beside him, not attempting to guide his chair, he noted. *Good.* He'd have had words for her if she had. His arms were strong—stronger now from weeks of wheeling the chair—and he only needed someone to direct him occasionally.

"Have I done something wrong?"

Had she? Aside from losing his fiancée. "No." He shook his head. "I came to tell you—"

"On your right," she interrupted. "There is a low branch sticking out. It will strike your cheek if you continue straight."

Theodore adjusted his chair and they continued. "I came to tell you that Mrs. McNeil assures me your work has been exemplary—something we both find rather odd for a woman in your position. But regardless, you have earned your ticket home, and one will be purchased for you first thing tomorrow morning when you are delivered to the train station in Inverness."

A slight pause met his announcement, followed by a quiet, "Thank you, milord."

She didn't sound thankful, rather sad. Disappointed. *Because she has not had time to accomplish whatever plot she'd planned here?*

"Where will you return to in England?" he asked. "Now that you are no longer needed as a chaperone."

"I have other duties awaiting me—similar to those I have performed here for the past week."

"Is that not highly irregular—a woman of your position employed as a maid?"

"A woman *in* my position has very little say or choice in her employment. I consider myself fortunate to have a roof over my head."

He stiffened at her reply and felt a twinge of guilt. Was it possible he had judged her wrong? Maybe her skills as a chaperone were so poor—obviously, given how she had bungled this opportunity—that she had little choice but to work as a maid. What else was a gently bred spinster of little means to do?

But there was still the matter of the telegram from Violet's father. "Are you employed in the household of Violet's parents, Lord and Lady Worthington?"

"I am."

Had he imagined that sad little sigh, so quiet and quick it would have been imperceptible to one not listening so keenly? "They are your relations, are they not? Violet is your cousin, you said." Some distant cousin once or twice removed, perhaps. But even so, a relation, nonetheless. Why, then, would they not support this elderly spinster cousin properly? Lord Worthington was certainly capable of it. *Because he does not trust her?* The woman had to have done something to earn that distrust and therefore become relegated to the position of a servant. Perhaps chaperoning his daughter had been Lord Worthington's way of giving the woman another chance. *And look what she's done with it.* Theodore felt his face warm as his ire rose yet again.

"Violet is my cousin. Lord Worthington is my father's elder brother. When my parents died, he took me in."

Brother? "Elder?" Theodore questioned, trying to make sense of what she'd said. This was no distant relation, and Lord Worthington was not terribly old—not even two score years older than his daughter. So the child of his *younger* brother would be— "How old are *you*?"

If she thought it a peculiar or inappropriate question, he did not detect such in her reply.

"I am six and twenty. Five years older than Violet. Unfortunately, we have never been close, though we have resided in the same household since I was twelve."

A surge of shock, followed swiftly by an awareness that had not been there a moment before, rippled through him. *Just twenty-six.* He'd believed himself to be speaking with a woman much older than himself. Certainly not one younger, one still of marriageable age, no matter what society said.

Instead of cooling his ire, this revelation only fueled it. He wheeled his chair faster. He'd bet that this *young* spinster had not ruined the opportunity presented to her as a chaperone. No, indeed. Quite the opposite, in fact. She'd manipulated circumstances to her benefit extraordinarily, getting rid of his bride-to-be while conveniently inserting herself into his path.

And he had nearly fallen for it—allowing her to stay the week, walking with her now, beginning to know her, even wanting to trust her.

"Tell me, Miss Worthington, do you enjoy living with your aunt and uncle? Do you like working for them?"

"I—I do my best to be grateful."

"You are unhappy, then?"

"There is a rock on your left, milord. You might wish to—"

"Do not attempt to change the subject." There were many rocks along the pathway. He'd grown accustomed to the constant jarring. "Are you unhappy with your circumstances in England?"

"I see not why it matters to you. The rock is—"

"It matters a great deal. I insist that you tell me."

"I cannot recall having *ever* been happy since my parents and brother died. You really must adjust your chair so—"

"You saw an opportunity and took it!" Theodore pounced. "A way out of a life you despise, with an aunt and cousin who hate you and an uncle who mistrusts you. You got rid of Violet and came here to try to take her pla—" With a jolt, his head snapped as his front left wheel struck something hard. A half second later he was airborne, launched up and forward out of his chair as it came to a jarring stop. Theodore's hands flailed wildly in front of him, bracing for an impact he could neither see nor protect himself from.

"Milord!"

He collided with something much softer than the pathway, caught in its folds as he crashed to the ground.

"Milord, are you all right?"

The frantic feminine voice in his ear roused him from the shock of his fall. "Miss Worthington?" Theodore braced his hands to push himself off the ground, only to realize that she was between him and the path. Outraged, he rolled to his right, freeing her. "What are you doing, fool woman?"

"Trying to prevent you from further injuring yourself." She huffed. "Since you would not heed my warning about the rock."

Beside him the sounds of her rising were apparent. Theodore lay blind and stunned on the ground, uncertain which of the many avenues flooding his mind to pursue. Anger seemed obvious, a cover for his humiliation.

"You ought to have said there was a *stone* in my path. A rock implies something small, negligible."

"Rock and stone are synonymous. Why would I have mentioned it if it were negligible?" Exasperation punctuated her every syllable.

She had a point, though he was reluctant to admit it. He listened as she shook out her skirts and presumably brushed dust from them—dust from the hard ground she had landed on. *Because of me.*

"Are you injured?" he asked, reverting to the gentlemanly course he ought to have chosen first. It was likely too late for that now when he'd been behaving as anything but one.

"You wouldn't care if I were," she said, her voice quavering again as he had heard it that first day in the library.

He wondered how he had ever assumed she was an older woman. Just now he could hear only youth and vulnerability and sorrow in her voice. *So much sorrow.* And he had caused at least a little of it.

"I would care." He sighed wearily, tired of the world as he now viewed it—blindly, through only a lens of mistrust and fear—and mostly tired of himself for the cad he had become. War did terrible things to a man, but he was no longer at war, and he needed to cease acting as if he were and stop blaming his poor behavior on his experiences there.

"*You* are hurt, aren't you?" Her skirts brushed his arm as she leaned over him.

Theodore shook his head. "I am well enough." He hoped. The sutures in his legs had long since healed, and with her cushioning his fall, it was doubtful any further harm had been done internally. Theodore leaned forward and sat up, then lifted each leg so that his knees were bent. He turned toward Miss Worthington, keenly aware of her hovering presence. Oddly, it did not bother him. He did not sense her pity, only a true desire to help if needed.

"Would you like me to bring your chair closer?"

"Yes, please." There it was, that quality that Mrs. McNeil had spoken of—a sense of knowing what one would request before he requested it. Only now, he did not find it so odd, but rather he appreciated that she had not tried to pull him up herself or run screaming for help.

"If you'll hold it for me, I can get myself into it again."

"It's right here." She took one of his hands and braced it on the wheel. "This is the right side, as it is facing you."

"Thank you."

Her hand lingered on his a second longer. "I apologize for my surliness. The fall did hurt, but that was no reason for me to be cross with you." She released his hand and stepped away again.

She had every right to be cross with him when he had been nothing but irritable with her since their first meeting. Theodore clenched his hand over the wheel, curling his fingers around it in an attempt to shake off the effects of her touch. It had been almost affectionate, and he fought against his warm reaction, against the desire to feel her hand on his once more. Miss Beatrice Worthington was not Violet. Nor did he yet trust her. Perhaps it was she, and not her cousin, who was the accomplished actress.

"I'm ready when you are," she said.

Theodore nodded. This was not going to be pretty. He could imagine well enough how repulsive his awkward movements might seem to her. *Good.* That might end her scheming if she'd thought to take Violet's place.

"You have a lovely garden here," she said as he began to position himself. "I haven't had too much time to appreciate it, but the wildflowers are simply breathtaking. Your garden isn't like most of those I've been to in England, with precisely trimmed hedges and pruned bushes, with not so much as the tiniest branch out of place. There is a wildness to the plants here. A more natural and simple beauty. Take those clusters of dark pink flowers growing against the wall over there . . ."

She prattled on about the plants she'd encountered in the past week, describing them in detail—clearly focusing on them instead of him—all while he struggled to pull himself into the chair. It was a process, maneuvering himself in front of the chair with his back to it, then using his arms to lift himself onto the seat. Twice he tried and failed. She said nothing each time but continued her litany of botanical observations. Instead of finding it irritating, he found himself grateful—and fully aware that she was doing her best to take the attention off him during his struggles.

At last, he was settled. He leaned his head back and would have been staring up at her, were his eyes not bandaged. "You can stop now, Miss Worthington. Though I appreciate your efforts at making an awkward situation less so."

"Was I that obvious?"

He chuckled. "Only a little." *A lot.* And he appreciated it.

"Well, you *do* have a lovely garden."

"I am not sure it has ever been so thoroughly esteemed by anyone before." He smiled of his own accord. "In addition to all this wildness"—he waved his hand about—"we have an elegant rose garden. Would you like to see it?"

"I would like that very much."

"I will show it to you, then." Theodore placed his hands on the wheels and started down the path, surprised to feel that he, too, would like that very much.

Five

THE ROSE GARDEN was as unique as the rest of the grounds. Like a traditional English garden, it was groomed. Unlike anything Beatrice had visited before, it formed a spiral, the neat path leading one in circles to the very heart of the garden.

"Oh my," she exclaimed, clasping her hands in delight as she took in the tall, newly opened blooms bowing toward the center of a tiny, circular courtyard. Two curved benches faced each other on the little terrace, only a few feet separating them. Beatrice seated herself upon the one opposite Lord Hughes' chair.

"This has become my favorite place of late—since the roses started blooming," he said.

With hands braced on either side of her on the bench, Beatrice leaned forward, eyes closed, as she inhaled deeply, the sweet scent making her almost giddy. "I can see why."

"It's a good reminder to me that I haven't lost all the joys of life," he said. "I am still able to enjoy the fragrance of roses, to savor the taste of Cook's fresh-baked loaves, to appreciate the lovely melody you were humming this afternoon."

Beatrice blushed and felt grateful he could not see her, then instantly felt terrible for having such a thought again. "The fragrance of this garden and the taste of Cook's fresh-baked bread are much more delightful than a few notes of an old song."

"What old song was it? I did not recognize it. The tune was unusual."

Beatrice wondered and worried about where he was going with the question. Thus far, everything she had told him he had twisted to use against her. She answered warily.

"It is an Indian melody. My mother used to sing it to me."

"Was she from India?"

Beatrice smiled. Had Lord Hughes been able to see her pale skin, he would have known that was impossible. "No. But that is where I spent my childhood. Father moved us there when I was just an infant."

"Did you like it there?"

"Very much." She dreamed of it still—her lavish bedroom and the four-poster bed with its airy curtains that were drawn around her each night, always making her feel as if she were a princess in some fairytale. The landscape had been so different in India—England was prettier, she now granted—but the sights and sounds and unique smells of her childhood held strong in memory. She had loved her home. Her parents. Her brother.

Lord Hughes cleared his throat as if something uncomfortable were stuck in it. "You said your parents perished when you were twelve?"

"Our home caught fire." Now she was the one with something caught in her throat. Fourteen years later, the memory still seared her heart as much as the heat had her skin that night. "I was the only one who survived. My mother pushed me out the second-story window of my bedroom."

"And you lived to tell of it? Obviously," he added quickly with a solemn nod.

"My arm was broken in the fall, made worse because I rolled on it in an attempt to stop it burning. The curtains were on fire, and they touched the side of my nightgown . . ." She didn't describe any more. It was enough for him to picture what had happened, and it was more than she cared to remember. Whenever she thought about it too long, she could feel the flames scorching her skin and remember the absolute terror of those moments. She still had the scars to remind her every day.

"My mother used a vase and then a candlestick to shatter the window glass. She helped me onto the ledge and pushed me. Then she went back inside to help Father find my brother. I never saw any of them again."

"Good God," Lord Hughes murmured. "What a terrible lot to have endured—and at such a young age." His lips pursed as if he were holding back something more. Though she could not see his eyes, it was apparent, in his shallow breaths and the slow shake of his head, that he was stricken by her tale.

She was surprised at the genuine grief lining his face. "It was. A lot." Aside from her uncle, he was the first person who had ever acknowledged such. Who had expressed any sort of understanding or considered that she'd not only suffered the terror of that night and the painful injuries she'd sustained but the loss of her entire family, the loss of her life as she had known it—forever.

"Afterward you returned to England—to your uncle's home?"

"It was a few months afterward. I was in hospital for some time. But yes, eventually, after arrangements had been made, I was put on a ship to England."

"By yourself? No one came for you?"

Beatrice smiled sadly. "No one came for me. Another family my uncle was acquainted with was traveling to England, and it was agreed that I should be under the care of their governess as well, for the duration of the voyage. So I was not entirely alone." Though she had very much felt she was.

Feelings that had been made worse by witnessing that whole and functioning family—what she once had but that had been taken from her. Beatrice recalled crying more on that voyage, particularly as they left India behind, than she had during her weeks in hospital. Before, she had been able to pretend she would be going home again, that her parents and brother were still to be found. Sailing away from India had made her loss real and permanent.

Across from her, Lord Hughes drummed his fingers on the arm of his chair. A contemplative expression pursed his lips, and she wondered and worried again what he must be thinking. Would he still honor his word to pay her way home tomorrow? She was reluctant to go, to leave this place of beauty and respite—even working as she had this week had felt rejuvenating—but at least at her aunt's home she knew the expectations, knew how to endure and survive. Here she remained uncertain whether he was friend or foe. Whether he would turn her out at once—as he had threatened that first day—or if he would show compassion. And how her heart might react to either.

"Did you not find a new family in your aunt and uncle and cousin? Were they not welcoming?"

"My uncle was." Beatrice chose her words carefully, as she always must, lest the truth of her living circumstances return to her uncle's ears, and her aunt make her life the worse for it.

"But not your aunt and cousin?"

"Milord, may I inquire as to why you are asking so many questions of me?" She stood abruptly, feeling suddenly trapped in the small space. Lord Hughes' chair stood between her and the exit, but perhaps she could squeeze by.

"I am merely trying to understand why I have never met or heard of you before," he said with far more patience than she'd seen from him previously. "When I made Violet's acquaintance, her parents were also in attendance at the Milfords' summer party. As a member of their family, it would seem that you should have been in attendance as well. That you should have had a Season—even if it was some years before your cousin's. And I should have remembered that or recalled your name or meeting you. The *ton* is not so enormous that most of us are not at least somewhat acquainted with the names of those in the various families. Yet I cannot recall having ever heard yours until this week when you presented yourself and told me of Violet's disappearance. I mistakenly—until this afternoon when you told me your age—thought you to be a much older relation, one far past middle age. Which would have explained my not knowing you."

"I can see how that might seem suspect," Beatrice said, attempting to view things from his perspective. "I can explain the reason for my absences and why you have never heard my name before—if you will allow me."

He nodded. "Please."

That word again. Beatrice closed her eyes briefly. His kindness was almost harder to bear. "I have never been included as part of my aunt and uncle's family. My uncle encourages it when he is home, but that is rare. He keeps his own apartment near the House of Lords and is very invested in his work there. My aunt . . ." What could she say that was truthful, yet would not come back to hurt her if Aunt Margaret heard of it? "When I first arrived back in England, I had little use of my arm. The surgery to mend it had not been entirely successful, and it was many more months before it could bend properly and I was able to use it to do things like eat or dress myself—simple tasks one does not think much of until they are suddenly impossible."

"I understand completely." The earl's mouth twisted in a wry smile as he patted his legs. "It is frustrating, is it not?"

"Very," she agreed. "I am most fortunate in that I regained the use of my arm. But even now, it does not look quite as it should, and I have some scarring." How strange it was to be telling this to him, to one who—had he been able to see—might have been easily repulsed by her oddity. Her aunt and cousin certainly were and had warned her repeatedly that any man who ever saw her arm would be doubly so. "To shelter me"—to protect herself from gossip—"Aunt Margaret has kept me away from events where I might be shunned."

"So you were never given a proper Season? You never attend *any* events with your uncle and his family? Even a country soiree was considered too much for you?"

She shrugged. "It has never been my choice whether or not to accompany my aunt and cousin, but the company they keep is often cruel. I am not certain that, given the opportunity to attend with them, I would have actually chosen to."

Lord Hughes nodded once more. "I understand that as well. It is partly why I have elected to convalesce here in the Highlands, away from the eyes of those who would judge and find me wanting."

"I do not find you so," Beatrice said, without thinking before her mind had considered the consequences of such an admission.

"Yet I have found you lacking at every turn, have not even had the grace to allow you to explain yourself, have not considered your words or position." He shook his head as if disgusted with himself.

"Until now?" she suggested, working to keep the hurt from her tone. His disbelief and easy dismissal of her that first day had stung, as had his complete ignoring of her the past week. They had not spoken once during her tenure working in his home, though their paths had crossed as she lit fires, cleaned, and even delivered his tray a time or two. Dare she hope his opinion of her had been revised? It ought not to matter if it had or had not—she was leaving tomorrow—but somehow, it did. She wanted just one person, wanted *him*, to know her heart. That it was pure and good. That she bade him no ill and had not consciously brought any upon him with Violet's disappearance.

Lord Hughes said nothing for several long seconds. Quiet shrouded the little garden. Even the birds and insects seemed to have taken themselves elsewhere. But it was not peaceful. Beatrice sat once more, tense and silent, wondering what he would say or do next. What did he think of her now? Her aunt was not here to plant the seeds of doubt and distrust that she had sewn so completely at home. There the neighbors had all heard how suspect it was that Beatrice was the only survivor of a fire that killed her entire family—a fire whose origin no one was quite certain of.

She'd heard the gossip and seen the fingers pointed on too many occasions to count. *Murderess. She killed her family. Watch out for her.* For years, she'd never understood what she'd done to unleash such hatred or why her aunt had gone to such lengths to promote such an awful rumor. Until that day when her aunt and uncle had argued loudly in his study.

Lord Hughes rolled his chair closer until their knees were nearly touching. "I owe you an apology—several, actually. I have mistrusted you, suspected you of misdeeds, and then today, accused you of terrible things. I have no excuse for that, but I wish to explain anyway. If *you* will allow it."

"Of course, milord." Beatrice's heart raced at his nearness, even as her feelings soared, then plummeted, then soared again at his words. He wanted to apologize—truly apologize— to her! *He suspected me.* He regrets his actions.

"Your news about Violet brought hurt and humiliation, both of which I reacted to with anger and sent hurtling at the messenger. I was too busy thinking of my problems to even consider yours, notwithstanding you had outlined them clearly for me. I am sorry. Truly sorry for my actions that day and this week."

"It is all right. You had reason to be upset."

He shook his head. "But not at you. For that, I apologize. As for suspecting you, since the war I have had difficulty trusting anyone. I am often fearful and think the worst of everyone. It is probably a blessing Violet did not come—for whatever reason," he added hastily. "I am not the man I was. I would only have disappointed her. I have disappointed you."

"You have not. I had no expectations of your character," Beatrice assured him. However, that was not entirely true. She'd believed she knew him quite well before coming. But he couldn't know that. Neither would she ever divulge how she had come upon such knowledge nor the way she had admired him for some time. She'd come close enough to such revelations with her admission a few minutes before.

"It has been the poorest behavior, severely lacking. Can you— *will* you—forgive me for it? For not believing that all you spoke and presented to me was truth and nothing more?" He held his hands out blindly.

"Yes." Her whispered word felt almost like a promise as she placed her hands in his. She'd already forgiven him, truth be told. He was hurting in body and soul, and she could not hold him fully accountable when he was already suffering. "Think no more on it, I beg you."

"You are too kind."

Beatrice blushed again. "You are the first person to ever tell me that. Or to apologize. I thank you for both."

"Will you allow me to show my thanks to you? For your courage and fortitude in coming here to face me?" His fingers folded over hers.

"It is not as if you were a lion in his den," she said, her heart light at their continued touch.

"Not far from it though." He growled.

Beatrice laughed. "Actually, a lion might have been more preferable that first day."

"Probably," he agreed. "You see, I had been so looking forward to the company. I needed someone other than myself to think of. I was eager to show my beloved Highlands to—"

"Your beloved," Beatrice finished softly as she withdrew her hands from his. She would do well to remember her place, and that it was never and would never be that of any Violet held. Even if she had thrown it away. Though Lord Hughes could not see now, no doubt he remembered Violet's blonde curls, her full lips, her clear blue eyes.

If he could see me . . . He wouldn't be likely to look twice. Brown hair, brown eyes, and a plain face did not attract a man. The only thing he might have noticed was the odd angle at which her arm hung—never entirely straight and the bend not quite natural either. It was her one remarkable feature—and not one she enjoyed receiving remarks upon.

"I *was* eager to share this place with Violet." Lord Hughes cleared his throat. "But she has not come—has found greener pastures, shall we say."

Beatrice stifled a laugh. "She is not a cow." Though the idea that he had nearly called Violet one made her heart light once more.

"A wild pony, then," the earl suggested. "Not wishing to be tied down to the likes of me."

"That is a rather good comparison," Beatrice agreed. "I am sorry to say."

He waved his hand dismissively. "That is in the past. I do not wish to speak of Violet any longer. I have spent the last week pursuing her whereabouts through various means, and nothing I have learned is encouraging. So let us move past all of that."

"All right," Beatrice said hesitantly. What did he mean exactly? Perhaps he intended to invite her to join him for dinner tonight, where they would speak of things other than his missing fiancée. She tried not to get her hopes up, but an evening spent in his company—just a few pleasant hours—would be a memory she might cherish in the future.

"I am wondering if—would you consider staying on as my *houseguest*, instead of a housemaid?"

"As your guest?" she asked, certain she misunderstood. "Beyond tomorrow?"

He nodded vigorously. "Say, for the next few months. You came here expecting a summer in the Highlands, did you not?"

"Yes, but—"

"Wonderful. It is settled, then." He wheeled his chair backward, away from her. "Shall we go in? It will be time to change for dinner soon."

"I have no other clothes to change into," Beatrice reminded him. "And as for staying the summer . . ." Oh, how she wanted to say yes. But how could she? It had been one thing to come here with Violet as a chaperone. With the two of them and Lord Hughes' current injuries, it had been *almost* permissible. Or so Aunt Margaret had somehow convinced herself when she had sent them off, sans an older traveling companion. Even Violet's maid had not come, as Lord Hughes had assured Aunt Margaret that he would provide one for Violet upon her arrival. Beatrice had half suspected she would be asked to serve as Violet's maid, though that would have made Violet's position—without a chaperone—that much more tenuous and suspect.

But then Lord Hughes and Violet were to be married at

summer's end. Perhaps, since they were already betrothed, there had been more allowance for this excursion. *Had been.* There certainly was not any sort of allowance for one now. To stay . . . would mean certain ruin. And while she ought not to care—society already thought so ill of her—she had to, for her uncle's sake if nothing else. *For Lord Hughes' sake as well.* Though, society never judged men in quite the same manner as they did women.

"I am flattered by your offer, but I cannot accept. Though I am quite past marriageable age, I am not so old that society would not judge me harshly for such actions. I am sorry for that, for I think I might have enjoyed your beloved Highlands and our time together greatly." Eyes stinging with regret, Beatrice slid past him and started down the spiraling path. Lord Hughes rolled his chair after her, not saying anything more.

What was there to say? Her brief summer had come to an end.

Six

THEODORE TOOK DINNER alone in his room, as he had taken to doing most of the time lately. Eating had become both tedious and embarrassing. It was amazing how much one's sight was necessary for such an activity. It was as Miss Worthington had said this afternoon. He had not appreciated the ability to complete simple tasks until that had been taken from him.

When his sloppy mealtime was complete, Theodore wheeled his chair to the opposite side of the large room where a divan, writing desk, and cushioned chair used to reside. Taking their place were two long, parallel bars, braced on poles that had been anchored to the floor. Before dinner, Logan and Ian, who had been recently hired as his valet, had helped him become familiar with the bars, and now it was time to try them.

Feeling his way with his hands, Theodore positioned his chair between the two, then clasped his hands on either side and pulled himself up to a standing position. He hovered there a minute, most of his weight still being supported by his arms. The doctor had warned him to take it slow, to try standing a little at a time each day before attempting to walk. But Theodore had no use for that advice. Life was passing him by while he sat blind and lame in a chair each day. *No more.* He was going to walk again if it killed him.

Gradually, he lessened the pressure on his arms and settled more onto his legs and feet. His right leg was stronger than the left, having sustained less injury. His left leg, he was fortunate to still be in possession of. He'd glimpsed it only once before passing out, and the gaping mass of tissue, blood, and bone had been utterly horrifying. He'd hoped for death in those seconds of agony. Later, he had awoken to find himself in a great deal of pain but still in possession of both life and leg—and utterly alone on the abandoned battlefield, his leg having been bound by some unknown soul. Theodore had cursed the man, whoever he was. Death had been beckoning, and the bound leg had no doubt slowed the process. He'd tried to undo the Good Samaritan's work but had fainted again with the searing pain and loss of blood.

All through the long, dark night the scene repeated. He'd awoken alone to excruciating pain and then sank into brief reprieves of unconsciousness. He wasn't certain how long he'd lain alone on that field, if it was hours or days.

His next memory was of blinding light—an explosion that simultaneously shook him awake and blinded him. He wasn't alone anymore but jostling along on a cart. The screams and cries of men surrounded him. His own joined them, a howl of pain and confusion.

Then, a miracle. A nurse leaned over him, whispering words of comfort.

"I can't see," he'd told her, clasping her hand as if it were a lifeline.

It was. He hadn't realized how much until later when news of Miss Nightingale's heroism and good works became more widely known.

"The leg's infected. It will have to be amputated," a male voice said.

"No!" Theodore struggled to sit up.

Miss Nightingale's hand squeezed his reassuringly. Her voice was firm when she turned away from him and spoke again.

"He's with the group that just came in—those that were blinded in the explosion. Will you condemn this man to being a cripple as well?"

"I've little choice if he wishes to live," the faceless doctor said.

"Wait, then," she insisted. "Give me forty-eight hours with him to improve his condition. If I cannot, or if he worsens before then, you may operate."

Theodore took another step, the pain shooting up his leg proof that it was still there. Miss Nightingale had performed the miracle—cleansing his wounds in a manner that made him wish for death again but that ultimately staved off the infection and saved his leg.

His next miracle had been the enterprising surgeon Dr. Hulke, who was able to repair the limb and even offered hope for a return of his sight. And the third blessing—being sent to the newer Renkioi Hospital, where conditions were greatly improved.

His initial recovery had been long and slow. For weeks, there'd been no escaping the pain. Theodore had clung to gratitude that he was alive—and to the memory of Violet and her letters, carried with him in his pocket and still in his possession when he'd been shot.

Theodore trudged forward, his arms bearing less of his weight. This afternoon, Miss Worthington had also reminded him of how thankful he ought to be, though he doubted that had been her intention. Hearing her story and imagining her loss and suffering at such a young age made him feel all the more ridiculous for his complaining. He'd seen men who had suffered severe burns, and he had always believed that to be the most excruciating kind of pain. A bullet might be removed, a wound closed, a bone set. But when one's flesh had been devoured by fire, there was no escaping the agony or the weeks of torturous treatments. It was one of many things he had witnessed that he knew he would never forget but wished that he could.

He took another step, this one more difficult. The doctor had suggested that if he were able to walk again, he would likely require the use of a cane the rest of his days. How was he supposed to hike the hills and moors he loved or hold Violet in his arms and dance with her when required to use a cane? How was he supposed to navigate the stairs in his house or climb into and out of a carriage or any other number of things? No, a cane would not do. Not if he could help it at all.

He took another step and then another. Beads of sweat sprang up along his forehead, though the room was cool. His left leg trembled. He forced it to move anyway. *All the way to the end of the bars.* To the window, then back again. That was his goal today. Perhaps a dozen steps each direction. That was all. Not so difficult.

Excruciating. His arms burned now too. He could not delay or he risked collapse. His right leg moved again. It was stronger than he had hoped. His left was far weaker. He lifted it anyway and set it down, wincing, then leaning his head back with a groan of pain. *Move quickly.* For the merest second, his left foot and leg carried the weight as he stepped with his right.

How many steps had he taken? He had to be nearly there. He tried picturing Violet in his mind, as he had so often during the ordeal of healing. He'd been doing this for her. He would walk for her. But her face blurred in his memory. He had none to replace it with but instead thought on the gentle voice of Miss Worthington as she had described the plants and flowers in his garden today. He doubted she cared for them *that* much, but in those moments of his shame and frustration, as he'd hauled himself back into his chair, she had chosen to focus elsewhere. She had understood what it was to be embarrassed at not having one's body perform as it ought. She had true empathy because she had experienced something similar herself.

It was then that he had decided to believe her. Before she'd answered all those questions about her past. Before he had realized that the telegram he'd sent to her uncle had probably been answered by her aunt instead. Before he'd realized what a life of loss and hardship she endured. He had believed her because her kindness had been too genuine—not dissimilar from Miss Nightingale's—too thoughtful to have been anything but the absolute truth.

A mere hour later, he had done more than believe her. He had desired her company and wanted her to stay the summer, to be his friend, to pull him from his own bleak existence. It seemed they each could use a friend, and he'd thought the idea rather brilliant. He had not expected her refusal. It had stung and served to convince him even more how very wrong he'd been about her. She'd not committed some crime, getting rid of Violet and attempting to take her place. She'd been as innocent a bystander as he, perhaps more so for being stranded without any means to get home or so much as a change of clothes.

He was beginning to think Miss Worthington's initial assessment was correct—he might be better off for Violet's having left him if that was the kind of person she was.

Theodore managed four more steps and then bumped up against the edge of the windowsill. *Thank you, Lord.* Arms shaking, he lowered himself to the floor, too exhausted to feel victorious or to contemplate the return trip. He turned his body and slumped against the wall, sweaty and breathless, his left leg throbbing. He'd have to ring for help. There was no way he could make it back to his chair on his own.

Theodore rested a few minutes, gradually feeling at least some of his strength return and then suddenly realizing his grave error. The bell pull, beside his bed, might as well have been miles away. Even if he had been near it, the cord did not extend to the floor, and he would not have been able to reach it, sitting as he was.

Sighing with exasperation at his own stupidity and weakness, he tipped his head back against the wall. He was going to need to hire more help. Logan, Ian, Mrs. McNeil, and the few other servants he employed managed the estate just fine. But they could not be expected to manage him as well, to help with his recovery, to read and write correspondence for him, to be here to aid him when he was down—which he suspected was going to be a frequent occurrence, given this first shaky walk. Little wonder Mrs. McNeil had suggested Miss Worthington stay on as a companion—

A slow smile curved his lips. *Miss Worthington.* It was the perfect solution.

Tomorrow morning—once Ian found him and helped him off the floor and into his chair—Theodore was going to make some changes to the staff. Including the *hiring* of one Miss Worthington and giving Mrs. McNeil a well-deserved raise.

Seven

BEATRICE TURNED BACK for a last look at Broughleigh. This morning, the stately manse appeared even grander than when she'd arrived. The buff stone appeared white, sparkling almost, with the sun shining directly on it and the backdrop of its wild and colorful gardens all around. A quick glance up and she noted that the windows were bare, devoid of the face she'd hoped to glimpse one last time. *It is better this way.* Better that Lord Hughes had not come down to breakfast with her nor to say goodbye. Had he done so, she might not have had the courage to actually leave.

All night she'd tossed and turned, asking herself why she felt so compelled to protect a reputation that was already in tatters, thanks to her aunt. But though people believed her a murderess, they'd never actually had any proof. If she stayed the summer as a guest of Lord Hughes, her virtue would be beyond repair—a fact that could only hurt her uncle. She supposed she felt loyalty to him because he had cared for her mother. He cared for her as well, like a daughter, even if he wasn't around much to show it. When she was younger, he'd often brought home sweets or ribbons or other small gifts—one for Violet and one for her, as if they were equals in his mind. Beatrice had never forgotten those small kindnesses. And his biggest one of all, granting her leave to accompany Violet this summer. Somehow, her uncle had persuaded Aunt

Margaret to allow it, and while time spent in Violet's company was never pleasant, and Beatrice had worried greatly over meeting Lord Hughes, it had been a holiday to look forward to, nonetheless.

A very brief holiday. Beatrice faced the carriage, then accepted the footman's hand and stepped up.

"Good morning, Miss Worthington."

Her foot missed the floorboard, and she nearly fell backward out of the carriage. "Good—morning." She regained her balance and took the seat across from Lord Hughes. "I did not expect you to accompany me to Inverness. It is not necessary." Just when she'd thought to have mastered her emotions, here he was to jumble them once again. But she could not honestly say she regretted his presence. Quite the opposite, in fact.

"I could not miss the opportunity for an outing," Lord Hughes said. "Though they are difficult for me at this stage of my recovery, they are also beneficial."

"Of course," Beatrice murmured. *He did not come for me but for himself.* Still, she now had the chance to study his face during their drive, to commit to memory the only man she had ever held feelings for.

The carriage door closed, and a minute later they were off, headed down the long drive. Beatrice did not allow her gaze to linger on the house. It was just a house, after all. It was the man in it who had affected her so.

Across from her, Lord Hughes reclined easily against the seat. His legs were stretched out in front of him. One hand lay palm up across his thigh, while the other rested on a basket on the seat beside him. "Forgive me if I fall asleep during our drive. I spent a fitful night without much rest."

"I am sorry to hear that." She did not share with him that she had experienced the same. "I hope your discomfort was not due to yesterday's mishap in the garden."

"If you are referring to the way my obstinate nature sent me vaulting from my chair, then no, it has had no lasting effects." A wry grin curved his lips.

"I am glad, and I am glad, too, that you seem none the worse for it in spirit." If anything, he seemed better for it, cordial in every way this morning.

"No, indeed. I'm still obstinate. It will likely take another spill or ten for the Lord to humble me and put me in my place."

Beatrice wasn't certain how to respond to that. If she agreed with him, it would be calling him stubborn and arrogant—which she rather felt he was, given their interactions this week. But it would be impolite to point that out. If she argued that he was not in possession of such traits, she would be lying.

Lord Hughes leaned forward, his face near hers as he whispered, "You were supposed to inquire about what kept me awake much of the night."

"Oh." Beatrice brought a gloved hand to her mouth to hide her smile, though he would not have seen it. "Pray tell, milord. What kept you awake during the long hours of the night?"

He leaned back against his seat once more. "I spent the night on the hard floor of my bedroom, seated beneath a drafty window where I was both uncomfortable and cold."

"That seems a rather poor choice of sleeping accommodations," she said, both amused and curious at the direction their conversation had taken.

"Aye, well . . . yesterday, I had walking bars installed in my room. I can brace my hands upon them and take steps. The goal is to exercise my legs until they are strong enough to move on their own without assistance."

"That is wonderful." Beatrice clasped her hands together joyfully. "I did not know your injuries were not permanent. I am so happy for you."

"Congratulations are a bit premature." He frowned. "I was able to manage a dozen or so steps but had not the strength to turn around and return to my chair. Hence, I was stuck for the night, as the bell pull was nowhere near me."

"How dreadful. I am sorry." How galling that must have been for him, not to mention miserable.

"It is all right. I have come up with a solution. Today, the bars are being relocated to the ballroom. I intend to hire an assistant to be with me at all times—both to aid in moving my chair as needed when I am at the bars, to read and write correspondence for me, and to walk with me in the garden each day. Logan has been helping with all those tasks, but he already has far too many responsibilities."

"I see. Is that why you are going to Inverness today? To find an assistant?"

He shook his head. "I believe I have already found one, but I need to persuade her to stay." He turned his face toward hers again, as if he could see her through the bandages covering his eyes. "What say you, Miss Worthington? Will you consider staying on as an employee? That is different from a houseguest. Your reputation would not be in jeopardy."

"Would it not?" Hope rose within her, light and soaring and threatening to lift her from the seat. He *had* come this morning for her. *To persuade me to stay.* It was only because he needed help, of course. But still—he had chosen her when he might have employed any number of other people.

"Other women of a similar age are employed in my household. And their reputations are not in question. Yours would be no different."

"I would have to be treated as an employee," she insisted. "I would keep my room downstairs and take my meals with the staff as I have been."

"Hmm." His lips pursed as he considered. "I do see your

point about the location of your room. But part of your duties would require you to take your meals with me. I cannot locate the items on the table as needed; I cannot tell you how many times I have knocked over my glass in the past week alone. In short, I am a nuisance and a burden to my already overburdened staff. They were all overjoyed to have your help this past week, but I believe you will give even greater assistance to me and them in this new position."

He spoke as if she had already accepted his offer. She supposed she had. It *was* a good solution. It would allow her to stay here, in this lovely, peaceful place, and to spend time with him. All while under the protection of employment.

"There is the matter of your salary—"

"Room and board would be plenty," she assured him.

Lord Hughes shook his head. "It will not. I pay my other employees well. In fact, Mrs. McNeil was given a raise just this morning. You will also be paid, beginning with last week's wages, which, as they will not be spent on train fare to London, should be used to purchase the things you need. I've instructed the driver to take us to what I have been told is the best modiste in Inverness, where you may purchase dresses and other garments as needed and desired. It is likely you will get messy at times, as you assist me—as I suspect you did yesterday, bracing my fall as you did—so you will need several dresses in your wardrobe."

"Several?" Beatrice laughed. "I haven't even agreed to this yet."

"But you will, won't you?" He reached blindly for her hands as he had done before, and she took them in her own again, at once savoring the warmth and humanity of his touch. She felt certain this was not usual behavior for an employer to engage in, but nothing was normal about their situation. He'd been wounded grievously, both in war and matters of the heart, and he needed someone to help him find his way again. *And I need him.*

No. She banished the thought immediately. She needed this summer, a few magical months in which to restore her soul after the years of battering it had endured. That was not too much to ask, to wish for, was it? Not too self-indulgent when, at the same time, she would be helping him.

"Yesterday, I felt a compassion from you, an understanding that none other has shown me thus far. Doctors have done all they can. My staff has been most patient, but *you* know what it is to have a body incapable of normal function. You understand the frustration and embarrassment that comes with such a challenge."

Beatrice nodded her silent understanding.

Lord Hughes continued, "You also know what it takes to overcome. You have suffered your own pain and humiliation and have not forgotten what it feels like to be in the throes of each."

"That is quite a lot you sensed in me yesterday when I am not certain I did much other than failing to prevent you from exiting your chair prematurely."

"My fault entirely. We have already established that I am most obstinate and often arrogant. You should know I am also moody as of late and melancholy frequently." His expression was that of a wounded puppy.

"Hmm . . . you make this position sound most appealing."

"You have witnessed me at my worst this week. But I feel that—around you—I might be able to return to my best again. I might reclaim the man I once was." He held her hands tight, awaiting her answer.

Beatrice breathed in deeply, striving to slow her speeding heart and to keep herself from reeling with the sudden giddiness that threatened her composure. He was being entirely serious, and here she felt like laughing with joy. "You *are* perhaps the most stubborn man I have ever met. And your arrogance . . ."

"I *know.*" He groaned. "Perhaps you will be able to teach me some manners as well."

"Perhaps."

"So you agree?"

His tone was so hopeful that she had little choice. "Yes." She laughed. "I will stay as your assistant."

"Splendid!" He released her and collapsed back upon his seat as if exhausted, though a smile lit his face. "Your first assignment is to accompany me on a picnic on the shores of the River Ness. We'll eat before beginning our shopping on High Street. It will be up to you to see that I remain presentable."

A picnic. Exploring a new city. Shopping. All of it with Lord Hughes. She could hardly believe it was true. But it was.

Eight

Miss Worthington gripped the handles on Theodore's wheelchair and forged on, over the grassy knoll toward the ruin of Urquhart Castle. "The ground here is so strange. Every step I feel almost as if I will sink, but then it springs me back up again."

"Unfortunately, my chair does not react to Scotland's moist soil quite so well." He grimaced as his hands pushed against the wheels, attempting to move them forward. "I should have waited in the carriage. You would be able to enjoy the views much better without me."

"Without my tour guide? I think not. You've yet to tell me the history of this castle. That is the price for my diligence"—she gave his chair a mighty shove and it rolled forward again—"in getting you up this slope."

"I believe ice cream would be an appropriate reward as well," he said, recalling her fondness for the treat on their excursion to Inverness.

"I believe I feel stronger already."

They trudged on until Miss Worthington proclaimed that they had come as far as they were able without her fearing for his life. "The ground is terribly uneven and slopes the other direction. I would not like to have to fetch you out of the lake."

"Loch," he corrected in an overexaggerated Scottish accent. "When in Scotland—"

"Speak as the Scots," she finished. "*Loch* Ness is the prettiest loch I've seen, and we passed ever so many on the journey from Edinburgh."

"Describe it to me." He requested such things of her frequently and appreciated that she saw the world—or at least this corner of it—through a wide lens of wonder and appreciation. She had a way with words that painted a picture so vividly that he hardly felt cheated having his eyes covered.

"The water is the deepest blue, making the loch appear both bottomless and mysterious."

He nodded. "They say it has more water in it than all the other lakes in Scotland and England combined. And, of course, there is the ancient monster said to lurk there."

"It looks as if it might hold such a creature." She sounded breathless, as if overcome by the possibility. "The hills surrounding the loch are as bright a green as I've ever seen and slope down to the edge and then simply disappear beneath the water as if they are the tops of grand mountains, rising from its depths. There is little shore, at least that I can see from here."

Theodore smiled, picturing it.

"The sky is a mysterious grey today, dark and brooding, as if guarding a mystery that we cannot see. It is the whole of it—the sky, green hills, and deep blue of the lake—that make it so very lovely."

"Tell me of the castle now," he said.

Still keeping a firm grip on his chair, she moved slightly. "Urquhart looks to have been made up of several parts as if there were many different outbuildings. Or perhaps it once was whole, and these piles of stone are all that is left, the rest having been eroded entirely."

"A bit of both, I believe," Theodore said. "It dates to the thirteenth century—as do many other castles still standing. It's our ancestors' fault that Urquhart is a ruin. The English laid waste to it in the late 1600s to prevent the Jacobites from using it."

"That is a tragedy," Miss Worthington said, her voice wistful. "It would have been a lovely place to live. I think I should have done little else but sit in one of the windows and stare outside at the loch all day, had it been my home. At least there is still a tower."

"You should walk down to it," Theodore said. "Leave me here and take a few minutes for yourself to explore." What he would have given to have been able to go with her, to run down the hill and scramble over the stones. *Someday.* By summer's end, would he at least be able to walk with her in the garden? Thus far, his progress had been slow—much slower than he had anticipated.

At least I will be able to see her by summer's end. He hoped. But what if the result of last month's eye surgery was not what he wished? It was strange talking with Miss Worthington and not being able to put a face to her voice. That he had no reference point, no idea at all what she might look like, bothered him even more than not being able to walk with her.

"I think I shall just view the castle from here," she said. "I don't wish to see the destruction up close. It is tragic what men do to one another and the land in times of war."

"I couldn't agree more," he said somberly, his mind instantly returning to Crimea.

"I'm so sorry." Miss Worthington's breath touched his face as she crouched beside him. "That was thoughtless of me. I didn't mean to remind you—"

His hand found hers on the arm of his chair and covered it. "You keep my mind from the dark places more than you can imagine. But they will always be there, lurking. And when they force their way out, it is good to know I have someone beside me."

"I am glad to be here."

"I hope so," Theodore said quietly. She had been here three weeks—two as his assistant. They had been the best two weeks he'd experienced since returning from the war, and perhaps even the best two weeks he'd had before it, including his time at the Milfords' soiree. Miss Worthington placed no societal expectations upon him. She'd not a false bone in her body nor hair on her head. She was not above doing even the most menial tasks and found great joy in the simple pleasures of life, many of which he had been missing out on before she came.

Humbling himself to accept her help hadn't been easy. But she had made it as painless as possible, sharing stories of her former mishaps when her arm had been healing and then laughing with him at his attempts in the dining room—most often a fiasco when he was left to his own devices. She encouraged him at the bars each day, praising his every step, urging him to take one more. She taught him how to function in his current dark world—how to use his fingers to count the spaces on the table and locate his glass on his own. The angle at which to hold his fork so he didn't stab himself in the chin every time. She was kind and patient and the godsend he hadn't realized he needed in his life. The weeks of summer were slipping away, and already he feared they wouldn't be enough.

Nine

"The rain has foiled our plans today, hasn't it?" Lord Hughes said as Logan wheeled him into the library.

"I suppose it has," Beatrice agreed, looking at the large drops smattering the windowpanes and thinking wistfully of their planned visit to Clava Cairns, the ancient burial site and circle of standing stones the earl had told her about, that would now have to wait. "In England, stormy days meant the choice between being trapped inside or walking in the rain."

"You chose the rain?" Lord Hughes guessed as he rolled his chair toward her.

"I did." She gave a determined nod of her head.

He sighed. "I'll have Mrs. McNeil locate the umbrellas."

Beatrice turned from the window to face him. "Perhaps later," she said. "I have another idea. We can play chess."

Lord Hughes's mouth opened in surprise, then his lips turned down into a pout. He placed a hand over his heart as if wounded. "You mock me, my lady."

My lady. He really shouldn't say things like that. "Not at all." She hurried toward him. "I have always wanted to learn to play and never had the opportunity. Today I do, and you can teach me."

"Hmm. The blind leading the blind, or something like that."

"Exactly." She beamed. "I'll get the chess board."

Two hours and two sandwich trays later, Theodore found himself in the midst of the most leisurely, yet most enjoyable game of chess he'd ever played. It was slow going of necessity, as he'd patiently explained each of the pieces, their positions on the board, their purpose, and their manners of movement, all while unable to see. It was a nice change of pace to be teaching Miss Worthington something. He wondered if that hadn't been her intent all along.

"Remind me again all the things this piece does and if it's very valuable."

Theodore held his hand out, and she placed a piece in it. His fingers traced the curves. "A knight. Somewhat valuable, yet also expendable. It is the only piece that can jump over another."

"Is it also the one that moves in an L? That is what I've written in my notes." Per his suggestion, she'd written a list of the pieces and the movements each made to refer to throughout the game and any future ones they might play.

"Yes, two over in either direction and one up or down."

"Or one to the left or right and two up or down," she finished, taking the piece from him.

"Yes, but it only captures what it lands on."

"It has just landed on your rook."

Theodore frowned briefly, then clapped his hands. "Well done . . . perhaps. Describe to me the board now so I may see what that move cost you."

"My brave knight to your queen." She surrendered it to him and made the move, playing for him as well. "I believe you are going to win."

"Technically, *you* are going to win," he corrected, "since

you have been playing for me." He reached for another sandwich, found one, then brought it to his mouth easily. A week ago, he might have knocked the whole tray over in his clumsy effort, but Miss Worthington had taught him how to gently search with his hands in a manner that helped compensate for his lack of sight. He was trying to repay the favor by sharing with her all his best chess strategies.

"It is a win that I am learning how to play at all. Thank you for agreeing to teach me."

"It has not been as frustrating as I had anticipated. You have done a good job being my eyes." It had been most enjoyable, sitting near her like this, chatting and eating and strategizing together.

"And you are an excellent teacher."

He shrugged. She was an exceptional student. "I have played enough in my past that I am able to picture the board in my mind. What I am *unable* to visualize and what I most wish I might is your face."

"Me?" Genuine surprise rang in her voice. "I should think there are hundreds of other things you might wish to see more. Why, the whole of the Highlands is magical, mysterious, stunningly beautiful. Each place we have visited or plan to visit would be far more fascinating to view."

He disagreed. "I can imagine those, particularly with your apt descriptions. But I cannot imagine you. You have not described *yourself* to me." Theodore leaned back in his chair, considering. "But that is a brilliant idea. Will you do just that— tell me what you look like?"

She did not answer at once, then, "I fear you will be disappointed." Her voice was quiet. "I am no great beauty like Violet."

"Violet's beauty did not travel beyond her complexion." He saw that now, how he had been attracted solely to her physical appearance and then swept up in her flattery of his. *As many men would have been.* As he might still have been, had he not been forced to see the world with means beyond his eyes. "I have seen your soul, Miss Worthington—Beatrice. May I call you that?" He had wanted to for some time and did not wait for her to answer his query in the negative. "You emanate both true beauty and joy. Did you know that is the meaning behind your name? Beatrice—bringer of joy or happiness."

"I did not. Where did you learn such a thing?"

"From a book, no doubt." Theodore turned his head, imagining the shelves lining the room. It was not as grand as the library at his English estate, but it still held a great many volumes that he had enjoyed over the years. "There are several famous Beatrices, from Shakespeare's *Much Ado About Nothing* to the Beatrice who serves as Dante's guide through paradise in *The Divine Comedy*."

"I have read neither," she admitted, sounding embarrassed. "Aunt Margaret grants me very little access to their library, even if I were permitted time to read."

A slow smile grew on Theodore's face. "It seems there is something else I can share with you—my library and my love of literature. We'll start today if you are not opposed to reading out loud to me?"

"Not at all. Would you like to begin now? I can put away our game while you decide on a book."

Theodore heard her rise but reached out and managed to grasp her wrist before she had moved too far. "The books can wait. They will still be here in a few minutes or whenever we are ready for them. Won't you tell me what you look like first?"

"Is that really necessary? I don't know what you look like either. Your bandages cover half of your face."

Did she really wish to see his entire face, or was that a ploy to get out of describing hers? There was only one way to know. "I'll take them off if you'll tell me of yourself."

"Can you? Is that advisable?"

Theodore shrugged. "It is only three more weeks until the doctor's visit in which he is to remove them. If I don't open my eyes, I cannot see that harm will be done—pun intended." He grinned.

"It's not amusing," she scolded. "I don't wish you to do anything to further harm yourself. If the bandages are to remain on longer . . ."

"Are you afraid to see me?"

"No."

"Only afraid for me to see you?"

She sighed. "Yes."

Theodore's hand slid down her wrist to twine her fingers with his, trying to reassure her. She had mentioned scars from her burns. Was that what worried her, that he would be repulsed by those? On the contrary, he considered them battle wounds and felt only admiration for her that she had survived. "I have put a great deal of trust in you these past weeks. You have seen me stumble and fall, you've seen me frustrated and angry, humiliated, hopeless. You have helped me to stand, wiped my face and shirt front when I was clumsy, tied my cravat, removed my shoes. You have turned away to spare me when you knew I was embarrassed. Can you not trust me now and believe that no matter what you tell me, no matter your appearance, I will still cherish our friendship?"

"Very well." She sounded resigned rather than pleased at his request. "What do you wish to know?" She sat once more, and Theodore released her hand.

"Begin here." He leaned closer, over the chessboard still between them, and reached out to where he imagined her head might be. His fingers brushed against something soft. He stilled and allowed his hand to rest. "What color is your hair?"

"Dark brown. Not golden as Violet's. It is straight, not curled. It is thick and so heavy that at times when it is pinned too tightly, it causes my head to ache."

"Do you let it down, then?" His fingers slowly moved over the silken strands, and he imagined long dark hair trailing to a woman's waist.

She shook her head and his hand fell away. "It is not proper for a woman to wear her hair down."

"Ridiculous rules," he muttered. "We've no use for them here. You should wear it down whenever you wish."

"Perhaps."

"Perhaps nothing. We don't stand on propriety here at Broughleigh. How many other men have you dined with who march their fingers across the dinner table in order to locate their wine glass and the utensils they are to eat with?"

"None, though there are some who drink much and ought to employ that tactic." She laughed lightly.

"Does your head ache right now?"

"A little."

"Take your hair down," he ordered. "I'll not have my assistant suffering with a headache."

"It is fine, really. I should not have mentioned it."

Shaking his own head, Theodore backed his chair up then rolled it around until he was beside her. "Turn around. So you are facing away from me. I'll do it for you." The prospect was at once thrilling and daunting. He'd never unpinned a woman's hair before, even when he'd been able to see what he was doing.

"I don't think—"

"Obviously, you don't if you wear a hairstyle that pains you. Turn, please."

"That was rather rude. You're being obstinate again."

"As are you. I'm waiting." He tapped a foot against the bottom of his chair.

"Hmph."

With what he guessed was a flounce and probably a roll of her eyes, she turned away. Slowly he raised his hands, then lowered them until they rested on her head. His fingers slid lower until they found the chignon at the nape of her neck. Gently he began searching for pins. It did not take long to find one and pull it out. He set it on his leg and resumed his search.

As the silken strands began to loosen, it became all he could do not to run his fingers through the mass and bury his face in its depths. Since their shopping expedition a few weeks earlier, she had been wearing a fragrance that both pleased him and drove him mad. It pleased him because he always knew where she was in a room now. He only had to follow her scent.

It was driving him mad because he found the floral bouquet stimulating. It had awakened in him something that had slumbered nearly three years, and he wasn't in a position to do anything about such feelings. Nor was he entirely comfortable having them about Beatrice when a mere month ago he had been betrothed to her cousin.

I am no longer betrothed. Last week, he had dictated a letter, formally ending his engagement to Violet based on her elopement with another man. He'd made sure to send it to her father this time. A few weeks earlier, writing a letter of that nature would have been unthinkable. But it had been accomplished with ease and had even brought relief. *That chapter of my life is closed.*

He removed another pin from Beatrice's hair and set it aside, then allowed the strands to slip through his fingers, taking great pleasure in the sensation. Without his sight, touch had become critical. He reached for her often, always grateful when she placed her hand in his outstretched one. That connection reassured him, comforted him. Anchored him. It reminded him he was no longer alone in a mad, dark world. He wasn't on his own, and the world was no longer dark. Somehow, in spite of his inability to see, Beatrice had brought him back into the light.

Beatrice, who was not only lovely in soul and had lightened his burdens but also had the softest, silkiest hair he'd ever had the pleasure of touching.

In front of him, she cleared her throat before whispering, "I believe that is all the pins, milord."

"Theodore," he said, feeling a sudden tightening of his own throat. With great reluctance, he forced himself to remove his hands from her hair. He had looked forward to many pleasures of married life, but he had never considered the simpler ones. What would it be like to have the privilege of brushing his wife's hair every evening before bed? To sit and talk with her at breakfast each day, to walk together in the garden, to strategize with one another over a chessboard? "Please call me by my given name as well."

Her skirts rustled as she turned toward him. "Only when we are alone. I am still your employee and should address you properly when in the company of others."

"All right," he agreed. With so few on staff and the absence of visitors from the outside, they were most often alone. "I want to—may I touch your face? So I can see—as much as is possible—what you look like?"

"Like other humans, I have a forehead, a chin, and a straight nose. Nothing remarkable, milor—Theodore."

He grinned to put her at ease. "Milord Theodore... I rather like the sound of that."

"*So* arrogant," she muttered, but he heard amusement in her tone.

Theodore lifted his hand hesitantly. "Please," he asked, at once serious again, the request rendering him vulnerable rather than arrogant. He had to touch her. He wasn't certain why; it was almost as if he needed to know she was real and not some figment of his overwrought imagination. Not the desperate dream of a man abandoned—both on the battlefield and by his fiancée.

In answer, her fingers curved over his, and she drew his hand toward her. She placed it on skin as soft and smooth as her hair had been silky. His other hand lifted of its own accord, and he found the other side of her face. His fingers lingered a moment before sliding over its contours. *Cheekbones, nose, forehead.*

"My eyes are also brown," she said as if she'd anticipated him asking.

He smiled, a picture starting to form in his mind.

In comparison to his own, her ears felt dainty. Her chin was firm. Her lips . . . His thumb lingered there, tracing their fulness. He heard her swallow and caught the sharp intake of her breath.

What am I doing? He knew what he *wanted* to do. Or what his body—his mouth— wanted to, anyway. But was it the right thing? *What are my intentions?* That he cared for Beatrice was absolute. She had become his best ally, his most noble of friends. That he was attracted to her was also obvious. And having never seen her, his attraction had to be true— more than a mere physical connection—did it not? *But if I kiss her . . .* It would be a declaration of much more than friendship.

Drawing in his own labored breath, he withdrew his hands from her face. "Thank you."

"You're welcome." Her whisper was so quiet that he scarcely heard it.

"Your face does not feel as if it is scarred. Have the years healed your wounds so thoroughly?"

"My face, thankfully, was never burned. It was my nightgown that caught fire. The scars still remain on my hand and arm, down the side of my body, and on my leg. Fortunately, few are where they are easily seen."

He wondered suddenly how she had fared that day at the modiste. He had not accompanied her into the shop, but he now realized it might have been a hardship for her to be measured and fitted for gowns and other clothing. Perhaps that was also why she had refused Mrs. McNeil's offer of an additional dress when she had first arrived.

He sought to reassure her that what she looked like did not matter to him. "Our scars are evidence of our triumphs. They show what we have overcome. You need not be ashamed of them."

"Yours were earned honorably in battle. It has been different for me. My aunt—" She broke off, and he imagined her shaking her head as she held back whatever it was she had been about to say.

"Your aunt what?" he prodded.

"I should not tell you. It would only cause problems if she found out, and—"

"Your aunt is not here. Nor does she have reason to ever be, as my betrothal to her daughter has been officially ended." He leaned forward, placing a hand upon Beatrice's arm. "Tell me, please." He had to know what troubled her. He had to know so he could fix it.

"She spread a rumor that it was I who—"

Theodore waited, hoping his patience would encourage her.

"It is too awful. I cannot say it."

His fingers slid to her hand. He grasped it tightly. "It may be that you will feel better for telling it."

"It may be that I will feel worse. That you will view me as others do."

"My opinion of you is based solely on our past month together. Nothing your aunt has said will sway that." He squeezed her hand once, then released it and leaned back. "But I will not force you to share something you do not wish to."

"I want to tell you, but I do not wish you to think the worst of me as everyone else does." The tremor in her voice filled him with sorrow.

"You are the first person—the only person, aside from my uncle—who has ever treated me kindly, who hasn't thought me a terrible person."

Had he not done just that upon her arrival? Theodore squirmed uncomfortably, regretful of those first days with her and the things he had said, the way he had behaved. If he was the kindest person she had known, then her life had to have been misery. *Years of it.* He'd had only months of suffering and yet look what it had reduced him to before she came. How had her years of loneliness and suffering molded her into the gentlest soul he'd ever known?

"Tell me," he said once more. "Trust me."

"I do." She reached for him as he did for her so often. He enfolded her hands in his, reassuring, promising that all would be well.

"My aunt—" Beatrice took a deep breath. "She told everyone that *I* started the fire that killed my family. Anyone who has seen my scars views them as well deserved and the mark of a murderer."

Theodore held back words not appropriate for polite society. "I might just become a murderer if I ever cross paths with your aunt again. What an abhorrent thing to do—and toward a child. What possessed the woman to say—? Perhaps she is possessed."

"Only *obsessed*," Beatrice said sadly.

"What do you mean?" Theodore tilted his head, his curiosity growing.

"She cannot forget the past. She is obsessed with my mother, or rather the relationship my uncle had with her. He courted my mother before he met my aunt. He even asked her to marry him, but she was in love with my father and chose him instead."

"Your mother spurned your uncle for his untitled younger brother?"

"She loved my father," Beatrice said, her tone defensive. "They went to India to get away from my uncle and the hard feelings between the brothers—or at least that is the story I've gleaned from the servants over the years."

"So, when you came back to live with him . . ." This was starting to make sense now. Albeit in an unpleasant sort of way. This was no fairy tale with a happy ending.

"I didn't know about any of this for a long time," Beatrice said. "I had no idea until a few years ago when I overheard my aunt and uncle arguing. She accused him of never loving her the way he had loved my mother. My uncle told my aunt that she was right—that he *didn't* love her."

"Seems the wrong thing for him to have said," Theodore muttered.

"It gets worse. She accused him of loving me in my mother's place. All because on the very first day of my arrival, when I was just twelve, he had said I was the mirror image of my mother."

Theodore felt as if he'd been struck by something sharp and painful. A direct hit to his heart. The feeling was not dissimilar from the way he'd felt upon hearing that Violet had eloped. Only worse, somehow. Had Beatrice's uncle transferred his unrequited feelings to her? Had he taken advantage of his guardianship?

"My uncle refuted her claims, but he stayed away even more after that. And he stopped bringing me gifts as he did for

Violet, stopped treating me as if I were his daughter. He hardly looked at me after that. It was only when he fought for me to accompany Violet this summer that I thought perhaps he still cared for me just a little. Either that or he simply wished to be rid of me, to have me gone from his sight."

The breath he hadn't realized he'd been holding escaped Theodore's lungs heavily. He brought Beatrice's hand to his lips and kissed it, so *very* grateful she was here with him and whole and well. That she had survived all her scars. "You will never, ever have to return to your aunt and uncle's house," he said, his throat thick with emotion. "To that place where others scorn you, where they cannot appreciate the truly beautiful person that you have become."

Ten

"If I am able to push my chair twenty steps across the lawn today, you should wear your hair down." Hands braced on the back of his chair, Theodore took another labored step.

Beatrice began unpinning her bun. "I have no doubt you will achieve your twenty steps, and my hair is already down." The July afternoon was warm and leaving it up would have been cooler, but since that day in the library two weeks ago, she'd been careful not to provide the earl another opportunity to be so close to her. *So intimate.* Feeling his hands in her hair and on her face had been the most frightening—*what were these feelings he evoked, and how am I ever to live without them, having now experienced such?*—and exhilarating experience of her life.

He reached out to her frequently, either for reassurance that she was nearby or for assistance getting into and out of his chair or accomplishing some other task. Each of those simple connections affected her deeply, starved as she was for any sort of care or warmth herself. But that afternoon had been different. He had merely wished to know what she looked like, but his touch had caused her to wish for things that could not be. *That he touched me because he cares for me. That he felt the same stirrings as his touch caused me. That he would not stop but would hold my face in his hands, lean forward and—*

"Ten steps—ha!" Beside her, Theodore grunted at the small victory. "Halfway there."

"Marvelous!" Beatrice clapped and relegated her scandalous thoughts to the back of her mind, where she hoped they would remain until tonight, when she lay tucked in beneath the luxurious bedding Theodore had had delivered to her room weeks ago, after she had agreed to stay.

She could not seem to help thinking of him each night, and while she ought not indulge in such thoughts there either, a lot of things about her time here were improper—from their familiar use of each other's given names to the long periods of time they spent alone together each day. But the staff either chose to ignore such or found nothing wrong in their conduct. She'd felt no judgment from any of them. Logan, Mrs. McNeil, and the others had been nothing but kind to her and grateful for all they perceived she had done for the earl.

"Are you still there? Or has my brown-eyed assistant abandoned me?"

"I am right here." Beatrice hurried to catch up to him and placed a hand on his sleeve for a brief second. "Isn't this so much better than walking between the bars?"

He gave a jerky nod. "Outside is better. Though more difficult. I am unable to support my weight on the chair as I can on the bars. I fear I cannot—"

His leg buckled and Beatrice reached for him, already too late to stop his fall. As he went down, his weight pushed the chair forward and it surged ahead, sending him sprawling.

"Theodore!" She knelt beside him on the grass, touching his shoulder and then head, checking for injuries. "Are you hurt?"

"Only my pride." He groaned, rolling onto his back. "And maybe my leg a little." He reached for his left leg, attempting to straighten it. "Hard to tell since it was screaming at me already."

"I'm so very sorry," Beatrice exclaimed. "I shouldn't have pushed you to walk behind your chair. I only thought that if you could learn to walk by pushing it around, that would give you more mobility. I thought the lawn would be a good place to start—less slippery than the floor."

"All good thoughts, if only my leg would cooperate. I am beginning to fear it never functioning correctly again."

"You've been walking on it scarcely a month," she reminded him. "Considering that you nearly lost it, your progress has been remarkable."

He frowned and his brow furrowed above his bandages. "I didn't realize I'd mentioned my injuries in such detail."

"You didn't," she admitted. By some unspoken rule, they never discussed Crimea or anything to do with the war or his injuries. Beatrice sensed he did not wish to talk about them, so she hadn't asked. But she knew. "I merely assumed that with an injury requiring surgery and this long period of recovery . . ." She bit her lip. She'd said too much. And also not enough. She needed to tell him the truth. *He will find out. He'll know what I did.* And then what? All of his kindnesses to her would be gone. He would think the worst of her, and his feelings would be justified. She would have to return to England, to her aunt bent on making her suffer.

Anything Aunt Margaret did to her now wouldn't come close to the sorrow she'd feel leaving this magical place. *Leaving Theodore.*

If I tell him myself. If I explain . . . might he understand?

"What do the clouds look like today? I feel the warmth of the sun, so I assume there are few."

Beatrice reined her thoughts back to the present and found Theodore facing the sky, his hands propped casually behind his head, a smile on his face.

All is forgotten. For now. He recovered from setbacks

much quicker than he had six weeks ago. His legs were strengthening, as was his spirit. More and more he was the man she had come to know before ever coming here, though the brooding had not left him entirely. She suspected it never would. Recovering from trauma and completely forgetting it were entirely different. In her experience, the latter rarely happened.

He cleared his throat. "The clouds? Are there none? Or have you gone? Where are you, my Beatrice?"

Right here, but I am not truly yours. "There are few today. They are white, fluffy." After nearly a solid week of rain, the day was bright, the sky mostly clear.

"Tell me something I don't know." Theodore moved one hand from behind his head to pat the ground beside him. "Lie down and look up as I am. It's the only proper way to see their true forms. Then you can tell me if there is an elephant prancing above us, or a Viking ship rowing toward shore."

Beatrice shifted off her knees and leaned to the side but did not lie down beside him. She craned her neck and studied the sky. "No elephants today but a lion's face, complete with a shaggy mane all around."

He nodded. "Good. I can imagine that. You've played this game before?"

"With my brother. I had forgotten until now." Wistfully she recalled that childhood memory as she gave in to the earl's invitation to lie on the grass beside him.

"Perfect. You can pretend I'm your brother."

"That is *quite* impossible." *For many reasons.* She turned toward Theodore and found him already facing her.

"You feel no affection toward me? Or is it simply that I do not resemble the lad? He had eyes you could see, I suppose."

She laughed at his overexaggerated expression of mock hurt. "Eyes, yes, but no teeth. I recall that his front two were missing around that time."

Theodore gave her a toothy grin. "Well, then, a point for me."

"Many points for you." Beatrice clamped her lips together and squeezed her eyes shut. Why did she keep saying such things?

Theodore's hand found hers and clasped it between them. "You have more points than you can imagine—were we keeping score."

Beatrice didn't trust herself not to say something else she oughtn't, so she turned her face from his and looked to the sky once more. "There is a wide cloud floating over us that reminds me of a loch, and on its far side, a cottage sits at the edge. A tiny spiral of smoke is floating up from the chimney."

Theodore gave a lazy, relaxed sigh. "I can picture that. It seems a very peaceful place."

"As is Broughleigh." Beatrice closed her eyes once more, utterly content in that moment, the only sounds being the harmony of their breathing. She could fall asleep this way, out here among the sweet grass, with the person she cared most for in this world beside her.

A loud wail, the first long note of a bagpipe echoed over them, breaking the silence and jerking her to her knees in a flurry of skirts and movement.

Still lying down, Theodore groaned. "Arthur."

"It's not evening yet. Why is he playing now?" Beatrice placed a hand over her thudding heart.

"Because he can?" Theodore suggested. "Who knows? He comes from a long line of pipers who've taken their jobs very seriously. Maybe today is a Scottish holiday or commemoration I'm unaware of."

"Or maybe he was warning us that we're about to have visitors." Beatrice looked past the hill where Arthur played to the road below and the plumes of dust billowing up behind the carriage coming toward Broughleigh, a familiar crest emblazoned across its side.

Theodore sat up, his shoulder brushing hers. "Who is it?"

Beatrice followed the conveyance's progress until it stopped in front of the house. The door opened, and a blonde head of curls poked out.

"Violet is here."

Eleven

"Bea dear," Aunt Margaret sang in her falsely sweet voice. "Fetch a tray of sandwiches for Violet. Our journey has tired her so."

Beatrice stepped away from the wall and smoothed the front of the apron she'd donned hastily before delivering the tea tray. Her hair was up once more, wound in a tighter knot than she'd worn all summer.

"Do not bother Cook," Theodore said, a bite to his tone that Beatrice had not heard for several weeks. "She is in the midst of dinner preparations by now. We keep only a small staff here," he said, his attention directed to the sofa where Violet and her mother sat.

Beatrice risked another glance at Violet and found her initial assessment correct. Her cousin looked unwell. Perhaps the journey *hadn't* agreed with her. She remained uncharacteristically silent and slumped on the couch as if defeated.

"If your home is so understaffed, isn't there something else Beatrice can do—some other task that does not require her to hover about, eavesdropping?" Aunt Margaret flitted her hand toward her as if trying to rid herself of an annoying insect.

Beatrice fought the feelings that reduced her to such a state and shrank back near the window. It might be easier if she left, but then she would not be here to defend herself if the truth came out. *And it will.* She'd always counted on that eventuality in her favor, that someday everyone would know she had not killed her family. But never had the truth of what happened that night been revealed.

Now, instead, the truth of her only dishonesty was threatening exposure at any second. It was like the boulders on the nearby hills. Enormous and seemingly randomly placed, they perched sideways, half in and half out of the earth, ready to thunder down the side of the hill at any second, taking up large chunks of earth as they rolled and destroying all in their path.

I don't want to destroy Theodore. I never meant to hurt him.

"Miss Worthington's presence is none of your concern. Why are *you* here?" Theodore demanded.

"So you and Violet may become reacquainted with one another before your wedding, of course." Aunt Margaret's tone carried the perfect balance of feigned innocence and her usual insistence.

"There is to be no wedding. Your husband should have received the documents formally dissolving our betrothal. Good day to you. Logan will show you out." Theodore swiveled his chair away from them.

Beatrice crossed the room so she might open the door for him as he exited.

"Now, see here." Aunt Margaret rose from the sofa, claws out like a lioness ready to pounce. "We know of no such letter and have come all this way at *your* invitation."

Theodore paused his progress and faced them once more. "That invitation was for the beginning of the summer. It was refuted when your daughter eloped with another man."

"Oh posh." Aunt Margaret waved her hand again. "There was no elopement. Violet is here now, is she not?"

"Where has she been for the past month and a half? What of the letter breaking our engagement? If I recall correctly, she had no use for a '*blind cripple*.'"

Violet winced.

"What letter are you speaking of?" Aunt Margaret demanded. "Did *you* actually read it? Or did you just take the word of that deceiver? The murderess," she added in a harsh whisper.

No. Beatrice pressed a hand to her mouth to hold in her cry of dismay. Her aunt was going to take it all away, these lovely weeks of summer when she and the earl had healed together. "Violet, for once in your life speak the truth," Beatrice implored.

"I have been—making my way back to you"—Violet glanced to her mother for approval—"after being tricked by my cousin into getting off the train."

HAVE I DONE the right thing? Tormented by his every decision the past week, Theodore gripped the back of his wheelchair and took another unsteady step. How marvelous that he was well enough to be pacing his room. How agitating that he felt like pacing in the first place. But the past week—with three Worthington women in residence at Broughleigh—would have tried anyone's patience.

Awkwardly, he turned his chair and started in the opposite direction. Today, in a few short hours, God willing, he would start to have some true answers. It had been all he could do not to take the bandages from his eyes early, to extract from his desk the letter Beatrice had read to him seven weeks ago—the letter her aunt and cousin insisted did not exist. He'd made sure the drawer with his papers had remained locked, and he had kept the key on his person at all times. The truth was soon to come out. His patience would be rewarded—or his heart would be broken once more.

He had allowed Violet and her mother to stay, worried that if he sent them packing, Beatrice would be persuaded to leave, too, in order to protect her reputation. Before he had gone inside to meet with their unexpected and unwelcome guests, she had all but begged him to treat her horribly in their presence. She was to act as a true servant, spoken to as such, and generally disregarded except when he was making a request of her. All in the name of protecting her from her aunt.

He'd hated every minute of the charade. He hated the way she was treated by her own relatives, particularly Violet, who ought to have regarded Beatrice as a dear friend or sister. Neither had he enjoyed the time he'd spent in Violet's company the past week. She now walked with him each day, but where he and Beatrice had soon felt comfortable around each other and enjoyed easy conversations, he and Violet found little to say. True, he was no longer the man who had swept her into his arms and across the terrace. But she was changed, too—and not for the better, as petulant as a child much of the time.

Theodore had retreated to taking meals alone in his room, using his blindness as an excuse. Meanwhile, his staff—including Beatrice—had been overworked meeting the many demands of his guests. Out of kindness to both Cook and Beatrice, he had sent her to work in the kitchen, where at least she might be spared from her aunt's and cousin's continuous barbs. It had meant he'd been devoid of her company as well, and he missed her keenly. His previous melancholy had returned, his days darker than ever, in spite of his fiancée's arrival.

At precisely one o'clock, Dr. Hulke arrived, having traveled from the Royal Ophthalmic Hospital in Moorfields. Theodore sat in his chair as the first layer of bandages were removed.

"We'll check your right eye first and see if this recovery in the Highlands that you insisted upon has done what we hoped it would," Dr. Hulke said cheerfully.

He had wanted Theodore to stay near the hospital, but as there was little to be done but wait and allow his eyes to rest, Theodore had seen no need to remain in England, not when a summer away promised more leisure.

"Well?" Dr. Hulke asked.

"I'm ready. Take the last layer off," Theodore said.

Absolute silence met his request. Then—

"It is off." The doctor's voice was somber.

Theodore reached up and touched the skin just below his eye. He forced his eye open and used his fingers to hold it there, but nothing changed. The dark persisted.

"I am sorry," Dr. Hulke said. "We always knew there was a chance this would occur."

Theodore nodded and swallowed the anger and overwhelming sorrow rising in his throat.

"I'm so sorry, darling. But it will be all right. I'll be your eyes for you."

It was all Theodore could do not to fling Violet's arm from his shoulders. "Not now," he ground out. Why were any of them here? Why had he thought allowing them to witness this *glorious* moment a good idea? "Get out," he said. "Everyone but the doctor."

Several sets of footsteps retreated, followed by the door closing.

"I *am* sorry, Theodore," Dr. Hulke reiterated.

Theodore nodded. "I know." He reached up to remove the bandages from his left eye himself. When the last was gone he waited before opening his eye, wondering why he was even bothering at all if his world was to remain forever dark.

"Go on." Dr. Hulke's hand on his shoulder offered comfort—or condolences.

Please, God. Help me accept what is to be. It was the only prayer to be had now, the only hope there was. Without his sight, his world would remain forever dark.

That isn't true.

Beatrice. She had brought him into the light again, even when he couldn't see. She had made life worth living again. He would have courage as she did.

Slowly Theodore opened his eye.

Twelve

THEODORE STARED AT the two papers, one a letter from Violet that he had received during the war, the other the letter telling of her elopement. *The handwriting is different.* His stomach turned over, accompanied by a feeling of utter dismay.

He'd been so certain it was Violet who had lied about the letter. *Not Beatrice.* Had he regained partial sight only to have his heart broken?

Pushing the letters aside, he held the candlestick over the open drawer and used his free hand to rifle through the papers there. He pulled the entire bundle out, set the candle down and began spreading the papers across his desk. *Eight.* The sum total of letters he'd received from Violet throughout the nearly three years they'd been separated. It wasn't a lot. She was not a prolific writer. Yet he'd loved each one of her letters, had treasured them and read them again and again.

The handwriting on each was as he remembered, the same carefully crafted script. It matched the writing on the first letter he had extracted. None matched the writing on the letter breaking their engagement, which meant it was Beatrice who had written such painful words.

Theodore turned away from the irrefutable evidence covering his desk. Violet had been telling the truth. It was as he had suspected at the beginning. She'd been a victim, and Beatrice—Miss Worthington—was the actress. *Maybe a murderess, too.* No. He couldn't believe that of her. He could scarcely believe this.

His mind returned to the first moments she had gained his trust, when she had gone on about the flowers in his garden, painting vivid pictures with her words, distracting both of them from the awkward task at hand as he'd maneuvered himself back into his chair. She had a way of seeing and appreciating the world that had brought him back into it. She'd brought him beauty and light, much as Violet's letters had done when he was in Crimea.

The letters. What if— Theodore swept the whole bundle from his desk, including the hateful one, calling him a blind cripple. He wedged the lot between his leg and the chair then wheeled himself toward the door. Earlier, after he had told everyone to leave, Violet and her mother had gone shopping for the day. Beatrice was working in the kitchen. The library would be empty. He'd only to get himself inside—without being seen. Excepting Dr. Hulke, they all believed him to be entirely blind now.

Instead, perhaps, I am just starting to see.

THEODORE WAITED ON the front drive, his eyes hidden behind the dark spectacles Dr. Hulke had left for him. When he heard the front door open and close, he refrained from turning to see Beatrice.

She stopped in front of him. "I was told you wished to see me, milord."

"You may cease the formality. Your aunt and cousin have left." He softened his voice at the worry in her expression. "You need never fear them again."

"Why have they—"

"I asked them to leave. Or rather, I insisted upon it. I may have even suggested that if they did not vacate the premises immediately, I would send their carriage ahead without them, and they would have to walk to Inverness on their own."

"Oh dear." Beatrice clapped her hands to her cheeks as she gazed down the drive.

"I suppose that was rather churlish of me," Theodore said, unconcerned. "Though somehow, it felt less so than when I once made a similar suggestion to you."

Beatrice smiled. "It appears we have made little progress with your manners this summer."

"I will likely require a great deal more work if I am ever to be considered a gentleman again," he agreed.

Her smile faded. "Oh, Theodore, I am so terribly sorry about your eyes." She clasped her hands in front of her and bent her face to them as if in prayer. "What may I—is there anything I may do for you?"

"Would you be so kind as to guide me to the rose garden?"

"Of course." She fell into step beside him, and they started down the drive. Theodore closed his eyes as he wheeled his chair, not wishing her to know his secret just yet.

They walked in silence, excepting Beatrice's occasional sniffle. It required a great deal of self-control for Theodore to refrain from looking up at her. Instead, he followed her directives that guided him safely into the heart of the fragrant garden. He parked his chair between two bushes, one ablaze in yellow and the other red. *Flanked by friendship and love.* That he had neither with Violet now was most apparent. *But what of Beatrice?* It was a question he suddenly longed to explore.

No. Not suddenly. That was not a fair assessment to either of them. The sight of her had not brought about these heightened feelings, though he wanted nothing so much in this moment as to look at her at his leisure, to drink in the sight of her and commit every detail of her beautiful face to memory.

But his feelings for her had been growing for weeks, one at a time like stones that were stacked one upon the other to build a castle. It felt like he had crested the top of the wall and seen the glorious views around him. And it was so much more than any disappointment he had felt over Violet, both today and earlier this summer.

But while his senses soared with sudden awareness, it appeared that Beatrice was not of a like mind but weighed down with some unknown sorrow. She had seated herself across from him, one hand pressed to her mouth as the other dashed furiously at quickly falling tears.

"Why are you crying?"

She pressed both hands to her mouth as if to stifle a sob. "I'm sorry. I did not mean to intrude on your enjoyment of the roses."

"You are not intruding," Theodore insisted. He had chosen this garden for more than its fragrance. It offered privacy from both the house and grounds and anyone who might be about. "Tell me what has caused your tears."

"Nothing—everything. I am just so sad. It is unfair. You are the one who ought to be crying, but I cannot seem to help myself. I so wanted you to regain your sight. I prayed for that even more than I prayed that your legs might be made whole. I think you might learn to live without walking again, but to be deprived of seeing the beauty of this world—" She leaned forward, face buried in her hands as sobs shook her slender form.

Her tears are for me. Theodore gripped the sides of his chair, then braced his weight on either side. He pushed up, almost easily, the weeks of practice in his room plus his eagerness to reach Beatrice making him fearless. Failure was not an option. It was his turn to be the strong one. He straightened, and his hands left the security of the chair behind. He took one wobbly step, then another, his gaze focused on the ground as he worked to lift each foot and place it carefully. Childlike he might be in his efforts at relearning to walk, but he was certain in his purpose. *Strong. Able. Still the man I used to be.* No, that wasn't right either. He was better now. Better for having temporarily lost both his sight and the ability to walk. Better for the summer he had spent with Beatrice.

She gasped. "Theo—what are you—you're walking!" She jumped up and reached out to him as if she expected him to tumble to the ground at any minute. Instead of taking her outstretched hands, he ripped the glasses from his face so he might look at her fully.

"What—no. You must protect your eyes." She turned toward the discarded glasses, but Theodore caught her arm, holding her in place.

"My eyes are fine. Or the left one at least." He caught her gaze for the first time, though truly he'd been looking into her soul all summer and she into his. "Beatrice." His other hand reached up to touch her face, skimming along the high plane of her cheek, down to her delicate chin, and up over lips parted in surprise.

"You can see?"

He nodded, a smile curving his lips almost as quickly as the one that had formed on hers. "A little. My left eye only. And my left leg can walk a little. So you see, no tears needed."

A fresh set—happy ones, he assumed—burst forth, sliding down her cheeks. She leaned forward, pulling him into a hug that nearly sent both of them toppling.

"Careful." He laughed and held her closer, as much

because he wanted to as to steady himself. "Haven't quite got my land legs yet."

She pulled back and stared at him, then reached a hand up to brush his cheek as he had hers. "Oh, Theodore. This is wonderful. A miracle. I am so happy for you."

"I am happy, too. But it would be a very good idea for us to sit now."

Still holding on to him, she stepped to the side, then helped him to the bench and sat close beside him, their knees touching as they faced one another.

Theodore took her hands in his, not for stability or reassurance as he had so many times before but because he had to touch her. He intended to hang on and never let go.

"Do you think you could be happy for *us*? Could you be content with a man who hobbles about with a cane and can only see with one eye?"

Her eyes widened and met his for the second time.

He nodded, affirming the question he read in them. Then, to make certain she understood him completely, he bent his head and touched his lips to hers—not briefly, but in a sweet, lingering kiss, a promise of things to come.

"I love you, Beatrice." His forehead touched hers as their breathing slowed.

She pulled away and looked up at him, not with the joy he had anticipated but with tear-filled eyes once more.

"I love you, too, Theodore. I have for so long. But I've done something terrible, and I have to tell you."

He extracted one of his hands from hers and reached into his pocket, retrieving two of the papers he'd brought with him to the library. "Would it have anything to do with these?" He placed the letters, plus the page of her notes on chess—which had proved her the author of all the letters, except the one stating that Violet had eloped—into her hand.

She nodded but would not look up at him. "I never meant to hurt you. I believed you and Violet would marry, and that would be the end of it. No one would be the wiser—or the worse—for my deceit."

"Why did you do it?" he asked. "Did Violet put you up to it?"

"No." Beatrice shook her head and finally looked at him again. "It was all my doing, my wrong. I was emptying the rubbish bin in her room one day and found your letter—I believe it to be your first to her. Thinking it had been discarded by mistake, I brought it to her."

"And—"

"She said she had no use for it and no intention of writing to you."

"So you decided to write for her?" Theodore asked, still not quite understanding Beatrice's motivation.

"I felt drawn to your words, and it felt wrong not to respond to you. You were in a strange place, facing grave dangers, and it seemed like you ought to at least have a few words of comfort from your fiancée. So I wrote that first letter and signed Violet's name. When your next letter came, she hadn't even bothered to open it when I found it discarded. I took it and opened it and read it, then wrote to you again. After that, I searched for your letters regularly. I am not certain I found all of them, and it wasn't always possible for me to write back to you, but I tried. I sensed that you needed to hear from Violet, that the thought of your fiancée caring for you and awaiting your return to England was what you needed to see you through."

"You have no idea how much I needed those letters, how much they meant to me." Theodore took them from her, refolded them, and placed them in his pocket. He treasured them even more now, knowing who their true author was.

"I'm so sorry." Beatrice searched his face. "Can you ever forgive me? I never meant to hurt you."

He took both of her hands in his again. "You did not hurt me. You saved me—in more ways than one. I cherished those letters and read and reread each beautiful word over and over again. They reminded me of home and gave me great comfort. And then, this summer, you brought me back into the world, reminded me of its wonder. You made me want to live again, Beatrice. I am only surprised now that I did not see the truth sooner. You truly are the bringer of joy and light, and the woman who I wish to spend the rest of my life with. If you will have me, with all my imperfections?"

"I think they shall go rather well with mine." She lifted her hand, and he glimpsed the scarring on the back of it and her wrist, disappearing into her sleeve.

He bent his head and placed a kiss there. "Battle wounds. But we have been victorious. And victory is sweet."

He kissed her again in the rose garden as the sun peeked from a cloud overhead, bathing them in the warm light of summer.

Dear Reader,

If you are like me, you find novellas wonderful for their intense burst of romance that can be devoured in one afternoon. However, you may also find they leave you wishing for a bit more with the characters it feels you've just begun to know. That was how I felt upon completing (already over my allotted word count) this story. To remedy that situation, I kept writing more of Theodore's and Beatrice's happily ever after. If you would like to read this as well, you may find it on my website at michelepaigeholmes.com. Search for the *Summer in the Highlands* book cover, and the link there will take you to a page titled "Wedding in the Highlands." I hope this epilogue will satisfy you as much as it did me. Happy reading!

Michele Paige Holmes is the author of eighteen published romance novels and at least a dozen more, as yet unpublished books lingering on her hard drive. She has also written five novellas for the Timeless Romance Anthologies. She loves history and all things romantic, though the reality of her life is often less so, with piles of laundry to be folded, meals to be cooked, and dishes to be washed. She finds those blessings too, or evidence of the blessings in her life—her husband, five, mostly grown children, and five charming, high-energy grandchildren (four of whom reside in her home).

She is married to her high school sweetheart, a true Ironman who considers doing ultramarathons and triathlons fun. The only time Michele logs serious miles is at Disney theme parks, but she and her super-fit husband have been happily married for thirty-five years, in spite of her lack of coordination and lagging fitness levels. She is happy to continue her role as cheerleader and race support.

While her husband is out running, biking, or swimming, Michele's furry companion Sherlock Holmes—a Cavapoo strongly resembling a teddy bear—keeps her company and keeps her feet warm during the cold winter months in Utah. In recent years Michele has enjoyed traveling to some of the locations she writes about. This summer she will be returning to Scotland to do research for upcoming Hearthfire Historical novels.

You can find Michele on the web: MichelePaigeHolmes.com
Facebook: Michele Paige Holmes
Instagram: Michele Paige Holmes
Pinterest: Michele Paige Holmes

www.ingramcontent.com/pod-product-compliance
Lightning Source LLC
LaVergne TN
LVHW021756060526
838201LV00058B/3118